Things We Burn

A JUPITER TIDES NOVEL

ANNE MALCOM

Cover Design: TRC Designs
Editing: Kim BookJunkie
Proofreading: All Encompassing Books

For all the mothers reading this at 3 a.m.
For all the mothers looking for a moment to themselves.
For all the mothers doing this without a village.
For all the mothers who feel like they're failing (you're not).
For all the mothers trying to 'do it all' (I have discovered that this is impossible).

For all the mothers.

You are doing amazing.

I love the surprise pregnancy trope.

I wrote it into my first book. Into countless books after.

I continued to write the trope when I got pregnant for the first time and then lost that pregnancy.

I continued to write it after three more miscarriages.

And, my fifth pregnancy, I wrote it again, with hope in my heart. That time, our little girl Juniper was determined to stay. I got to write about pregnancy from real experience.

That book is *Method for Matrimony*, in case you haven't read it.

None of my books have explored postpartum. I had never experienced it until this past year, the year it took me to write this book. That is an unheard of length of time for me.

But I was a new mum trying to soak up time with my baby. I was (still am) a new mum trying to survive.

We don't see a lot of real talk when it comes to postpartum. We hear about the 'magic', the unconditional love. And that's there for sure. But it's also hard. Really freaking hard. You feel isolated.

Alone. Like you're failing. Like every other mother in the world has it figured out apart from you.

At least that's how I felt.

Before I had Juni, I would look at mothers with children, smile, then go back about my day. Now I see them, doing the hardest job in the world, and I want to scream *I'm one of you. This is so hard, you're making it look easy. I see you'*.

So, if you're a momma reading this, *I see you*.

My books have always been about escape, love, romance. But I've always wanted to help people feel less alone. That's what I wanted, more than anything with this book. To celebrate mothers. To speak to them. To remind them that this is hard and you're doing fucking great.

I didn't have a 'village' once my mother and aunt flew back to New Zealand. I had an amazing husband. Who heavily inspired Kane. But that was it. And it wasn't enough. We're not meant to do this alone. I wrote Avery the village I didn't get, that many women don't get.

Anyway, enough rambling. On with the book.

"CAN WE LEAVE YET?"

My best friend side-eyed me. "We only just arrived."

"Yes, I came, I saw." I waved my hand at the crowd.

"You're also supposed to conquer."

"I haven't got the energy to conquer," I whined. "I worked more than I slept this week."

Exhaustion had settled deep into my bones, making moving my limbs, talking, and worst of all, socializing, seem torturous. I was already fantasizing about my bed and the six hours of sleep I'd be able to grab if I left at that instant.

"Then it's all the more important for you to be here right now." Kiera reached forward to a waiter with a tray of champagne, taking two glasses. "You are in dire need of a life." She handed me a glass.

I took it on reflex more than anything else. Champagne was the last thing I wanted right then. What I really wanted was a warm cup of tea and my bed.

"*This* isn't the kind of life I want." I gestured around the room with my glass.

The room was full of very impressive looking people. People in expensive outfits with glossy hairstyles—both the men and the women—and glowing skin, who were laughing and generally looking fabulous.

I doubted I looked fabulous. Kiera had tried to get me into one of her short, tight, sparkly dresses. Though my best friend was a force of nature, I was not a short, sparkly dress kind of woman. She knew this, yet she pushed me to wear some scrap of fabric I doubted would cover enough of my body to keep me out of a police car for indecent exposure.

Instead, I'd worn a pair of black, low-waisted slacks and a black halter, relenting by wearing a pair of Kiera's shoes. They were much too high and uncomfortable for someone who had already been on her feet for at least twelve hours today.

I had no idea what I was thinking. About the shoes or letting her drag me to the party.

Oh yeah, I knew what I was thinking. I hadn't been laid in months, and I was looking for some real human contact and an orgasm that didn't come from my vibrator.

This party was really the wrong place to go for that.

Sure, the men here were handsome. If you liked them with fake tans, perfect hairstyles, sculpted muscles and a mouth full of teeth too white and straight to be anything but veneers.

I liked my men a little more ... rugged. The kind of men who wouldn't notice that I hadn't had a haircut or color in months. That my eyebrows weren't groomed and I was neither tanned nor flawless. That I was not a size zero nor even a size six. The kind of man who didn't notice all that stuff and really only cared about whether I was borderline attractive—which I thought I was—and consenting—which I also was. Almost every man here had a supermodel type on his arm or was ogling one of the many supermodel types who filled the room.

It was not my night.

At least there was wine.

I sipped it. Expensive wine too.

I wasn't a big drinker, mostly because I didn't have time nor the inclination. But some of the perks of my job gave me access to some of the most expensive booze on the planet. Sure, it was good. I enjoyed the ritual of it. The history. The way it paired impeccably with food. But I wasn't about to spend a thousand bucks on something I was going to pee out later.

Just when I was about to write this party off as a fail, my eyes found silvery-blue ones.

The most striking color I'd seen on a man. Or a person, for that matter.

And they were looking at me.

Me.

In a sea of gorgeous people.

Standing beside Kiera—the tall, stunning woman who had made men walk into walls from staring at her before.

He took my breath away.

And not just because of his eyes.

There was a whole lot more going on.

A face, for starters.

One that was not polished nor tanned like the others in this room. It was olive-colored, though in a more natural way. He looked like he was Italian or Greek and spent hours in the sun. Weathered. Even from across the room, I could see creases on his face.

He had dark, glossy black hair that brushed his eyebrows. It was messy, tousled and long enough to communicate it was overdue for a cut. His nose was crooked. Like it had been broken and then never healed quite right.

There was a scar going through his lips, one that marred them just a little. Not enough to turn his attractive mouth into a grimace. Nor did it obscure his ability to smile. Which he was doing right now.

Though you could call it more of a smirk.

A smirk that did things to my ... lady bits.

They had been sorely neglected by members of the male sex. Things were dire if a *smile* was doing it for me.

Although this was no regular smile. This dark-haired, rugged, square-jawed man was something else. And he definitely didn't look like he belonged here at this party.

Most men were wearing collared shirts, if not expensive suits.

He was wearing a simple black tee and black jeans. Though he made them look like they were worth a million bucks. He had tattoos scattered up and down his arms and one crawling up his neck, if I wasn't mistaken.

He was tall. Towering, one might say. I didn't think a man's height overly mattered to me before. But it did now.

He must've been over 6', and he was full of corded muscle. Not bulky but defined. His biceps were stretching the sleeves of the tee he was wearing. And not because he was wearing a size too small either.

I would've liked a size smaller because then I would've seen the outline of the six-pack he most definitely had.

"Holy shit," Kiera breathed from beside me. "That's Kane 'The Devil' Rhodes."

I reluctantly wrenched my gaze away from my man to look at where my best friend was gazing.

Except she was looking at *him*.

"You know him?" I asked, a little disappointed. I recognized the way she was looking at him, and I immediately felt a stab of aggression toward my best—and only—friend in the world. That did not make sense. For me to feel territorial over a man I didn't even know, for me to feel disdain toward the one person on the planet I had that I didn't outrank or was blood related to.

"Of course, I do," she hissed, still staring, openly.

Kane 'The Devil' Rhodes still had his attention firmly in our direction. It felt like a game, a challenge, that unrelenting stare.

My gaze darted down to my glass. I did not shy away from eye contact, didn't blink first in games of power moves. Until then.

"He's only the biggest thing in extreme sports right now," Kiera babbled, unaware of the turmoil swimming through my mind. "He just cleaned up at the Motocross Championships."

Puzzled, my attention went to her. "Since when do you follow sports, extreme or otherwise?"

As much as I loved my friend, and I did, dearly, she was not someone who had varied and eclectic interests. She loved parties, expensive shoes, going to the spa and steamy romance books. Not that there was anything wrong with those things.

In fact, she had a lot more going for her compared to me who didn't have *any* interests. Beyond my job, though more than one person—people I'd dated—had called it an obsession.

Sad, really.

"You do not have to follow sports to know who Kane 'The Devil' Rhodes is," she scoffed, as if it were obvious.

"Why are you calling him by his full name?" I asked, genuinely confused. "And what is with 'The Devil.'" I air quoted. "It sounds like the name of some Disney channel character in a teen sitcom."

Kiera rolled her eyes then glared at me. "If you actually lived outside of that small, steaming kitchen you cage yourself in, you would know that he's kind of a celebrity in all spheres. On account of him being fucking hot and a total badass. He's dated countless models and actresses, and he is literally *fearless*. He has medals and awards in like three different extreme sports. He competed in the winter Olympics after breaking his arm in the qualifiers and brought home the silver. Brings new meaning to the term 'daredevil.'"

"You sound like you're reporting for an entertainment channel," I told her, failing to be impressed. I'd met many people who were famous, talented and world renowned in their field. More often than not, they were obnoxious assholes. You had to be in order to get to the top.

I supposed I was one too.

She shook her head. "No, I just live in the real world," she snapped, though not unkindly; it was just her brash way as a native New Yorker. "One where Kane Rhodes is currently king. And apparently, he just dumped his latest—oh, my fuck, he's coming over here, he's coming over here." She readjusted her dress so her already well-exposed breasts spilled out further.

I didn't do anything to alter my appearance. It was what it was these days. Though I did wish that I had washed my mousy-brown locks and done something other than take them out of a French braid and kind of spritz the curls a little. They were just touching my shoulders, the volume of the curls softening my face somewhat but also not looking anywhere near as polished and shiny as everyone else's at the party. I'd tried products to tame the frizz, the fly-aways, spent money that made me wince. But my hair always ended up the same. Wild, unruly and easier to shove up into a bun. What I was used to since it needed to be tied up for work.

At least Kiera had done my makeup.

I'd initially thought she'd gone way overboard with the blush high on my already round cheekbones, and she'd made the liner on my eyes too dark, causing my shadowy-brown eyes to look almost black. Then she'd swiped red lipstick over my lips—my most hated feature, even though Kiera told me she paid a hefty amount to get fillers to look half as natural and full as mine.

The top I was wearing was Kiera's. Though we had the same bust size, we did not have the same waist by any stretch of the imagination. The fabric was silky and had a lot of give, but it still clung to my torso in a way that made me slightly self-conscious. My stomach was not washboard flat, and my hips were wide. I had the traditional hourglass shape. I'd never really tried to lose the extra pounds I carried because it was my body's natural shape, and eating was part of my job.

It wasn't that I thought I was some wallflower; I understood I had all the features that made me conventionally attractive. I had curves that a certain kind of man enjoyed. But I never felt comfortable with them, never felt like they matched up with who I was. I was not the sex kitten type person that my full lips, hourglass figure and dark gaze communicated.

Maybe, deep down I wanted to be. I'd never felt comfortable with sexuality or femininity. I'd shoved it down whenever my mother tried to address it, further bolstering the distance between us.

Hence why I wasn't used to wearing a whole lot of makeup, and I didn't recognize myself when Kiera had finished with me.

I kind of looked ... sultry, I guessed? Who could tell?

Kane 'The Devil' Rhodes did in fact seem to be making his way over to us, though. And it made sense that he was doing that because of my petite, curvy and knockout bestie with the greatest tits you could find in this room.

"He's coming over here," Kiera repeated. "Oh my god, I wish I was filming this."

Of course, she did. Kiera had a social media presence that had taken off. She'd recently been able to quit her job in cosmetic sales to pursue it full time. That was where the tickets to this swanky party had come from. Perks of the job.

I watched the crowd part for this man, people staring as he walked by. Some were even gaping. A couple of people not so discreetly filmed him.

My attraction to the man waned some. Anyone who garnered attention like that would likely have an ego the size of Texas.

Though my attraction waned, it didn't fizzle out completely. No, my heartbeat thundered by the time he stood in front of us.

"Hi."

His voice was like honey. Or whisky. Something smooth and impossibly rich and manly at the same time. But with an edge. A rasp.

My skin prickled with the single syllable greeting.

That was not directed at my best friend.

But me.

Or maybe the person behind me.

There was no way for me to check without it being obvious.

I was pretty sure it was me, though, because he was standing close to me. Like really close. Much closer than was polite.

I could smell him.

He smelled of a woodsy aftershave and something else. Something that wasn't manufactured and didn't come out of a bottle. That was all him.

I could bathe in that smell.

Pheromones, I reminded myself. Pheromones. It was a natural phenomenon, designed by nature. On a cellular level, we must've been somewhat compatible. That was it. It didn't mean anything profound. No fireworks nor love at first sight that Hollywood tried to peddle.

No, we were animals at our cores, a chemical reaction to satisfy an ancient urge to further the species.

"Hi," I replied reflexively, trying to get my bearings.

I wasn't someone who was shaken easily. Working in some of the most chaotic and high-profile kitchens in the country will do that to you. If you were going to crack under pressure, you did it about the first year of working in an actual restaurant environment. Usually the first month. I had seen too many mental breakdowns to count and been on the edge of a few myself. There was a moment when you were sweating, when Chef was screaming at you, when your fingertips burned because you hadn't yet scorched the feeling out of them, when you couldn't remember the last time you slept and you seriously thought your heart was going to explode. That was the moment when you walked out of the kitchen forever. For your own sanity.

Or you held on to your shit by the tips of your seared fingers, embraced the part of you that thrived off this chaos and pulled yourself together. I was proud to say I got my shit together years ago and hadn't come close to losing it since.

Yet here I was, having heart palpitations because a hot guy said hi to me.

Pathetic.

I'd been around plenty of good-looking people, plenty of men with attitude and charisma that made them more attractive than they should've been. The restaurant world was driven by men like that, ones who had power, were used to women falling at their feet and saw women who didn't as people to be conquered.

Once... Once I'd let a man like that conquer me, and I'd promised myself I would never let that shit happen again. I'd never be charmed by talent and power and wealth.

That reminder hardened me ever so slightly.

"I'm Kane." His eyes twinkled, that smirk still in place on his face.

"I've heard," I replied, my voice somewhat cooler now. I'd found my trademark calm. A couple of seconds too late, but better late than never.

He raised his brow playfully. "You've *heard*?" His eyes were electric blue. The tattoo on his neck was a delicate sparrow, juxtaposed by hard cords of muscle.

There was no way to catalog the rest of the tattoos—of which there were many—without it looking like I was gawking.

I nodded, taking a small sip of the champagne in my hand. Not because I was thirsty, but because I needed something else to do other than just stand there and look at him. I forced myself to make the sip slow, almost lazy. "About ten seconds ago."

His brow stayed raised, and his smirk stretched into a full-on grin. "You've known who I am for ten seconds?"

I shrugged. "Give or take."

He ran his hand through his dark hair. Now that I was up closer, I could see it had a wild curl to it. There didn't seem to be any product taming it. His tan skin was smooth but also weathered in a way that communicated he didn't slather expensive products on his face. And the lines around his eyes and forehead said he didn't inject Botox like many of the men at parties like this did. There were thin streaks of silver in that inky hair, barely noticeable to the naked eye, but I was making it my business to catalog every inch of him.

His left hand had a tattoo on it, a vintage looking compass with script around it I couldn't read. The tattoos on his arms weren't a cohesive sleeve; they were unevenly spaced, and although I couldn't peer closely at them, I could see they varied in intricacy and style.

I pegged him to be my age, maybe a little older than my thirty-five years.

"Well, you seem to have me at a disadvantage since you've known who I am for about..." he looked to his wrist where an expensive looking watch sat. "Twenty seconds ... *give or take,* and I still don't know who you are."

He was flirting. That much was obvious. Just because I hadn't been laid in a while didn't mean I was naïve. I watched the mating dance at the restaurant every single night. People were always screwing each other... Front of house, back of house—everyone dipped their pen in the company ink.

Except me and a handful of others who had learned our lesson the hard way and kept our work life and sex life separate. Which, in a job like mine, meant that you didn't *have* a sex life because you dedicated your life to your job.

It hadn't bothered me. I wasn't a sexual person.

Or at least I'd thought I wasn't.

Feelings and hunger were waking up in places I didn't even

know I had inside me from just this man's proximity and his play-ful, charged gaze.

"I'm not known for bringing new meaning to the term 'dare-devil,' so it makes sense you wouldn't know who I am," I replied, a hint of teasing in my tone. A very slight hint. I had somewhat of a dry, cold sense of humor that a lot of guys—most guys—did not understand or like.

They thought I was mocking them, and their fragile egos did not react well.

Kane, on the other hand, seemed absolutely delighted. He chuckled. Low and throaty, a sound that ... did *things* to me. I squeezed the stem of my champagne glass.

"Seems you've learned a lot about me in a short amount of time." He met my dry teasing tone with one of his own. "I'm impressed."

I shrugged in response.

I got the impression he had a lot of women falling over them-selves or throwing themselves at him. Not that it wasn't tempting. But again, I'd been around too many men like that, and I hadn't so much as blinked at them in years.

Kane, on paper, should've been just like the rest. Handsome, rich, flirty, charismatic. I was inoculated to all of that. Or I'd thought I was.

It turned out he was a different strain of man entirely.

"If you know even a little about me, you may know that I'm not left at a disadvantage for long," he murmured, reaching forward to take my champagne from my hand—our fingers brushing in the process and my body jerking at the contact—before lifting it to his lips, right over top of the imprint of my bright red lipstick, and taking a long sip.

I watched his throat move as he swallowed, enchanted by the muscles in his neck, the bobbing of his Adam's apple, the rough stubble covering his bronzed skin. The sparrow on his neck moved its wings.

My haze lasted for about a second.

Until the music and the voices of the party filtered back in, and there was movement to my right.

Kiera's eyes were darting between the two of us, holding her own glass and wearing what could only be described as a shit-eating grin.

She'd watched and heard the whole exchange. Of course, she had. She'd been standing right beside me the entire time. I'd just forgotten about her presence.

A dick move.

Kiera talked a mile a minute and mingled with the rich and famous on the regular, and not once had she left me standing awkwardly at her side.

"This is Kiera Graves," I said quickly, focusing on my friend. I waved at the man still holding my champagne glass with lips slightly reddened from the transfer of my lipstick. "As we've established, this is Kane Rhodes."

I had angled my body to face both of them, giving Kane my side and, therefore, not putting myself at risk of ogling him like a love-struck teenager while he drank my wine. A gesture that was so inti-mate and sexual I could barely breathe.

Kane did not seem perturbed; he merely changed his position, coming to stand beside me, so close that our bare arms brushed.

My body stiffened.

I did not like my bare skin brushing someone else's like this. I had an odd thing about touching. About *this* kind of touching. Not quite intimate but familiar in a way that made my skin crawl.

No one, not even the scant amount of lovers I'd had, could touch me in that way. Except Kane could.

A complete stranger.

It didn't make my skin crawl.

No. It sent heat sparking up my arm and into every nerve ending in my body.

"And you don't know her name," Kiera nodded to me, still grinning between the two of us like a Cheshire cat. She was enjoying this. Because she'd never seen me in this kind of situation with a man. She'd never seen me in *any* kind of situation with a man.

I'd met her after all the drama with the man I didn't speak of. Had only mentioned it to her once when she'd gotten me drunk on grappa on the one vacation she'd forced me to take in Corfu.

Kane looked at Kiera when she spoke, maybe out of politeness, but his gaze didn't stay on her for long. As if it were magnetized, it floated back to me with a sultry warmth that made the back of my neck hot.

"Unfortunately, not yet," he replied.

"Well, then I'm not doing my job in promoting her," she frowned.

Kiera was not a publicist by trade, but she tried very hard to be my publicist, agent and manager all in one.

"No, I'm just doing my job in sabotaging your efforts to promote me," I countered, focusing on Kiera and not on the man staring at me, whose arm was still brushing mine.

Kiera's scowl deepened, but she kept her attention on Kane. "Avery Hart is the best chef in New York. Which means she's the best chef in the world."

I rolled my eyes. Kiera was of the opinion that New York was the best city on planet Earth, and if it didn't happen in New York, then it didn't happen at all.

"I think many chefs in New York, and in France, Italy, Japan and practically all over the planet would beg to differ," I told her, my ears already hot. I bet they were turning red. I loathed when the conversation veered to me in this way. I should've been used to it. Part of the game was playing into praise and giving interviews, though I had strict guidelines to determine which ones I'd participate in.

Pretty much being whenever the owner of my restaurant vaguely threatened me into doing them so the restaurant got more buzz.

Not that it needed it.

Our reservation list was booked two years in advance. No amount of social cachet or fame could help you jump that list.

Kane's eyes were still on me. I could feel them. It was a surprise I wasn't just melting to a puddle at his feet.

"A chef." His voice tickled my skin. "I consider it a crime that I haven't eaten your ... food, Avery Hart."

My body might've twitched, had I not had exquisite control over my reflexes.

He'd paused on purpose, to make the not so vague sexual innuendo. If any other man had uttered that sentence, it would've come off as sleazy and gross.

With Kane, it was only riveting and charming.

I forced myself to straighten my back, my brain battling against the reaction of my body. Over how easily this stranger had power over it. The lack of control was what snapped me back into my usual façade. I cleared my expression and stared at Kane, forcing myself to ignore the heat in his eyes.

Ensuring that my hand didn't shake, I reached out and took my glass back, maintaining his gaze as I took a long sip.

He didn't speak, just watched me drink, his eyes traveling to my throat as I swallowed.

"You won't eat it for another two years," I told him after I swallowed. "That's if you call the restaurant right now and ask for a reservation. Sorry to disappoint."

"I have an inkling you are many things, Avery Hart, but I know you'll never be disappointing," he snickered without missing a beat.

I opened my mouth to sling a cold retort, even with my body

close to spontaneous combustion, but Kane didn't give me the opportunity.

"Kiera Graves, you strike me as a woman who can handle herself," Kane stated playfully, eyes still darting from her to me.

Every time that azure gaze zeroed in on me, my knees quivered, and my stomach felt like it was bottoming out.

"Oh, I can take care of myself," Kiera countered with a gleam in her eyes. One that usually signaled trouble.

"So you wouldn't be cast adrift if I were to take Avery away with me." He stepped even closer, our arms no longer brushing. They were now pressed together, and I could feel the warmth of his body, smell the depth of his cologne mixed with a scent that couldn't possibly be mixed in any laboratory. A scent that was only biological.

I had a nose—part of the job description. Taste was arguably the most important, but every sense was part of the cooking and consuming experience. So maybe my nose was more sensitive than the layperson's.

Or maybe it was something utterly and wholly innate that made my entire body jerk when his smell hit my nose.

Or maybe it was the warmth of his body, the sheer size of it, big, powerful and all-consuming.

Maybe it was the words he said, the words that it took a second to process.

"I would have to *insist* you take Avery away with you," Kiera answered. "This isn't really her scene." She waved her hand at the party.

"Avery walks and talks and has an opinion of her very own," I informed the both of them, my voice sharp, cold despite the fire in my veins.

I was the 'Ice Queen,' after all. A title coined by some disgruntled staff in my kitchen. Or maybe it had been an old lover; I didn't know. But the title stuck.

The Ice Queen of Inferno.

A rather tacky title some second-rate newspaper had run, cobbling together quotes from the scant amount of interviews I'd done to create a 'profile' on me. They'd also interviewed people who I'd fired from my kitchen, all of which did not have nice things to say about me.

Neither of the people in front of me blanched at the tone that sent grown men running away from me in the kitchen. Both of them just grinned. Kiera's playfully and knowingly, and Kane … with pure lust.

The man in question turned to face me fully, the front of our bodies mirror inches apart. Much too close for people who had only learned each other's names … minutes? ago.

My breathing turned shallow at the closeness that should've been far too intimate for strangers, yet I leaned into it.

"Do you, Avery Hart, want to leave this godforsaken party full of vapid idiots—present company excluded—and come home with me?" Kane asked, eyes twinkling with sensual promise and mischief.

There it was. Plainly. Come home with him. No bullshit. No, he was saying exactly what he planned. Desire was threaded into his gaze, into his proximity and in the chemistry between our bodies that didn't make a lick of sense.

I was about sense. Logic. Weighed risk. The only excitement in my life happened in the kitchen. I was strict about that. Nothing unexpected. Nothing chaotic. Nothing dangerous.

Kane 'The Devil' Rhodes promised nothing but chaos. Danger. I should turn my back on him.

Instead, I looked up at him and uttered a single word.

"Yes."

I hadn't thought my body could have any more of a visceral reaction to a person, hadn't thought Kane could radiate any purer sexual or masculine energy.

I'd been wrong.

The second the single syllable exited my mouth, all playfulness left his gaze.

He was a portrait of desire. Ravenous hunger.

For me.

He didn't hesitate, his arm wrapping possessively around my waist, resting his palm on my lower back.

That area burned with what felt like a brand.

"Kiera, it's been my pleasure." He gave my friend brief eye contact before moving us away.

I didn't say anything to her, letting myself be taken by Kane. A quick glance over my shoulder showed Kiera grinning ear to ear, raising her glass to me in a toast.

Whipping my head back around, the throngs of people I'd previously had to weave through parted for us.

They parted for *Kane*.

Everyone melted away from this man's path, eyes following us. I didn't miss the way people zeroed in on him. They whispered to each other. Some even snapped photos on their phones.

Even that didn't jerk me out of my daze. I was a private person. I didn't have social media, something that confounded Kiera every day of her social media obsessed life. I didn't like photos being taken of me. Not because I had some kind of murky past with an old boyfriend looking for me or something dramatic. I simply didn't like attention. Which might've confused people considering the culinary world was filled with narcissistic attention seekers looking for fame. But there was also a decent amount of us there for the passion, the art of it.

The attention should've made my skin crawl. I should've pulled out of Kane's grip and slunk out of the spotlight. But I didn't. Couldn't. Not just because his grip was vice-like. But because I didn't want to.

I cast my gaze down from the prying eyes and phones but otherwise let the moment be captured. Surely, these people were acting like sheep; one sports fan took a photo, then the person beside them followed suit because they didn't want to miss out on capturing the moment they brushed elbows with someone famous.

The photos would sit on the phones, forgotten by the next drink, I was certain.

Suddenly, we were no longer in the overly warm and crowded room that smelled of salmon canapés and too much aftershave; we were in the crisp New York air, the smell of crushed leaves welcome to my senses.

We passed the valets and people coming and going in a haze. I was concentrating on putting one foot in front of the other, trying to remain composed as the heat from Kane's body merged with the chill of the autumn air.

The party was held on the Hudson, in an industrial district that was quiet at night. The city never slept, but parts of it lay dormant, waiting for someone to rouse it. Rounding the corner, past the bustle of the party, the road was desolate, no rogue partygoers, no cabs, no one. Except me and Kane.

A man I'd just met.

Taking me down a dark alley.

Granted, he was supposedly very famous and hadn't exactly taken me by force, but I knew how quickly situations could change. Fame and the spotlight did not turn scoundrels into gentlemen. Quite the opposite, in fact.

Despite my initial reaction to the man, unease prickled up my spine.

As if sensing me tensing, Kane stopped, so I stopped with him.

"This is me." He motioned to a motorcycle that was parked along the brick side of a building. My knowledge of motorcycles was slim to none, but I could tell from the sleek shape, the color and the gleam of chrome that it was probably an expensive one. One he'd left on an abandoned side street of the city. The flippancy of someone with too much money or the ego of someone who thought they were untouchable, I didn't know.

"You want me to escort you back to the party, I'm happy to do it," Kane offered.

I tore my gaze off the bike and focused on him. The night was thick and closing in fast, but there was enough glow from the streetlights to show the sincerity on his face.

Though I didn't know anything about the man beyond his name, nickname and profession—if *daredevil* was a profession—I got the impression he was somewhat experienced with women. The wantonness in his gaze, the ease in which he'd sauntered over to me... The fact that he was rich and famous and handsome. Yes, he'd had experience.

But he wasn't assuming because I'd said yes in a crowded room while holding a drink meant I couldn't change my mind before going to a second location with him. He was making sure I still wanted this.

Kane Rhodes was sexy.

Kane Rhodes establishing consent was somehow even sexier.

"No," I stated firmly, squaring my shoulders. "I do not want to go back to the party."

It was the safer option.

But tonight, just for tonight, I wanted to dance with this devil.

Although he might've just asked the gentlemanly question, the grin that stretched upon his face was most definitely devilish.

His grip flexed at my hip.

"Don't worry." His tongue darted out to wet his plump lips. "I won't go too fast."

"You better go too fast," I raised a brow at him. "I'm expecting you to live up to your reputation."

He blinked at me, then his face got hungry and sexy, and my pussy pulsated.

Actually pulsated.

I didn't think men could literally make that happen.

"Jesus," he muttered, grabbing the back of my neck and yanking me to him so our lips crashed together.

My body responded to him immediately and violently. I was ready to climb up his body like it was a tree, so I could grind my pussy against his hard cock.

I knew his cock was hard because our bodies were pressed together.

He was well-endowed.

Very well-endowed.

"I need to get you home," he rasped against my lips. "Or else I'm gonna bend you over this fucking bike."

Another pussy pulse. In fact, that may have been a full body pulse.

"I am gonna do that." He brushed hair from my face before tucking it behind my ear. "But maybe not right outside a party full of assholes." He nodded his head in the direction of the thumping music.

I didn't quite know what to say to that, so I didn't say anything. Keeping my mouth shut was good because I feared I would tell him I didn't care about the assholes and beg him to fuck me against the bike right there and then.

And although that prospect was erotic and exciting at that moment, a voice at the back of my head told me I'd eventually regret doing something like that.

Me getting bent over a motorcycle was not the kind of publicity I wanted.

He moved backward, but not before kissing me quickly again on the lips, slipping his tongue in once more so I could taste the champagne he'd sipped from my glass.

I stood rigid and somewhat unsteady on my feet as he stepped away and did something near his bike.

"Helmet," he said, slipping something tight onto my head.

I didn't complain, though I worried about the helmet hair I'd be sporting when we got to our destination. Never in my life had I worried about how my hair looked more. And I was not a woman bothered by that kind of stuff.

But safety was more important. I'd always muttered curses about the motorcyclists I saw on the highway doing ninety without helmets.

Safety.

A good thing.

"Hop on," he said, once he was situated on the bike.

It occurred to me then that I didn't know this man. I knew that he was some kind of famous daredevil and people seemed to be impressed with him. I knew he was a great kisser. I knew he possessed the ability to make my pussy pulse.

Other than that? Nothing.

He could be a serial killer.

Or just a really big douche.

I didn't hesitate.

I hopped on the bike.

Two

I DID NOT HAVE a misspent youth.

My youth was uneventful and full of semi-normal things. Well, not so 'normal' since my father died when I was thirteen, but I did my best not to think about that. Even then, I shoved my grief away. I studied a whole lot. Had a few friends. A part-time job, a boyfriend or two because I thought I had to, though they never really excited me. I went to prom.

I did not go through a rebellious stage. There was no partying, no yelling at my mother, no bad boy boyfriend. Sure, I really liked Jess on *Gilmore Girls* and had my very first orgasm thinking about some leather-clad rebel on a motorcycle promising me a wild time.

But I did not bring those fantasies to life.

Mostly because we didn't have leather-clad, motorcycle-riding bad boys in my small town in New Hampshire. And by the time I moved to the city and had access to a larger pool of men, I was already working in restaurants most of my waking hours. There simply wasn't time to indulge in relationships.

Therefore, I had never been on the back of a motorcycle.

It turned out I liked it.

He drove fast. Too fast. Just like I'd requested.

We took turns at dizzying speeds.

The wind bit into my body, cold and fresh and hurtling through the clothing that wasn't suitable for a bike.

Kane was warm, hot, an inferno against my front and my arms which were tight around him.

It was the most reckless thing I'd ever done, getting on the back of a bike with someone I barely knew. Holding them in such an intimate way. I could feel his rock-hard abs underneath my hands and felt the utterly wild urge to dip my hands lower, to the buckle of his belt. Lower even then.

I didn't, of course. But I wanted to. My pussy, throbbing from the roaring vibration of the bike underneath me, wanted me to.

The city passed by in a whirl of lights. He wove through the New York traffic with ease, taking it at speeds that likely weren't legal and definitely weren't safe.

But I trusted him.

I'd gone insane.

I trusted a man I'd just met, a man who was nicknamed after Satan himself.

I did not have a death wish, and I hadn't thought I had a wild side. But there I was, hurtling through the city on the back of Kane 'The Devil' Rhodes's motorcycle.

We stopped in front of an old brownstone, Kane somehow finding street parking right away, which was near impossible, even for a motorcycle.

My heart was roaring as loud as the bike when he turned it off, my breaths coming in hard pants as he got off and then took the helmet off my head.

I was dazed and didn't even think of the hair I'd worried about a lifetime ago. My head whipped to him, standing on the curb, staring at me.

"That was amazing," I told him, exhilarated.

He was studying me with a light furrow to his brow like he was surprised or trying to figure something out. Trying to figure me out. There was still heat there. That liquid heat in his gaze, in his body, a sexiness that just dripped off him.

The sounds of the city were nothing but a muted roar for a handful of seconds as I let myself get lost in him, my blood still singing from the high.

"Not my place." He jangled the keys as he nodded up to the brownstone, jerking me out of my daze. "I let my publicist talk me into getting my apartment renovated." He let out a sigh that was somehow masculine. "Yeah, I know I sound like a fucking douchebag that I not only have a publicist but let him dictate how I decorate my house, but ... whatever." He shrugged. Again, it managed to be sexual and masculine and made my already raging libido spike higher.

"Anyway, I'm renting this." He waved to the brownstone that was in a quiet neighborhood—by New York standards, which meant it didn't have *Sex and the City* tourists posing in front of it— and cost some serious money.

Not that that was something that impressed me much, but I noted it.

The daredevil business paid well, apparently.

A hand at the small of my back sent sparks down my spine. "Just 'cause I rent the house doesn't mean I'm not going to own your pussy in every room," he murmured against my neck, leaning down so his lips brushed my skin.

I wasn't expecting him to say that, not after talking about publicists and renovations.

So my knees turned to jelly, almost collapsing to the sidewalk. Except Kane didn't give me the chance to, luckily. He slung me into his side and walked us both to the brownstone.

We went up the stairs, and he unlocked the door, but I barely noticed it over my galloping heart.

The clang of the front door closing and shutting out the street noise sent my heart sprinting and my vision danced with spots. The silence was oppressive, and I suddenly regretted my decision. I was not the type of woman who had one-night stands with famous athletes who effortlessly exuded sex. He might've done this many times before. I hadn't. I wasn't a sexual person, and I would be awkward and likely disappointing.

I opened my mouth to spout off an excuse and get out of there, but I didn't get a word out.

Kane grabbed me by the back of the neck and kissed me.

All of my doubts disappeared into a puff of smoke. A ball of freaking fire.

Suddenly, I was a sexual person. All I was was sex, instinct, hunger, desire.

His hands tangled into my hair, roughly pulling at the strands with the perfect amount of pressure. A spike of pain shot through my scalp, but it wasn't uncomfortable.

The opposite, actually. It only served to light up nerve endings in my body that were already singing, *submitting* to Kane.

The kiss was tongue and teeth. Kane's canines grazed my lip so hard the metallic tang of blood mingled in our mouths. He leaned back, a predatory smile on his face as he licked his lips.

"So far, I fucking love the taste of you," he declared, voice thick and raw.

He didn't give me time to return the compliment because he was kissing me again. His hands were at my ass, and I instinctively wrapped my legs around his waist as he lifted me up, having never made such an attempt before because I hadn't been so taken over with desire. And because I hadn't been confident that the man had the strength to hold me.

Kane had the strength to hold me. I didn't question it for even a second.

There was no hitch in his breath, no pause in the beautiful

assault on my mouth as he walked us in what I guessed was the direction of a bedroom. I didn't care where it was as long as it had a horizontal surface.

As my legs tightened around him, my core ached for friction as I began to grind myself against his denim-clad erection like some horny teenager.

Kane let out a growl and ripped his mouth from mine. One of his hands remained on my ass, the other cupped my chin, eyes cerulean fire as they zeroed in on me. "Was planning on takin' you to a bed, but fuck. I can't wait another single second to get inside of you."

My mouth went dry at his words, thirsty, desperate for him to sate me.

I clung to him as he lowered us effortlessly onto the floor. My back hit fabric, a rug, most likely. There was somewhat of a cushion against the hardwood floor but not much. I didn't mind the hard surface, though, not with Kane hovering over me, his lips moving down the column of my neck.

He kneaded my breasts as he kissed me, teeth again grazing my skin.

I practically swallowed my tongue when he sucked at the delicate skin of my neck.

"I'm not gonna do it because I know you're classy as fuck, but I'm just lettin' you know it's taking me great restraint not to mark you," Kane told me against my neck, pressing delicate kisses downward, contrasting with the scrape of his canines against my skin.

I arched my back as he made his way to my nipple, pulling aside the fabric of my top to expose it.

Mark me... My mind was delayed in processing his words, likely because all of my other senses were screaming.

With a hickey, he meant. The thought alone should've made me recoil. It was juvenile and archaic. But some part of me, a large part of me, wanted that mark. And if he'd asked, I would've said yes.

Luckily, he seemed to have more presence of mind than I did.

"Incredible tits, Avery Hart," Kane told me, looking up at me.

My hands tangled in his hair, I'd been desperate to run my hands through it, touch him.

His mouth went to my other nipple where he spent his time sucking, grazing his teeth.

"If you're not opposed, I plan on coming on them at some point this evening."

A jolt, right to my core.

"I'm not opposed." My voice was little more than a rasp.

He showed his teeth in a wicked grin. "Good. Now I'm gonna make you come with my mouth because I need to taste you when you come apart. Then I'll be fucking you till I'm the only one who can put you back together."

My body jerked with the words, my mind racing. Fear speared through my spine at the words. The oath. I had spent my life ensuring I was put together, not so much as a loose thread showing. I didn't want anyone, let alone a man having the power to take me apart. It should've sent me running. But it didn't. More heat flooded between my legs and I found myself wanting to give Kane that power. I wanted to be undone by him.

His hands went to my hips then, expertly undoing my pants.

"Hips up, baby."

I obeyed wordlessly, watching him through hooded eyes.

He took both my pants and panties off at the same time, tossing them over his shoulder.

Then he pushed apart my legs, placing the heels of my feet flat on the floor.

I gasped at the position, at the intimacy of it. No one but my gynecologist had been this up close and personal with my vagina. It was only because of her that I knew that everything was normal ... down there. But still, amongst all of my feelings of desire, I felt incredibly self-conscious with a practical stranger's gaze on the most intimate part of me.

What if he didn't like the way it looked?

A shallow thought, but one I wrestled with, nonetheless.

Kane licked his lips. His piercing eyes met mine just as I was about to slam my legs shut, army crawl to my pants then make my escape.

"Gorgeous fucking pussy, Avery Hart. Not that I expected anything less."

Then he dove in.

My tense body, ready to bolt, melted as soon as his lips fastened onto me. As they moved over the intimate skin of my pussy. I'd expected him to be as frenzied and borderline violent as he had been when he was kissing me. He was slower. Purposeful. Impossibly precise. As he changed his rhythm, his lips and tongue were learning me, torturing me. Then his finger slipped inside me.

I arched my back, crying out and clawing at the threads of the rug I was lying on.

Kane slowly picked up his pace, as if he could sense my body building up to climax. Already, I felt like my skin was too tight for my flesh, like I was too sensitive, like I might not be able to handle the intensity of the orgasm that was coiled inside of me.

Kane kept going, holding on to my thighs with enough force to imprint his fingertips into the soft skin. Hopefully, there would be a mark there, evidence of this, what I already knew was going to be the best orgasm of my life.

Kane's finger was no longer inside of me, both of his hands now on my ass, lifting me so he could ... *bury his face there*. So he could devour me.

The gesture, the wildness of it, the intensity of his tongue now at my clit broke me apart. I didn't know what sounds I made, if I made any sounds. It would've been impossible for me not to since I needed some way to release the pleasure that overwhelmed my entire body.

I didn't know how long it lasted, but I knew that Kane's tongue was still there, his mouth was still there, meeting the thrusts of my hips, the quivers of my body.

Slowly, I came down, and the room reappeared around me. My eyes opened, and I looked downward. Kane was still in between my legs, his eyes locked on mine.

Slowly and deliberately, Kane leaned in again and inhaled. I didn't think my spent body had it in me to do more than breathe heavily, yet I trembled in delight. It was such an unexpected and sensual act. It was ... dirty. Magnificent.

In my haze, Kane had traveled up my body, exposing himself enough so his hard, bare cock brushed against the impossibly sensitive flesh on my pussy.

I gasped out loud against his mouth as he braced himself above me with one hand while using the other to drag my leg up the side of his hip, opening myself to him further.

His mouth brushed against mine.

He tasted of me.

Me and him.

And I was someone who used taste as a vehicle for a prestigious career. It was my most utilized sense. And the explosion of us on my tongue was unlike anything I'd ever tasted.

Kane's expression was something like the cat that ate the canary except the canary was me, and he was no cat. He was a lion.

"Yeah," he hummed. "You like that." He pushed his cock against me so my eyes rolled to the back of my head, and my back arched.

"You're gonna fuckin' love this, Avery Hart," he growled.

Before I could question what he meant, he was inside me. His cock filled me, to the brim.

Instead of clawing at the no doubt expensive rug I was lying on

—I was being *fucked* on—I slipped my hands underneath Kane's tee to claw at his back. He hissed in pain—and hopefully, pleasure—and drilled into me harder.

I tore at the skin of his back like I was a frenzied animal. Because I felt like an animal. That's what our coupling had made me. I'd been stripped down to the core, exposing that I was just a hedonistic creature, ripping at him in lust, desire.

Kane was relentless in his thrusts.

"Harder," I groaned.

Kane didn't hesitate to heed my command.

He slammed into me so I saw stars. So impossibly hard that my spent body tensed again, coiling up. He was big. Very big. On the verge of uncomfortably large. Especially with the power in which he was pummeling into me.

But the discomfort somehow made it rawer; it took the edge off a pleasure that might've been too much otherwise.

It turned out, I needed a little pain with my pleasure.

In other words, he was made for me.

Kane's face hovered over mine, his mouth touching mine but not exactly kissing me. We were close, breathing, panting into each other's mouths. Another animalistic, carnal thing that shouldn't have been as impossibly sexy as it was.

I was no longer clawing at his back, my hands were just resting there. My hips were meeting his, thrust for thrust, chasing the orgasm I didn't feel like I would survive.

The rug was burning the exposed skin of my back. More pain. The perfect balm to the overwhelming pleasure, to carry me a little longer.

Part of me wanted to stay there, on the floor of that brownstone, with a rug burning my back, with Kane 'The Devil' Rhodes inside of me, on the edge of an orgasm that would ruin me. I didn't want to go back to my life. The one I loved. The career that was more than my passion. It was my identity.

I wanted to stay there, on the floor with a stranger inside of me for reasons I couldn't fathom.

But as stubborn as I was, I wasn't in control at that moment. Something bigger than me was. So Kane's thrusts took me over the edge. When I cried out, his mouth covered mine. There was a grunt against my lips as I milked Kane of his own release.

I lost all sense of time, of place, of anything but the waves crashing over me.

In short, even in that moment, I knew Kane Rhodes had ruined me for all men.

Three

THAT WAS the best sex I'd had in my life.

Not that I'd had particularly mind-blowing sex in my life.

I hadn't thought I was *capable* of having mind-blowing sex. I was always too in my head, too particular, not sexual enough.

Or so I'd thought.

I'd just never been with someone who could take me out of my head, show me what I didn't know I wanted, somehow who knew my body, knew how to make it sing. Make me scream.

Scream his name.

I'd done that.

My throat even felt hoarse.

I might've felt ashamed if it were with anyone else. But Kane was so wild, he was so free, confident with his pleasure, being in an animal state with him felt completely natural.

Even though we were practically strangers.

Maybe because we *were* practically strangers.

There was a freedom in that.

He didn't know me. Hadn't slogged through the required amount of dates I required before I slept with someone. Hadn't

32

formed the idea of me as being maybe conventionally pretty but also somewhat cold and unemotional as many of my old boyfriends had.

"I feel like I have to fuck you politely," one had said.

Kane most definitely didn't fuck me politely.

"I feel like you're grading me and making me a failure at having sex," another had told me.

If Kane thought I was grading him, he didn't make it known. And he sure as hell didn't fail.

We hadn't spoken. Not apart from the name screaming, and his exceptional dirty talk that made my toes blush.

The sex had concluded. At least I thought it had. But then we'd done it again. And again.

Once on the floor of the entryway, once on the floor of his bedroom and once in the actual bed.

My body was incapable of producing more orgasms, I was sure. And as impressive as Kane was, I assumed he'd need a cooldown period of some sort.

We were both fully naked, both flat on our backs, staring at the ceiling, breathing heavily, covered in a thin sheen of sweat.

I wasn't self-conscious about my perspiration. Kane's tongue had already tasted it, and it hadn't seemed to put him off. The opposite really; he'd loved the carnal act of licking my sweat, and despite my penchant for cleanliness in all areas of my life, I'd loved it too. It felt lascivious and dirty and *right*.

Nor was I self-conscious about the long period of silence we enjoyed as the dust settled. It was nice. I didn't feel the need to stroke his ego, to tell him how amazing he was, didn't feel insecure about my performance since he'd made it abundantly clear he'd enjoyed himself. He obviously didn't feel the need to talk either.

Until now.

"Do you like fettuccine?"

I opened my mouth, searching for a response.

Though it stood to reason Kane would speak eventually, that was most definitely not what I thought he'd say.

There was only one way to answer when Kane 'The Devil' Rhodes asked you if you liked pasta after he'd fucked you three times.

"Yes."

"Great, stay here. I'll whip us up some."

Kane leaned down to kiss me.

Not a peck on the lips kiss. He kissed me. Completely. With vigor.

I got the impression Kane didn't do anything by halves.

That impression was helped when his hand trailed down my naked body to cup me possessively between my legs, fingers exploring the area that was sensitive yet immediately wet for him.

He grinned wickedly as he pushed off the bed and put those same fingers in his mouth.

"Babe, I make a bomb ass fettuccini, but I don't think I'll ever taste anything as fucking spectacular as that cunt."

My eyelids fluttered.

Vulgar. Vigor. I liked it.

"Well, maybe once you try my food you'll have a different opinion," I replied, my voice lazy, soft almost.

His grin turned cheeky and playful. "I don't doubt your capability in the kitchen, but I do doubt there's a plate on Earth that can rival *that*."

With that parting note, he got out of bed and left the bedroom. I could only guess that he was going to cook fettuccine naked.

Not something that would've been appealing to me in any other circumstances. It was unhygienic and impractical. But the image of Kane doing it was very appetizing indeed.

I sank back into the bed and stared at the ceiling.

He'd ordered me to stay here. No one ordered me to do

anything. It was the other way around. Even in the bedroom ... up until now.

I'd happily and without resistance submitted to Kane. I enjoyed it immensely, being able to let go of the reins and just enjoy the ride. No pun intended.

But now that the sex had concluded—at least for now, though a carnal and greedy part of me wanted more—I did not want to heed orders. I did not want to stare at a ceiling and guess whether Kane was downstairs cooking naked. I wanted to find out for myself.

Kane, in fact, was cooking naked.

It was the view of his ass, his muscular and tattooed back at the stove that greeted me when I walked into the kitchen—not naked.

I'd put on a tee I'd found in a suitcase discarded in the walk-in closet, clothes spilling out of it. Kane was just staying there, after all, and it didn't surprise me that he wasn't the type to keep everything neatly folded.

I was the type to keep everything neatly folded and organized. Everything in my apartment and kitchen was color-coded, alphabetized, systematic. Messy men irritated me. Kane did not. For whatever reason.

I'd grabbed the first shirt I could find. It was soft from countless washes, worn so much the print had faded into nothing. It smelled faintly of laundry powder but mostly of him. Because of our height difference, it hit me mid-thigh. I had curves that meant I was never the woman who put on her boyfriend's clothes and was dwarfed by them. Not that I was the type to put on my boyfriend's clothes. What was the point in that? I had clothes of my own. I'd always thought it was a ridiculous thing that only happened in cheesy rom-coms.

I got it now. The act of wearing a lover's clothing after they'd just owned every inch of your body. When you smelled of sweat and sex and him.

Yes, I got it.

I put on panties, though. Another thing I didn't get. Walking around without underwear. It seemed impractical and unsanitary. Especially after sex. Even protected, which Kane luckily had the foresight and sensibility to ensure because I hadn't even been thinking about condoms. I had no memory of him putting it on the first time, but I'd been a little preoccupied. Even though I was on birth control—for practicality's sake more than anything—I had never been so reckless or so intimate with someone to have sex without a condom.

My bare feet didn't make a sound on the hardwood floors, nor on the plush rugs as I followed the telltale signs of pots clanging in the kitchen.

My body felt relaxed and at home as I entered the kitchen to the smell of onions and garlic.

I didn't say anything to Kane as I watched him move about the kitchen. He did it like he'd done everything else, with confidence, an ease in his movements. My eyes traveled over the tattoo on his back. It was the one piece on his body that was cohesive. It looked like it could've been painted on the ceiling of some old church in Europe. In the middle of his shoulder blades was a heart shape, wings behind it and various knives stabbing into it, blood dripping from the heart. Cherub-type angles were on either side of the heart and on the bottom, holding a chalice as if to catch the blood. Flames burned around the scene.

I didn't know why, but the tattoo seemed beautiful yet somehow sad. I ached to know the history of it.

"I told you to stay upstairs," Kane said as he turned toward me. Though I hadn't spoken, Kane must've sensed my presence. He was grinning. He didn't look like the man who would have such a sad scene immortalized into his back. "You're a woman who doesn't do what you're told... I like that."

I found myself grinning back even though I wasn't someone who easily smiled. People, mostly men, often commented on my perpetual 'resting bitch face.'

That didn't bother me. Women who didn't smile on command, who didn't walk and talk the way men wanted them to, and most especially, women who had power, were more often than not labeled as bitches.

I looked around.

The kitchen was nice, like the rest of the brownstone. All renovated with hardwood floors, expensive art, tasteful furnishings. The long space contained quartz countertops and stainless steel appliances, everything top of the line and sparkling clean. Everything except where Kane had been. That area was an explosion of ingredients, chopping boards, plates.

I kept an impeccably clean kitchen. Didn't tolerate any kind of mess. My staff knew their station had to be spotless at all times. This was absolute chaos to my relentless order. Yet for some reason, it didn't set my teeth on edge.

I perched on the barstool at the kitchen island.

"I'm not one to do as I'm told," I agreed. "Nor am I someone who lays in bed while someone else cooks for me."

I didn't add that I'd never had the opportunity to lay in bed as someone cooked for me. It felt a little pathetic.

His mouth twitched. "Well, we're gonna have to change that, aren't we?"

My stomach dipped at the way he said it. So offhand, as if there were going to be opportunities for us to change that, chances to use the royal 'we.' I told myself not to read too much into it.

"Wine? Beer?" He nodded to the wine fridge beside the subzero.

I licked my lips. I was thirsty. Not that I was a big drinker, but right then, a crisp, cold beer suddenly sounded appetizing.

"Beer," I responded. "But I can get it."

"Keep that luscious ass in that stool." He pointed at me with a spatula. "I got it."

I pursed my lips. It went against everything in me to not just heed the command but to let someone run after me, let alone a man. I was about power balances, not owing anyone anything, not seeming weak, vulnerable.

An intuitive voice inside of me told me that Kane was the most important person to guard myself against, yet I ignored it. I kept my ass in the stool as he strutted to the fridge to get me a beer.

I watched his naked body move. It was covered in tattoos and scars. A lot of scars. I'd noticed them when he undressed, but I had other things to concentrate on at that point. I didn't really think about what being Kane 'The Devil' Rhodes meant. But it meant pain, by the looks of those scars. Risk.

The scars, the tattoos, the muscles, the bone structure all spoke of a dangerous life, yet the cheeky grin he wore spoke of something else too. Something more playful. Safer. Or maybe that made him all the more dangerous.

The hiss of a bottle opening sounded before Kane rounded the island to place the beer in front of me, pulling up my hair to kiss the back of my neck.

I shivered.

The casual affection was unnerving.

But what was more unnerving was that it felt natural. Right.

"Gotta say, babe, I thought of you as more of a fine wine type of gal," he said, walking back to the pan where he resumed the process of cooking.

I put my shaking hand around the bottle dripping with condensation, taking a long drink to wet my dry throat.

I contemplated his words. "I suppose that aligns with what little you know of me." I wiped the wetness from the bottle onto his tee. "I don't mind wine, especially the expensive stuff. It's my job to know it, pair it with the dishes I serve. Well, it's technically my sommelier's job, but I don't hand over reins easily."

"Well, that tracks with what *little* I know of you," he teased, looking over his shoulder at me.

The underlying assumption being he thought of me as a control freak didn't feel like an insult. Kane didn't seem to feel threatened by the control I liked or my 'abrasive' personality, my inability to go with the flow—all things previous boyfriends had been vocal about.

Then again, he'd just met me, and I'd uncharacteristically gone with the flow, so he hadn't really had the full experience. My throat clenched at the thought of someone obviously reckless and free like Kane knowing the real me... My schedules, my routine, my order. He would not like that.

For the first time in my adult life, I wanted to change myself for a man. A man I just met.

I shook that feeling off, taking a sip of my beer before putting it down. "I don't drink often," I continued, my voice notably cooler. "I don't enjoy it. Being drunk."

To my surprise, Kane nodded, sipping his own beer. "Yeah, it's more fun to do crazy shit sober. Doing anything with a buzz just kind of ... cheapens it. For me anyway." He shrugged. "Each to their own, though. I'm not saying I haven't gotten fucked-up. I have. Plenty. But in my old age, I enjoy making decisions based on needs, not on a chemical reaction to booze. And it would've been a fucking tragedy if I hadn't been sober for the last two hours."

I crossed my legs, needing friction as all of my hastily-gathered cool melted.

"I don't know about wine pairings, but I'm thinking beer and pasta go pretty well with mind-blowing sex." His voice was thick with mischief and lust.

There was nothing I could say, so I just nodded my head and watched him cook.

He didn't press the conversation further.

It was nice, lapsing into comfortable silence, no need to force conversation.

I didn't remember a time in my life when I felt more relaxed.

Though my instincts told me to get up, to clean up after Kane, to take over, I ignored them. I just sat and watched Kane "The Devil" Rhodes cook me pasta.

Naked.

I filed that away in my memories, knowing even then that it was something I'd revisit long after he'd forgotten about me.

* * *

I placed my fork in the center of my clean plate, licking my lips. I hadn't thought I'd be able to finish the mountain of pasta Kane had served me, but I was obviously hungrier than I'd realized.

"That was amazing," I said honestly.

He smacked his lips, his own plate empty too. "I get the chef's stamp of approval?" he asked without self-consciousness.

I nodded. "You definitely do."

In more ways than one, was what I left unsaid.

I leaned over to get his plate, stacking it with mine. "I'll get the dishes."

Kane caught my wrist. "Fuck the dishes. They'll still be there in the morning."

My eyes went to the chaotic kitchen, to our plates. Again, it went against all my instincts to leave such a mess.

"Give you a little brain aneurysm thinking of this sitting overnight?" Kane teased, this thumb gently rubbing the inside of my wrist.

I looked at him. He was smiling. Again, he wasn't put off by my obvious Type-A personality. He seemed to find it … endearing?

I smiled back without even meaning to. "Maybe."

He didn't reply, just looked at me with too much knowing and tenderness.

Suddenly, I was uncomfortable under that gaze. Uncomfortable in his shirt, with a stomach full of his food. It was easy. Too easy.

"It's late." I yanked my wrist out of his grasp, voice cold.

It was the middle of the night. I wasn't tired. Though I should've been. I'd been up since dawn, worked to get everything prepped at the restaurant for one of my very rare nights off. I was on my feet for hours out of the day, and I wasn't athletically fit. Then there was the physical exertion of the sex.

Despite that, my limbs tensed, ready to bolt. "I should go."

Kane quirked a brow. "Babe, I'm far from fuckin' done with you." Clearly, he was not bothered by my tone, my change in demeanor. Not threatened by it. He nodded his head to the dishes. "That was just to fuel the tank. You want to go?" I'd opened my mouth to argue, but he spoke first. "Really want to go? Or you think you should? Just like you think you should do the dishes?"

My spine straightened at the way he spoke. Plainly, challenging me. But there was no judgment or malice.

I chewed my lip. An anxious tic from my youth that I hadn't done in years. He was picking away at me, at the shields I'd thought were iron but he tore down like they were made of paper.

"Yeah," he nodded, even though I hadn't actually said anything.

With ease and strength, he tugged at my barstool, turning it to face him. He cupped my face. "Just for tonight, I'm gonna push against all that order inside of here." He stroked my temple. "Gonna give you a taste of chaos."

And then he kissed me. With chaos.

And all of my doubts went up in flames.

* * *

Kane's tongue between my legs woke me up.

He didn't even say good morning.

Just dove. Right in.

"I've got to go," he rasped, mouth still glistening with ... me.

I deflated, my limbs boneless as my body twitched with aftershocks.

Of course, he was eager to flee.

I'd literally fucked him on the first ... not even date. We shared less than one drink together and one bite of a shitty appetizer and a midnight bowl of pasta.

I'd traded jokes and small talk full of sexual innuendo, got on a bike with him, then let him fuck me on the floor of his entryway.

Then on the floor of his bedroom.

Then in his bed.

Yep.

That sent a message.

One that did not coincide with us sharing breakfast together.

One that did not coincide with anything more than a one-night stand. One of the best nights and mornings of sex I'd had.

Ever.

A frantic sort of panic clutched on to my lungs, making it hard to breathe for a handful of seconds.

I'd never see Kane again.

Yes, I'd only met the man the previous night, and I certainly didn't believe in love at first sight—I knew I wasn't in love with him. But I was in .... *something* with him. I felt changed in a pivotal way. It felt wrong and strange to go back to my life from before without Kane, without him touching me, looking at me.

I shook myself from those thoughts.

I was not being myself.

I did not get wrapped up in men.

I did not let men twist me up and ruin me.

"Yes, so do I. I've got to get to the docks." My voice was cold.

His brow quirked playfully. "You work at the docks too?"

I got up from the bed, wanting to hide my nakedness with a sheet but unwilling to seem self-conscious. Being comfortable in my skin was a power move, so I gritted my teeth and didn't think about the cellulite on my thighs or the likelihood that Kane bedded women who didn't have a speck of it. "I need to get the catch of the day so I can plan my menu from there."

Kane didn't hide the way he stared at my nakedness. It was clear he was not looking at my cellulite. No, it was with sheer desire that his eyes skimmed my body.

My skin prickled at his hungry gaze.

"Don't you have people to do that kind of thing?" he asked, sounding genuinely curious as he rested his elbow on the bed and leaned into his hand. "You're the boss, aren't you?"

"Yes," I told him, trying to act comfortable that this seemingly benign conversation was happening with both of us naked. "That doesn't mean anything, though. If anything, I need to work harder than anyone else."

Kane's flirty smile faltered, replaced with an expression that was impossibly intense and probing.

Luckily, it lasted only a moment before the smile returned.

"Well, far be it for me to keep you from your fishing." He held out his hand to help me up.

Again, panic swirled beneath my sternum at the prospect of going about the motions of getting ready to leave. Internally scolding myself, I pushed past it.

By the time I'd used the facilities and the toothbrush I found in the bathroom, Kane had brought up my clothes from last night.

He was wearing underwear. That was it. I restrained my urge to drool at his six-pack, his tattoos, inspect his scars. There was no point in doing that, trying to learn more about a man I would never see again.

Instead, I took my clothes.

He sat on the bed and watched me dress. "What does your normal day look like?"

The simple curiosity in the question took me aback. He wasn't asking because he felt like he should be polite and pretend to care about it; he genuinely seemed like he wanted to know.

"It depends on the day, but usually, the first thing I do is source protein for the restaurant. If I want to or have the time, I may go to look at artisan producers of ingredients. Then I go to the restaurant to get started on prep, and I'm there till close." I kept my tone brisk as I pulled my halter over my head. I knew I'd have to stop at my apartment to change. Not to shower, though. I wanted to smell like Kane all day.

"What does *your* normal day look like?" I asked him as I put on the last of my clothes. I'd obviously forgotten what I told myself moments ago when I'd decided I didn't need to learn more about him.

He showed his teeth, creating a smile with an edge. "Baby, I haven't had a normal day in my life, and if I've got anything to do with it, I won't have one till the day I meet the reaper."

We couldn't have been more opposite if we'd tried. Completely wrong for each other.

"I'll walk you down, get you a cab." He pushed off the bed then went to the closet, presumably to retrieve something from his exploding suitcase.

"You don't have to; I'm quite capable of hailing a cab," I called to him, suddenly feeling awkward and needing to get out of there so I could get distance from him. Surely, once I was out of his orbit, sense would return, and I'd realize he was just another man. A handsome one, a muscled one, and one with a talented tongue, but a man, nonetheless.

"I know you're quite capable." Kane emerged as he pulled a shirt over his head, wearing cut-off sweats. "But grant me the boon, at least."

He was charming. Effortlessly so. And I felt myself falling for it. "Fine," I huffed.

He walked me down the stairs with his hand on the small of my back, my steps becoming heavier and heavier.

Kane's gait was easy, unhurried, casual. Of course, it was. He'd likely done this dance countless times, hence why he was so effortlessly likable. He wasn't holding on to last night like it was something sacred. It was a night of passion, of fun, of chaos that was nothing but another night to him.

I strove to treat it as something similar for myself. A taste of his life, of recklessness. I could channel it into my food. Store last night away somewhere like I did all the other complicated experiences in my past.

The air was crisp, the morning light still emerging, though the city was thriving as it always was. The flurry helped center me. Though I didn't love chaos, the wildness of the city helped to center me. I wasn't a New York native, but it had been home to me for almost my entire adult life.

At the curb Kane whistled, and within seconds, a cab was there.

My heart hammered.

Kane took my hips, pressing our bodies together so he could kiss me. Fully.

Despite my panic, I returned the kiss with fervor.

The horn of the impatient cab driver ended the kiss. Cab drivers in New York didn't care about life-altering moments. I was sure they were immune to couples thinking they were main characters in some love story by now.

Kane smiled against my lips. "I don't think the cab driver will take lightly to me fucking you against the hood of this car like I'm tempted to, so I'm gonna have to let you go."

My body sailed with lust at the mere mention of such an act. For anyone else, it would be nothing but a ridiculous comment. For Kane, I wouldn't be surprised if he was into that kind of thing.

I wasn't into that kind of thing, I reminded myself.

I put on my mask of indifference, trying to step back from Kane, but he held fast.

He cupped my face. "I'll be seeing you, Avery Hart."

It sounded like a promise.

But it was just another line. We didn't exchange numbers, make plans. He was being polite.

"I'll be seeing you, Kane 'The Devil' Rhodes," I replied back with a flippancy in my tone I was proud of.

He held me a beat longer before opening the door to the cab. I all but fell into it, forcing myself not to look at Kane again as he closed the door then banged the top of the car.

My body sank into the faded leather of the seat.

I wouldn't be seeing Kane again.

A good thing. Since he was the antithesis of everything I was. A near miss. That's what that was. A brush with a meteor that very well could've leveled me. I closed my eyes, sinking back, inhaling the smokey smell of the cab while running through my day. I forced Kane from my mind, promising myself I wouldn't think of him again.

KANE

I hadn't wanted Avery to leave. Watching her get dressed, walking downstairs and hailing her a cab had gone against all of my better instincts.

Not that I thought I had better instincts.

The sheets smelled of her. My mouth tasted of her. As soon as she left, I felt the urge, the fucking hunger to chase her down the street and fuck her against a brownstone. Fuck who was watching.

In fact, the thought of doing it, doing her in the street, had my cock standing at attention. Not that it wasn't already painfully hard from her walking around naked, apparently not feeling the need to cover up. If I had it my way, that woman would not wear a thing to hide the perfection that was her body. Her curves.

Except the thought of another man glimpsing the dark pink of her nipples or the hair covering her pussy had me clenching a fist. I was not jealous. Not by a long shot. All of my relationships—if you could call them that—had been open. I wasn't into chaining a woman to me, and I sure as fuck didn't want chains. It didn't bother me that the women I was with were also with other men— sometimes other women. It comforted me. I didn't want the pressure of being their one and only. Much too dangerous.

But the thought of another man, or woman, touching Avery, tasting her, even fucking holding her hand… I shuddered with fury.

A shower. A cold fucking shower was what I needed. Giving in to the fury licking at my throat would do nothing for me. Would ruin years of work.

The cold shower did little to help. I made myself come against the spray thinking of Avery. Not of her tits nor her ass nor her cunt. But to that half-smile of hers that I got the sense people didn't see often. I felt possessive over that smile.

"You're late," Julian, my publicist informed me when I called him.

He was on the set of the fucking photoshoot I'd regretted agreeing to since I woke up with Avery's body in my arms this morning.

"I need you to get me into a restaurant," I said in reply.

"And I need you to get to 450 West Thirty-One Street five minutes ago. Have you even left yet?"

I'd closed the door to the brownstone just seconds before he posed the question. I had the urge to buy it off of Kris now that I had the memories of fucking Avery in the entryway.

I'd have to pay over market because the fuck liked to make money, and he'd sniff out that it was personal. But I didn't give a fuck. I wanted to halt all renovations on my penthouse, sell it and move into the place where I'd first tasted, first owned, Avery Hart.

"It's called Inferno," I said, jogging the few feet to my bike.

My cock twitched at the memory of her behind me last night, her heat pressing into me. I'd been sure I'd have to ease her into the ride; she was uptight—in a way that made me desperate to unwind her. Classy. She was not someone who looked used to being on the back of a bike. She'd surprised and delighted the fuck out of me when she'd demanded I'd go fast.

Trust... She'd trusted me with her life within ten minutes of meeting me. And that was something I'd gathered was out of character for her.

"Are you fucking with me?" Julian practically shrieked.

I considered what it was about me that made a woman as beguiling and interesting and in control as Avery Hart to trust me. "No, I need a table there tonight."

"You are not shitting me," Julian muttered. "The waiting list for Inferno is two years long."

Though I expected some kind of waiting list, that gave me pause. When she'd said that last night, I thought she was teasing me. Clearly, she wasn't. Avery was good at what she did. Powerful. Talented. I liked that.

"You good at your job?" I asked Julian.

I could almost feel his chest puffing up. "I'm the best in the fucking business."

"Well, get me that table." I fingered the leather she had sat on last night, imagining fucking her against it at some point.

"It's impossible."

"Buy the fucking restaurant if we have to," I demanded. "I'm getting that table."

I got on the bike.

I wasn't done with Avery Hart.

Not by a long shot.

AVERY

MY MIND WAS ELSEWHERE during the dinner service.

Which was a bad thing.

No matter what was going on in my personal life—though I hadn't had one to speak of in years past—the kitchen melted all of that away. There was nothing but the task in front of me, the three other tasks ahead of that and the various elements that had to be started and finished all at the same time in order to create the perfect dish.

Running a kitchen of this caliber, keeping the food up to my standards, was a constant, back-breaking task. It required every shred of my attention and energy. It was not for the fainthearted and not for people who wanted to live with a work-life balance.

Work *was* my life.

I'd liked it that way.

Until Kane had fucked me thirteen ways from Sunday, and I hadn't been able to get him out of my head.

Luckily, I was practiced enough at this menu that I could work with my distracted mind. Luckily, I had a staff that I'd handpicked, hand trained and who all could theoretically handle the night should I suddenly drop dead or take a sick day—which I never did.

I seared a wagyu, thinking about the chances of seeing Kane again while also checking on the scallops to my right.

"These are done in three seconds," I told Ferris, my sous chef.

"Yes, Chef," he replied dutifully, taking them off exactly three seconds later.

My attention went to where Hallway was plating.

"That quail egg needs to be three centimeters to the right," I told her.

"Yes, Chef," she said, taking direction without pause.

I thought of Kane.

He'd taken me to a temporary home, he'd had to leave in the morning, putting me in the cab without asking for my number. The recipe for a one-night stand.

What was I to expect? He was some famous daredevil playboy. He wasn't going around looking to settle down.

Nor was I.

"A guest wants to come back to compliment the chef," Michelle, my front of house manager, informed me.

I glanced up from the plate I was garnishing to show her my raised brow.

I did not entertain shit like that. A lot of chefs reveled in the attention, especially if it was from some prominent person or another. I did not.

There was a reason I was back here making the food instead of out there serving it and interfacing with people. I wanted to feed people, give them experiences. I did not want anything else. Not to mention that there was still thirty minutes of service remaining, and I did not have a second to spare. Every moment in my kitchen was precious and accounted for. I expected all of my staff to treat time as the priceless commodity it was, to not waste it. And I did not expect anything of my staff that I wouldn't expect of myself.

Michelle knew all that, of course. She'd been working with me for years and was excellent at her job.

"I know, I know." She reached over to grab a linen to start wiping plates before service.

Michelle didn't have idle hands. No one in my restaurant did.

"But this guest was *very* insistent and somewhat famous."

I rolled my eyes as I moved from plate to plate. "They always are." The restaurant was the best in the city, had a two-year waiting list for a table, and despite my distaste for the practice, celebrities constantly tried to jump that line. It was the game, and I had to play it, though.

"This is different," she spoke as she wiped. "This is one you want to let compliment you."

Again, I didn't stop moving. Stillness for me was death but I did note her tone—somewhat dreamy which was almost unheard of for Michelle. The woman was not prone to emotional outbursts of any kind. She was straight edge, calm and collected under even the most stressful of situations. She was the most valuable person in the restaurant and one of the few people I trusted implicitly.

"Fine," I sighed.

I didn't check my appearance, didn't round to the other side of the kitchen where waiters were expertly and dutifully taking plates and shouting out tickets.

I didn't look up as the door to the kitchen swung open, and a large body walked through it. A flash of black. Tall. Male. That was all I noticed.

Whichever celebrity or politician or millionaire who wanted to show off to his friends about 'knowing the chef' was going to be offended that I didn't look up to greet him, and I didn't care. Letting him in my kitchen was all I could do. Using power and influence to gain access to the place I considered my sanctuary pissed me the fuck off.

"I need three more scallops," I called out, frowning at the sear on the plate in front of me.

Not right.

"Yes, Chef!" Ferris replied.

I pulled a ticket. "Two wagyu, one scallop, one risotto," I read off. "I need them yesterday; we're two minutes behind on service."

Two minutes. An age in my kitchen.

"Yes, Chef!" my team called back.

The clang of pots and the sizzle of pans sounded around me, noises I barely heard anymore, but noises that comforted me with their chaos.

Two minutes behind. My team could make that up. But I was going to be delayed by the person now standing in front of me. He hadn't spoken. Probably because he expected me to look up, fawn over him.

Still, I worked at plates.

"Impressive."

The single word had me freezing. For three seconds. Three seconds with my hand hovering over the plate, not doing anything at all.

I'd never frozen for that long in a kitchen.

Not since...

I didn't think about that.

The deep voice washed those memories away. The tenor of the single word. The way it boomed right through me. It was liquid sex.

Slowly, my eyes moved up.

Kane was standing there, dressed in a black tee and jeans.

The restaurant had a dress code—something I didn't approve of as it was classist and elitist, but once again, I had to play the game—and it was famous for enforcing it upon even the most powerful of guests.

A football player had thrown a tantrum last year when he wasn't let in because he was wearing sneakers.

Expensive, designer sneakers that cost more than the host's monthly take-home, according to him.

He was not only refused a table but banned indefinitely.

People tended to adhere to the dress code.

Not Kane.

And somehow, he'd been let in without incident.

Maybe it was the electric presence, the cheeky smile, the charisma he had about him that was somehow both effortless and powerful. Warm too.

Hot.

Even though I'd spent my adult life in sweltering kitchens and hadn't broken a sweat, suddenly my upper lip felt moist.

A few seconds. That's all I paused in shock for. It might as well have been hours in my world.

"Chef?" Ferris prompted, looking uneasy. I'd never spaced out in my kitchen. My chefs knew to rely on me, and I could tell by the concerned tilt of Ferris's mouth that he was slightly worried.

Regaining my senses, I stepped back so he could plate the scallops I asked for.

Wordlessly, I finished dressing the plate then tinkered with the placement of the scallops, tweezing on a garnish before a final wipe down.

"Away on fifteen!" I yelled, mentally calculating the amount of scallops we'd plated tonight with how many I'd gotten from the docks this morning.

"We've got three orders of scallops left," I told Angela, our head server.

"Heard, Chef," she replied, expertly balancing plates before floating toward the restaurant at a brisk pace.

I forced myself to keep working despite Kane watching me.

"I don't want to interrupt ... *Chef*," Kane drawled.

My toes curled at the title I'd been addressed by for years, by countless people. No one had ever made the deferential term sound sultry, dirty and impossibly sexy.

Kane managed all of those things, said in the same tone he'd murmured naughty things to me last night, with the gaze that communicated he knew what it felt like to be inside me.

The clang of the kitchen brought me back to earth, and I jerked, looking back down at my plates.

"You're busy," he continued.

"I've got twenty-seven minutes left in service," I informed him. My voice was crisp, cold, not betraying my simmering insides. I felt panicked at being put off-kilter in a kitchen, *my* kitchen, by a man. My guard was up. It needed to be up.

"Then I'll be back in twenty-seven minutes," was his reply, not obviously perturbed by my icy response.

"I have to close down the kitchen after that," I said, talking to the plates.

"Behind, Chef," Ferris announced softly. I knew my second was hovering because he was worried, protective, even though he was younger than me. He'd been in my kitchen the longest. We weren't friends by any stretch of the imagination—by design, I wasn't friends with any of the staff—but there was mutual respect there.

I stepped aside for him to plate my wagyu.

"Well, I'll be here until the kitchen is closed, then." Kane's response was slightly playful, yet with a sensual edge and an iron foundation. He was making it known that I wasn't going to be able to dismiss him.

"Fine." Frustrated and secretly excited, I let out a sigh. I said the word as a dismissal, focused on the plates, refusing to look up.

I held my breath for ten seconds, waiting, stealing myself.

When I looked up, Kane was gone.

I didn't know whether I was relieved or disappointed.

Luckily, I didn't have time to examine my feelings as the chaos of the kitchen required my full attention.

Not for the first time, I was infinitely glad about that.

* * *

I was on edge the remainder of service.

It didn't help that I heard the murmurs of my usually professional staff about Kane's appearance. It seemed even the people who worked long hours in my kitchen and weren't prone to pandering to celebrity diners somehow not only knew of extreme sports stars but were also impressed by them.

That intrigued me. I hadn't been aware that 'extreme sports'— whatever that meant—were popular enough to permeate my kitchen.

Again, I didn't let myself get intrigued. I couldn't slip. Wouldn't. Though none of my staff were brave enough to ask questions, I could tell they were curious.

Like the well-oiled machine we were, my staff made quick work of cleaning the kitchen and completing end of day tasks.

I let everyone go, but Ferris still lingered.

"I'm fine, Ferris, go home," I told him.

He hesitated for a split second, peering at me with his brows knitted together.

"Yes, Chef," he nodded, turning and leaving me. Alone. In my kitchen. Which was usually my happy place. The quiet, the clean juxtaposing with the rest of the night. I would run through the tasks I needed to do then check over everyone's stations, even though I knew they'd be spotless.

Sometimes, rarely, I would share a drink with Michelle at the bar once the guests had left.

Tonight, the quiet kitchen did not calm my heartbeat. Anticipation curled up my back like a snake, my palms sweating. Michelle had already cleared it with me that Kane stay and be informed when the kitchen was closed down. She'd assured me she'd send him back. And she'd had a glimmer in her eyes, the slightest teasing, but other than that, she said nothing. The consummate professional.

I held my breath as the doors to the kitchen opened and closed.

Kane was in here.

There were not dozens of other people coming in and out, no one shouting tickets, no plates to distract me. Just him and me.

And he looked as good as he had when he first came in. Better. His forearms were defined and sinewy, peppered with tattoos. His hair was ruffled, messy. There was a large shadow of dark stubble on his angular jaw, making him look all the more rugged. His eyes... They were what captivated me. They were zeroed in on me with a different intensity than before. Heavier. He'd seen me in the kitchen. Seen me as a powerful woman and it hadn't scared him away.

No. If I was reading him correctly, it excited him.

His eyes ran up and down me. I wasn't brave enough to hold his gaze and just let him look at me, so I kept wiping at surfaces that were already gleaming.

He settled on a stool in front of the plating counter, lazily leaning against it as he cradled his chin in his hands, watching me.

"Your food is good," he said.

The compliment was simple. Too simple, my ego would say. My food was not just good. It was fucking great. Extraordinary. Some of the best food to be plated on the planet.

It was that way because food was my life. I'd spent years honing my skills. Hours upon hours tweaking singular elements on each dish, traveling the world to pick up flavor profiles and cooking techniques.

My food was not merely *good*.

People had said many great things about my food over the years.

Yet somehow, Kane's simple, unadorned compliment meant the most.

He said it with a kind of concrete intensity that glued me to the floor. That made my insides do somersaults.

"Thank you," I replied, my voice wispy.

I was glad I had the act of polishing the stainless steel countertops, or else I might've felt awkward.

Awkward.

Like I was a pimply teen at a dance, and my date's hand was on my lower back.

"I figured you'd have people to do that." He gestured to where I was polishing. "You doin' this for our benefit?" he asked.

Our.

A single word. Our. Intimate somehow.

I tried to remain emotionless, knowing the counters were pristine, and all my jobs for the night were done.

Never someone to put off the difficult things, I abandoned the basket of soiled kitchen linens and faced Kane without anything to occupy my body.

His attention was squarely on me. As it had been since the moment he walked through the doors to my kitchen. Before, though, I was busy. I stole glances at him, of course, but there was never the opportunity to just stand under his gaze.

My palms were sweaty, heartbeat thrashing.

"No," I said, my voice even ... ish. "I finish out the night myself."

He tilted his head. "Every night? You? Alone?"

I nodded once. "I don't do anything in this kitchen I don't expect my staff to do."

Something flickered in his eyes. Something hot and hungry.

He got up from his stool. "We're going to revisit you bein' here past midnight alone at a later date."

My cheeks heated at the possessive lilt to his tone and the gist of what he was saying.

I was about to tell him that we were not going to revisit anything of the sort because this was my kitchen, and I called the shots here.

But I stopped myself. It was second nature to put on my ice queen persona, to establish that I was not going to be ordered around or dominated.

A part of me, one that Kane had awakened, wanted to let go of that persona, wanted to try something different. I wanted to submit.

So I tried something different. I didn't lash out with my ice-tipped words. I let the first thing come to my head, then I said it.

"I googled you," I blurted.

Kane merely blinked in response. To be fair, I didn't give him much of an opportunity to respond since I launched into my next sentence within seconds.

"It is kind of a douchey thing to do," I clasped the back of my neck. "Googling someone. But I did it. And I figured it may make me somewhat less douchey if I informed you that I googled you."

I wiped my palms on my pants. They were sweating. I did not get sweaty palms. Sweaty palms meant nerves. Nerves meant you were second-guessing yourself. Your ability. There was no room for that in my kitchen.

Yet there I was. Sweating.

Nervous.

Kane, the handsome prick, did not seem nervous in the slightest. His body was relaxed, his expression lazy yet aware at the same time, his eyes sparkling as the side of his lip turned up in a smirk that made my panties damp.

Not from sweat.

"What did you find out?" he asked, seemingly unbothered about my googling.

I studied my fingernails for a moment, scrambling to find my cool. "That you have two Olympic medals."

He shrugged. *Shrugged* at the mention of Olympic medals.

"One, technically," he corrected.

I frowned. My brain might not have been firing on all cylinders right then, but I'd eaten up any and all information about this man with ravenous hunger and good recall. I was sure it was two. I'd even fact-checked my original source. One couldn't always trust Wikipedia.

"Silver doesn't count." He casually thrummed his fingers against the stainless steel.

I regarded him. Though he still had a mischievous glint in his eye, he was being serious about the medal thing.

I pursed my lips. Most people would try to argue with him on the point. Merely getting to the Olympics was kind of a big deal, let alone coming in second. At least that's what *most* people would think.

But most people hadn't competed at the utmost levels. Only the 1 percent of the 1 percent had. Most people didn't do that because you had to drive yourself half crazy to get there. You had to sacrifice a lot. You had to be brutal with yourself. And you had to have one pursuit: to get to the top.

If you got second to the top, you weren't satisfied. Because what you turned yourself into to come in second meant you only mattered if you came in first.

Or maybe that wasn't everyone.

I, at least, understood the sentiment of what Kane said, so I didn't argue with him.

His lips quirked ever so slightly in response to my silence, and I wondered if he'd received the predictable response when he'd said similar things to people in the past.

"What else did you find out?"

I sank my teeth into my bottom lip. "More accolades and wins for various extreme sports, along with multiple disciplines, which I understand isn't common."

He shrugged. "I learn fast and get bored easily."

There was no arrogance in his tone. But there was a confidence. One that was supremely sexy instead of annoying.

"Anything else?" He slid off the stool then stepped toward me. *Prowled* toward me would be a better description. "Because if not, I'm gonna do something in this kitchen that none of your staff are gonna do. Ever."

My heart was now in my throat.

"Gonna fuck you on that counter you just polished so good."

"That's a health violation," I informed him lamely after realizing my mouth had dropped open. I couldn't think of anything else to say.

Well, there were plenty of things to say. There were people in the front of the house, finishing up. They could come through the door at any moment. They weren't likely to, but it was a possibility. I was a professional. This restaurant was my life. Doing something like fucking a patron, a celebrity, in my kitchen could ruin everything.

I could've said any of those things. Instead, I mentioned a health violation.

"I don't give a fuck." Kane bared his teeth.

Then he kissed me.

I melted into the kiss. Immediately. Every single reservation I had about his plans drifted away. It was right, impossibly right, for him to take me right here in the place I held most sacred.

He worked at my chefs' whites. Tore at them.

I helped him get off my shirt, giving him access to my bra, my nipples.

I gasped as his lip fastened around one, my hands tangling in his hair.

"You okay with this, Chef?" he paused to look up at me. His voice was thick and guttural.

"Yes," I panted down at him without hesitation.

His hand went below the waistband of my pants, inside my panties. "You okay with this?" His fingers worked at where I was wet. Soaking.

"Fuck yes." My eyes rolled to the back of my head.

He leaned in to nibble on my ear while he rubbed at my clit. "You okay if I bend you over that same counter you were so carefully using tweezers to garnish an hour ago?"

No reservations. "Yes."

In one blink, one ragged breath, I was whirled around. My hands found the stainless steel before Kane's palms were on my hips, pulling them back, lifting my ass upward. He kicked at my ankles to spread my legs then hurriedly dragged down my pants. I stepped out of them automatically, feeling euphoric at being naked. In my kitchen.

Kane had one hand on my hip, holding me in place as I heard the telltale crinkle of foil.

His palm found my pussy, circling my clit so my knees buckled.

Then his finger was gone. His cock was there. Filling me. To the brim.

I opened my mouth to cry out, despite knowing people were within yelling distance.

Kane's palm covered my mouth, muffling my scream.

Clean enough so I could see Kane's distorted reflection in the surface, I stared at the stainless steel as he pounded into me.

"You're the boss in here, Chef," he grunted in my ear as he fucked me. "Got me so fucking hard, seeing you command this kitchen."

My body coiled, ready to come in seconds as him bending to whisper in my ear changed the angle, getting him deeper.

"I like to know that you're the boss here, and that you'll think of me taking you." He reached around to find my clit. "Want you to plate every dish and remember *this*." He found the perfect spot, and I exploded.

My teeth bit into his palm on reflex as I hurtled into the abyss.

He continued pumping, grunting in pain or a release of his own —I didn't know, I was too far gone.

By the time he stopped, I was ready to collapse against the counter.

Covered in sweat, I was gasping so heavily, my breath was fogging up the surface.

Kane's lips latched on to my neck, kissing me there, licking at the perspiration.

I shivered in delight.

Carefully, with the utmost gentleness, he pulled out of me. Still, I whimpered.

He held on to me, bracing me as he, presumably, took care of the condom then buttoned his jeans.

"Step in, Chef," he said quietly.

I looked back to where he was crouched, at my ankles, holding my pants and panties, ready to put them on for me.

"I can do it," I protested, even though my limbs were lead.

"You can," he agreed. "But let me."

I relented without a fight, stepping into my pants and panties before letting him pull them up. After pulling my body upright, he put on my shirt again, buttoning with steady, tattooed fingers.

I watched, still trying to catch my breath.

One of those fingers went under my chin, tilting it upward.

His ice-blue gaze smoldered with intensity.

"Chef, that was indescribable," he murmured before he gently laid his lips on mine. "I'll wipe down the counters, ensure you don't get a health violation. Then you're gonna come home with me."

Even though this was my kitchen and I called the shots, all I did was say, "'Kay."

$$Five$$

WE WERE BACK at Kane's borrowed brownstone. After having sex in my kitchen. Something wild and irresponsible ... two words no one would use to describe me. I didn't feel guilt or shame over the act, even though I thought I would. I took my work seriously, my kitchen seriously. It was like my church in some ways. Yet it wasn't sacrilege to do what I did with Kane

Especially when he worshipped me.

Once he was done cleaning up our 'mess'—not that there was any visible evidence of what had taken place beyond some palm marks—he walked me to his bike, which he'd somehow found a parking spot for in the alley that adjoined our kitchen, where the dumpsters were.

I didn't ask him how he parked it there. Didn't ask any questions, actually. I just got on the back of his bike.

This time, we didn't have sex in the entryway, though I stared at the rug, ornate and very expensive looking. Again, no evidence of what had taken place on it last night, but my cheeks warmed at the memory.

"You eat?" Kane asked, smirking as his eyes followed mine.

I contemplated the question, unable to orientate myself between his sexual innuendos, unyielding carnal desires and then questions about my basic needs.

He toyed with strands of my hair that had escaped my tight bun after riding on the back of his bike. "You spent your entire night cooking for other people, cooking for me. After seeing you move in that kitchen, I'm going to assume you didn't feed yourself."

Kane was perceptive. And it did something to me to know he'd given this some thought. Been thinking about me beyond just being someone he was having sex with. This was a nurturing energy that I didn't expect from the daredevil who emanated sex and danger.

"I ate earlier," I told him. Not a lie. I ate like I normally did—a snack, usually, depending on how busy it was. Maybe some protein.

Kane stared at me, inspecting my more than ample curves that communicated I wasn't exactly starving. "Not enough," he decided.

Then without saying anything else, he directed me to the kitchen I'd been in in the early hours of the morning.

"Ass there." He sat me in a seat before rounding the island to the fridge.

"I'm afraid that I'm not going to be able to create something anywhere near your level," he said from the fridge. "But I do make a mean sandwich." His arms were full of what looked like assorted meats and dressings. "That good with you?"

I didn't know what to say. This man had wanted to feed me, to cook for me, two nights in a row. No one had done that for me in my adult life.

"People usually urge *me* to cook for *them* when they find out I'm a chef," I chuckled.

"I'm not surprised." He plonked the ingredients onto the counter without ceremony. A bottle of mayo rolled toward me.

I rolled it back, and Kane caught it.

"But I'm not looking to have you work when you're around me, Chef," he said. The title made my fingertips clench the island. It was one I'd heard all my life but it was always used to establish deference, distance. Now it was used to create an intimacy I hadn't known with another person. "I'm not gonna be another person wanting things from you. And this is also purely selfish on my part. I want you to have energy to go upstairs and ride my cock."

Cue pussy tingles.

"You gonna let me make you a sandwich?" I nearly swallowed my tongue as I watched his tongue dart out to wet his lips.

I nodded curtly.

Then, after eating his—admittedly delicious—sandwich, I went upstairs and rode his cock.

* * *

I wasn't practiced at 'riding' men.

Arguably, the act itself should've been part of my cache—it communicated control, agency, things I needed inside and outside the bedroom.

But it also required confidence.

Something I had plenty of outside the bedroom.

Inside, not so much.

My mother had more recently turned into someone who was 'free' in discussions of sex and anything else. But this identity was new. It had started after my father died, while I was starting to distance myself from her.

Before that, sex and even periods were something talked about in metaphors, with a heavy dose of embarrassment.

I'd therefore slunk away from sexuality, even though I got breasts early, which only made things more uncomfortable for me.

I'd focused on my goals, concentrated on my desire to be a world-renowned chef and hadn't deviated. Losing my virginity had been awkward, painful and unpleasant.

Every dalliance afterward had been variations of the same. I'd let men take charge, hoping that one of them would clue me in as to why everyone seemed so obsessed with sex. None of them had.

Until Kane.

Now I got what all the fuss was about.

I didn't feel self-conscious about my size and whether I'd be too heavy for him. Though for a second, I was concerned about my lack of experience and whether it would show. But Kane kissed those doubts right away. My body took over, my instincts. I reveled in watching the pleasure on Kane's face as I moved up and down, the new angle a perfect fit for me and capable of giving me an orgasm within minutes. I'd raked my hands down his chest, covered his tattoos. He'd pulled my hair free from its bun so it had brushed his skin. Our lips crashed against each other's, our damp skin grinding.

Yes, I was now a definite fan of this position. Though I suspected any position with Kane would be enjoyable.

I'd cleaned up then gone back to bed in nothing but my panties. Kane was naked. The second my knee had hit the mattress, he'd grabbed me by the waist and tugged me to him.

I was half splayed on top of him, his arms tight around me. Possessive. Warm.

Kane wasn't so much of a cuddler but a claimer. Every inch of my skin felt like it belonged to him.

I liked it. It didn't make me feel suffocated or submissive. It made me feel something else. Revered? Safe? I didn't want to inspect the feelings a man I'd known for only two days was giving me.

It was late. I'd been up early, worked all day and barely had any sleep the night before. I'd had very athletic sex. Twice. Technically, I was exhausted. But my body also felt wired. I didn't want to sleep. Who knew what tomorrow would bring? It wouldn't bring Kane and me in this bed with the world ceasing to exist outside. Normally, I sank into bed, eager to go to sleep, then to get away from the quiet of the night and back into the bustle of my kitchen.

Not this night.

Kane was still awake too, if the tautness of his muscles and the way his grip around me hadn't relaxed was anything to go by.

"What made you want to be a chef?" he asked, breaking the thick, comfortable silence between us. He'd obviously sensed I was awake too.

I looked up at him, resting my face in my hands.

"What made me want to be a chef?" I repeated.

"The way you move in that kitchen…" His thumb brushed my bottom lip. "It was magnificent to watch. It was like you were born to do it. Like it was effortless."

I laughed. "No, I was just trained relentlessly in some of the toughest kitchens in the world, drilled to make it look effortless."

"You can't train that, the way you were," Kane disagreed tenderly. "That's something in your blood. Was one of your parents a chef?"

The mention of my parents gave me pause, momentarily shoving me back behind my shields, into the cool embrace of my ice queen persona.

But Kane's warm body, his firm hold and the sincere curiosity behind his question gently coaxed me back.

I cleared my throat. "No, my parents weren't. My father was an amateur chef, a foodie. He's where my love of it stemmed from, but it grew into something bigger than that for me."

I was anxious to get off the topic of my parents, especially my father, so I did something I rarely did; I babbled without thinking entirely about what was coming out of my mouth.

"Food is chaos and control in one. You get to nourish people and give them an experience they'll never forget. There are rules. Some you can't break, some you absolutely can and have to if you want to be remembered. But there is order underneath it all. Or that's what I like to think."

I shrugged, feeling self-conscious about what I was saying.

"You don't want to hear this." I looked downward at the comforter.

Kane stopped playing with my hair so he could tilt my chin upward.

"I want to hear everything there is to know about you," he said softly. "Every word."

Again, he was being completely sincere. He wanted to know me. He was interested.

"Continue," he demanded.

"Um, well… I just, like it. Like the order and the chaos. Like that I can be comforted and surprised in the kitchen, and it gave me something I wanted—no, something I needed. Without it…" I traced the ridges of his abs. "Without it, I don't know who I'd be."

I stopped talking because I needed to take a breath.

"Aside from Kiera, I don't have friends," I confessed. "No interests, hobbies. I don't travel unless it's for work. I don't take vacations. I don't really speak to my family. So this is it. Inferno is my life. Food is my life."

It was a rather shameful admission, one I hadn't fully intended on giving. Kane, by all appearances—and some hefty googling—had a full life. Bursting at the seams, really. He didn't specialize in a single profession. His main sport seemed to be motocross, but he also had Olympic medals for snowboarding, and he raced cars 'for fun' yet had qualified for some of the top races in the country.

He'd climbed Everest, for heaven's sake.

In addition to those accomplishments, he had what appeared to be a glittering social life. He was pictured with countless celebrities at parties, on yachts, walking down the streets of various cities with his arm slung around the shoulders of famous models and actresses.

Yes, it was rather shameful to admit to this man that my kitchen was all I had.

I was attempting to burrow into myself, hiding behind my shields.

But Kane flipped us so I was on my back, and his body was covering mine. He braced himself on his forearms, his lips inches away, barely brushing mine.

He stroked my eyebrow, searching my face.

"I've never had a passion like that," he murmured quietly. "Never had something so deeply embedded in the core of me." He clicked his tongue. "At least not in the past."

My throat burned upon hearing that last sentence. It couldn't mean what I thought it meant. It couldn't mean me. No. Absolutely not. I was hearing things.

"It's precious, something to be immensely proud of that you have that talent," he continued, his voice low. "I find you very fucking impressive, Avery Hart." He moved so I could feel his hardness pressing into my core.

I gasped, instantly responding.

His lips pressed down on mine, kissing me slowly, purposefully, lazily. But it was also a claiming. His kiss felt like a brand.

With devastating slowness, he pushed inside of me.

My body writhed with the unexpected pleasure of it. I arched my back against the bed, clawing at the sheets as he took his time filling me.

Once he was fully seated, he didn't give me the friction I sorely needed. Everything inside me felt raw. Not just from the sex earlier in the night but from the admission, from opening up in a way I hadn't before.

This didn't feel like the sex we'd had before—hot, animalistic, carnal. No, sex after learning personal details was intimate in a way that felt terrifying and exhilarating at the same time.

"Chef, open your eyes."

I hadn't realized I'd squeezed them shut.

Slowly, I heeded his request.

Kane was hovering above me, taking in all the details of my face.

"I like you, Avery Hart," he whispered. "And I consider it a great fucking honor to have my cock inside of you."

Though the admission was tender, serious, I couldn't help but let out a small giggle.

A giggle.

I didn't giggle.

I rarely laughed.

But a giggle was something that feminine, carefree women did. I was not that.

Yet there I was, giggling with Kane inside me.

Not likely to be good for his ego.

I waited for his eyes to shutter, his body to tense as he lashed out at me for the giggle.

But instead, his lips stretched into a large grin.

"Like that." He nuzzled my neck. "Hearing you happy like that while I'm inside you."

He moved, and my giggle was gone, replaced by a moan of pleasure.

"Yeah," he said, more seriously. "Like the laughter, but I'm gonna aim for the screaming of my name now."

And he got it.

I screamed his name, but it also felt imprinted on my insides.

Kane turned up at the restaurant again the following night. After dinner service. He just sauntered in the back entrance as though he owned the place, had every right to be there and had done it a million times before.

It wasn't easy to just walk in the back door, or the side door that led to the dumpsters and the alley. I'd ensured that, for the safety of my staff. There was a keypad on the exterior door, and there were security cameras and multiple people whose job it was to notice if there was someone at the back of house who wasn't supposed to be there.

Kane had, apparently, charmed his way back there.

I wanted to be mad about it. I really did. Except the vision of him watching me go about my end of night chores as if I was performing a strip tease sent all logical thought from my head.

"Hey, Chef," he murmured when I looked up to see him standing there.

And there went my cool. The greeting sent fire into my veins.

His hair was long enough to be pulled back into a man bun. I hadn't liked that kind of thing. But pulled back, it showed off his angular chin, clean shaven this time. His heavy brow, contrasted by those electric-blue eyes. The crooked nose, and the scar on his lip was more prominent somehow.

He managed to look menacing, mysterious and mischievous all at once. Oh, and masculine. Hugely masculine. I noted his tattooed hands had nails that were painted black. Something unexpected, yet he pulled it off, and it only added to his appeal. His effortless style.

Meanwhile, I was in my chef's whites. My face was likely flushed from the heat and the business of the kitchen. No gloss on my lips, no mascara to help make my brown eyes 'pop' as Kiera said. But Kane was looking at me as if I were dressed to the nines.

I bit my lip and finished my chores in record time. We didn't have sex in the kitchen again. It felt like a one-off. A sacred memory. A pivotal one.

I walked with him to his bike as if it were a foregone conclusion we were going home together. All of the dating advice from people like Kiera would go against this. Play hard to get, establish space, boundaries, independence. Don't make yourself too available for him. She'd drilled such things into me many times.

But I didn't want to play games with Kane. He seemed unflinchingly honest with me. Treating this, us, like it was natural. As easy as breathing.

And nothing came easy to me before, most especially relationships.

So I was going for it.

"What's your address?" he asked, leaning me against the bike. He'd kissed me senseless prior to this, so I didn't have the wherewithal to do anything but rattle off my address, let him put a helmet on me and get us on the bike.

Riding through the city on Kane's bike had quickly become my favorite thing in the entire world. The cool breeze, the lights flashing by, the roar of the bike. I had no responsibilities but to hold on to Kane and let him take the wheel. It was thrilling.

Peaceful.

Peace...

Something I'd never known until I met Kane "The Devil" Rhodes.

* * *

"This is your place, huh?" He had walked inside, doing a slow spin to take in the entire area. It didn't take more than a spin. And it didn't need to be a slow one either.

My studio apartment was big by Manhattan studio apartment standards. The sleeping area held enough space for a queen bed, two side tables, a trunk at the end and even a set of drawers stacked neatly underneath the large window that looked out at the skyline.

The entrance separated my sleeping area from my living area, which consisted of a green velvet sofa that had admittedly seen better days but was soft and comfortable and covered with throw pillows and blankets Kiera had bought. Kiera bought most any and all decorative objects that didn't serve as a direct function of the apartment.

I was a bare bones kind of woman. I didn't spend a lot of time on the couch, certainly not enough time to flip through hundred-dollar coffee table books or burn candles that likely cost the same.

My flowers were fake, which again, was Kiera's doing, only after she fought relentlessly to get me to brighten up my space with fresh flowers. I didn't see the point when they'd eventually die.

So because of my friend, my apartment had a *slight* bit of personality and wasn't totally devoid of warmth. The personality wasn't my own, though. It was borrowed from my best friend, who knew me well enough to make it look like me. Or attempt to. My personality and interests were one in the same: my job. I didn't have time for much else and didn't define myself by anything else.

The kitchen was small, with new appliances that I'd purchased when I'd bought the apartment. I hadn't bothered to do much other than that, so the shiny appliances looked out of place against the faded linoleum and yellowing paint.

I had never been self-conscious about my apartment. When I was outside the kitchen, I found myself around a lot of wealthy people—despite my best efforts. Regardless, I had never felt pressure to live up to the expectations of others.

I didn't feel the need to own outrageously expensive bags or jewelry. I liked good quality clothing, but it was simple pants, shirts, tees. I hadn't needed to prove myself to anyone. My food did that.

With Kane's eyes on my living space, I wasn't embarrassed about how small it was, how all of the furniture was second hand... But I was mindful of the quiet markers of wealth I'd caught off the man. The expensive but not splashy watch, the low-key but well-made clothes. The general way he carried himself. Oh, and the fact that he was world famous.

He was renting an entire brownstone. His *penthouse* was being renovated, no doubt by some outrageously expensive interior designer. Not that he seemed like the kind of person bothered by all that, I just knew that's how celebrities rolled.

I didn't feel judged, having the rich and famous daredevil in my compact apartment. But I felt ... naked. And the man had seen me naked. I wasn't someone who considered her apartment her sanctuary or anything. I wasn't someone who searched for sanctuary, beyond my kitchen. Chaos, noise, movement ... that was what I relished. Therefore, I wasn't in this small and quiet apartment more often than I needed to be.

It was with Kane's presence that I realized I didn't have a space that reflected who I was. Unless you counted the huge, gleaming kitchen and the stainless-steel appliances, cleaned to the point of shining every day—everything cold and hard and lifeless. Until I got in there and sparked the fires, brought in fresh produce and scented the air with food. Which I hadn't done in a long while, admittedly.

"Not impressive enough for you?" I asked him without snark. I was genuinely curious as to what Kane thought of my apartment. I didn't think he was the kind of person to judge based on possessions, but I couldn't know him completely in the short time we'd spent together.

In my experience, people with money and power were excellent at putting on acts. Some of them were genuine and good people. Most had been at some point before the opulence and the sharpness of the world turned them into something entirely different.

Kane's eyes shot to me. "I'm *plenty* impressed by you, Chef, and I'm not someone impressed or otherwise by real estate. It's just ... not what I was expecting."

I leaned against the counter. "Interesting. And what were you expecting?" Again, I didn't ask the question with any bite or offense; I was simply curious as to what kind of image Kane had built of me.

He moved to my bookshelves which contained countless paperbacks that had been bought with good intentions yet hadn't been touched, and recipe books so worn, some of the covers had been almost ripped away entirely.

I didn't cook using recipes often these days, but starting out, I made it my mission to learn everything I could. It was the old adage, 'you've got to know the rules in order to break them' or some such thing. I wanted to know food, cuisines, front and back. Every technique, from every culture, I took it upon myself to master.

"Well, from what I gather, you're somewhat of a celebrity chef..."

"Ugh, I am definitely *not* a *celebrity chef*," I rolled my eyes, spitting out the two words with distaste. "I have not appeared on a single reality show bearing my name, I don't judge cooking competitions, and I haven't slapped my name on a line of subpar cookware sold at big-box stores."

I had been offered each of those things, with money that made Kiera's eyes pop but hadn't swayed me in the slightest. Kiera had tried to convince me the first few times I got the offers, but now she understood the answer would always be no.

Kane winked at me. "Okay, tell me how you really feel."

I smirked. I guessed that was a little snarky. "I'm not judging chefs who go that route—"

"Yes, you are," he interrupted. "Which is fine with me. You don't have to get political with your answers. I like the truth."

I licked my lips. His eyes followed that movement, and my nipples pebbled. "Okay, I do judge them," I admitted slowly. "But I'm sure they judge me on my snobbery about how they earn their living."

"Or maybe they're insanely jealous of your principles."

I shrugged. I didn't have friends amongst my contemporaries in the culinary world. Partly because I didn't party like a lot of them did, and I wasn't friendly. But also because the world was competitive. "Doubt it."

"Anyway..." He peered at me after putting a book down, his eyes twinkling. "I won't say the C word since I now know it's a trigger, but from what I understand, you're a *well-known* chef at a restaurant that charges fifty dollars for a salad. I can't presume to understand how payroll works, but I do know it's your name on the door."

I nodded, understanding where he was going with this.

"Though the neighborhood is good," he continued, speaking of the Upper West Side. "And I know the criminal cost of rent in this city, I'm guessing at this stage in your career, you could get a one bedroom if you wanted."

There was no judgment, just curiosity. Kiera had said the same thing, many times, urging me to go apartment hunting with her.

I shrugged. "I like the building. It's close to the restaurant, and I don't need more than this." I gestured around my living room slash kitchen slash bedroom.

After putting down a well-worn recipe book, his piercing eyes searched my features. "You really mean it."

I nodded. "I don't say things I don't mean."

Though Kane made it his business to really look at me when he was staring, the weight of it, in my apartment of all places, was suddenly too much.

I moved to the kitchen, deciding I needed to busy my hands, even though they'd been busy all night. I couldn't just stand there with Kane ogling at me.

"What are you doing?" he asked, looking down at the counter.

"Making dinner," I explained, following his eyes.

"*Dinner?*" he repeated, his lip curled in disgust. "This is what the Michelin Star chef cooks herself for dinner?"

I bristled, leaning back and folding my hands across my chest. "There is nothing wrong with a humble peanut butter and jelly."

"You're not wrong," he agreed. "I've consumed many in my life and have been perfectly satisfied. But I've also eaten your food which made me realize that I'd never been truly satisfied until I put something you made in my mouth."

My knees trembled, and my stomach did a weird flip thing all the way down to my pussy.

Kane looked up at me, his irises dancing with hunger and mischief and palpable sexual energy. "You are capable of creating greatness. And you deserve to eat better than peanut butter and jelly."

I stared at him, slack-jawed for a second or two. Then I composed myself, clearing my throat. "I cook food all day. Wonderful, complicated food. Every waking hour is concerned with menus, with the most minute details from where the fish is obtained to the garnish on the plates. Whether or not parsley puree should be squeezed, spooned or left off completely. I do not have the energy to make any more decisions about garnishes and proteins. It's cliché, but I'm sure it's on par with the house cleaner living in a mess or therapists being craziest of them all. I'm sure with your chosen profession you take it easy when you're not racing motorcycles or hurtling down the side of a mountain or whatever. You're more careful."

Kane had been staring at me intently as I spoke, hanging on every word. I'd never had anyone, let alone a man, listen to me with such rapt attention.

Okay, that was a lie. Everyone in my kitchen listened to me like that, taking notes of the most minute details.

But a man, a romantic partner, never had. Granted, I didn't have a whole lot of experience with romantic entanglements, but the few I'd had rarely listened without a phone in their hand, one eye on the TV or just a general glazed look in their eyes.

The weight of having the attention of a romantic partner, of a man like Kane, was hard to stand under.

He didn't speak for a long time, just stared with his intensity, with that smirk that held something deeper, something more reverent and something all too heavy for a Tuesday evening.

"I was more careful when I didn't have an audience," he said finally. "But I'm beginning to understand there's nothing careful about me right now. I've never been in more danger than standing here in this apartment."

My heart tried to escape my chest. I got his meaning, what laid beneath his words.

Me.

Us.

Was there an us?

He left the words hanging there for a long time before he rolled up his sleeves, striding toward the kitchen to open the fridge.

He surveyed the contents, clicking his tongue.

I couldn't be entirely sure what was in there—maybe an old takeout box or some expired condiments. A bottle of champagne that Kiera had put in there, since she was of the opinion that one must always have champagne in the fridge 'in case of emergency.'

"You're a chef," he chastised, popping his head over the door. "And this is what you have in your fridge?"

I couldn't deny it, so I didn't respond.

He looked from me to the fridge then went to my cupboards.

"Well, I do love a challenge," he muttered as he leaned into the fridge and grabbed the champagne. "Open that, won't you, Chef? Then go and relax, although I have a hunch that word isn't even in your vocabulary. Sit, watch your man perform a miracle if you must." He winked. "Otherwise, drink, read, watch TV. My only requirement is that you get off your feet."

I looked at him as he opened cupboards until he found a frying pan, setting it on the stove. He didn't ask me where anything was.

I was still holding the champagne.

He looked over his shoulder at me, raising a brow.

"I'm hoping to fuck that you have proper glasses for that." He nodded to the bottle. "I'm a heathen; I'll drink out of a coffee mug if I must, but you deserve better."

"I have glasses," I replied robotically. I did because like the champagne, Kiera ensured that I had champagne flutes. I also had

Bordeaux, pinot and cabernet glasses. Not because I drank a lot of wine but because on the off-chance I did have a glass—usually with Kiera—I needed to have the proper vessels.

Same with all of my pots, pans, knives and cutlery. Everything was top of the line, out of place in the faded-paint cupboards.

"This is for a celebration," I finally said, referring to the champagne.

"Every day we're walking this lump of rock hurtling through space is a time to celebrate," Kane quipped. "And finding you on this hunk of rock is reason to celebrate. Open the wine, Chef."

The last part of his sentence was uttered lower, his tone sultrier.

I did the only thing I could do. I opened the wine.

* * *

"This was amazing," I said honestly as I set my napkin on my empty plate.

Somehow, Kane had made a meal for us using the scant amount of ingredients in my kitchen. Linguine. With caramelized onion, garlic and some fried pancetta I had in the fridge. Simple. But everything done right—the exact balance of flavors, the pasta perfectly *al dente*.

"Glad you liked it, Chef," Kane replied. "We're going grocery shopping tomorrow, to ensure you have food in your fridge to sustain life."

I gaped at the offhand comment. *We*. Plans for tomorrow. I had a million things to do for the restaurant tomorrow. Like I did daily.

But I couldn't say no to going grocery shopping with Kane. Something so pedestrian. Something so … normal.

"People, men most especially, don't cook for me," I said instead of addressing the grocery plans. "And if they do, they don't do it three nights in a row."

"There a question in there, Chef?" Kane asked, lazily playing with a tendril of my hair.

He did that, touched me. Often. As if it were normal. As if he were unable to keep his hands to himself. Even when we sat at my already compact table, he'd wrenched my chair closer to his so our sides were pressed together.

"Why?" I asked.

There was a lot more than a question about the food in that word. Why was he here still? Why me? In my googling, I knew I looked nothing like the women he usually dated. Models. Stunning, shiny, slim.

I was not ugly, but I was not stunning. Definitely not shiny. I always had more than one hair out of place, too busy to be worrying about beauty routines. And despite the sporadic nature of my meals, I was not slim. Food was my life; I needed to actually consume it in order to be good at my job. Plus, I had a naturally curvy body. Being slim wasn't in the cards for me.

Kane, although he hadn't known me for long—four days, was it only that?—seemed to understand that the single word wasn't a simple question.

He stared at me, still toying with my hair. "Because, Chef, I've never tasted anything like what you cook. Never looked into someone's eyes and wanted to drown in them. And I've never felt more anchored to this hunk of rock than when my hand is on you. When I'm inside you."

My chair screeched as he snatched me from it. I was straddling him in a couple of heartbeats. He was already hard.

"You're addicting, Chef," he murmured, lips brushing mine. "And I'm not at all mad about that."

Then he kissed me. Hungry, claiming, without reservation.

I kissed him back with the same fervor, grinding against him.

He stood without obvious effort, and I instinctively wrapped my legs around his hips. Never breaking the kiss, he walked us through my apartment.

"Though I plan on fucking you on every surface of this apartment, I think we'll be conventional and start with the bed," he growled against my mouth. "My woman's had a long day, and she needs comfort. And multiple orgasms."

"I should shower," I gasped as he threw me down on the bed. "I've been working all day."

The past few nights, I hadn't thought about the reality of sleeping with Kane after such long days, but I was suddenly self-conscious. He didn't shy away from oral sex, from inhaling my scent, and surely it couldn't be … pleasant.

"We'll shower." Kane bared his teeth. "Together." He leaned over to take off my pants then inhaled me over my panties. "But I like this smell. Fucking love it. I'll show you just how much."

And he did.

Then we showered.

And it wasn't until I was just falling asleep in his arms when I realized he'd referred to me as 'his woman.'

Six

A BANGING on the door filtered through my unconscious brain.

I was warm. Comfortably toasty. Encased in Kane's arms, as I had been the entire night. His grip didn't even relax in his sleep; he held me tight to him although I could feel that he was still asleep by the even cadence of his breath. How he was sleeping through the banging, I didn't know. Then again, if he lived in New York for any extended period of time, he was likely used to loud and strange noises at any point of the night. I also had the inkling that Kane didn't live a quiet life in general, therefore, he was used to noise.

I didn't exactly live a quiet life either, but as a rule, I slept lightly. That rule was challenged these past nights with Kane, as I'd slept deeper than I had in recorded memory. Of course, that also could've been because he had fucked me into sheer exhaustion.

The banging didn't let up, nor did Kane rouse.

"I know you're in there; I tracked your phone!" a voice boomed throughout the two rooms of my apartment, coming through the front door. A familiar voice.

I sighed, knowing she'd never let up.

I carefully pulled myself out of Kane's arms. He tensed for a split second before making a sleepy groan and turning over to push his face into the pillow.

Though there was the urgency of the banging and the yelling, I couldn't help but take a beat to admire Kane. He was now splayed on my bed, his large body taking up the entire surface. His hair brushed over his face, features completely and utterly relaxed. The sheet barely covered his naked body, exposing the muscular skin of his arms and torso, peppered with both scars and tattoos. His tattoos were haphazard, chaotic without rhythm or sense, different styles, different vibes, different messages.

There was an intricate image of a man riding a bull in exquisite detail, a crudely drawn knight holding a sword, a snake eating its own tail, a straight razor dripping with blood. A motorcycle. Just to name a few.

It should've looked messy and incoherent, but it only made him all the more impressive and wild. He'd told me about some of them, the cruder ones were from bets he lost. Which showed who Kane was. He'd put ink on his skin for life because he lost a bet.

I felt a stab of envy toward him in that moment, the freedom he must enjoy, feasting on life. I felt a stab of envy toward whomever was going to end up with him. It surely wasn't going to be me. This ... *thing*, whatever we were, was going to be short-lived. We were much too different to survive beyond the wild sex and pasta at two a.m. phase. I had to remember that Kane was a man who obviously jumped into experiences with both feet, and those experiences burned bright and hot, but something—someone—would come around to capture his attention again.

I jerked as the pounding intensified in tempo and volume. With a pit in my stomach, I snatched Kane's tee from its spot on the floor, throwing it on before running out the door of my bedroom, already realizing that soon, Kane's presence in my bed and in my life would be nothing but a memory.

"You fucking *bitch*!" Kiera shrieked when I opened the door.

Kiera was known to be enthusiastic, but she'd never cursed at me at six in the morning. And she was never known for a visit at six in the morning unless she'd been on a bender the night before and was craving shakshuka.

She looked sober and pissed off. And incredibly put together for the early hour. Her red bob was straight and glossy, her delicate face covered in expertly applied makeup as usual. She was wearing a pantsuit with no shirt underneath and sky-high heels. Unsurprising for Kiera—she lived in heels. I didn't know how she did it. Why she was this dressed up this early in the morning was anyone's guess. She might not have made it home from the night before.

"Do you not reply to texts or phone calls at all anymore?" she snapped, hands on her hips.

"I'm sorry," I said sincerely. "I've been busy."

Kiera had called and texted a whole lot since I left with Kane the night of the party. I'd been meaning to get back to her, but I couldn't figure out how to explain everything that had happened inside a text or a phone call. On top of that, I was caught up in the hurricane that was Kane, and whatever free moment I had when I wasn't at the restaurant, I was with him.

I'd left my friend at the wayside, and I was plagued with guilt. I wasn't blessed with having friends. I wasn't the kind of person with the ability to make friends. Kiera was it for me, and I'd neglected her.

"*Busy?*" she shrieked. "When you first didn't reply to me after leaving the party with Kane 'The Devil' Rhodes, I thought you were getting banged seven ways from Sunday, and I was happy to leave you to it." She dragged a hand through her ruby locks. "But then, enough time passed that I figured even The Devil's stamina would've failed him, and your general addiction for work would've pulled you out of his clutches. And still, nothing." Her hands flew back onto her waist, one hip cocked out. "I toyed with the idea that he had accidentally killed you in an asphyxiation kink gone wrong, but then your restaurant didn't close, therefore, I surmised you were alive. Just *ignoring my texts*."

Kiera's eyes were narrowed, her nostrils flaring, and she was gesturing wildly like she did when she was excited or pissed.

"I get that you're not into girl talk, but even you, Avery Hart, understand that I, your best friend, at the very least deserve proof of life, if not details of length, girth and preferred positioning." She yelled the ridiculous words with passion, so I bit my lip, struggling not to laugh.

Kiera was half Italian, half Irish. She was known for her temper. As she was exhibiting then. Laughing at her would not be the smart decision. And though part of me wanted to laugh, I could see the hurt underneath the yelling. Kiera might've had a more active social life than me and many friends, but I knew she also considered me her best friend. Me not confiding in her, ghosting her, would never go down well. She didn't care about the sex details—well, some of her did. Mostly, she felt abandoned. I knew her well enough to understand that.

The apology was on my lips when Kane spoke. "I think you have me to blame."

Kiera had her mouth open, obviously ready to continue her tirade. Her eyes widened as they went toward the owner of the deep voice, still raspy from sleep. Then those eyes went down.

I followed her gaze, or tried to. Kane was right at my back, and his hand had slid to my hip, underneath the tee I had on to settle inside the band of my panties. It was a lazy, possessive gesture that he didn't seem bothered to be doing in front of Kiera.

Kiera, who was struck dumb and currently staring at Kane. Ogling at him would be a better descriptive. Ogling at him standing in his underwear.

It was a sight; I'd give her that.

"She's been busy with work," he explained, rubbing my hip

bone with his thumb. "And when she wasn't busy with work, *I* kept her busy."

Kane made no effort to keep the innuendo out of his tone.

Kiera blushed.

Kiera. The woman who talked about every kind of kink under the sun in mixed company, who was not ashamed of her sexuality.

"Well," she huffed out, the wind quite obviously out of her sails. I waited for her to say more, but she didn't, she just kept staring.

"How about I get dressed and go get us all coffees and pastries? Give you two the time to discuss, what was it? Length, girth and preferred position?" he asked, teasing in his tone.

"Caramel latte, oat milk, four shots," Kiera said without missing a beat. "And some kind of chocolate pastry thing. I have a feeling this conversation requires sugar, caffeine and maybe a defibrillator." She winked at me before sauntering through the door.

"Nice ass!" she called back at Kane.

"I like her," Kane murmured into my hair as he pulled me into his heat.

Despite the strangeness of the situation, I found myself relaxing into his embrace.

"You don't have to go get coffee," I told him. "You can just … go." I was giving him the escape hatch I sensed he might desire. None of my previous partners had liked Kiera. And though I adored her, she was a lot. Especially at six in the morning. Maybe closer to the truth was I didn't want Kiera to see this and ask questions I'd been ignoring.

"Are you fuckin' kidding me, Chef?" Kane pulled me back to arm's length. "I ain't going anywhere. Mostly because I haven't gotten my fill of you this morning, and also 'cause I'm looking forward to drinking coffee with you and your friend and grilling her for all the information."

He kissed me. Firm. Open-mouthed. Tongues. Like my best friend wasn't right there in the living room.

I kissed him back.

Enthusiastically.

Then he let me go and walked back into my bedroom.

"Girlfriend, watching that almost gave *me* an orgasm," Kiera pretended to fan herself before sitting back on the sofa and crossing her legs.

She was grinning, making no qualms about the fact that she'd been watching.

"I'm officially not mad at you anymore," she announced as she patted my sofa. "Now get your ass over here and give me every goddamn detail."

* * *

An hour later, the coffee was gone, and our croissants were no more than crumbs on plates on my coffee table.

I was sitting tucked into Kane's chest, not really by choice. When he'd come back with coffee and breakfast—looking far too sinfully attractive in his shirt, jeans, tousled hair and a cheeky grin—I'd attempted to put a sensible distance between us. He was having none of that, grabbing on to me and hauling me across the couch so I was almost sitting on his lap.

Kiera watched this happen with the same gleam to her smile that she'd had the entire time she was here.

I had given her a complete rundown of the past four days. Had it only been four days? Trite as it was, it truly felt like a lifetime. Like Kane had changed something fundamental inside me.

I was plagued with romantic notions I'd been certain I was immune to.

Yet there I was... Instead of getting ready for the day, getting to the restaurant, keeping my orderly and important schedule in place, I was lazily drinking coffee in Kane 'The Devil' Rhodes's arms while shooting the shit with my best friend.

My best friend who had never sat casually in my apartment drinking coffee and eating breakfast with any of my boyfriends. Never smiled and laughed warmly, joking with them as she had been with Kane for the last hour.

It felt easy. Nice. Kane was just as engaging, asking Kiera questions about her life, meeting every one of her sarcastic quips with jokes of his own.

"I'm having a party," he said. "Well, my agent is making me have the party because of some fucking booze he talked me into endorsing. To be fair, it's fucking great shit; I'd never promote something I didn't actually like. Plus, the owner is a friend I owe a favor to, and I love a party." He hiked up a shoulder. "Obviously, Chef is coming. And I would be honored to have you there to liven up the place." He winked at Kiera.

I craned my head to look at him. "*Obviously*, I'm coming?"

"Yeah. You're my woman." He looked down, unaware or unbothered by the bite in my tone as he smiled lazily. "Want you there."

My mouth went dry at 'my woman.' It had me momentarily stunned. He'd said it last night too.

I was only stunned momentarily, though.

"I have a job. I can't take the night off with no notice." My spine was straight, tone chilly.

Kane didn't so much as flinch. "Yeah, which is why I scheduled the party for this Monday."

I gasped in surprise. The restaurant was closed the third Monday of every month. Completely closed. We weren't open for service every night, but there was always work to do. But those Mondays were a black day for everyone. It was so I could test out new menus, for the staff to have a proper break and to have the opportunity to deep clean or redecorate whatever Heidi decided to redecorate at the time.

The fact that Kane not only knew the restaurant was closed and had organized his party to be on that particular night was a huge gesture. Maybe a sweet one. If it weren't coupled with him also making a decision for me.

"I could be busy," I informed him coldly.

"*Are* you busy, Chef?" His eyes glittered, obviously amused with my irritation.

That only served to irritate me more.

"If you are, I'll simply change the party," he continued as if it were no big deal.

I bit my lip. That tic had returned whenever I was around Kane because I was never in control when I was with Kane.

"Oh, for fuck's sake. You're not busy, Avery," Kiera chimed in.

I shot her a death glare. Even though she seemed immune to them.

"I get it. You don't like a man making plans for you. Which I wouldn't recommend doing again," she told Kane. "On account of Avery not only being a massive control freak but also a woman with agency who is entitled to make her own plans." She gave him a jaunty smile. "But on this occasion, I'll allow it."

"Will *you* allow it?" I wanted to strangle my friend.

"Cut the shit, Chef," Kane grasped my chin so I was looking at him. "You're sexy as shit when you're pissed, something I'm gonna keep in mind, but we're gonna have a good time. You're gonna have a good time, and I'm gonna show you off." He leaned in to kiss me, grazing my lip with his teeth as he did so.

All thoughts of arguing with Kane flew out of my mind.

"You gonna battle me some more—which I welcome—or you gonna come to the party?" he murmured.

"I'm gonna come to the party," I whispered, almost in a trance.

"Okay." Kiera clapped her hands together and stood. I jerked back at the sudden sound to look at my best friend. "I'd like to stay, and I mean that. I could watch this," she motioned between me and Kane, "like I watch a *Real Housewives'* reunion—with delight and rapt attention. But alas, I have things to do." She pointed to Kane. "You live up to the hype." Her gaze returned to me. "I'll be here Monday to get ready for the party and to pre-game. If you keep getting all that good sex you're obviously getting, you won't even need makeup." She blew me a kiss then sauntered out the door.

"So that's Kiera," I pressed the heels of my palms into my eyes.

"Fond as I am of her company, she sorely delayed the way I wanted to wake up."

In a heartbeat, I was flipped onto my back on the sofa, Kane hoisting my legs upward and moving himself downward so he was right between my thighs.

He looked up at me with fire in his eyes. "Planned on tasting you first thing in the morning, so the first thing you screamed was my name. But I'll take having the taste of you on my tongue for the rest of the day."

Within seconds, my panties were off, and Kane's mouth was on me.

I was lost in pleasure, but not too lost to try to imprint the feeling into my mind, knowing it was temporary.

* * *

The next night, Kane stayed over at my house again.

Again, he cooked for me.

We'd gone grocery shopping after he'd buried his face in between my legs and made me scream on my sofa. After he'd then bent me over that sofa.

I'd gotten dressed in a daze, let him convince me to delay my errands for the restaurant for a morning of grocery shopping.

It wasn't hard to convince me.

I'd put on simple clothes. Jeans and a white tee, thrown my hair up into a messy ponytail. I slapped on tinted moisturizer that doubled as SPF because at my age, you knew the importance of

SPF. My skin was largely lineless because of this. Well, and good genes and ensuring that I wasn't out in the sun often, always in a kitchen filled with heat and grease that kept my skin from drying out.

"Ready," I informed Kane, snatching a pair of black designer sunglasses from my dresser. Kiera gave them to me. No way would I have spent $500 on sunglasses, but I liked them.

Kane glanced at me as I slipped on a pair of sneakers. He was lying in bed shirtless, reading one of the paperbacks I'd had in the apartment for decoration up until that point.

His phone was on the nightstand beside me.

It touched me that he was reading in his downtime instead of scrolling his phone like 99 percent of the population did these days.

I'd only seen him on his phone to answer a text or call, and that was only a couple of times. Otherwise, he wasn't on it.

"You're *ready*?" He dog-eared the book then put it on the nightstand. His eyes raked over me as he got up to snatch his jeans. "Jesus, I thought I'd have at least another ten minutes. Chicks take ages to look as gorgeous as you do right now."

The compliment was offhand, easily given, and it tickled the back of my neck. Still, I rolled my eyes. "You're biased because of the sex we just had."

Kane pulled his tee over his head then grasped my chin, face uncharacteristically serious. "Chef, I'm not biased. You're gorgeous. It's off-putting, just how stunning you are. Yeah, at the party with the makeup, the top that did great things for your tits ... you looked hot. But hot is a dime a dozen. You, in your chef's whites, in your kitchen, face flushed, eyes wild and alive—that's beauty. You on top of me, riding me with your hair wild—that's beauty. You now..." He tugged my ponytail. "Beauty," he whispered, then his lips were on mine.

I lost all sense.

"You're kind of beautiful too," I whispered back.

He smiled. "I know I'm meant to say that I prefer ruggedly handsome or masculine, but I like that you think I'm beautiful."

He kissed my nose.

"Now, let's go get some groceries so there's something living in your apartment that isn't just the bacteria on old Chinese takeout."

So we did.

We walked a handful of blocks together, in the daylight, Kane's hand in mine. Easy as can be. Natural. We got lost in the crowds of other people going about their days. I got lost in the notion that Kane and I were just a man and a woman grocery shopping together.

It was that simple.

And that complicated.

My fridge was now bursting with all sorts of fruits, vegetables, cold-pressed juices. Apparently, Kane was a juice guy. But also more champagne, beer, copious amounts of candy bars because clearly, he liked cold-pressed juices and sugar. A man of extremes.

The dinner he'd made was baked salmon and salad.

It was delicious.

Then he took me to bed.

And I'd woken up with him.

"You gonna overthink this?" he brushed hair from my face.

"Overthink what?" I blinked up at him, my voice lazy and satisfied and unfamiliar.

Relaxed.

That was the word.

I'd never sounded or felt so relaxed in my life.

Prior to this, to us, I woke up grinding my teeth, not giving myself a second to lay, to scroll or doze or do whatever it was people did in the mornings. I was up, mind calculating the things I had to do, the places I had to go and the amount of time I had to do those things depending on the menu for the evening.

I didn't have days off.

Not even today. Theoretically, I should've been up thirteen minutes ago. I should've been getting my coffee from the cart on the end of my block then heading to the docks to see what was freshest. Then it was to the meatpacking district for the New Zealand lamb I'd been waiting on from a supplier no one else knew about.

Then it was straight to the restaurant for prep.

I didn't have a free minute, let alone thirteen of them. Especially since I had taken the morning off yesterday to grocery shop.

Yet I didn't get up. I wasn't entirely sure I could get up, and not just because of my boneless limbs. Because Kane's arms were around me. Tight, vicelike. It should've made me feel caged, claustrophobic, panicked. It had with every other man who'd tried to hold me in any type of way.

Not with Kane.

"Overthink *this*." Kane's fingertip brushed what I knew was the crease between my eyebrows as I contemplated my relaxed state. "I already see you doin' it."

I chewed on my lip. He wasn't entirely wrong. Although I was overthinking, it was a lot less than I normally did.

"I'm not gonna play games." He cradled my cheek. "Have in the past, I'm not gonna lie. I've been an asshole, selfish, letting myself get caught up in bullshit." He spoke plainly without adornment. "I was not a gentleman, and I don't intend to be with you." His other hand cupped me between my legs, and I let out a sharp breath of pleasure.

He grinned wickedly.

"Not in the bedroom ... or wherever I feel like fuckin' you." He swiped his tongue along his teeth. "But the second I saw you, I knew that there was no way I was playing any type of game, wasting any time to make you mine. Initially, though... Gonna be honest, Chef. I wanted to fuck you, and I didn't think too far ahead of that. But it didn't take long to understand that I didn't just want to fuck you. Wanted to make you mine. And I saw it in your eyes too.

Whatever the fuck it is between us is intense as fuck. Doesn't make much sense. It's out of both of our control. And you're about control, Chef. Saw it when I walked into that kitchen, making me hard as a rock. I like seeing you in control, showing your power. But neither of us have power over this, and I'm expecting at some point that's gonna freak you out. Make you want to run."

His hand flexed at my hip as if he were expecting me to run right there and then.

"Not gonna let you do that, Chef," he added quietly. "Unless it's what you truly want in here." He tapped my chest. "Not here." He tapped my temple. "I'll let you fight it only so I can fight back with you. But I won't let you leave out of fear. Sayin' that plainly because I'm not doing bullshit with you. So you wanna run, or you want to sink into this?" His finger slipped into me.

My eyes rolled to the back of my head. But he didn't move his finger, didn't give me friction for release.

No, he just left it there inside of me, waiting.

He let all of those words hang, let them settle, resting on my chest like a weight.

And I couldn't breathe for a few seconds. Kane was right. A primal part of me wanted to fight against this. Wanted to run as far and as fast as I could. Because I knew that this was real, that this was something. We were something. Something that might burn fast and hot, might peter out and leave us both unscathed and satisfied. Or it could break me irreparably.

My body tensed at the mere thought of that. I had worked far too hard to craft a life for myself that was secure. I'd ensured that I could not be ruined, could not be hurt by anyone, especially a man.

Every relationship I'd had prior to this could only be loosely defined as a relationship. The stakes had been low. There were no feelings involved. No danger.

Kane was telling me that I couldn't control this, that he wouldn't let me run. He'd chase me. And he wasn't saying it in some toxic male kind of way. He was stating it as fact. As sure as the sky was blue, Kane was going to chase me if I ran from this out of fear.

As sure as the sun rose in the east and set in the west, Kane knew that I was his.

Yes, fear—a foreign and poisonous invader in my veins—urged me to run. To shut down and to convince this man that all of his feelings were one-sided and that I would not be submitting to him.

I opened my mouth to say that. To spout lies that would keep me safer than the truth ever could.

"I want this," I said instead, moving my body against his finger. My eyes found azure fire. "I want us."

His arm tightened even further. Tight enough to bruise. His gaze turned intense, claiming.

"Good," he growled. "Now let me make sure you feel me in you all day before you run around the city."

Seven

KANE and I had spent every night together since we met. Since the talk we'd had in my apartment, I decided to do the unthinkable... Lean into the chaos.

He did what he had done since the first night at my restaurant, waited for me to close up, eating the plate of food I regularly prepared for him before closing the kitchen.

I liked that he fed me when we got to my place, but I also loved the intimacy of feeding him. It wasn't something off the menu; it was whatever I was feeling at the time.Stuffed zucchini flowers, seared venison and mushrooms, cottage pie, freshly made pasta and pesto. More simple and provincial things than what I served in my restaurant. Heartier fare that I'd enjoyed across the world.

Every time he ate, he made sure to communicate just how much he enjoyed my food. And even though I had had thousands of people say similar things, it made my night. Well, various things made my nights these days, all of them connected to Kane.

My staff were used to him by then, no one asking questions. Not even Ferris. I'd told Michelle the most, that we were together, nothing else. That pleased her. But she didn't press. She never did.

She'd brought out a glass of whisky for Kane at the end of service, one finger. He thanked her, joked with her and my staff who were friendly but kept their distance.

Kane asked me why they didn't ask questions, why no one took photos. I momentarily paused at the question, wondering why on earth they would take a photo of us. Then I remembered Kane was famous.

It was easy for me to forget since I hadn't known he was famous when I met him. I didn't go on social media—didn't have social media—and didn't read the kind of magazines he graced the covers of.

And whenever we were together, it was late at night, going straight to my apartment—apparently, he liked my tiny place better than the behemoth brownstone. Then he'd cook for me, something simple but delicious. Steak and salad. Spicy shrimp. Grilled cheese. And we'd have sex. A lot of it. At some point, I'd fall into unconsciousness, and then he'd wake me, either in the middle of the night or in the morning or both to fuck me again. Then, while I was getting ready, he'd get us coffee and pastries from the café on the corner. Then we'd part.

When I asked him where he went while I was working, he shrugged his shoulders, saying the gym or doing whatever publicity shit his publicist had organized for his 'break' before he went on tour in preparation for the X Games. He rode in tracks and entered events all over the country.

That hung over my head, the looming date of Kane's departure. Sure, he owned an apartment in New York, but from what I could tell, he was usually on the move. Always competing somewhere, if not jumping out of planes, off bridges, riding motorcycles through South America, driving Jeeps on two wheels in the Middle East.

Somehow, I'd caught him on a rare occasion when he wasn't defying death but living the semblance of a normal life.

Well, whatever *normal* looked like for a famous daredevil.

He was obviously used to people taking photos in his presence, hence his question as to why none of the staff did it.

"Well, we have rules about doing such things in the restaurant. We do have many clients more famous than you," I teased.

"Don't hurt my precious ego," he teased back, a hand splayed over his chest. "But I'm not a client. And I'm pretty sure that not everyone here is such a militant rule follower like you, Chef."

I stiffened at his words. That's what I was, wasn't it? Type A, a rule follower who lived by schedules, by the clock. It had worked for me most of my life; it had been what kept me sane, that control. Now Kane seeing me that way had me suddenly uncomfortable.

I shook that feeling off.

"I'm sure they break rules sometimes, but not with you." I looked down at the filet I was seasoning. "They're far too afraid of me to snap a picture, considering I'd know it came from this kitchen when it came out." I didn't add that the position in my restaurant was too precious to risk a photo of him for. It sounded a little arrogant, even to me.

Kane's eyes danced with amusement. "Scared? Of you?" He pulled me into his arms, kissing my head. "I like that," he murmured against my hair.

"Are *you* scared of me?" I asked, teasing once more.

Kane pushed me back to meet my eyes, all amusement gone from his. "I'm fuckin' terrified of you, Chef."

I swallowed the lump in my throat, feeling like all the air had gone from my lungs. This ... thing between us had been all about feeling alive. About animal instincts, wanting each other. Though I had fleeting thoughts of just how deep I was in in such a short time, I quickly pushed them away.

Yet here was Kane, bringing it to the forefront, making these issues impossible to ignore. This thing between us was moving past infatuation and turning into something else, something more permanent. Something that would mark my insides like scars when it was done.

"You overly tired, Chef, or you want to come out with me tonight?" Thankfully, his question broke the seriousness of the moment.

I should've been tired. My work schedule was as grueling as it always had been, I was used to that. But I was also used to falling into bed as soon as I got home. Not riding around the city on the back of a motorcycle then getting fucked into oblivion for hours every night.

"I'm not tired," I replied honestly. When I was with Kane, it was the same feeling as when I was in the kitchen, like my body was electrified, like nothing else existed.

Except the kitchen was orderly, it had rules, structure. I was in control.

Kane was chaos. There were no rules with him, and I most certainly wasn't in control.

"Want to go out with me?" he asked.

The control freak in me wanted to first ask where we were going, especially because I was only wearing the jeans I'd taken to change into for the ride and a leather jacket Kane had unceremoniously bought me a few days ago. The leather was buttery-soft, but it was also warm, chasing away the bite of the autumn air. It fit me perfectly and was exactly my style—classic, understated. A thoughtful, powerful gesture from Kane that only added to the proof this was more than a thing.

Though the leather jacket was undoubtedly nice, I worried about my attire if we were going to be around people in cocktail dresses.

Kane always wore a variation of his all-black clothing, usually motorcycle boots and a band tee, a jacket of his own. But even I could recognize everything he wore was expensive. I could tell you exactly how much black truffles were going for at any given moment, but not those kinds of things.

I bit my tongue, swallowing all the questions on it and looked up at Kane.

"Let's go."

* * *

"*This* is where we're going?" I looked at the exterior of the bar. I tried to hide my distaste, but it didn't quite work. Not that I was a snob. Or I supposed I was, by occupational hazard more than upbringing. We didn't grow up rich, but I was never aware of money worries. My father, ever the practical man, had a healthy life insurance policy, and both my sister and I had college funds.

I had never gone out to a bar—I'd gone to wine tastings to find the best wine to pair with dishes. Learned from top sommeliers. I'd gone to cocktail lounges to attain techniques I utilized in my kitchens. Every trip was for a purpose, not for leisure.

"No cloth napkins or silver spoons here, Chef," Kane joked. "You scared?"

I narrowed my eyes at him. "Of course, I'm not scared." I straightened my back and walked into the bar in order to prove my point.

The music was blaring at a level you could hear on the streets, the source being a band playing on a tiny stage at the back of the tiny bar. The space was cluttered but not crowded. Despite the small space, no one so much as glanced my way when I walked in, even when I felt Kane's warmth behind me, hands on my hips and his lips brushing my neck.

I shivered.

It took me a second to process the dim lighting, the noise, the sticky floor, the weird mix of smells—peanuts, beer, sweat, smoke.

And then Kane's scent curled up in it all, his lips on my skin, the intimate touch.

Once I'd processed all of this, I recognized the band playing was good. Great, actually.

I wasn't into most things pop culture. Music was the exception. It was something I'd shared with my father, something that wove in and out of every one of my memories. My kitchen always had music playing. Not at a high volume, because we needed to hear each other, the tickets. But once service was over, I turned it up so it could wash over me, help me come down from the high of each night.

I'd had it playing the nights Kane watched me cleaning, yet he hadn't commented on it.

"This place has some of the best undiscovered bands in the country." His lips brushed against my ear as he spoke, sending goose bumps down my arms. "Unquiet Mind played all their original stuff here before they got huge."

Unquiet Mind was one of the few commercial bands I actually enjoyed. Even though they were one of the biggest bands in the world, I still found their music authentic, powerful. They hadn't sold out. They were on the playlist I'd played that first night he'd come into my kitchen.

"Figured you'd like them." He nodded to the band playing a mix between rock and folk music. Hard and lyrical. "Figured you'd like a place that didn't have cloth napkins and dress codes. Or at least it'd take you out of your comfort zone so I could watch your eyes light up."

My palms were sweating, realizing just how much he saw me.

"Let's get a beer." Hand on my hip, he directed us to the bar.

He nodded to the bartender, and once he arrived, leaned over, presumably to give him our order.

Kane didn't make a move to make further conversation with me. He merely lifted me onto the barstool in front of him and slung his arm over my shoulder, half around my neck, toying with the neckline of my tee.

He was obviously relaxed, at ease.

I was still tense, unsure of how to act in a scene like this. Unsure of how to act as Kane's 'date' in a place like this. I didn't have experience in dive bars with sticky floors.

The beer he handed me was cold, crisp. His lips at my neck were warm, electrifying.

"Breathe, Chef," he whispered. "Listen to the music. Drink your beer."

The instructions were simple, and though my brain tried to fight against them, I did as he asked.

* * *

I didn't know how long it had been since we arrived. I had two beers. The band was still playing. The music was good. Great. It took me away from reality, allowing me to enjoy the moment.

Kane didn't move from behind me, continuously laying his lips on my skin, moist from the beer, mixing with my sweat from the warmth of the bar.

"Let's go," he said as I finished my beer.

The band was winding down, and it must've been late. Going was the sensible thing to do, I was sure. But I didn't want to leave. A part of me wanted to sit there on that stool, with a beer and Kane and an indie band forever.

But I got up, because deep down, I was a sensible person.

Instead of leading us out the entrance, Kane took my hand and pulled me deeper into the bar.

Though I was confused, I didn't ask questions. I was riding the buzz of the music, the beers, the new location. I trusted Kane to take me wherever he wanted us to go.

We got a few glances as we made it through the crowd, but no one did a double take. Either the patrons of this bar were too drunk, failed to recognize him or didn't care that there was a celebrity in their midst.

The thump of the bass still sounded once we made it to the back where the restrooms were, but it was quieter.

Before I could even wonder what was happening, Kane pushed me against the wall and plastered my body with his, grasping my neck and putting his mouth on mine. He tasted like beer and him. His kiss was hungry. Ravenous. I didn't hesitate to return it. I realized I was hungry, *ravenous,* too.

Time unraveled as we kissed, his hand in my hair, running down the side of my body, underneath my tee and to my breasts, kneading, tweaking my nipples.

"Need to fuck you, Chef," he breathed against my ear. "Can take you home, to the bathroom, or we can do it right here, against the wall." There was a challenge in his voice, a sexual dare.

I knew that Kane would never try to convince me to do something I wasn't comfortable with and wouldn't say anything if I requested he take me home, to privacy, to the familiarity of my bed.

The corner we were in was somewhat secluded from the main bar, the hall to the restrooms to the left, presumably a storeroom to our right. But to enter either, you had to walk past us.

Anyone could walk past. See us. At least the bathrooms offered an ounce of privacy. Not exactly sensible but more sensible than an open hallway.

"Here," I whispered, barely recognizing my voice, my request.

Kane's teeth grazed my ear. Without pausing, he turned me around, my palms instinctively bracing themselves against the wall.

His hands pulled back my hips, before he kicked at my ankles, telling me to spread my legs apart. Fingers rushed to my jeans, undoing them quickly, roughly, with urgency.

I was already soaking when his hands went to my panties, caressing me there.

My body responded so viscerally to the simple touch, my knees shuddered.

The thump of the music vibrated against my palms, my heart thundering in my chest.

Anyone could walk by at any moment. Yes, the light was dim, the hour was late and whoever did walk by was likely sporting some heavy beer goggles. But we were still playing with fire.

That only made me burn hotter.

"Never had better pussy than yours," Kane murmured against my ear, fingers going inside me for a few seconds before they were gone and my jeans were around my ankles.

He shifted my hips, placing me in the perfect position for him. He didn't ease in, didn't bother with foreplay. There was no time for that. This wasn't careful, tender. This was hunger, getting our needs met knowing we could be interrupted, caught, at any moment.

I let out a cry as he filled me.

Though it hopefully merged with the music, I was louder than I'd expected.

Kane's hand went to my mouth, lightly covering it so he wasn't completely silencing me.

He pounded hard, relentlessly, hot breath against my neck.

My body met each of his thrusts, building up to an impossible crescendo.

I tasted the beer on my tongue, I breathed in the heady smells of the bar, of Kane's scent mixed in with them. I let myself go, awash in sensation.

Kane was a wild animal, slamming into me.

Then I was gone, flying through the air, riding a wave of complete pleasure. In the hallway of a dive bar, with Kane fucking me against a wall, I felt myself fall.

For Kane.

Eight

AFTER A DIZZYING RIDE through the city, our bodies still sticky with the sweat from earlier—the mere thought of what I'd done made my toes curl—we were tangled up in my bed, on our sides, facing each other.

I would have usually showered after coming home, to get the heat of the kitchen off me, the specific scent of it. But now it was mixed with Kane, me, us. I wanted to imprint that into my sheets.

Though it was so late it could be classed as 'early,' I still wasn't ready to sleep. I was ready to dive deeper into this. Into Kane.

"Why do you do this?" I asked, tracing the scars on his body, a roadmap of the injuries, the evidence of his brushes with death. The scar on his lip—from hitting a half pipe the wrong way when training for the Winter Olympics in New Zealand. The jagged mark on his bicep—from tearing layers of skin almost down to the bone when he hit the concrete while riding BMX.

Though I couldn't see it, I knew there was an ugly mar on his calf from almost being torn to pieces when his dirt bike landed on him after coming down wrong.

The scars made up a story of what he'd survived, sure. But they also taunted me with the fact that he danced with death for a living.

I'd only known him for a short time, but the idea of this earth spinning without Kane Rhodes walking on it made my skin prickle with sheer panic.

"Why do you do things with such high stakes?" I asked him, trying to swallow that terror.

He continued drawing circles on my navel for a few seconds before replying. "I had a shitty childhood," he said to my belly button. "A really shitty childhood. Cliché, which fucking sucks that the experience is so common, but such is the world. Deadbeat dad. Mom who was trying to make ends meet with two boys and not even a high school diploma. She did what she had to do, kept thinking the next man who came along would be the one. The one to save us." He looked up at me. "My mom was, and still is, a romantic, you see." He sucked his teeth. "Romantic love is her top-tier, a man to worship her. Further up than her sons' well-being."

I ground my teeth. Even though there didn't seem to be resentment in his tone, I instantly bristled toward his mother. No one would ever describe me as maternal, but even I knew that children came before romantic love. Keeping children safe came first. Baby Kane had deserved unconditional love, and I hated that he didn't have that.

Not knowing my interior thoughts, Kane kept speaking. "She thought it'd happen. A happily ever after, someone would save her, save us." He shook his head, a small, sad smile on his face. "The world quickly showed her the reality. Not every boyfriend was bad. Some were okay. Nice even. Somehow, the nice ones lasted the least amount of time. And somehow, she married the worst of them all."

Though his tone was light-hearted, I could feel the change in him, the tension in his body.

"Knox, my brother, knew there was something wrong about him from the start, even though he went out of his way to talk to us, made an effort." Kane's palm crept up to my chest, though not a sexual touch. No, he laid his tattooed hand over my heart. "Knox tried to warn my mom off, warn me off. I guess I was kind of a romantic too. I was waiting for the guy to take over, take care of my mom and show us how to be men. Thought we'd found him. It wasn't until after they got married that he changed, showed us who he really was."

Kane sucked in a long breath. Deep, as if he were trying to gulp in the air he couldn't get while drowning in the memory.

"Knox protected me from the worst of it," His easy tone vanished, pain so deep in his words that I could feel the point of each letter. "He offered himself up when it became clear that he married my mother not because he wanted her, but because he wanted ... us."

When the realization of what he was saying hit me, I tasted bile. My stomach lurched with the knowledge of what Kane meant.

This man, this monster, had married Kane's mother to get close to two small boys.

His eyes were clear and strong, remaining glued to mine. I forced myself not to let my horror and pain show on my face. "That fucked with me, for a long fucking time. Not only did I not know how to be a man, I felt like I *couldn't* be because of what happened to me. So I chased down every single thing I could find that made me look more masculine. I rode dirt bikes, I got in fistfights, I raced cars. And doing that shit when you're a dumb kid full of pain and unhealed trauma is the quickest way to get yourself arrested. So I did. Coupl'a times."

His eyes bounced between mine, gauging something. I didn't know what, I was still trying to digest the horrific information he'd served up.

"One night, I was drunk. Reliving shit that had happened. I was angry. Jesus, it was like a dragon was inside me. Like I was a dragon. It was bursting out of me." He squeezed his eyes shut. "Some guy bumped into me. Said something smart. That was it. His sin. Got in my space, touched me, made me feel like less of a man. So I did what I thought would make it so no one could ever confuse me for any kind of victim again. I beat him half to death."

The silence in the room after that was oppressive. Even more oppressive than when he talked about the abuse. I could feel it. His shame. Guilt. He was coated in it.

"Pure luck the guy survived. Wasn't brain damaged for life. He's now blind in one eye, though." He rubbed the bridge of his nose. "I had a record at that point. Was officially an adult. No money. I would've gone down for a decent amount of time, possibly ten years for attempted murder with my record. But Knox was there again, saving the day. He got the money for a hotshot lawyer who got it down to six months."

His eyes were swimming with a pain that seemed so foreign on his handsome, easygoing face that it took my breath away.

"Six months was nothing compared to what I was facing. But fuck, Chef, it was the worst six months of my life. It took me right back to being that kid with no control. Constantly on guard for danger. No power. For me, being in a cage was worse than death." He shook his head, and I swore to God, it looked like he was trying to shake demons free.

"But I got out," he sighed. "I lived. Was lucky. And then it was more luck that had me falling into a situation where the shit I did to chase away my demons—jumping things, riding things fast, dancing with death—that shit actually became a career."

My ears were ringing from the flood of information. The pain that Kane offered up, unadorned, without shame, without me having to pry it out of him. With absolute trust.

Kane wiped my cheek with his thumb.

I'd let a tear fall, and I hadn't even realized it.

"Don't need you to cry for me, Chef," he murmured. "Love that you feel that deep, but know that I've done a lot of work to repair the shit that asshole broke. Therapy. All that shit. Healed as much as I could. Well, I suppose if I was truly healed, I wouldn't be making my living jumping shit and playing out being a tough guy. Because if I look tough, fearless, I'll never be the victim again. Never watch my brother be the victim in order to protect me." He let out a cold laugh. "Not that he's going to ever be the victim."

"What happened to your brother?" I asked, my heart breaking for the boy I didn't know. My soul was in tatters, in agony, grieving for the boy who had turned into the man I loved.

Kane's features fell, obviously stricken. In pain.

"My job dances with death, Chef. On the legitimate side of it. For the world to see. His does too. But the world doesn't see what he does. He's taken himself so far into the shadows, I'm bracing myself for when he doesn't return."

Worry and love for his brother were physical things. I could taste them.

"And your mom?" I probed, unreasonably angry, furious, at the woman for putting her sons through that.

Kane smiled. It was a terribly sad smile. "She lives in Phoenix. Right now, at least. Waits tables. I bought her a house, fully paid off so she wouldn't have to do that anymore, but she's a creature of habit." He brushed the inside of my thumb with his wrist. "I personally think she's punishing herself. For our childhood, what she put us through."

I pursed my lips, a cold part of me thinking that waiting tables in Phoenix was far too light a punishment.

"I can see that," Kane murmured, brushing my lips with his tongue. "Your fire, ready to breathe it for me."

I frowned, not realizing I was that transparent. I never normally was.

"I've forgiven her, Chef," he said quietly.

"You've forgiven her?" I repeated. Forgiveness wasn't something I was entirely practiced in.

He nodded. "Therapy, inner-self work and generally realizing my mother is just another broken human being who was trying her best with the hand she got. I either blame her and don't have a mother or forgive her and get a mother who I accept as a flawed person. Knox isn't of that same opinion. They don't speak."

I tried to school my expression. I would likely act like the shadowy Knox who I liked although Kane alluded he was a criminal.

"So that's, in a nutshell, why I do it." Kane smoothed hair from my face. "Jump things, race things." He gave me a blinding grin. "And 'cause it's fun."

I shook my head, unable to do anything but smile back in the face of all the trauma Kane had laid out.

Kane arched his neck, giving me a gentle kiss. "It made me who I am, Chef. All of that. Plenty of times I've wanted to wish it away, but now more than ever, I'm happy I went through it because no other story would've led me to be here, in bed with Avery Hart."

Before I could formulate an adequate response, Kane kissed me, ending the conversation.

* * *

We arrived at Kane's party late, Kiera and me. Although I was itching to be the first to arrive, to see Kane, even though I'd woken up with him that morning.

I missed him. Such a foreign concept. Such a terrifying one. Where I felt off-kilter going not even twenty-four hours without someone.

Without a *man*.

Long-honed instincts inside of me told me to erect my walls, to step back, to retreat into that cold, unfeeling persona I'd crafted so exquisitely over the years.

But there was another side of me, another piece of me that Kane had revealed. A piece that wanted the danger and chaos and intoxication that came with being with him. I felt more alive than ever before, all of my senses engaged at all moments.

And then there was what he'd shared with me, offering his pain up so freely, sharing his trauma with me without agenda, with such vulnerability it obliterated my walls.

"You're glowing," Kiera informed me as she was doing my makeup at the apartment. She was drinking the champagne from Kane's and my latest grocery trip. The very fancy kind. We'd argued over who would pay. He'd won.

I had a tequila on the rocks, unearthed from the depths of my freezer.

I wasn't normally one for hard liquor, but I was going to be attending a party. Full of people I likely had nothing in common with, people Kane knew as acquaintances at least and friends at most. I wanted to … impress them. I wasn't versed with impressing people with social interactions; I let my food do that. I didn't normally care if people liked me, therefore, I didn't have the social skills to make that happen.

Hence the tequila.

"I'm not glowing," I argued. "You're just seeing me through rose-colored glasses because Kane charmed you, and you're a romantic. And because you live in rose-colored glasses."

It was something of an enigma that Kiera and I were even friends. Her the eternal romantic, an optimist. Warm, charismatic, extroverted and glamorous. Me, pretty much everything the opposite. Our friendship was happenstance, her answering my ad for a roommate in an apartment in Chelsea I couldn't afford. Initially, I'd written off the girl wearing bubblegum-pink lipstick, in six-inch heels who spoke loudly and giggled easily. I figured she'd get on my nerves. Except she was the only one who answered the ad apart from a guy who asked me where I put my worn socks.

Kiera it was.

And somehow, that crazy bitch pulled out of me a similar kind of softness and fun like Kane had. We'd been friends ever since.

She paused, mascara wand in hand, leaning back in order to give me a sharp look. "I may live in rose-colored glasses, but I'm seeing you clearly, baby. You are glo-*wing*." She winked, regarding me with more scrutiny that had nothing to do with my makeup and everything to do with how well she knew me.

"You like him," she hummed. "Actually *like*. For more than the no doubt wild sex that is working better than any $500 face cream. This man is under your skin."

My cheeks heated, hearing her say it out loud. I didn't know why it embarrassed me. Human beings were allowed to like people, fall in love. It was a rite of passage. But for me, it felt like a weakness.

"I do," I said instead of denying it. It was exceptionally hard to say, even to Kiera who had never judged another person in her entire life.

I expected Kiera to smile, to throw a party in the streets. For years, the eternal romantic had wanted me to find something with someone, even though she herself hadn't had a relationship that lasted longer than a season.

Except she didn't smile, her eyes were not light and teasing. "I can't believe I'm telling you of all people this, but be careful, Avery."

A boulder landed in my stomach. "I've been careful all my life." I felt defensive, evident by the bite to my voice. "I think I'm entitled to take a risk or two."

"You are," she nodded. "But you're my friend. I see past that tough exterior and know there's a soft heart in there. I don't want it damaged any more than it has been. I want someone to take care of it, be gentle with it. And Kane 'The Devil' Rhodes is not known for taking care or being gentle. Nor is he known for long and steady relationships."

She was speaking the truth, stating the words I'd whispered to myself, the ones I'd tried to drown out with the noise of the kitchen, the sounds of life with Kane.

Now that we were in the quiet of my apartment, with nothing but Taylor Swift singing about small men, the words hit their mark.

Still, I felt cornered, not ready to face up to these facts. And I was mad at my best friend. I opened my mouth to say something rash, something I'd likely regret, but she held up a hand, maybe reading my expression.

"That's all I'm going to say on the matter," she told me. "And I'm only saying it because I love you. Because I have a slight amount more experience on men in general and a certifiable PhD in assholes. Not that Kane is an asshole," she added quickly. "He seems the absolute opposite. But sometimes those ones, the ones who masquerade as bad but seem good, are the ones who do the most damage." She drained her drink. "Okay, that's it, that's enough of my not so sage wisdom and my protective friend routine. I know you can look after yourself, and I'm here cheering for a happy ending. If not, an ending on your terms. And just to let you know that if he hurts you, I'll cut his motherfucking balls off and let you make arancini out of them." She smiled sweetly. "Now, let's make you the hottest bitch at the party."

Though there were a lot of things I could've said to my friend at this moment, some of them good, some of them bad, and some of them far too honest, I simply sipped my drink and let her change the subject.

Her words settled at the base of my spine, though, along with an overwhelming sense of dread.

You could hear the music from the street.

Not something that surprised me since I didn't think Kane did quiet, understated parties.

The brownstone was filled with people, throngs of them, all drinking, laughing. All in different types of clothing. Some were dressed in cocktail attire, dresses, heels, suits and open collars. Most were on the more casual side, which is what I'd erred to.

Deep brown slacks, some trendy tennis shoes that Kiera had given me that I liked, but once I found out the price, I decided that they would be my one and only pair.

Deep brown tee, a similar color to the pants but not exact. That's what my off-duty wardrobe was—shades of monochrome, easy clothes I didn't have to think much about and would work if I was forced to attend something to promote the restaurant. If it were something fancier, I'd swap the shoes out for low-heeled pumps and the tee out for a blouse.

I didn't look out of place exactly, but I did have a moment when I thought back to the photos I'd seen of Kane when I googled him. The kind of women he was photographed with. Slim, perfectly put together, expensive clothes, shoes, showing a lot of skin, sky-high heels. He would be better suited with someone like Kiera who was all of those things.

"Fucking *finally*!" Hearing the familiar voice, my entire body simultaneously relaxed and tensed in anticipation. Before I could blink, I was hauled into a warm, hard body, and a mouth was slammed onto mine.

Despite the crowd, the doubts and fears swirling in my stomach, I kissed Kane back. Enthusiastically. So enthusiastically that more than one onlooker whistled, and I knew one of the whistlers was Kiera.

"You're late, Chef," Kane murmured against my mouth, acting as if he didn't have an entire audience, as if we were in the room alone.

His eyes only saw me.

And it made me feel like the little girl I'd never been. The little girl my sister had been, a romantic, dreaming of the man who would look at her like she was the only person in the room.

He leaned in to brush his lips against my ear. "Can't wait to get inside that pussy."

My body twitched in anticipation.

Okay, so not *exactly* what my romantic little sister would've imagined her white knight saying.

But that was good.

I didn't want a white knight.

"Kiera," Kane addressed my best friend, who was grinning at him despite the wariness she obviously felt. He slung his arm casually, possessively around my shoulders.

"You look lovely," he said, paying my friend the compliment she deserved.

She'd gone ... less casual than me.

Her cropped bob was curled in messy beach waves, her makeup was sultry. The neckline of her sequined dress was plunging, showing off her ample assets. Kane's eyes stayed at her false lash-framed irises.

"You're not too bad yourself," she replied.

He smiled cheekily. "I try."

"Like your ass in these pants." His hand lazily went down my back. "We'll have to make sure you have them in every color."

I couldn't help but grin. "I already do."

"Perfect," he licked his lips then looked to Kiera. "We have drinks, food, celebrities and many men who would hit on you ... with your consent, of course. You think you'll be okay on your own? I just must take Chef to the bathroom and have my way with her."

My cheeks flamed, and I really wanted to be embarrassed, but I wanted him to do that too. Just as he'd appraised my outfit, I'd done the same to him.

He was wearing an Unquiet Mind band tee, his inky hair was

long and wild, drooping over his left eyebrow. His dark jeans and Dr. Martens accentuated his strong legs and perfect backside. The black polish on his fingernails had chipped, and a handful of silver rings adorned his long fingers.

He looked like Kane. Attractive, edgy, hot.

Kiera's eyes alighted with glee. "Of course, bang away." She waved her hand. "I'm in my element here."

Before I could say anything, Kane whisked me away, back through the throngs of people, nodding and greeting various people who acknowledged him but not stopping for anyone. Not until we'd gone through the rooms to a bathroom that was on the other side of the brownstone. Not the main one guests were using, but there were people milling around. It wasn't exactly private.

Which was what got my heartbeat thumping.

Just before we could get to the bathroom, a man stepped in front of us.

He was one of the fewer people wearing a suit. No tie, though. Grey, expensive by the look of it, pale-pink dress shirt unbuttoned to show a tan and hairless chest.

He had perfectly styled short hair, a color brown that seemed too rich and perfect to be natural, although I suspected it might've been colored based on his overall appearance. Obviously fake tan, leather loafers, flashy watch, a mouth full of veneers showcased with a fake smile. He was conventionally handsome with a strong jaw and classic features, but his eyes were dark, beady, and something about him was off-putting.

"There you are," he sighed, eyes on Kane.

I expected Kane to dismiss him the way he had all of the people who had tried to get in our way, but he didn't.

"Brax, bro, this is Avery, who I've been telling you about. Avery, this is Brax, my manager."

Brax's eyes rested on me for a split second, casting up and down, what I would bet was a faux smile on his face. "Nice to meet you."

His tone dripped with dismissal. I could tell he didn't think I was worth his time. I had a lot of experience with men looking at me like that.

"We're so close to signing the Adidas deal," he spoke to Kane as if I weren't there. "There are some execs here, want to meet you, photo op, and then we'll be in for a three-year contract."

"I'm busy right now," Kane said, holding on to me.

Brax's eyes darted to me, irritation flickering in them before flashing a too white smile. "It'll take five minutes. I'm sure *Avery* can entertain herself for that long. We've got a great buffet." He looked at me as he dragged his hand over his jaw.

The way he said my name made my lip curl. Before now, I'd had a placid expression on my face because even if I got the sense this was an asshole in a suit, he was connected to Kane, so I was going to be polite.

But my eyes narrowed at what was left unspoken. He considered me to be just another bimbo. And if I wasn't mistaken, a bimbo who wasn't as skinny as the other bimbos.

I didn't know if Kane picked up on the insult since Brax delivered these subtle insults the same way a woman might. And the truest skill of that insult was to ensure no one but other women understood it.

The tilt of Kane's head, the clench to his jaw and the general energy around him communicated that he at least read the dismissal of me.

"*I'm* entertaining Avery," he bit out. "You do whatever the fuck you want with those corporate fucks. I'm going with my woman, and you're getting out of my way."

Brax's megawatt smile dimmed for only a millisecond.

"Of course. We'll touch base later." He quickly stepped aside, immediately submitting to Kane, but the edge to his smile told me I needed to look out for him.

He was a weasel.

Kane didn't hesitate to continue our journey, nuzzling my neck.

Despite Kane's touch and my body's instinctual reaction to it, I couldn't help my feeling like I was covered in a thin layer of grease and oil.

But then Kane pulled me into the bathroom and his lips plastered over mine, with fire and heat, and that oil burned right off.

Nine

"AS MUCH AS I love you in fucking pants, Chef, I've gotta say that a skirt would make for easier access." Kane was buttoning my pants in a gesture that was strangely intimate, despite what we'd just done.

Had sex. In the bathroom of his party. He'd done it in front of a mirror, my hands on the quartz sink. I'd watched him fucking me, hard, quick, hungry. His hand had red bite marks in it from where I'd sunk my teeth into it at the peak of my orgasm.

"I'm not a skirt person, but I think I could be persuaded to make an exception," I answered before I could realize I was, theoretically, against a man telling me what to wear.

But I'd discovered I liked, really liked, semipublic sex. And I wanted to do more of it with Kane. Logistically, skirts made sense.

Kane took hold of my waistband and yanked me so I was flush with his body. "As much as I fuckin' love that you'd make an exception for me when I get the feeling you don't make exceptions for anyone, I don't want you to. Like the pants." His hands ghosted over my backside. "They're you, and you can get on the back of my bike."

My gaze swam in his, utterly lucid with the knowledge that I was falling in love with this man. No, I had fallen. Long ago.

Kane walked us out of the bathroom and I didn't even bother to look around to see whether anyone had seen us go in together. I didn't care.

His gaze wandered behind me. "Okay, now you're gonna meet my brother."

My head whipped behind me, my gaze searching through the throngs of people to land on a cutting figure in a black suit, taller than the others, who seemed to stand out on presence alone. That could only be Kane's brother.

My head snapped back to Kane, eyes narrowed. "Kane, the first time I meet your brother cannot be when I look like I've just been fucked in a bathroom," I hissed, trying to smooth my hair, which was no doubt a mess.

Kane chuckled, arms around me as he walked us in the direction of the man in black. "Oh, Chef, the absolute best and only time I want you to meet my brother is when you are red from coming around my dick, and my cum is dripping out of you. Otherwise, the fuck may get some ideas about stealing you from me."

His words were crass, but they were true. The first part, at least. My face still felt hot; therefore, it must've been red, and the wetness in my panties communicated our lack of condom and my lack of responsibility since we'd used one the first two times then never again.

Kane had been hovering above me, eyes locked with mine in question when he'd pressed in, bare.

"Yes," I'd breathed at his silent request.

And that was all the permission he'd needed before rocking my world. Bare. I didn't regret my decision, not for a moment.

Irresponsible. All of this was irresponsible.

But it was fun, and chaotic. An adventure. Meeting family,

meeting someone so important to Kane, made it real. Made it much too terrifying.

"Kane," I tried to fight against him, but he was too strong.

And he ignored me, so before long, we stopped. In front of the man in black.

Shit.

There was no escaping it now.

"Chef, this is Knox." Kane nodded toward the man in front of us.

Knox.

His brother.

The one who'd put himself in an unimaginably horrific position to save his brother from the worst of sexual abuse when they were young. Although the man in front of us looked like he'd never been a helpless child. No, he looked like he sprouted from the ground with fully formed muscles. Everything about him seemed cold. Menacing. A primal instinct inside me told me this man was dangerous. Very dangerous.

He had the same eyes as Kane, sparkling sapphires. Though Kane's were full of life, mischief and fire. Knox's were flat and lifeless, like those of a predator.

He had the same angular jawbone as Kane, lips that had a similar curve but no scar, no upward tilt of a smile. I knew he was older than Kane only because Kane had told me. Whereas Kane's face was tan and weathered with lines from laughter, smiling and the sun, Knox's was almost porcelain, no lines to be found.

His brows were dark and heavy, his hair an inky curtain over his face.

Unlike his brother's casual attire, he was in a suit. I could tell it was expensive by the fit of it, like it was made to fit over his slim but muscular body. There were no tattoos on him to be seen.

The two men couldn't be more similar yet different at the same time. The sun and the moon.

"Knox, this is my Avery." Kane's introduction contained a possessive warmth, his finger brushing my bare arm.

"Avery Hart," Knox said, eyes unnervingly focused on me. "I've eaten at your restaurant. It's good."

Just like his brother, the single positive word to describe my food did not come out lackluster. No, it seemed like high praise coming from him. I got the sense this man did not throw out compliments.

"Thank you." My words felt heavy. Not just because of the compliment but for what he sacrificed for Kane. Resulting in Kane being able to smile easily, still love and have intimacy I felt certain the man in front of me wasn't capable of.

Whether he understood the gravity of my thank you could not be seen. His face remained an impassive mask.

"I see Brax is still here," he addressed Kane. Displeasure was evident in his tone.

Kane's smile dimmed only somewhat, but the dim told me something. "Come on, man, he's a good friend."

Knox's scowl deepened. "He's not your friend, brother. He's a leech."

This was obviously not the first time they had had this conversation. It interested me. My instincts with men were usually pretty spot on. I had disliked Brax upon meeting him without anything to back that up.

Though I didn't doubt Knox was a dangerous man, I got the sense he cared about his brother, would do and had done anything for him. That made him a good man in my book. And I trusted Kane's judgment.

Kane laughed. It felt forced. "Leeches make good managers, doing all the blood-sucking while I keep my hands clean."

Knox's lips didn't so much as twitch. This was definitely not a man who smiled often. Or ever.

Thinking of his past and about what Kane had alluded to about his present, I felt sad. Not sorry for him, since this kind of man was impossible to feel pity for, the emotion would bounce off his hardened shield. Just sadness.

"Leeches suck all the blood they can get, and they latch on to those closest to them, draining them before they realize it's too late."

My throat constricted as a tense moment passed between the brothers. They stared at each other, Kane's lip curled, Knox's nostrils flaring. I hated knowing that someone so obviously fake, a manipulator, was a thorn in the side of a relationship so powerful.

But Kane just smiled, yet once again, it seemed a little forced. He clamped his hand on his brother's shoulder.

I didn't miss the way Knox stiffened at the simple contact.

"We've gotta get you a woman, bro. So we can get you off blood and leeches and on to fucking in a bathroom and feeling like you could take on the fucking world."

And just like that, the tension broke.

Though I got the sense the battle wasn't over. Not by a long shot.

* * *

The evening went great. One could almost say I enjoyed myself, especially with the sojourn in the form of the quickie in the bathroom with a party full of guests a few rooms away.

Yes, it was out of my element, but Kane was at my side, and Kiera was there too, fluttering like the social butterfly she was while also keeping a sharp eye on me should I need rescuing.

Kiera was a dreamer at heart, but she had also told me, "White knights are bullshit. The people who will save you are your girlfriends."

Although she accepted Kane, though she liked me being in a relationship so far out of my comfort zone, she was protective, as the conversation earlier had communicated. She didn't trust easily, especially not men.

I didn't think I did either, yet there I was, throwing my everything into Kane, into his world.

That was not me.

Though I was enjoying the vacation from being Avery Hart, the talented chef with the ice queen reputation.

Except you couldn't take vacations from yourself, especially if you had any brush with celebrity.

Knox had left shortly after our meeting. Before leaving, he told me, "I'm glad you're with my brother," nodding sincerely. "Finally, he's made a good choice. I'm hoping he doesn't fuck it up."

I took that as Knox giving me his blessing. I felt strangely proud.

Kane had many friends, all of whom seemed fun, chaotic and ready for a good time. All of them were welcoming to me, with an air of almost amusement, as if they were used to entertaining Kane's flavor of the month.

We were speaking to Cleo Locke, one of the few female motocross riders in the sport who was really making a name for herself. She was an enigma with her pixie cut and delicate features. In her pretty, flowing, pastel dress paired with combat boots and arms full of tattoos. Her energy was warm, welcoming.

Kane hadn't even introduced me properly before her eyes lit up with recognition.

"I know you! It's been at the edge of my mind since you arrived," Cleo snapped her fingers. "You worked as Gerald DuBois's protegee."

My smile froze on my face, and my body turned rigid.

"I know now, of course, that you have your own very famous restaurant and are a force of nature, but I ate at his restaurant in Paris—fucking loved it—then bought his book because I love biographies, and you're mentioned in it," she gushed. "You're one of his proudest accomplishments." She rolled her eyes. "Yes, the man can cook and did great things in the culinary world ,blah, blah, blah," she flapped her hands. "But really, a man taking credit for a woman's achievements... Aren't we past that?" She shook her head, unaware that I had stopped breathing.

I didn't dare look at Kane. The second I'd gone still, his grip had tightened around me, and his head had tilted downward in my direction. He'd already clocked my reaction on body language alone —I wouldn't give him my face.

"I stopped reading the book there and then," Cleo continued. "And then I tried to find *your* book, but you don't have one, and you have very few published articles and pictures of yourself, hence the fact that it took me a hot minute to put a face to the name. Anyway, a long-winded way of saying I'm a big fan. I've only had the pleasure of eating your food at Gerald's restaurant, but Inferno is on my bucket list. If my schedule can ever line up with a reservation."

My mouth had gone dry. I forced my hand upward so I could take a sip of my drink before speaking. "We'll exchange numbers." I hoped my voice didn't betray anything. "You can tell me when you're in town, and I can see if I can make something work to get you in for a meal."

It was not something I normally, if ever, did—yielded my power in order to get people into the restaurant. One, because I didn't like it, and two, because if I set any kind of precedent, people wouldn't leave me alone.

I didn't quite know why I did it with Cleo. Maybe because I liked her on sight, maybe because she'd seen through Gerald. Or maybe because she reminded me a little of my sister Maisie, with her wild energy and easy smile.

"No shit?" Her eyes lit up. "That would fucking *rock*." She dug into her purse, grabbing her phone for us to exchange numbers.

By then I was recovered enough to look up at Kane and hide my discomfort. Unfortunately, he had a crease between his brows, obviously holding on to the moment when I'd stiffened.

He opened his mouth in question, but luckily, we were interrupted by Brax.

"Kane, we've got a sponsor over here we need to talk shop with." Brax looked at me with a fake smile. "You don't mind, do you? I'm sure you'd find it boring."

Any other time, I would've treated Brax's casual belittling of me with one of my patented stares and a cold quip, but I'd already pegged the man as an arrogant asshole.

"I'm not talkin' shop," Kane bit out. "And Avery isn't going anywhere."

"It's fine." I held up my drink, thankful it was half empty. "I need a refill and to find Kiera."

I all but ran from them at that moment.

I could tell Kane wanted to pull me off to a quiet corner to discuss the conversation with Cleo, but this was Kane's party. Therefore, there were no quiet corners. Usually, that would've irritated me. But for current circumstances, it suited me.

The party went well into the night, with people getting rowdier and rowdier. Kiera left at some point with a famous actor. She gave me a cheeky grin, and I couldn't help but smile back. It did help that I'd had two margaritas. Which was a lot for me.

I wasn't drunk. But I was less tense. I needed something to take the edge off, especially after the mention of Gerald.

Kane nursed the same beer the entire night. He made a good show of smiling and joking easily with his friends, but I didn't miss the sideways glances, filled with concern, he sent my way. I did my best to ignore those glances and try to make it look like I was having fun.

The last straggler had filtered out and Kane dragged me up to his room at the brownstone.

"As much as I'll try to convince you to sleep in tomorrow, I know that's an ill-fated journey," he said on the ascent up the stairs. "So bedtime it is."

I smiled. "Since when do you dictate my bedtime?"

His hand ghosted over my ass. "Whenever the fuck I like, Chef."

I didn't argue, though the principle should've made me bristle.

He stayed in the bathroom as I went about my nighttime routine, washing off makeup with the face wash I had at home. He'd noted every one of my toiletries in my bathroom and then bought them for me to have here.

Likely, he had an assistant buy them, but the gesture was pivotal. Romantic.

I tried to ignore it, feeling suddenly delicate without the sounds of the party and disturbingly sober in the overhead lights of the bathroom.

"Something triggered you tonight," Kane said from where he was perched on the side of the bathtub. "When Cleo mentioned that chef."

My stomach dropped. I'd hoped that Kane hadn't noted my reaction. The music was loud, we'd been drinking, and the environment was chaotic.

I glanced at him in the mirror. I considered trying to lie, brushing him off. I was an expert at throwing people off the scent when they tried to prod into my personal business. My family didn't even know about this.

Not even Kiera.

She knew the basics, she knew something had happened, that a man hurt me, but I hadn't been able to tell her the entire story.

I'd buried it, deep, unable and unwilling to drag it up into the light. Especially not into these bathroom lights in front of Kane.

It might've been the margaritas. It might've been my suddenly soft heart. Or that Kane had shared about his trauma so easily with me. It might've been because I was exhausted from keeping it inside for so long. Whatever the reason, I started talking, washing my face as I did so.

"I was young," I said, rubbing at my face a tad too vigorously. "I'd studied at the culinary institute in France and after, I'd promptly been offered a position working under Gerald DuBois at his Michelin star restaurant in the heart of Paris. It was a big deal."

I clenched my teeth and wiped my face with a washcloth, thinking of the girl I was then. There were no tears of joy at the offer, no hysterics of any kind. Even as a teenager, I was serious. I was happy at the offer, of course, but not surprised. Hadn't this been what I'd been working toward my entire life? I'd put the effort in and got the intended result.

The hysterics were reserved for my mother who had sobbed happy tears on the phone when I told her. I'd quickly found reasons to end that phone call. I didn't do well with emotions, especially hers. Too many bad memories attached.

"He had a reputation," I continued, patting my face dry. "For being a misogynistic asshole. Not something unique in the top tiers of the culinary world or the world in general," I added dryly with a bitter smile.

Though looking at the man who should've embodied toxic masculinity, I couldn't find a trace of it in him. He was masculine in every sense of the word. But no misogynist.

"I expected that," I continued, spritzing my face with toner. "I considered myself able to handle such things. If you can't handle pressure and a stripping down of everything you are, then you aren't capable of being in those world-class kitchens. But the asshole everyone said he was didn't materialize. He was hard on his staff, expected perfection, but I respected that. And he treated me with respect. Was patient. Impressed. Gave me freedom with new dishes, responsibilities that I didn't expect to get being so new. Which didn't earn me friends in the kitchen."

I took a deep breath, putting down the toner before toying with a moisturizer.

"I guess I considered him a mentor. Almost a father figure. Which, in hindsight, is an insult to my father's memory."

I gulped down fire and shame, remembering how part of me had wished for a man like that as a father instead of the easygoing, loving and jovial man I remembered. Because if I had a tough, stern and cold father, maybe it'd be easier to lose him.

"I stayed late often. To clean up, scrub ovens, counters, to experiment with recipes of my own. Gerald had given me free rein of the kitchen after service... A huge gift."

I thought back to the serene nights, the sizzling of the pans, the clang of pots and the faraway noises of Paris. I stayed until after midnight plenty of times, even when I'd have to be up at six to prepare for service.

"I was always alone in the kitchen," I rubbed lotion onto my neck. "Gerald was always at events and parties, being celebrated. He liked that. Bathed in the attention and praise he got for being a genius."

I rolled my eyes. I'd always found him a little narcissistic and pompous. But again, to survive and thrive at that level, you always had to have a certain level of narcissism and delusional belief in yourself.

"But then one night he was there," I whispered.

I still smelled him. Expensive port and aftershave couldn't cover the bitter twang of sweat.

"He'd been drinking. But he wasn't drunk. Not that that would've been an excuse for what happened next," I scoffed.

Kane had been intently listening, his elbows resting on his knees. That was his way. When I had his attention, I had all of it. He hung on my every word. Previously, I'd liked that. But at that moment, I didn't.

I was suddenly aware of my body, of his body, of the story that

I'd shoved down so deep that it tore out bits of me while coming back up.

Kane pushed up from where he was sitting, crossing the short distance between us. He gently angled me away from the mirror to face him, his breath on my face, his enticing scent mingling with that of my memories. "What happened next?" he asked quietly.

Kane was hyperaware of everything. Of minute details. Of gestures I made, expressions, the tone of my voice. He had learned who I was in the short time we'd been together. Actually, knew me.

I swallowed past the lump of dread in my esophagus. The memory had made nausea swirl in my gut. I regretted going there. Thinking that I was strong enough in Kane's arms, his presence. But I also knew I couldn't let myself retreat. Knew Kane wouldn't let it go now.

The only way through was forward.

"He, um," I pulled in a long breath. "He came on to me. Not very elegantly either."

There was the smell of the port. What I'd been cooking. Beef Wellington. Something I'd never put on a menu since that night.

His hands were fumbling, invasive straightaway.

I'd swatted them off, tried to push him away even as he backed me into the door to the walk-in freezer.

I hadn't been aware enough of my surroundings, of him casually talking to me with a strange gleam in his eyes, herding me to an area of the kitchen where I couldn't escape from.

I hadn't thought I'd need to be on guard in a way a woman needed to be on guard—when she was walking to her car at night, when she was breaking up with someone unpredictable, refusing the advances of someone at a bar.

No, I thought I didn't need the skills each woman unfortunately learned, not with this man. One I trusted. One old enough to be my father. A mentor.

After that night, I didn't think there was such a thing as a man I could trust. Or feel safe with.

"You know you want it," Gerald had whispered, lips against my neck. "I've seen the way you look at me."

"No," I replied, quietly at first, trying to push his roving hands away. "No!" I said louder as his hands crept even lower. "I don't want it. I don't want you."

I'd thought a lot about those words. Whether what happened next was my fault because I'd said it so plainly, without adornment or gentleness to stroke his ego enough to hide the straight up rejection.

I'd wondered if there was something I could've said, something I could've done to make him stop.

It was only in hindsight, with time to pad me from the trauma, that rage replaced those feelings of blame and guilt. It was not my responsibility to let him down easily so he wouldn't assault me. There was nothing, absolutely nothing, a woman could say to make sexual assault her fault. Nothing she could wear. No looks she could give.

No.

The single word was enough.

It was enough to make what he did a crime.

"He didn't rape me," I forced out the words. "Didn't get that far, at least. But he ... did enough."

Gerald's fingers, dry and probing, making their way past the elastic of my pants, pushing my simple cotton panties to the side before pushing inside.

It hurt.

It shocked me.

I left my body, not entirely understanding what was actually happening to me.

But then I did.

And my knee went to his balls.

His finger left me in a rush, brutally, causing more pain, but it gave me the opportunity to run.

I squeezed my eyes shut then forced myself to look at Kane. His face was a cool mask. "I came back to the kitchen the next day. I don't know what I was thinking. Don't know why I didn't report it to the police." I couldn't keep Kane's eye contact, my gaze flitting around the bathroom skittishly. "Because I was in a foreign country, was what I told myself," I sighed. "Because it would draw attention to me in a way I wouldn't like. I would never ever be able to make a name for myself as a chef. I'd always be the girl who accused Gerald DuBois of sexual assault. I wouldn't be believed. I'd already assumed that much. It would be he said, she said. The student of the great man who was nothing but ordinary. I wanted him to pay. I did. But I didn't want it to be at the expense of my career. My future."

Shame bloomed in my cheeks.

"It was selfish and cowardly," I admitted in a small voice. "Going back into that kitchen was, second to watching my father get buried, the hardest thing I ever did."

I'd thrown up in the alley before I walked in.

"But I went in," I whispered. "And he was there. And he looked at me, smiled tightly, politely, acting like nothing ever happened. Although I was no longer his golden student. Much to the delight of the others in the kitchen. I made sure I was never ever alone in his presence again." I clenched my fists at my sides. Kane was close to me but he wasn't touching me.

"I finished out my time there then left. Worked in other kitchens. Buried myself in that."

Though I didn't feel brave enough, I looked at Kane. His face was still expressionless. But he was shaking with what might've been rage, his chest rising and falling quickly.

I felt awkward, unaware of what to do with my admission out in the open air. Air that was stagnant after being buried for so long.

Kane jerked, as if I'd thrown water on him. His eyes lost that glazed look to them, and he squinted at me. His fire was back, mixed with a kind of rage I'd never seen on his face.

He cupped my face in his hands. "You, Avery Hart, are many, many things. Two things you absolutely aren't are selfish or a coward." His words were steely, hard as iron. "I'm not gonna lie, Chef, hearing that makes me want to make calls, get on a plane and go kill the fuck with my bare hands. I know that's my ugly, baser nature speaking, but fuck if his death doesn't sound sweet to me."

He took in an audible breath, never breaking eye contact.

"Spent my life working on that. That rage that put me in a cage. That turned me into someone I don't want to be, so I'll continue working on that. Moreover, I will not make this about me. I'll say it plainly, Chef. I'm sorry that happened to you. So fucking sorry. Men are scum. And I don't mean 'some men,' I mean most of us. Almost all of us." His thumb brushed my bottom lip. "But I'll endeavor to be worthy of you. And I'll treasure that you felt safe enough with me to tell me that just now."

My heart danced at his tender, sincere words. I wanted to cry. Sob against his chest. Kane would let me, that I knew. He wouldn't be afraid of my tears, my feelings.

But I didn't want that. There was still a stubborn, maybe emotionally stunted part of me that thought tears equaled weakness. So I held on.

Kane was watching me, searching my expression as if he were waiting for me to take the lead on what to say next.

When I didn't speak, he stroked my temple. "What do you want from here? I can run you a bath. Get you in the shower. Put on a movie. Whatever you need."

I rubbed my lips together. "Sex isn't anywhere in that list," I pointed out.

He grinned slowly, but it was muted. "After sharing that, dredging that up, I didn't know if you'd want to be touched like that right now."

I nodded, a gesture meant to push back the tears again more than anything. Kane was so considerate. Thoughtful. Empathetic.

I clutched on to the hem of his tee, tugging it up. He let me pull it over his head to reveal his tattooed and muscled torso.

"I need to be touched right now," I told him, kissing his neck. "I need you."

His eyes lit up. "Tell me what you need from me, Chef."

I kissed along his jaw, looking up at him. "I need you to bend me over that sink." I nodded to the sink in question. "Then I need you to fuck me, and I want to watch it in the mirror."

A groan rumbled from Kane. He took hold of my hair, roughly wrenching it back.

"Oh, Chef, I can do that."

KANE

It took an hour after Avery went to sleep for her muscles to relax. Even after I fucked her in the bathroom, watched her break apart, there was so much tension coiled up inside her.

She was waiting. For me to ... punish her for her admission? For me to look at her differently? Like she was dirty. Weak.

I was only guessing because that's what I'd been waiting for when I'd told her about my past. She was the only one, beyond a therapist, I'd ever told. I wasn't ashamed of it, but there was still a little toxic part of me that felt shame. Like I wasn't a man by admitting I was a victim.

But Avery made me feel like more of a man than I'd ever felt. There was no pity from her. Only fire, burning hot in her hazel gaze, fire she wanted to breathe on my mother, the man who hurt me. I could feel it, her need to avenge me.

It hadn't emasculated me, my woman wanting to fight for me. Fuck no. It confirmed that I'd chosen the right woman.

I was trying to stop myself from breathing my own kind of fire now. Once I'd been sure Avery was asleep in my arms, relaxed, I'd scrolled until I found every piece of information I could on Gerald DuBois.

Pompous asshole.

There were plenty of bullshit articles praising him, about his contribution to the culinary world. And plenty of those articles mentioned Avery. How he'd 'discovered her', 'turned her into the chef she was today'. I'd wanted to hurl my phone at the fucking wall.

No one had discovered her, and sure as fuck, no one but her made her into the chef she was.

Once I'd calmed my heart rate, I kept looking, learning.

Though I hadn't jumped on a plane to France … yet. I wanted to know thy enemy.

He was my enemy.

Avery was everything to me.

Fucking everything.

I knew it scared her, *we* scared her. It scared the fuck out of me too. But I was never one to run away when I got scared. I made a career off that shit.

So once I was done looking up Gerald DuBois, I emailed my jeweler.

Avery was not a flashy diamond kind of woman. I'd need something she could wear in the kitchen.

I'd work on it, we had time.

Because I planned on having a lifetime with Avery Hart.

Ten

AVERY

WE HAD one more night before Kane left.

One more night after his party, after my unexpected admission. I felt like I'd purged. Like something rotting inside of me had been removed. Kane didn't look at me differently, didn't treat me differently, like I was broken.

His last night was the same as any other night. He lingered, eating his duck l'orange with a chocolate cake I'd whipped up earlier —I wasn't the best pastry chef but I was known for that chocolate cake, and I knew Kane had a sweet tooth, which he'd declared almost as tasty as my pussy.

I'd grinned at that, after closing down the kitchen and walking to the alley with him.

"You up for another trip, Chef?" he asked when we made it to his bike.

My skin tingled with the offer, excited and hungry for another risk-filled dalliance. Although part of me was greedy for just him and a bed.

Yet I nodded.

Kane kissed me hard and quick before putting on my helmet and getting me on the bike.

I pressed close to him as we rode through the streets. The air had more of a chill now, so Kane ensured I wore more layers, even though he was only wearing a thin tee and a leather jacket.

"Do as I say, not as I do," he'd joked when I'd pointed that out.

The motorcycle was my preferred mode of transportation. I had no idea how I'd go back to the subway or cabs. Two weeks. Two weeks without Kane. The thoughts followed me through the city until we stopped at a curb.

I got off the bike, looking at the businesses around us. Most of them were closed up, except the one with the flashing neon sign —*Inked*—which I guessed was our destination.

Kane's hand closed firmly around mine, lifting our intertwined hands to kiss mine before walking us into the tattoo parlor.

"William," Kane grinned at the man at the counter before clapping him in a man-bro handshake.

"Rhodes," the tattoo-covered man greeted, smiling. The smile looked at odds with the rest of him. It was warm, boyish even.

And he was not boyish. Even sitting, I could tell he was well over 6′. He was wearing a black tank top that showed off bulging muscles and skin that was covered in tattoos. I couldn't find a piece that wasn't inked. The tattoos ran up his neck and covered his shaved skull. There was script underneath both of his eyes.

The eyes that were blindingly green, moving from Kane to me. His smile remained for me. Again, warm, friendly.

"William," Kane waved to me. "This is my woman, Avery—"

"Hart," William finished for him. He stood, rounding the counter so he could come shake my hand. "I know who you are. I'm a big fan."

I felt my eyes widen, taken aback. I could count on one hand the amount of people who had recognized me on face value. I didn't do press. The handful of interviews I did rarely included a photo—on my insistence—and the ones that did were not really indicative of how I looked on a daily basis because of the makeup and the lighting and the general polish.

But it had happened, mostly by cooking students who followed the comings and goings of the culinary world and read the publications I was featured in. Never by six-foot-something giants covered in tattoos.

"Your food is incredible," he added, still shaking my hand enthusiastically. "Your twist on duck l'orange was revolutionary."

I smiled. Genuinely. Despite finding it hard to take compliments—even though I teetered between overly cocky and battling imposter syndrome—somehow, William made it easy.

"Thank you," I told him. "That dish is a particular favorite of mine."

He nodded, finally letting go of my hand. "It's my death row meal. Along with your twist on Mille-Feuille. Paired with a bottle of Villa Wolf Gewürztraminer."

It was surreal to have this man talk about delicate desserts and a white wine that presented first with flowers on the palate. I instantly liked him.

"What are you doing with this gutter rat?" he asked teasingly. "He wouldn't even know a soufflé from a soup."

Kane laughed good-naturedly and had been watching the exchange between the two of us with a warm smile on his face.

"She's slumming it, and I'd appreciate you not pointing it out since I'm planning on holding on to her until she comes to her senses." Kane squeezed my hand.

William shook his head. "Avery Hart is nothing but a master of the senses, brother, you're fucked."

Kane's eyes twinkled, then went serious. "I surely am."

The jovial atmosphere left for a moment, leaving me feeling overwhelmed by the seriousness of the moment. We were no longer caught up in a chaotic and adventurous fling. It was something ... more. And it scared the shit out of me.

A clap jerked me from my thoughts.

"So what are we in for today?" William asked, looking between the two of us. "Avery, you looking to get some ink?"

I laughed at the absurdity of that. "Me? No."

I didn't judge anyone with tattoos. In fact, I liked them a lot. I was fascinated with Kane's. Part of me wanted to be a person who could cover her skin in something so permanent. Most of the chefs in my world had at least one.

I just didn't think I could pull it off. Tattoos were at direct odds with everything I thought about myself.

"One day," Kane said, rubbing my arm, and I gasped at him in shock. "But no, today, you've got the pleasure of permanently scarring me."

"Great," William stood from his seat. "Come on back."

And just like that, we were walking through a large room that smelled of antiseptic and ink, buzzing mingling with the hard rock playing over the speaker.

Surprisingly, the tables were separated by partitions, and a lot of them were occupied. Not sure why I was surprised. Just because I didn't consider getting a tattoo at midnight didn't mean there weren't plenty of people who did.

That fascinated me, people who lived lives like that. I was jealous of that freedom. Then it dawned on me... That was Kane. Rather glaringly obvious, since I was in a tattoo parlor with him at midnight, and he was on a first-name basis with those who worked there.

William led us to the end of a partition to a table covered with plastic, the walls covered by various posters of dragons and mythical creatures, pictures of tattoos. On a shelf beside the tattoo table sat a stack of worn paperbacks.

Curiously, a lot of them were culinary related, biographies on some of the greats.

"Take a seat." William nodded to a chair beside the bed.

"You know the drill, brother," he said to Kane.

As I was about to let go of him to sit down, Kane's hold flexed on my hand, and he dragged me to him so our mouths crashed together.

He kissed me hard and passionately, and though I was aware of the other man in the small space with us, I kissed him back with the same fervor.

Sitting once he let me go, I looked down at my lap. My ears became hot, knowing we had an audience, one who actually knew who I was, but William hadn't so much as blinked, busy putting on latex gloves.

"What are we doing today?" he asked Kane. "Got sketches from some billionaire after you lost a bet again?"

Kane chuckled, the sound low and throaty.

"Nah, this one's simple. 'Yes, Chef,' right here." He whipped off his shirt then pointed to the empty spot on his left pec.

My heart skipped. My mouth went dry.

Had he just said what I thought he did?

He stared at me, an easygoing expression on his face as if it were totally normal for him to get a tattoo that was about me—on his heart no less—after however long we'd been 'together.'

Was I missing something? Had I been out of the game so long that tattoos of names of lovers were no longer a faux pas? Surely not.

Or maybe it was Kane. William had just said he permanently inked his body when he lost bets, so maybe it meant something different to him.

His eyes went to mine, and something passed between us.

No, it didn't mean anything different to him.

He was getting me, inked on his body.

I watched it happen.

Then, after shooting the shit with William, sharing a beer and talking about food, we left. We rode through the night, back to his brownstone where he made slow and purposeful love to me with my name inked on his chest.

We didn't speak of it.

I told myself I didn't need to, the look, the act said it all.

But mostly it was because I was too damn terrified of what it meant.

* * *

I didn't see Kane for two weeks after that night.

Two agonizing weeks. I worked fourteen days straight—not uncommon for me—and I did twelve-hour days—also not uncommon. Every second was busy, full of decisions, of menus, of practice plates, of sourcing the exact fish I needed at the docks and negotiating prices.

There was not a moment to think about a romantic entanglement.

Or at least there shouldn't have been.

But every minute, every second, Kane was there. At the forefront of my mind. His rough, callused hands running over my skin, his cock pumping inside me, his arms crushing me to his body in his sleep.

And every time I heard, "Yes, Chef"—which had to be hundreds of times a day—my pussy tingled, and my knees weakened, thinking about the rough and guttural way Kane said it. Then my mind flashed to those two words, inked into his chest.

I missed him, to put it simply. Even though it was infinitely more complicated than that. It felt like my cells were dying without him. Like I wasn't entirely alive.

It was an obsession we had for each other, pure and simple. It couldn't have been healthy, it sure as hell was dangerous, and it was bound to burn itself out at some point. But I couldn't find myself caring. For once, I was being reckless with my time, my energy and my heart. I'd deal with the fallout when it came.

I did find myself watching the clock like a hawk all day, waiting for the time to strike so I could leave the restaurant with enough time to go get ready and make it to the arena.

Kane only flew in today. Because of the way his schedule worked, he had to go straight to the arena to prepare. I could've seen him before the show, but that would've meant I would've had to leave the restaurant even earlier. And I needed to be there to prepare, to school my staff, to basically control everything I could. It was enough that I was taking time off for a man.

Unheard of.

It was my challenge, my punishment to myself, that I would not get to see him until after the show.

Kiera was coming with me. Because Kane offered her the tickets as well, and I didn't like the idea of going alone. I was not a person who enjoyed crowds or had been to any kind of event like this.

I needed Kiera. And she was more than happy to oblige.

She also helped pick my outfit.

No, she *bought* my outfit.

She was already at my apartment when I got there, waiting at the door with a large shopping bag in one hand and a bottle of champagne in the other.

"Outfit," she announced, holding up the bag. "Dutch courage." She held up the champagne. "Since I'm betting you're close to breaking out in hives at leaving the restaurant on a Saturday night in order to go to a place that is so far out of your comfort zone it may as well be another planet. Which Jersey technically is."

Not for the first, or even the hundredth time, I was infinitely grateful that the universe brought me a friend like Kiera.

A friend like Kiera who somehow knew exactly what kind of

outfit to put me in for attending an extreme sports event where I was *dating*—that seemed far too pedestrian of a word for what Kane and I were doing—one of the biggest stars in the show. One of the biggest stars on the planet right now. Despite not having any social media accounts or time to follow entertainment news, I scrolled religiously, reading articles on Kane blowing through the globe, flying through the air on a motorcycle, walking through the airport in Wayfarers, face in a phone, texting me.

Well, at least I assumed he was texting me since we'd rarely gone more than an hour without some kind of contact, unless he was actively competing.

Which was tonight, the last of the Supercross events he was competing in.

Kiera and me. Because no way could I fathom going to this event on my own. Me. Who ran kitchens all over the world. Me, who had done everything alone since I left home at seventeen.

Jeans. That's what Kiera had bought for my first public appearance as Kane's girlfriend—if that's what I was—and for the first time I'd see the man in weeks.

I owned jeans. Didn't think that they were particularly spectacular or special.

But these jeans were something else. They fit me like a second skin; the denim was faded perfectly and sculpted my butt in such a way that I thought it was witchcraft. She had also got a simple white tank. Again, it didn't sound like anything extraordinary. But something about the thick, ribbed fabric, the way the sleeves curved slightly inward to be more flattering on my arms to accentuate my chest and flatten my stomach.

Then she put me in simple sneakers and slung a bunch of gold necklaces around my neck.

And she tamed my hair into slightly more manageable but still wild curls. Did makeup that was subtle but made my eyes pop and my lips look impossibly perfect. My green eyes were almost glowing, the high blush on my cheeks emphasized the cheekbones and made my heart-shaped face look both sultry and soft at the same time.

I hadn't admitted it to myself, but I wanted to look good for Kane. I wanted to look like I deserved to be with the famous, devilishly-handsome superstar. Though I wasn't a jealous person, I was mindful of him being 'on tour' for the past two weeks. I didn't exactly know what that entailed, but I could only imagine there were plenty of attractive women in his vicinity. Women with smaller waists, bigger boobs and much less complicated backstories. I didn't think that I had the ability to be insecure about such things. It turned out I'd never cared about anyone enough to be insecure about them.

Kane hadn't given me any reason to be unsure. He'd been in constant contact, calling me the second he woke up and the second he went to bed. At all hours.

Yet I couldn't help feeling doubt.

That he'd see me, and I wouldn't be what he remembered. That I'd be a disappointment. That I'd been a novelty. One he got caught up in, and once he had distance, a plethora of slim, beautiful uncomplicated women around him, he'd come to his senses. I knew an outfit and hair and makeup couldn't completely dispel such feelings, but they helped.

Kiera also helped by providing me with endless chatter throughout the trip, barely giving herself a chance to take a breath, and not requiring me to do more than nod and look out the window while picking at my cuticles.

We were escorted from an entrance at the back by large men in suits. Kane had given us the option to be in some private box, but I wanted to be as close to him as I could. Not that I could be that close to him while he was tearing around a track on a motorcycle. And I wanted the true experience of what it would be like to come as a fan, to be on the ground.

Our section was cordoned off from the rest of the general

public, with seats and a refreshment stand. I didn't know if this was the norm or something Kane had organized for us.

Brax was there. On the phone when we arrived, his eyes running over me dismissively, Kiera sleazily before he gave us a patronizing nod and returned to his phone call. He hadn't gotten off that thing since we arrived, which I was glad about.

"Yep, you were right," Kiera said in my ear as we settled ourselves in the seats. Her eyes were on Brax. "Total asshole. My detector has taken a while to calibrate, but I can spot them from a mile away now. Unless I'm sleeping with them."

I suppressed a chuckle. She wasn't wrong. Not that I socialized with her 'boyfriends'—though that was a generous term for them— but I'd heard about them plenty, had had a crying Kiera on my couch and in my kitchen eating chocolate mousse cake many times.

I nodded in agreement, deciding that I was going to ignore Brax if he was going to do that to me. I'd stopped forcing myself to be polite to assholes long ago.

I looked around at the arena. It was much like any sporting venue stadium with the staggered seating, the thrumming crowd. But instead of a baseball or football field, there was a large dirt pit in the middle, with various hills and valleys—the 'track,' I assumed.

My eyes traced over the various slopes and ramps with interest. Not having anything to compare them with, I could only use my imagination to figure out what they would be used for. Jumping through the air. On motorcycles. My nails bit into my palms, thinking of Kane doing that. He'd been doing it for weeks and survived—he'd been doing it for *years* and survived—but still, dread curled up my spine.

Then I moved my attention to the stands. People were still filtering in, but the entire place was packing up. Quickly. It looked like every one of these seats was going to be filled. How many were there? Thousands. Tens of thousands?

"Wasn't extreme sports like a '90s thing?" I asked Kiera, leaning over in her direction while staring at the crowd.

Kiera scoffed, downing her drink before looking at me with an arched brow. "Honey, where have you been for the past five years?"

"In a kitchen or sleeping," I replied. She knew this.

"You don't scroll through social media, like at all?" Her nails drummed on the screen of her ever-present phone. I couldn't even be sure I'd brought mine. I must've. I was keeping better track of it now since it was my only line of communication to Kane. Plus, I wanted to ensure the restaurant could reach me in case of problems. Not that I could do anything in New Jersey.

I wanted a night out like a normal person. A normal person who was going to watch her kind of boyfriend perform motorcycle tricks in front of thousands—*tens of thousands*—of people.

"I only have social media because you made me one, and I only follow you. I haven't gone on since you created the profile," I informed her, something again, I thought she knew.

Her horrified face told me that my best friend had been ignorant of just how unaware I was to the goings-on of the virtual world.

"Babe, I knew you were not a social media addict, but I didn't think you were off the fucking grid."

I rolled my eyes, taking a sip of my drink before scanning the area again. People were still taking their seats, the music pumping over the speakers, but there were also people seemingly finishing setup on the track.

My stomach felt like it was trying to climb up into my throat.

It must almost be time.

I looked back to Kiera. "I don't think I can be classified as 'off grid' just because I don't know about influencers ... aside from you, I mean."

"I'm the only influencer that anyone needs to know about." She gave me a sly smile. I knew it was a joke, because despite the seemingly vapid title, my friend was a deep person who struggled with a lot of insecurity. All of her makeup, her online persona was just that... a persona she wore to survive her insecurities.

I knew a thing or two about that.

"But we're not talking about makeup gurus or lifestyle vloggers here," she continued. "We're talking about *culture*."

I pursed my lips, gesturing to the track. "You're going to classify *this* as culture?"

"Oh, I'm sorry, did I miss your weekly pilgrimages to the Louvre or the Met?" she asked dryly. "Or did I neglect your love of the opera and classical music?"

I smiled at my friend's gentle ribbing.

"Like it or not, darling, pop culture is the culture of the time." She nodded her head to the arena. "Which happens to include super-hot dudes riding on motorcycles and jumping shit. Which people have dug in a big way for a long time. Although I'll give it to you, it used to be a certain societal niche that enjoyed things like X-Games. But the sport has had somewhat of a resurgence. Not entirely because of Kane Rhodes, but let's just say this stadium would not be at capacity if it weren't for him."

She wasn't wrong. I'd been ignorant of him and the power of social media for a long time, but since I'd been researching him, I couldn't deny the league of fame he was in. It was hard to remember when I was with him. Because he wasn't Kane 'The Devil' Rhodes when we were together.

I still didn't know how I felt about that. We'd enjoyed a relationship in the shadows, drinking coffees together in the early morning, no realities of who we truly were in the daylight.

That time had ended. I was with someone famous. Hugely famous. He had millions of followers on social media, was photographed wherever he went. And whenever a woman was with him, she was picked apart.

By accident or grace, that hadn't happened with me. Yet.

A deep dread rolled in my stomach, knowing it was just a matter of time before that happened unless I ended it. I had a small amount of attention and fame, but I had managed to remain uninteresting enough that people didn't want to know about Avery Hart the person. Any kind of attention that Kane enjoyed, even an ounce of it, was too much for me.

Yet there I was.

"That purse is ridiculous," I muttered as Keira took longer than she should've trying to arrange her phone, lip gloss and credit card just so the thing closed.

"This is not just a purse," she said, aghast. "This is the Fendi Baguette from the *Sex and the City* movies. Do you know how hard these are to get? It's a collector's item."

I rolled my eyes. Another way that Kiera and I were vastly different—I did not get excited over purses, certainly not overpriced ones that the designer paid big bucks to put in a movie in order to create a false scarcity and try to justify the price tag.

Not that I would ever say that to Kiera, never judging her for the things that made her happy. She worked damn hard for every cent she made.

"It's my thurdy gift to myself," she declared, admiring the bag. I took back every judgmental thing I thought about it. If something as simple as a bag could bring that look of childlike joy to my friend's face, who cared about the price or the false scarcity?

"You're thirtieth?" I echoed. "It's a little late for that, isn't it?"

Kiera shot me a vicious gaze. "It absolutely is not a little late for that since I'm only *twenty-nine*."

I kept my lips pressed shut. Kiera had been twenty-nine for three years. Another thing I didn't understand about women—how we were desperate to seem younger, not just denying the aging process but spending thousands on making it look like we were perpetually in our twenties.

I held up my hands in surrender. "Okay, so you're twenty-nine, and it's an early thirtieth gift."

"*Thurdy*, not thirty," she said.

"Thurdy?" I repeated.

She nodded. "A thurdy gift is something a woman in her thirties or older buys for herself. It's most often rather expensive and from a casual observer's gaze impractical, but it brings her joy and signifies the life she's building for herself." She grinned at me. "I coined the term. Think it'll catch on?"

The roar of the crowd jerked us from our conversation. Music was playing so loud it became a second heartbeat inside my body. I watched in awe as bikes sped by, unaware that was possible.

Then Kane was announced.

The crowd went wild. I could feel the change in energy. The power that he wielded.

"Fuck yeah!" Kiera shouted from beside me, grinning widely at me and quite obviously embracing the energetic atmosphere.

I couldn't embrace anything.

My heart stuttered as Kane went through the air at a height that seemed inconceivable. It only resumed at an uneven beat when he landed back on the ground, wheels first, carrying on the track at a dizzying speed.

More roars. My pulse was racing at a speed that made me feel like I'd just drank four espressos. I was more wired than I had been in any kitchen.

And that was just from watching.

I felt excitement, I felt dread, I felt immense fear. That was Kane. Doing this. And he did this constantly. Rode hand in hand with death. This was the man I was with.

I loved it. Hated it.

Music boomed through the stadium, his bike flipping and flying seemingly with the rhythm. He hung off it, holding on to the handlebars with one hand in a move that seemed to defy physics. It was like a dance. It was an art, I realized. Not just someone hopping on a motorcycle to prove they were a man, like Kane had told me.

No, this required skill. Though the ones who came before him were impressive, there was a tangible difference. I understood why he was so famous. Because he was the best in the world. He made it look effortless.

I couldn't take my eyes off him. I was almost having fun.

It didn't happen in slow motion. It was a frantic, horrible, terrifying blur. He was up in the air one moment, just like before. But unlike moments earlier, he didn't land smoothly with a cheer from the crowds. No, he crashed.

Crashed.

A normal word from the past. I'd heard about people getting hurt, killed in accidents before, and I'd had a detached kind of sympathy for them, knew crashes happened. They were a part of life.

But not this life.

Not my life.

Not *Kane's* life.

Surely, that couldn't have been what happened, but it seemed like all sound had been sucked from the stadium. I was in an abyss. Everyone around me ceased to exist.

There were no more screams, no more pulsating crowd. There was nothing but the replay of Kane in the air then being on the ground.

I started moving, obviously. Because at one point I was standing in our little section, and then I was moving. Sprinting. Pushing past people, elbows, hips, arms. Then I jumped over fences, over the barriers between the course and the crowd.

I couldn't be sure how long it took me to get from my spot to Kane. There were already people around him, but not the paramedics who needed to be there. Not the army of people who needed to be there to ensure Kane was okay.

I half collapsed, half skidded on my knees when I made it to him. I noticed from a faraway place that there was a dull sting in my legs. But that was nothing compared to the burn in my lungs as I struggled to breathe around the image of Kane, prone, lying on the ground.

Brax was there.

I didn't know why Brax was there and not an army of doctors. I didn't know how he'd gotten there first. Maybe because there was a portion of time between the crash and me moving when I froze. When I was a thirteen-year-old girl being told her father was dead. I was experiencing loss again, preparing for it. Brax hadn't done that. He'd obviously moved quicker than me, and I didn't like that.

He was trying to pull off Kane's helmet.

"You're not supposed to do that," I hissed over the buzz in my ears, swatting his hands away.

Brax glanced up at me. Still in the midst of this, there was a cold annoyance in his gaze. And in that moment, I loathed him. I wanted to stab him in the eye, punch him in the face. I wanted to hurt him. I wanted to kill him.

"He's good, he's fine. Aren't you, bro?" His tone was infuriatingly casual, light.

"You don't just fucking 'rub some dirt' on this situation," I snapped at Brax. "He fell. From the sky. On a motorcycle."

My eyes turned to Kane, though I was terrified to look at his face in case it was pale and lifeless or there was blood coming out of his ears.

But I locked on to sapphire eyes. Open. Awake. Aware.

A part of me relaxed. Slightly. My teeth were no longer in danger of immediately snapping from the force I was grinding them.

"Chef." Kane's voice sounded normal. Not like he'd plummeted from ... how many feet in the air on a motorcycle?

I crawled closer to him, not glancing at Brax but having the strong urge to elbow him in the gut. Or in that pretty face of his. How is it he was here first? Protecting his investment.

I swallowed my bitterness toward Brax to focus on Kane.

"Kind of envisioned being a bit more impressive the first time you saw me ride," he joked. He sounded like himself, but there was a tension to his voice, a straining around his eyes that told me he was in pain.

"I'm plenty impressed," I said honestly, forcing myself to be calm. "You fell from a thousand feet and are talking to me, still handsome as ever."

He let out a laugh that turned into a cough that sounded wet.

My heart dropped out of my chest, right there onto the dirt.

I ripped my eyes from Kane's to look for someone to help so I wouldn't watch him die there, in front of thousands of people.

Like I'd conjured them, the paramedics made their way to us.

"Give us some space, please," one of them said.

Though it felt wrong at the very core of me, I let go of Kane's hand and stood up to let them do their work.

Brax was somehow beside me.

He touched my shoulder in a way that maybe was supposed to be reassuring, but it felt controlling, his hold was too firm, bordering on painful.

Kane's eyes were on us, on me, which was likely why Brax made the gesture, to keep up appearances.

I didn't flinch out of his grip as I so wanted to; I didn't want to give Kane a reason to worry about me.

"Her knees," Kane gritted out as they lifted him onto a gurney.

I frowned at him. His helmet was intact, but maybe he was concussed.

"Her fuckin' knees," he repeated, pointing to me. He waved his hands at the paramedics, shrugging them off. "I don't want anyone fucking touching me until they look at my woman's knees."

When all eyes turned to me, I looked down. My jeans, my magical jeans had ripped, and sure enough, there was blood dribbling down my legs from two grazes I'd obviously sustained when I'd skidded against the rocky surface.

They stung faintly.

"You can't be serious," I huffed, taking the chance to pull myself from Brax's side to walk toward Kane. "You just crashed from fifty feet in the air. I just did what most third-graders do on a daily basis."

"You're bleeding," Kane argued, his voice steel. "Take care of her first," he ordered the paramedics.

They didn't look happy about it, but it seemed they also couldn't resist the authority in Kane's tone because they made a move toward me.

"Do not even think about it." I held up my hand. "Toss some Band-Aids my way while we're in the ambulance, and you're taking care of him." My voice had its own authority. I might not have had muscles nor been a man, but I'd controlled kitchens for years.

"I'm not letting anyone do shit to me while my woman is bleeding." Kane was obviously not letting it go. His eyes twinkled as they focused on me, but I could see the pain ringing in them. "I'm a stubborn son of a bitch, Chef, and I haven't lost a battle of the wills yet."

I squared my shoulders. "Well, you've never engaged in one with me."

Then, with effort, I tore my eyes from him to focus on the paramedics who were watching us both. "I understand he is a brute, a famous brute and can be somewhat convincing in a hardheaded kind of way, but he's also just sustained a serious injury. And I'll tell you right now, if you even *think* about tending to me before him, I'll make sure to sue you for negligence." I'm pretty sure that I couldn't do that, and I did feel vaguely guilty for threatening people who saved lives on a daily basis, but panic was crawling up my throat, and I had no other option.

"Tranquilize him if you need to," I added when I saw Kane's lips part to argue. "I'll do it myself if I have to." My voice was cold, calm and utterly unyielding. I focused my gaze back on Kane, prepared for a fight, knowing I was going to win.

Kane's face was still hard, mostly from pain at that point. At least that's what I was guessing because his eyes had turned soft. Tender.

"Fuck, I love you," he said.

I blinked.

He just said he loved me.

After crashing a motorcycle from a dizzying height.

While on a gurney.

With a crowd full of people watching.

Granted, they likely couldn't hear him, but the paramedics could.

I could.

He must've had a head injury.

I swallowed the butterflies in my throat and steadied myself as the world had gone and tilted since he uttered that sentence.

"If that's true, you won't say another word, and you'll let these nice people take care of you," I ordered stiffly.

If Kane was upset about me not returning the words, he didn't show it on his face. He just smiled lazily. "Yes, Chef," he replied dutifully.

I sagged as the paramedics took this as permission, instantly getting to work on him. Although I rode in the ambulance, I opted to do so in the front. There was no room for me back there. Not with all the equipment, the people trying to help Kane and with those three words.

I was done for.

Kane was alive. For now.

But I feared our relationship was terminal.

Eleven

CONSIDERING HOW IT HAD LOOKED, Kane got off easy. A lot of bruises, a broken wrist and a ruptured spleen were what he had to show for crashing into the ground on a motorcycle flying sixty feet in the air.

I'd vocalized my shock at his injuries and lack of life-threatening ones. Kane had shrugged. "What can I say? I know how to crash, babe."

It terrified me how blasé he was about death, his proximity to it.

It terrified me and shook at drawers I'd closed, locked and forgotten about inside myself.

The urge to run from him, from this, was tempting. Especially with the 'I love you' hanging in the air. My relationships ran their course far before such things could be uttered. I made sure of that.

We were in a private room at Mt Sinai. The room didn't look so much like a hospital room but a suite at a hotel. I guessed that was what power and money and fame got you. Before this happened, I ranted on about the inadequacy of care in this country, but as horrible as it made me, I was grateful for the treatment Kane was

155

receiving. That Kane had the best doctors in the country making sure they didn't miss anything. Making sure he didn't die.

I slept there.

Not on the lush pullout bed across the room. No, Kane had demanded I curl up in the —admittedly bigger than regular— hospital bed with him. I'd fought him on it at first, but he'd simply said if I didn't, he'd get up and go to the pullout. It wasn't a bluff.

I wasn't exactly hard to convince.

I wanted to be close to him. Feel his skin, smell him, have his heart beating against my cheek.

Which is how we went to sleep, until Brax woke us up in the morning with the clearing of his throat.

Seeing the man at all, let alone first thing while feeling emotionally hungover, was not my favorite thing to do in the morning.

I tried my best to plaster on a façade for Kane's sake.

It helped that Knox was at his side. His eyes were on the two of us. He wasn't smiling, but the edges of his lips were almost turned upward. An almost-smile.

The warm look I gave him was not forced.

"Don't get enough attention as it is, brother?" Knox asked dryly.

Kane leaned over to kiss my head before replying. I self-consciously tried to sit up, feeling uncomfortable, cuddling in bed with him with the two men standing over us.

Despite his injuries, Kane's grasp was firm, so I couldn't move unless I wanted to fight him and risk hurting him. So I relaxed back.

"Maybe I just wanted the good drugs without the judgment," he teased. "And to get Chef to try out her hands at being my nurse." There was a sexual innuendo that I didn't think I would have a carnal response to, but damn, I did.

I didn't miss the way Brax rolled his eyes.

"Just came to ensure you're okay," Knox said.

"Got nine lives. You know that, brother," Kane waved off his concern.

Knox's lips were no longer turned up. "You're fast runnin' out of those."

There was an uncomfortable moment before Knox said, "Avery, take care of him." The request felt sacred somehow, like he trusted me.

"Of course," I told him.

He nodded once, didn't acknowledge Brax, then left.

Brax tried to stay. Tried to go over interviews he'd scheduled.

"Not doin' any of that shit," Kane interrupted him.

"Kane—"

"I'm not doin' it," Kane repeated, not hiding the impatience in his tone. "I'm tired. I'm getting too old for this shit. This," he gestured to his arm which was in a cast, "is not gonna be a money grab. No publicity bullshit. I'm gonna stay in New York with Chef until I feel like going back."

"But we've got the Winter Games. I've already got a physical therapist who said if we work hard, you'll be in fine shape for them," Brax pushed, splotches of red creeping up his neck.

"I don't do *fine*," Kane barked. "I do it when I want to. If my body is ready by then, it is. If it isn't, then it isn't. Ain't pushing shit. Deal with it."

The disdain in Kane's tone was unmistakable.

It was shameful for Brax. To be dismissed. I didn't know if that was something that happened often, but I doubt it since Kane was so easygoing. I knew it was doubly embarrassing to be shut down publicly, though, in front of me.

For a split second, Brax's gaze shot to me, and I felt the pure loathing in it.

I remained placid, even though that made my fingertips numb.

Brax blamed me for this. However insane that was. When a man felt emasculated, he usually looked for the nearest woman to blame.

I made a mental note to be careful of Brax. He'd want to punish me for this.

He looked back to Kane, wearing a tight smile. "I'll take care of it. You may want to take care of this."

He threw down the rolled-up newspaper he'd been holding.

Kane was on the front page.

With me.

I widened my eyes in horror.

Then I looked up to Brax who now had a self-satisfied smirk on his face.

"I'll leave you both," he said before turning on his expensive loafers and leaving.

I couldn't see him, but I knew he was smiling because he'd landed a blow. One of many to come.

* * *

Kane grinned at the photo that was plastered on pretty much every news site—I'd found this out by frantically googling, noting all the missed calls from the restaurant and people who had seen it. I'd deal with that … later.

It was a picture of me. Me after pushing past every official and kneeling at Kane's side, his arm reaching up to my face.

"Fucking love this photo," he muttered.

I gaped at him. "You love a photo in which you are suffering from a ruptured spleen and narrowly escaped death?"

I hated the photo. All it was was a snapshot of the most terrible moment of my life.

Kane's gaze softened as he must've heard the pain in my tone. "I don't love it of me, although I do look handsome." His fingertips trailed over the image of my face. I'd expected it to be contorted in worry or horror, but my features were calm, eyes intent on Kane.

Except my hands. They were gripping on to the sides of his helmet for dear life.

"My warrior woman," he murmured. "You leapt through crowds, security, bounded onto that track without hesitation."

"You can't know that," I argued.

"Seen the videos."

I cringed. There was a video. Of course, there was. This was the age of social media, of the viral posts. Everyone wanted their fifteen minutes.

"I've never had anyone care about me." He grabbed my cheek, not unlike he had when he was lying there. "Other than my brother, but that's different. We cared about each other because we were all we had. I've never had a woman care about me enough to run through a stadium without pause and stare at me with utter calmness while ordering me to live."

My throat constricted at the intensity, the palpable sincerity in Kane's words. This was him. Unafraid to jump in the air on a motorcycle, unafraid to speak his feelings, to show his emotions.

"You can consider that a standing order," I told him. "Because I love you."

The simple words took everything to say, to admit to myself. Loving someone gave them power. Loving someone meant indescribable pain if you lost them.

Kane's eyes swam with emotion that hit me square in the chest. Tears he didn't seem embarrassed of swam in those endless eyes of his.

"Greatest gift I'll ever get, hearing those words." His thumb brushed my lips.

And there I was. Done for.

* * *

Kane was in the hospital for two more nights. He discharged himself against the doctor's wishes. Against my wishes.

We'd argued about it.

And though I'd dug my heels in and put on my ice queen façade, I'd lost that one.

"I've spent plenty of time in a room I couldn't leave," was his explanation. "I know my body. And, babe, I'm rich. We need a doctor, I'll hire one to come to the apartment."

It would've sounded obnoxious and arrogant coming from anyone else, but not Kane.

And I couldn't argue against him not wanting to feel caged again.

So I didn't fight him being released.

I was surprised and elated when he discharged to my place instead of his. Although I did try to point out that his borrowed brownstone had much more spacious bathrooms and more room in general. He could technically walk, but I could tell that each slow step pained him.

"That place isn't home, Chef. And even if that fuckin' penthouse wasn't being remodeled, that place wouldn't be home either. Especially after that fancy designer is done sucking all the personality out of it. Your place, to me, is home." He grasped my neck. "*You* are my home."

And what could I say to that? My apartment had never felt like home either, until I walked in with Kane, carrying his duffel—which he insisted on, despite his bodyguard, Mike, following us in.

Mike was necessary because of the paparazzi. They had been camped outside the hospital in droves. They followed our SUV from the hospital to my apartment, swarming us in the lobby.

I'd gone from spending time alone with Kane to seeing the full brunt of his fame, turbocharged by the accident and the photo of us going viral.

I supposed it didn't help that I had a small dose of fame being a chef. Nothing like Kane, but things did come up if you googled my name.

Heidi, the owner of my restaurant, had called countless times, leaving messages about Kane having a table at the restaurant as soon as he was healed.

I loved Heidi. She was a self-made woman who gave me the freedom to design a menu and run a kitchen, only requiring that I do the bare minimum interviews for publicity. But she was a businesswoman, meaning her respect for my privacy only went so far. And with me and Kane being on the front page of … everywhere, this gave the restaurant even more social cachet.

Kiera had already reached out to me to let me know the countless offers I was getting for sponsoring cookware, for magazine pieces, social media deals. She knew that I'd refuse them all, but she wanted to let me know I was officially 'on grid.'

My mother and sister had called too.

I was putting that, all of that, away in the back of my mind to focus on when Kane was not still pale, walking slowly and carefully in a cast.

Even though he was far from fragile, considering we had sex the moment Mike left the apartment.

He didn't go far, though. He was posted outside the front door.

It was all surreal. The security guard, the throngs of people outside my apartment building. The articles crawling over the internet like locusts. The missed calls and texts. The only ones I'd returned were from my mother and sister, hoping to stop them from calling or even worse, showing up unannounced.

Neither of them were extreme sports fans, but they were both mothers, and my own mother seemed to be trying to make up for the failures she thought she made with me after my father died. My sister, well, even though she was six years younger, she too wanted to take care of me.

I didn't let either of them my entire life, and I wasn't about to start then.

Plus, I had a tatted daredevil to take care of for the foreseeable future. That was my priority. I pushed all the other stuff away into folders in my mind.

"Right," I said, closing the door. "You, there," I pointed to the couch. "I'll get food, water and set up your pills with a chart to track when we dose and how much."

I turned to get started on those things, trusting Kane's ability to shuffle the short distance.

But he grabbed hold of my hand with his uninjured wrist.

"No, you're not doing any of that." He swiped his tongue along his lip. "We're going to the bedroom, and you're gonna ride me." His tone was drenched in authority. Desire. Hunger.

And although plenty of my own desire cropped up at his words, I swallowed it down, bugging my eyes at him. "Kane, you can't be serious. You're technically supposed to still be in the hospital right now. You have instructions to do nothing strenuous."

Kane wasn't swayed, stroking the inside of my wrist with his thumb. "That's why you'll be riding me, doing all the work." He winked.

"I'm too heavy for that," I groaned.

Kane's gaze darkened, and his brow furrowed. "You are not too heavy for anything," he snapped. "Most especially riding my cock. You gonna argue some more, or you gonna make me prove my point by carrying you to the bedroom?"

Hands on my hips, I glared at him. He wasn't bluffing. "Kane, you cannot carry me. You were discharged from intensive care an hour ago."

"Don't care if I was pulled back from the gates of Hades two seconds ago, I'll be carrying my woman to the bedroom."

When he bent as if to do it, I held up my hand to stop him. "Fine," I snapped. "We'll go. But I'm not happy about it."

He grinned in satisfaction. "Oh, yes you are, Chef. I can tell that pussy of yours is already wet."

I pursed my lips.

He wasn't wrong.

"Come on," I huffed.

Kane chuckled as we walked to the bedroom.

"What's so funny?" I barked over my shoulder.

"You," he replied as we entered my bedroom. "Acting all pissed about riding my cock when I know you're as desperate for it as I am."

Again, I kept my lips a thin line, sucking in a breath through my nostrils. "I don't want to hurt you."

Kane cupped my cheeks, tilting my head upward. "Only way you could hurt me, Chef, is if you leave me to walk this world without you. You gonna do that?"

I almost flinched at the intensity in his words, the possessiveness. Sure, Kane had been plenty possessive before, but this was different. Much different.

"No," I said without hesitation.

His lips pressed into mine. "Good," he growled against my lips. "Now ride my cock."

* * *

"Chef."

I was coated in a thin layer of perspiration, riding Kane.

He was right. My body had been desperate for this. Aching. Yes, I'd been ready and happy to forgo my own needs for Kane, but I was selfishly elated to know that he'd needed this. Us.

I'd realized we hadn't done this since before he left. Since before I'd watched him tumble through the air, since I'd spent time thinking I was going to lose him.

I rode him harder, desperate for the fullness of him inside me, the friction, the aliveness and the free fall of another orgasm.

"Chef," Kane repeated in a low grunt.

I stared down at him. He was clutching my neck, eyes on me.

They were clouded with desire, cords in his neck protruding, telling me he was close to finishing. But the ferocity of his arousal was something else. That same intensity as before, only deeper. Unending, it seemed.

"I love you," he murmured, low and deep.

My body twitched as the words branded me.

"I love you," I panted.

He hauled me down for a kiss.

"Milk my cock, then."

And I did as requested.

* * *

After we were done, I cooked Kane lunch. It was the first time I'd cooked for him in my apartment. It felt ... odd. Domestic, somehow. When I was in my kitchen at Inferno, I'd cooked him versions of the dishes we made there—heartier, with much bigger portions, but they were still sophisticated dishes. I'd been hiding behind techniques and fanfare.

No longer feeling the need to hide, I didn't do that this time. Kiera had already stocked my fridge before we got back, so it was overflowing with all the things I'd requested and many I had not.

Champagne, beer, caviar and also packaged snacks that a third-grader might eat. I'd shaken my head with a smile, thinking of my friend as I began making something.

It wasn't from any of my recipe books. It wasn't something I learned to cook in professional kitchens.

No, it was my mother's chicken soup.

"It's a well-worn cliché, but it's true," she told me, chopping celery.

"Chicken soup, the kind full of nourishing and warm ingredients, helps soothe illnesses and injuries, and it warms the soul."

I didn't know why I made it, serving it with crusty French bread. Maybe because I wanted to take care of Kane, which didn't come natural to me, so I borrowed from my mother.

Or because I was practicing some kind of therapy on myself since these past few days had made me think of her more than I had in years.

I'd served up a heaping bowl of soup with bread for Kane and given myself a much smaller portion. My stomach was still churning from everything that had happened the past few days.

"You're not eating enough." He frowned as his eyes shifted between our bowls.

"I'm not recovering from a ruptured spleen and broken bones," I informed him snippily. "Eat your lunch."

He grinned. "Heard, Chef."

I smiled into my bowl.

We were in the living room after I cleaned up and forced him onto the sofa with an old paperback from my bookshelves, since he didn't watch TV. A benign fact about him that I found incredibly charming.

"Babe, you gotta get to the restaurant," Kane said, glancing up at the clock and shifting in a careful way that told me he was in pain.

"I'm not going to the restaurant." I looked at the clock too, to calculate how long it had been since his last dosage.

Since we were within minutes of his next dose, I went to where his pill bottles were lined up in order to get them ready.

A hand at my wrist stopped me. The one that wasn't in a cast, and regardless of his injuries, the grip was ironclad.

"You're not going to the restaurant? For me?" Despite the strength of his grip, there was something vulnerable in his tone. Something small. With a stab to my heart, I thought of the story

Kane told me about his past, about not feeling loved, special. A little boy whose mother chose her own happiness before him.

"Yes," I said, my voice as soft as I'd ever heard it. "I'm not going to the restaurant because you are more important."

He didn't say anything for a long moment, just stared at me. "Love you, Chef."

My heart pounded at the weight of those words. He said them with such power, such certainty it took my breath away.

It was like in each different situation, environment, the words meant different things, settled in different places.

"I love you too," I forced myself to reply, the words hardest to say this time around, for whatever reason.

Something was slotting into place. Kane was slotting into place. His presence, the way he smiled, the way he spoke to me, the way he kissed me. In that moment, it truly fit into me, permanently.

A large part of me panicked and wanted to run. But the whole world was watching now, so there was nowhere to run to.

And even if the world wasn't watching, I knew I wouldn't run.

That scared me even more.

* * *

"I need to get out of this apartment," Kane declared.

It was the next day, late afternoon. Kane had slept over twelve hours. I had gently roused him to give him his medication, he'd slurred some unintelligible words then hit the mattress again.

I slept little. Not only did I have alarms for medications, but I was also watching Kane, ensuring his chest was rising and falling, chewing my nails while worrying about him.

Chewing my nails. A nervous habit I'd stopped the moment I stood in my first professional kitchen and the head chef took one look at my hands and told me I wouldn't last the day if I had to deal with stress by gnawing on my body.

I'd scrolled through my texts, shooting messages off to Kiera to let her know everything was okay, thanking her for the food.

Though my fingers itched to do so, I did not look at the numerous articles about Kane and myself.

I'd already made the mistake of looking at social media when Kane posted the photo of the two of us with the caption 'My Chef.'

It had millions of likes. Millions. The numbers didn't mean much to me, but Kane was famous. It came with the territory, I guessed.

The mistake was looking at the comments.

I'm surprised the fat pig managed to run to his side without passing out.

Kane usually dates models, what gives?

He can do better, she needs to stay in the kitchen.

I thought I was unaffected by mean comments—I'd had plenty in my time. But my stomach had pitched, and I'd bitten my lip until I tasted blood before forcing myself off social media.

I was not a self-conscious person, especially about my appearance. If someone I respected said something negative about my food, that hit. If someone I didn't know, didn't respect, insulted me about my appearance, it rolled right off my back. It was pedestrian, tactless and weak, to make insults like that.

I didn't know why the comments bothered me. Maybe because there were thousands like that. Thousands.

That's what I was in for, being with Kane. Constant attention, constant dissection. It made my skin crawl. The spotlight was already singeing me to the bone.

But that bone, that charred bone, already belonged to Kane.

I was stuck with him. Branded by him.

So like I was practiced at doing, I shoved those thoughts away, those comments, those fears.

I let him sleep. Woke up and rode him—not before performing oral sex, an act I'd never enjoyed until Kane—then made us coffee and breakfast.

Normally, we'd go to the café and bakery on the corner to sit outside, despite the crispness to the air, to drink our coffee and eat our pastries. But not with Kane's injuries and not with the paparazzi.

Ferris was running the errands I normally did for the restaurant, and it made my hands itch and pulse spike. I'd trained him for such things. He'd come with me on numerous trips so the restaurant wouldn't burst into flames if I was ill or died suddenly.

Still, I was firing off text messages to him all morning, ensuring he was doing everything right. Which he was—I'd trained him well.

Then there was the act of being in an apartment with Kane with nothing to do. We'd had sex twice, and it was great and lasted a decent amount of time. And I was cooking breakfast and lunch, cleaning up afterward which killed time too. But even after all of that, I was left with an exorbitant amount of free time.

A cleaner came in once a week, so I couldn't go and scrub toilets to keep my hands busy.

"Chef, relax. You're giving me a heart attack with all that tension," Kane instructed from the sofa, paperback in his hands. He'd already tried to convince me to go in to work, but I'd refused. Firmly. He'd relented, allowing me to cook, clean, care for him.

Until now.

"Relaxing is not something I'm trained to do," I informed him.

He laughed. The sound was deep and throaty and oh so sexy.

"Not many people need to be trained to do it, but I'll consider it my honor." He patted the sofa beside him.

I went to him, and he instantly pulled me into him, kissing my head and inhaling. "You smell like you, food and sex," he hummed. "My favorite."

I sank into him, enjoying the hardness and softness of his body, his own scent ... for about a minute.

"What now?" I asked, tensing.

Kane laughed again. "There is no *what now* when you're relaxing. That's the point."

"Right," I said, my voice strained. I waited another minute. "I don't like it."

Kane burst out laughing now, wincing at the full body shudders. I scowled at him, not liking him being in pain.

"This may take a few sessions," he conceded.

"Or never," I scoffed, trying to get up. Kane's arms tightened around me.

"Where you goin'?" he asked into my hair.

"I'm making you a chocolate cake."

"That's not relaxing."

I gave him a side-eye. "It is to me."

He watched me for a moment, eyes dancing with amusement. "I'll allow it, Chef." He leaned in to kiss my nose.

I rolled my eyes, and he smirked, leaning back to go back to his book as I prepared to make the cake.

That filled in some time. Though the cake wasn't overly difficult or extravagant, so it was already baked, chilled, frosted and eaten before we went to sleep, the dishes used to eat it on washed and put away.

Wiping some frosting off his lips, Kane said he needed to get out.

I'd tried to argue against that, since he'd just gotten out of the hospital, but Kane made it clear he wasn't budging on this choice.

Though I was hesitant about the world outside, I sagged in relief.

"I'll get my purse," I practically jumped to my feet. "Where are we going?"

"Closest bar to get a beer," was his response.

I froze. "You're not supposed to drink with your medication."

He arched a brow. "That's just a recommendation from tight ass doctors; it won't kill me."

I scowled at him. "No, it may not, but it can interfere with the medication's effectiveness and can slow the healing process."

"Chef." Kane stood, making his way to me where he settled his hands on my hips. "The crashes and injuries I've had, I could almost get my PhD in medication. Trust me, a beer isn't gonna do shit beyond sate my thirst. And when you have one too, it'll help you obtain that mystical act of relaxation we're looking for."

I chewed on my cheek as I considered that. I was a rule follower. And it said on the labels to not drink alcohol. I didn't think doctors put that on there for shits and giggles.

Then I looked around the four walls of my apartment, and they suddenly began closing in.

"Okay, I'll get ready," I conceded. "One beer, though." I pointed my finger at him.

"Yes, Chef," he replied dutifully. Then his brows furrowed. "Get ready? You said you were going to get your purse. You don't need to get ready; you look great."

He looked down at my body lazily as if to prove a point.

I was wearing jeans—because I didn't own sweats, hadn't had the occasion to wear them, although after today, I got the appeal. My jeans were not the magic jeans Kiera bought me. These were regular, worn jeans, paired with a plain black tee and a cashmere cardigan.

My hair was pulled up in a low bun, tendrils escaping out, and I wasn't wearing makeup.

Normally, I wouldn't think twice about leaving the house like this. Normally, I didn't have thousands of people saying negative things about my appearance.

But then I looked at Kane, saw the hungry glint in his eyes, the appreciation. All of the comments melted away.

So I got my purse and jacket while Kane grabbed his coat, then we walked out.

Kane made casual conversation with Mike, who had refused to come inside and sit down but had accepted coffee, lunch and chocolate cake. I was happy to hear he hadn't slept against the door.

Mike was tall, muscles on every inch of his body, had close-cropped hair and an overall air that spoke to being former military. He looked menacing, deadly. But he was friendly, even though he barely smiled.

He'd also done well at scaring the scant remaining reporters lingering outside my apartment. They followed us down the street, though, at a distance. It was harder for paparazzi in New York; too many people and too many other important events to cover. I tried to act natural, tried to relax under Kane's arm around my shoulder. He didn't seem bothered, nor did he seem in pain, even though the walk to the bar was half a block.

I saw that he'd lost some of his color when we were seated, and his smile seemed strained.

"Kane," I hissed. "If you push yourself too hard..."

"The day a walk to a bar with my woman pushes me too hard is a day I'm getting put in the ground." He reached over to take my hand. "That day isn't coming for a long while."

I didn't smile at him but forced myself to relax somewhat.

The waitress who came to take our drink orders spoke solely to Kane. I might as well have been invisible. Though Kane wasn't having that, barely looking at her, his hands constantly on me. He was polite to the waitress but also made it clear that her heavy flirting and pushing her chest out was going nowhere.

Our beers arrived, and I sipped mine daintily, not wanting to be impaired while taking care of Kane.

He didn't force conversation, seemingly content holding my hand and drinking his beer. He also ignored the people who had taken photos of us on their phones.

I tried my best to do that too.

Then I tried to mimic him, enjoying the silence, the beer, listening to the low music and conversations around us.

I failed at that. My eyes darted around the bar and my fingers twitched.

And then I thought about things to say. I didn't do small talk.

"I lost my father when I was thirteen," I blurted in the dead voice I always used when speaking about this subject. Though I had spent my entire adult life telling strangers and friends my father was dead, every time I said it out loud, it stung. The little girl inside me who wanted her father, hurt so desperately, it was hard to keep the tears in.

But I'd trained myself. To lock that down. Keep my voice even. No tears. Tight smile and a thank you when people told me how sorry they were.

Kane didn't have pity or sorrow in his eyes when I spoke, didn't rush to give condolences. Nor did he seem surprised at the information coming out of nowhere.

"You were close," he surmised.

I nodded, releasing a heavy exhale. "My mother and I had a ... difficult relationship. Have a difficult relationship," I corrected. Even after years passed, me no longer being a teenage girl clashing with her mother, we never really repaired things. Because it was more than that. Deeper than that.

And although my mother tried hard—still trying to this day to bring me close, I had my walls up. Didn't let her or my sister Maisie in.

"My dad was my best friend," I added with a smile. "He was the one who taught me how to cook, developed my love of food. We'd spend Sundays cooking together, Saturdays going to new places to try new food." I could almost taste the Ethiopian we had on a rainy afternoon, the spices hitting my palette.

I pulled at a thread on my cardigan. "I felt like he understood me in a way neither my mother nor my sister did."

My mother and sister shared the same interests, they were emotional, they liked to watch rom-coms, go shopping. And though they always invited me along with them, I always felt out of place.

"Your sister younger?" Kane asked.

I nodded. "Six years." I thought of Maisie. Was it the distance between us in age that made us so different? "She's got two kids," I told him, thinking of my nephews. When was the last time I saw them? One Christmas ago? Two? "Had the first when she was twenty, with a colossal asshole, the second after she got rid of the colossal asshole at twenty-three."

My sister being a young mother, staying in the same town we grew up in, further solidified the relationship between my mother and her. The two of them talked to each other daily, and my mother was over there constantly, to see her grandchildren.

There was a stab in my heart, thinking of the family I'd put myself on the outside of.

"The guy she's with now. He good to her?" Kane asked.

I toyed with the label of my beer, discomfort swimming through me. "From what I can gather. I've met him a couple of times. He doesn't drink too much or give my sister black eyes, so that counts as a win."

Anger blazed in Kane's gaze. "Tell me someone dealt with him, and if they didn't, I'll make a phone call."

He was serious. I didn't know what a phone call would entail, but there was a violence simmering below the surface of Kane's expression that I'd only seen when I'd spoken about Gerald.

Whether or not his fury was because of his mother's past or because he cared so much about me, I didn't know. He wanted to avenge a sister he'd never met, he was a good man.

"No, I dealt with him." I looked away from his intense scrutiny, taking in the bar's decor.

When he cleared his throat, I looked back at him. The violence remained in his expression but the corner of his mouth was turned up. "You *dealt* with him?" he asked.

"You're not the only one who can make phone calls to teach assholes lessons." Though I didn't make a whole lot of friends throughout my culinary career, I'd given and gained respect from people along the way. Some of the people were Italian. Old school Italian who'd promised if I needed any favors done, they would be there as a thank you for putting in the right words for them at the right restaurants. I hadn't expected calling in those favors until seeing my sister's black eye.

I hadn't lost a wink of sleep over her ex-husband's stay in the hospital with two black eyes of his own and broken bones, delivered in order to get the message across.

My sister, to that day, thought he was mugged.

Kane inclined his head. "Color me impressed. Your dad would be proud."

That hit me square in the chest.

"Maybe." I took a swig of my beer before chewing at my lip once again. My father had been fiercely protective of us both. He'd been larger than life in many ways, but I didn't once remember him raising his voice nor condoning violence.

Kane leaned across the table then grabbed my face. "Your dad would be fuckin' proud, Chef."

I wanted to burst into tears. I didn't. "He wouldn't be proud to know I only talk to my mom and sister twice a year," I whispered. "Christmas and birthdays. I don't even call them on the anniversary of his death. I send flowers."

I picked at the label on my beer bottle, unable to look at him while I admitted the shameful thing I'd carried around for years.

"They do something. Every year. And they invite me. Every year." I shook my head in disgust at myself. "I just don't have the courage to go. I don't think I belong with them. It split us in two. My father dying. Them on one side, me on the other. And maybe a part of me likes it that way because I don't have to be as close to them, so it won't hurt as much if something happens to them." I looked up at Kane. "Which is why you make me want to run. Because if something happened to you, it would destroy me."

There it was. The admission of all admissions. The most I'd laid myself bare to a man ever.

Though I'd never been close to this fear of losing another man since my father, since I realized men I loved could be lost.

Kane didn't break my stare. There was not an ounce of judgment for my abandonment of my family. "It is my singular duty on this planet to keep you intact, Chef," he murmured. "It's also my duty to make promises I can keep. I can't promise nothing will happen to me. Even if I was an accountant, I could get hit by a cab crossing the street." He picked up my fingers to kiss them. "But I vow I'll do everything in my power to ensure I stay here with you."

It was a pretty promise. A lovely one.

But nonetheless, the reality remained... I would lose Kane.

Maybe not to the grave, like my most recent fear. But a small, intuitive voice inside me told me I would lose him.

One way or another.

Twelve

KANE HEALED QUICKLY.

At an almost superhuman rate.

"Babe, my body is used to trauma," he said when I commented on how impressive it was to have him moving around like normal in less than two weeks. "Healing physically, I'm fucking aces at that. Emotionally ... I'm still workin' on that." His tone was teasing, but I didn't miss the undertone to it.

He hadn't been trapped in my apartment, per se. After the beer pilgrimage, we left every morning to get coffee together at my favorite café. The first few outings were a circus, paparazzi, strangers on the street recording us with their phones. I felt suffocated, trapped.

Even Kane, used to the attention, had a rigid jaw and an uncharacteristic scowl on his face. He'd almost gotten in a fight with someone who made it past Mike and got too close to me.

I hadn't read the news since Kane's accident, didn't look at the articles about me. There were many. It was a *phenomenon*, according to Kiera. Us as a couple. It was now 'lore,' she said, whatever the heck that meant.

But the internet moved quickly. The story of our relationship died down, the focus on Taylor Swift being in town. I wanted to send her a box of chocolates to thank her.

We got to the point where Mike didn't have to follow us everywhere. We could get coffee without being harassed, go grocery shopping together without camera flashes going off. We resumed benign tasks I either had avoided or didn't do all together. But with Kane, I loved it.

I couldn't take any more time off from the restaurant, despite Heidi's understanding. The control freak in me wouldn't allow it.

So I went back.

And Kane still came to pick me up. Every night.

Not on the bike, though. He drove an SUV and grumbled about it every night. He spent a lot of his days inside reading—he was cleared for the gym but certainly not the more extreme pastimes he enjoyed. We had more sex than ever. That took the edge off but didn't help entirely.

I could see it in him, a restlessness. Kane was not one to be confined. He was not designed to live a normal life. He couldn't be content getting coffee, grocery shopping, reading, watching me cook. Granted, we were having adventurous sex, a lot of it, but he needed more.

I understood it. It scared me. Because although I didn't have a traditional life, I had a routine, roots here in New York. My restaurant was my home. It was what fed the beasts inside me. I couldn't leave it. Not even for Kane.

And Kane couldn't leave his nomadic, thrill-seeking life.

Not even for me.

Something I was unable to deny for much longer. It was growing between us, like a tumor, that truth.

On top of that, Heidi had been capitalizing on the restaurant's fame. The constant paparazzi, the now three-year waiting list. It was already popular, but this was new heights.

So when Gerald DuBois was in America filming his documentary and wanted to come cook with his former protégé for a night, she couldn't say no. She didn't ask me because she assumed I'd be thrilled. I had said nothing but positive things about my time at his restaurant, the few times I was asked when I was younger. I'd done that because I thought that's what I needed to do in order to escape his wrath, to prevent him from blacklisting me in the culinary world. That was then.

Now, I said nothing, feeling immense guilt over those lies, wondering if I'd influenced some young girls to want to work with a predator. It was a weight I carried with me everywhere.

I hadn't told Kane about Gerald, there was no point. He was going to be here for one day, one night. In my kitchen. The thought made my vision tunnel. The kitchen that I had worked myself to the bone to earn. The place that I made safe for everyone who worked there. It was clean in every sense of the word, and I was proud of that.

His presence would sully it. Tarnish it in a way that I couldn't wipe away.

If I let it, I reminded myself. I wasn't some naïve, powerless nineteen-year-old anymore. I had become somebody. And he knew it. Perhaps it pissed him off, but he wasn't a danger to me.

If Kane knew he was here, there would be plenty of danger. He'd spoken about how hard he worked to contain the anger inside of him. He was intense about me. Possessive. Though he was progressive, a feminist, I knew that the primal side of him wouldn't be able to hold back, wouldn't hear reason if he knew about Gerald.

Safer and saner for all involved to keep this from him. I didn't like lying to him—omission counted as lying in my book—but I felt like it was a lesser evil at that point.

I could survive one dinner service with him. Sure, I likely could've feigned illness or straight up refused to share my kitchen. It wasn't unheard of in the culinary world full of egos. The staff who had been with me for years might've raised eyebrows, since I wasn't known for overly dramatic behavior, but no one would've guessed the truth. The truth that felt bitter and rancid in my insides, the guilt of carrying it around with me a physical thing.

It was too late now to 'out' Gerald.

Or maybe it wasn't. This was the age of women coming forward and speaking about their abuse, bringing down powerful men and ending their reigns of terror.

Yes, plenty of brave women had done that. Not without attention, though.

And it was the attention I couldn't stomach. Having to be the 'face' of it.

It was cowardly.

I hated myself a little for it.

Yet not enough to speak. Especially not after I'd gotten a taste of it with Kane. And that was by association. I couldn't do it, have it all focused on me.

It was my rebellion then, to stay in my kitchen, stand my ground and refuse to let Gerald run me out.

Even though I was terrified.

Kane noticed it, as he noticed everything about me.

"Chef." The word was gentle, tender, concerned.

I refused to meet his eyes in the mirror as he came up behind me, his arms wrapping around me.

In every other circumstance, Kane's arms around me were comforting, grounding, safe. Yet that night, they made my skin feel too tight for my body and my stomach turn.

"Chef," he said again.

Reluctantly, I looked up at him in the mirror.

"What's happening?" he asked. His finger brushed the sides of my uniform open so he could stroke my hip bone lazily.

I sank my teeth into my lip until I tasted blood so I wouldn't flinch away from a touch that would usually set my body alight.

"The restaurant," I said, unable to lie to him. "Tonight is going to be a lot. Special guests who think a lot of themselves, making my life harder than it needs to be."

There. Not a lie.

Yet I still felt the truth sticking to my insides like tar.

Kane smiled at me in the mirror, but it didn't quite reach his eyes. He saw me, knew me, even after a short time. And I knew him too. I knew he was weighing whether he should push it, probe more.

But that wasn't Kane's style. He'd wait until I was comfortable. Or he'd accept that I wasn't ready or willing to tell him something.

I did not deserve him.

"You want me to come in there, rough 'em up?" he teased, nuzzling my neck. "I can blow off this event; I've been looking for an excuse."

My lungs seized at the thought of Kane in the same building as Gerald.

Kane had imprisoned his dragon when Gerald was a two-dimensional asshole living on another continent. I did not want Kane near Gerald. Didn't want him to breathe the same air, and I certainly didn't want to create any drama.

"No, it'll only make things a lot more complicated with Kane 'The Devil' Rhodes in the building," I replied. Again, not a lie.

It was a blessing in disguise that Kane had let Brax convince him to go to some event that night. I knew part of it was him going crazy, being stuck in the city, unable to do anything dangerous. I didn't like that Brax was involved, but it would keep Kane from the restaurant.

Kane sucked his teeth. "Although I like to make things complicated, I don't want to do it for you." He brushed his lips against mine. "But I'll come pick you up at closing time. We'll take a ride. Then I'll find a nice little alleyway where I can fuck you on the back of my bike."

Technically, Kane had not been cleared to be on the bike. But he was on it anyway.

Although my libido was quelled at the prospect of the night ahead of me, a tiny ember burned at Kane's promise.

There it was, something to focus on to get me through the night. Gerald would be long gone by the end of service. He'd be unable to keep himself from the front of house, the attention.

"That sounds perfect."

I'd go into the restaurant early, prep, claim my space, and by the time Gerald sauntered in, I'd be myself, I'd have my power.

A few hours of service and this night would be nothing but a memory.

* * *

My skin was stinging as I stumbled into the alley, daylight assaulting me. I squinted against it, my eyes adjusting. My heartbeat was still in my throat, and it took me a couple of seconds to focus.

In those couple of seconds, someone had come rushing toward me. Though it made no sense, I thought it was Gerald—even though this figure was much larger and coming from the street, not from inside the restaurant.

Regardless, I let out a cry and flinched away from the strong hands curling around me.

"Chef." Kane rubbed my arms, pulling me close to him. "Baby, it's me."

I relaxed instantly, my breath blowing out in one heave. I was safe. Kane was there.

It felt like moments prior I'd left him in my apartment, so sure, so confident that I was untouchable now with age, with the illusion of power.

Kane kissed my head and gave me a much-needed moment to find myself.

After that moment passed, he held me at arm's length, eyes scanning over my body as if checking to make sure I wasn't bleeding somewhere. His gaze lingered on my stinging cheek, and his face went blank. Utterly blank.

Yet his eyes were cerulean fire.

"What happened?" Two words. Cold. Demanding.

Dazed, I just blinked at him for a bit. I should've asked him why he was there, how it was that fate had intervened to have Kane there at that moment. Eventually, the words seemingly came out on their own. "I, um, it's... Gerald. He's here for an event at the restaurant tonight. He wasn't supposed to be here. No one was. And..."

The events of this afternoon mashed together like a lucid nightmare. Me thinking I was claiming some sort of power by getting there early to prepare. Gerald obviously thought the same thing.

I turned because I felt him rather than heard him.

He was the reason I was always on guard, even in my own kitchen.

"Avery," he drawled. "It's been a long time. You look ravishing."

I wanted to gag with his eyes on me. My hands froze from where I'd been chopping herbs, the knife in my hand clattering onto the cutting board.

He strolled around the large kitchen, making a show of cataloging the appliances, dragging his finger along counters to check for dirt. He grinned, holding up a finger. "Sparkling clean," he reported in his thick accent. "I'm not surprised. You've earned, what, two Michelin Stars since you've taken over this kitchen? I'm so proud of you."

The words rang in my ears as I tried to adjust to the reality of seeing Gerald in my kitchen, my safe place. My success. My powerhouse.

He'd aged. Obviously, he had. It had been over a decade since I last saw him in person. Of course, I hadn't been able to avoid seeing his smug face in magazines. But those pictures had been airbrushed and retouched.

Now he looked ... old. The drinking, the late nights and the stress of the restaurant business had taken its toll. His hair was still peppered with gray but mostly dark brown. Which meant he likely got it colored to look just the right amount of sprinkled with gray. He'd obviously had Botox since his skin looked overly tight and shiny, his dark brows just a little too manicured.

Conventionally, he was attractive. The perfectly-trimmed mustache, full lips, structured jaw, broad shoulders. He was tall and trim, except even his exquisitely tailored suit could not hide how the paunch of his stomach was hanging over his belt.

I'd been captivated by him. Not by his looks or the accent or the way he carried himself. No, by his food. By the way he'd redefined cuisine, the flavors he married, the flavors he created.

I'd been so enamored by the flavors he created that I'd missed how rancid he was on the inside.

But I would not make that mistake again. Not in my restaurant.

Or that's what I'd told myself.

Until I'd frozen, like a deer in headlights, letting him corner me. In *my* restaurant.

Acid churned in my belly at the memory.

"He touched you," Kane bit out, jerking me out of my trance. He brushed his hand over my cheek with a featherlight touch, but somehow, there was force behind it.

My hand lifted to my cheek.

"He, um … slapped me. When I told him I wouldn't be letting him rape me." It wasn't quite that simple, in my brain I knew that, but I couldn't pin down the subtleties of the conversation, how it had gotten to that point … again. It was like my mind was shielding it from me already.

I quite obviously didn't have my wits about me when I'd said that, because if I had, I would've worded it differently. Or I would've waited until Kane wasn't in the same vicinity—or country —as Gerald before I told him.

As it was, I wasn't thinking. And it ruined everything.

There was a pause after I uttered those words. A split second. One I would think of often afterward, after everything fell apart.

The pause was a knife cutting through the life I'd been living up until that point, a clean slice where I'd be able to pinpoint the last moment Kane was mine and I was his.

Kane's face contorted, turning him into someone—something I didn't recognize.

"Stay here," he growled, sounding barely human before he let me go and ran into the restaurant.

My ear was still ringing from the slap, from the shock of the encounter and then from Kane's transformation, so I hesitated, standing in that side alley holding my cheek and staring at Kane's bike.

I couldn't say for how long. But it couldn't have been more than a minute. Surely not.

It was a crash that mingled against the faraway city sounds at the mouth of the alley. The crash and what sounded like a roar coming from the kitchen. The sounds that wrenched me out of my trance.

I ran, my heart trying to escape my chest and my cheek smarting as I rushed back into the restaurant, looking for the cause of the clamor. It was coming from my kitchen. My solace. My domain. My sanctuary.

Where, once again, Gerald had tried to victimize me.

Where Kane had Gerald on the ground, hitting him. The sounds of knuckles against flesh were a dull, wet thud.

And he didn't stop hitting him.

Not for a long time.

Thirteen

KANE WAS ARRESTED.

Once the police got there, that was.

Right before that, Kane had been staring at Gerald's battered face. Then up at me.

When our gazes locked, I flinched. The burning in my cheek was nothing compared to the agony in my soul caused by that look.

Kane was no longer a rage-filled animal. There was no fight left in him. No, there was only love, naked, wretched love on his face. It wasn't that tender, playful love I'd grown accustomed to. No, this was something ugly. It was spattered with blood and resignation over what had happened here.

Kane had beaten a man because of me. He'd let go of the control he'd held on to so tightly since the last time he'd been locked up. And he was sober now, you could see it in his face. He saw his fate ahead of him. Police. A young, fit man covered in blood. An older, paunchy man battered from his fists.

There was a knife, one I'd used for herbs, lying on the ground. Kane was bleeding—I hadn't realized that at first, since he was covered in Gerald's blood. A flesh wound on the meaty part of his bicep, but it horrified me.

Gerald, at some point had tried to stab him. The police kept asking whether it was before or after the beating started; that was an important detail.

Before was what Kane said.

Would they believe him?

Did I believe him?

Would it matter in a court of law?

I had to swallow bile once I realized what that meant for Kane.

My feet were leaden as I tried to step toward him. And my mouth was dry, unable to find words.

Kane had been the one to call the police. Once he'd stopped hitting Gerald. Once the man's handsome face was no longer recognizable and Kane's knuckles were crimson. He'd ripped his stare from mine, got his phone from his pocket then called them, voice even, calm. Blood dripped from his hands as he held the phone to his ear.

He dropped the phone beside him once the call was made. Still, I couldn't move. I was cemented in place, horrified at my body's response, the freezing. Somewhere, deep down, I was screaming at myself to move, to hug Kane, to tell him I loved him, to do something. But I didn't. I just stayed there. Useless.

And then the police crashed in. It was only mere minutes after calling them. Who knew if they were in the area or it was a low crime day. Maybe it was luck. If you could call it that.

Once they took statements, the police didn't look at Gerald with much sympathy, nor did they look happy about putting Kane in cuffs.

But their hands were tied. It wasn't self-defense, nor was Kane 'saving me' from any kind of assault. It was revenge, pure and simple.

It was attempted murder, someone said, somewhere.

I told them about the knife, that Kane had been stabbed. That must've meant something.

I tried to hold on to all the details, hold on to my trademark calm. This is when it was needed most. But my kitchen was a mess. There was blood splatter on the floor. It was cluttered with strangers, officers, paramedics. A lot of them. I didn't know if it was because of the restaurant or Kane's fame. It didn't matter.

The man I loved was getting cuffed and hauled away.

Gerald had already been taken away by paramedics. Not in a body bag.

Kane hadn't killed him.

That was good.

Not because I wanted Gerald alive—a cold part of me would've liked to see him dead—but because I didn't want that piece of shit to turn Kane into a murderer.

"Chef," Kane's voice brought me back to the moment.

I'd just been standing there, numbly watching them put shackles on Kane. Powerless. I was powerless there. Because of Gerald.

"We're gonna be okay," he said, eyes on me. "You're gonna be okay. Call my brother. I love you."

"I love you," was all I could croak back.

Then he was hauled off.

Standing in my kitchen, I realized my life had just imploded.

Kane had said to call his brother.

I wanted to. I so dearly wanted to. Knox, although terrifying, had a strong presence, like he could take care of anything. The same demeanor Kane had. Like if there was a meteor headed toward Earth, somehow, they'd take care of it.

A meteor had already hurtled into my life, leaving nothing but rubble. And I had no way to contact Knox.

I had to take care of it. Had to take care of Kane.

That ripped me out of the hideous mental coma I'd been in since Gerald stepped into my kitchen.

I'd jumped into action, looking up the best lawyer in the city, calling them despite it being the middle of the night by the time I'd given my statement to the police countless times, called Heidi to let her know what happened in the kitchen and that the restaurant would be closed.

That should've all come second. I should've called the lawyer first. That was logical, yet all logic had abandoned me.

"Ms. Hart, yes, we've already been in contact with Mr. Smith," a woman told me as if it were midday.

I blinked in confusion. My head was pounding, my ears ringing and my stomach clenching from the lack of food I'd imbibed all day. I didn't dare eat. I knew I'd vomit it all up. "Mr. Smith?"

"Braxton Smith, Mr. Rhodes's manager," the woman clarified.

Brax.

I hadn't called him. I wanted him as far from this situation as possible. But somehow, he knew. He already had his talons in, one step ahead of me.

This wasn't a competition, I reminded myself. The fact that Brax was getting lawyers together, getting organized, meant that Kane was going to be okay. As much as I didn't like the man, Kane was his paycheck, and he wouldn't earn him money from behind bars. Even if his intentions were nefarious, the overall desire was the same. Get Kane out of jail.

Jail.

My mouth was sandy at the thought of it.

I hadn't had a wink of sleep all night. After the lawyer's office promised me a meeting the next day, I'd spent what was left of the night going over every second of what had transpired, trying to figure out all the ways I could've avoided this horrible situation.

I could've told Kane the truth at the start. I could've refused to cook with Gerald—despite my pride. I could've been brave and actually spoken up about him all those years ago.

Yes, there were many paths I could've taken that would've spared Kane from this. But I hadn't. I hadn't dwelled on the 'what ifs' since my father died. I'd promised myself not to do it again.

So when the sun rose, I put on my clothes—slacks and a white blouse, sensible-heeled shoes, pulled back my hair and did my best to cover the bags under my eyes with makeup. There was a faint bruise underneath my eye, a redness to my cheek that still lingered.

There was just a lone photographer outside my apartment, telling me the news hadn't broken … yet. I hid behind dark glasses, but I didn't need to since he didn't even seem to recognize me without Kane. How quickly I sank into obscurity without him. Obscurity. Hadn't that been what I wanted?

Yet without the presence of him, I felt less than invisible.

Self-pity does not become you, I told myself.

That wasn't who I was. I sucked it up and dealt. Got things done.

Brax was at the lawyer's office when I arrived.

That irked me for reasons unknown. Well, not really *unknown*. I didn't like the guy. Which wasn't exactly fair. He'd been in Kane's life for a lot longer than I had. Kane was a good judge of character, he was a good man, and he trusted Brax.

I needed to as well.

Yet disgust snaked down my spine when he pulled me into a hug in the plush reception area.

He smelled of expensive cologne. Too much of it, yet not enough to mask the bitter undertone of sweat.

"You didn't have to come," he said, releasing me but holding on to my upper arms for a fraction too long, his grip just a little too tight. "I've got this under control." He lifted his hand up to smooth his already perfect hair.

"Of course, I had to come," I argued, my tone a little sharp. "I'm…" I pursed my lips. Saying I was Kane's girlfriend sounded juvenile and nowhere near important enough of a title for what we were.

But we weren't engaged. Weren't married. Hadn't been together all that long. By all societal standards, I *was* just a girlfriend. I had no legal rights in this situation. The reality of that made my skin clammy and my heart rate spike.

After years of experience in busy kitchens, I managed to keep my expression neutral and calm, maintaining eye contact with Brax.

"Of course, I had to come," I repeated my earlier statement. "This is where I belong, making sure that Kane is going to be okay."

"Darlin', that's my job," Brax chuckled, the sound faux and condescending. "Don't you worry—"

"My pretty little head about it?" I tilted the aforementioned head sideways to regard him.

His smile dimmed somewhat. "Now, that isn't what I was going to say."

I folded my arms across my chest, already missing Kane like a limb, my mind overcome with worry about him. "That was the sentiment," I retorted coldly. "I know you've had a relationship with Kane for years, and I respect that. Kane respects you, trusts you. So I respect and trust you. But that doesn't mean I'm going to sit at home and wring my hands. I'm going to be involved." I ensured my tone was authoritative, without holes for emotion to slip into.

Men like Brax caught those holes, used them as openings to bring women down, make them second-guess themselves, make them submit. I'd failed once already with a man like that, and I wouldn't again.

He contemplated me with that slimy smile and calculating gaze before reaching out to squeeze my hand. His grip was sweaty and too firm.

"Of course," he said easily. "Of course, Kane wouldn't want it any other way. Especially considering…"

"Considering what?" I asked sharply.

"Well, this wouldn't have happened if he hadn't come to the restaurant. Not that it's *your* fault," he added quickly. But that's exactly what he was saying. He was probing for weakness, for the blame I felt over the situation.

I thought I'd buried that blame deep, but it seemed I was wearing it like a sign.

Before I could open my mouth or worse, burst into tears, a voice interrupted.

"Ms. Hart? Mr. Smith? Victoria is ready for you."

We looked at the man in a sleek suit, chiseled jaw and a warm yet professional mask.

I straightened my spine again.

"Ladies first." Brax held out his arm, greasy smile back in place.

For Kane. I'm doing this for Kane, I reminded myself.

I stepped in front of him and followed the man in the suit.

Victoria Steele was younger than I expected her to be. Maybe my age. Maybe even younger. Her porcelain skin didn't have a single line in it that I could see. She was harshly beautiful. Everything about her features was sharp, high cheekbones, piercing eyes rimmed with black liner. Her lips were painted blood-red, dark hair pulled back to further define her features. She was also incredibly petite in an impeccably tailored, white suit, diamonds adorning her wrists.

From my research, she was the best defense lawyer in the city. In the country. She had graduated from Harvard Law, had come straight to New York City to work at one of the top firms and was made partner within a handful of years. One of the youngest partners in history. It was impressive.

Her corner office was large, filled with light, although it was coldly appointed—no pictures of family, of children. Though I knew better than anyone that to get to the top of your industry, you didn't have time for family.

I appreciated that she shook both of our hands, not smiling, taking stock of us. The small curl to her lip after she regarded Brax gave me the hint that she was practiced at reading people and had gotten his number straight away.

"Please, sit." She pointed to the sofas instead of the chairs in front of a large oak desk.

I hated Brax being next to me, sitting closer than he needed to. The sofa was large, yet he splayed his legs open so they almost brushed mine. Taking up space. Daring me to cower into a corner.

I gritted my teeth and stayed where I was.

Victoria watched this carefully from her spot on the sofa across from us, her legs crossed. "I'm not going to bother with small talk. I'll just say that Kane is currently being held, and I'm in talks with the D.A. about what they plan on charging him with."

I appreciated the lack of small talk; I needed all the information on where Kane was and how to get him out.

"He's not going to go to jail, though, is he?" I asked. Or begged.

She looked at me with an even gaze devoid of sympathy. That was good, right? You didn't want a lawyer easily swayed by emotions. You wanted a stone-cold killer.

"Normally, in a situation like this, considering it's been established that Mr. DuBois came at him first with a knife after assaulting you, I would say we had favorable odds." She didn't break eye contact. "Still, the beating would've been tricky, but nothing I couldn't handle normally."

"Normally?" Brax asked from beside me, steepling his fingers and leaning forward. "What's not normal about this situation except that Kane has a fuck of a lot more money and influence than most average Joes who get in a fight over a woman."

My body stiffened.

Over a *woman*.

Dismissive. Almost derogatory. As if the woman in question wasn't right beside him. As if the woman in question didn't matter at all.

Victoria's eyes hardened ever so slightly at Brax's words, briefly sliding to me before refocusing on him. She didn't like him. I could see that through her veneer. She was a senior partner at one of the top law firms in New York. I had the sense she might've encountered many men like Brax before.

"Well, let's start off by saying the fight was *not* on account of any woman," she said before turning her gaze back to me. "None of this was Avery's doing. She did not ask for DuBois to assault her, nor did she ask for Kane to assault DuBois in return."

The tips of Brax's ears went pink. "Of course, not."

She acted as if he didn't speak.

"Secondly, although Mr. Rhodes does have considerable influence that comes with being a public persona, so does Mr. DuBois."

"He's a fucking *chef*," Brax scoffed. "How much influence can you garner by grilling people some fucking steaks?"

My hands fisted on my knees.

"Shit, sorry, I didn't mean..." Brax turned to me, and I waved him off despite having the urge to slap him.

"Mr. DuBois's influence on the cultural world is a little more than grilling some steaks," Victoria countered dryly. "Chefs who operate on the level that he and Ms. Hart operate on feed governors, presidential hopefuls, lawmakers, CEOs and ... district attorneys." She clasped her hands in her lap. "The kind of culinary experience provided by someone of that caliber creates a gravitas and a power that may not seem obvious to people like you, but is considerable, nonetheless."

I bit back my smile. Yeah, I liked this lawyer.

Though Brax kept an easy expression on his face, I didn't miss the way he moved his jaw, grinding his teeth. He did not like being talked to like that by a woman.

Go figure.

"Okay," he replied through gritted teeth. "But again, the publicity around this... Kane is pretty beloved, and he has his share of powerful friends."

Victoria nodded. "I'm aware. I've already spoken to some. But we have had a confluence of ... bad luck, for lack of a better term when it comes to this situation and the timing. The D.A. is looking to make a name for herself. She's new to the role and is trying to shed the office's reputation for being 'soft' on people of influence. And the judge we've been assigned is somewhat known for carrying out sentences to teach privileged kids lessons."

Brax dragged a hand down his face. "Kane is not a fucking kid."

"Nor was he privileged," I added. "He grew up in poverty, worked his ass off for everything he has, volunteers with what little free time he does have, and donates 40 percent of his paychecks to charity."

Brax's head snapped in my direction. I didn't look at him, but I assumed he was surprised I was privy to that information. I was just the girlfriend after all.

Victoria nodded. "All relevant details that I will be using to argue on his behalf. And I'm great at what I do. The best. I'll do everything in my considerable power to ensure he gets off with a slap on the wrist, a fine, some community service. I'll do my best to push for DuBois getting charged with assault, both toward you and for stabbing Mr. Rhodes. I win cases. That's why I'm here." She held her hands out to gesture to the sleek corner office with views of the city.

"But I don't do bullshit," she continued, her focus back on me. "And I'd be bullshitting you if I said for sure that I could guarantee we'll get out of this lightly. With Kane's record, the judge, the D.A., there is a very real possibility that he could be facing prison time. Despite my best efforts. Mr. DuBois is not dead, which is our only saving grace in this situation. But he's much older than Mr. Rhodes and is still in an induced coma."

I wanted to vomit. Not at Gerald being in a coma. For all I cared, he could stay that way forever. But he needed to wake up. For Kane's sake.

"Well," Brax stood up after a few beats of silence. "We'll go somewhere else to find someone who can win."

Victoria didn't look perturbed. In fact, she almost looked like she expected it.

"You can try," she shrugged. "I'm the best. Which is why you're here in the first place. Because I'm the best, my time is limited and expensive. I'm only doing this as a favor to Avery."

I recoiled.

Her gaze softened somewhat as she gauged my obvious confusion. "I've had the pleasure of eating your food a handful of times," she explained. "I have … wonderful memories connected to it. You gave me something special."

Though I'd had many people tell me they liked my food in the past, it hadn't affected me like this. To be fair, I was taken off guard, and being in such a high-stress situation, I almost wanted to cry. Almost.

"Thank you," I replied, my voice even. "That means a lot." I looked up at Brax. "We're going with Victoria."

His brow twitched. There was no smarmy smile in place then. "Did you not hear what she said? She may not be able to keep Kane out of prison."

I nodded, keeping my cool although my insides felt like dust. "I heard that part. I also heard that she's the best at what she does, and

I believe her. If we go somewhere else, not only could Kane go to prison, he could go for a lot *longer*."

Brax's eyes narrowed. "This is not your decision to make."

Dread flooded my veins. It wasn't. I didn't know how all of this worked, but I guessed that Brax had power and access that enabled him to make these kinds of decisions. That was his job, wasn't it?

"Actually, it is," Victoria saved me from having to respond. "I've already been to visit Mr. Rhodes, and he informed me that Ms. Hart has power of attorney over all decisions pertaining to this case and his representation."

It was the second time in as many minutes that this woman had caught me off guard. Kane had said that? Something bloomed within me. I didn't have a ring or any kind of title to prove that I was Kane's, but he'd found a way to make it clear even from behind bars.

Brax looked like his head was going to explode, his chest rising and falling rapidly.

"Fine," he bit out. "But if Kane goes to jail, make it known that it was your choice." He pointed his finger violently at me.

Then he stormed out.

* * *

Everything passed in a blur. Quickly. Far too quickly.

The trial was expedited. Bail was refused.

On account of Kane's 'resources' which included access to a private jet. He was a flight risk.

Victoria fought. Hard. I could see she was a force of nature in the courtroom. The problem was not just the D.A., who was indeed trying to make a name for herself. It was also the judge who had a bone to pick with those in the public eye. He didn't even try to hide his contempt for Kane.

There was bias there. Even I could see it. Victoria was outraged.

She fought the judge tooth and nail on every ruling, to the point of being threatened with removal from the courtroom multiple times.

In our meetings, I could see her trademark cool was being replaced with pure fury. I knew that fury would hit its mark, knew that those responsible would pay.

But that would be after Kane served time, that much was clear. Kane had already been found guilty of aggravated assault. The only victory that Victoria had gained was getting attempted murder off the table.

Gerald making the first move with the knife, stabbing Kane, seemed to do nothing to affect any charges.

"I'll make it my mission for the rest of my career to end that judge's tenure," she said through her teeth as we awaited sentencing.

Gerald didn't die. That was our one saving grace. He was even out of the hospital. Somehow, he hadn't been charged either. And he'd been on a press tour not only to besmirch Kane's name but mine too.

I'd finally found the courage to tell my story. To say who Gerald truly was. That courage was fueled by a desperation to punish Gerald, to wipe the label of 'victim' off his smug face and ensure Kane was not painted as the villain.

Kiera and Victoria set up the interview, with a female journalist at a well-respected publication, a New York institution.

I'd been nervous. More nervous than I had been in my entire life. I was almost drenched in sweat by the time they arrived at my apartment—we'd forgone her office on account of the subject matter. But Kiera was there. She was always there. Through the entire process, since I'd called her after I'd walked out of the lawyer's office that very first day.

"You're doing the right thing," she assured me.

"I know. My problem is, I should've done this over a decade ago. It was the right thing then. Now..."

"Now it's the right thing too," she squeezed my bicep. "You do not place blame on yourself for how you deal with trauma men give you. Absolutely fucking not. You survived. You thrived. You created a powerful life for yourself in order to ensure you didn't get victimized again."

Her words struck true. Not just for me, but it made me recognize the similarities between my and Kane's stories. Yes, the timelines, childhoods might've been different, but we'd both been victimized in different ways, both chasing power over our lives to deal with it. Mine with order, his with chaos.

And now his power was being taken away from him.

Again. And there was nothing I could do about it. I was powerless too. So I had to talk.

The interviewer was kind, fair, detached yet not unfriendly. She asked tough questions but ones that needed to be asked.

Once the article came out, the previously wild media circus turned nuclear. People had already swarmed the courthouse, my restaurant, my apartment. The news cycle was never-ending, obsessed with the story of Kane ruining his career because of being tangled up with a chef.

I'd been painted as the villain as, of course, only a woman could be responsible when two men battle.

But the tides changed with the interview. Sure, there were plenty of assholes who said I must've been 'asking for it,' more who said I was making up lies. But not many. Especially after the interviewer found more of Gerald's students who had similar if not worse experiences. None of those women worked in kitchens again.

He stopped giving interviews then. He was fired from his restaurant, dropped from sponsorship deals. His life went up in flames.

It might've been satisfying to see if my own life wasn't burning to cinders too. I wasn't sleeping. Mike followed me everywhere since I was never not stalked by paparazzi.

My staff was quieter around me at the restaurant, the environment of my kitchen forever changed. I went through the motions every service, unable to stop staring at the spot where my life had changed forever. There were no blood smears there, it had been cleaned to shining, but I couldn't stop seeing it.

My food was still good, it must've been. Not because of me but because of years of honed instincts, of highly trained staff who could run my restaurant without me.

I'd only seen Kane once.

Once. I didn't know how the justice system normally worked, but surely, this wasn't right.

"You're too thin, Chef," he said the second after he'd hugged me, inhaling my hair. Kissing my neck. My mouth. My forehead. "You need to take care of yourself."

I took stock of him. He was still built with packed muscle, still devastatingly handsome, but his eyes were bloodshot, dark circles rimming them as if he weren't sleeping.

"I'm fine," I said, taking a seat next to him. "I'm focusing on you."

I'd promised myself I wasn't going to show weakness, wouldn't give him any reason to worry about me, but I'd wanted to crumble right there and then, seeing him locked up like that.

"And I'm good, not goin' anywhere." He squeezed my hand. "We need to get you in a new apartment, one the press doesn't know about. One with more security."

"You're worried about *my* security right now?" I scoffed, shaking my head. "No, we're not doing that. You're not pulling the protective alpha move, especially not right now when *you* need protection."

He raised his brow playfully, a shadow of who he used to be. "You think these are just for show, Chef?" He flexed his biceps. "I can take care of myself if I must, but that's not even an issue since they've got me segregated." He scoffed at that. "Could do with some conversation, some distraction, even if it is dodging a shank."

My blood went cold. "We do not joke about you getting shanked."

His expression cleared immediately. "Heard, Chef." There was a pause, the room far too quiet, too cold. Too sterile. I wanted to be in a bed with Kane. I wanted the noisy New York streets, I wanted coffee and reading the newspaper together as the city woke up.

I had the strong sense that I'd never get any of that again.

My lungs spasmed at the prospect.

"I saw the article," Kane said, toying with our intertwined fingers. He hadn't let go of me since I walked into the room. His hands on me were both a balm and torture. We could touch, hug and give chaste kisses but nothing else. I wanted to bury myself in him, but I couldn't.

"So fuckin' proud of you, Chef." His eyes were clear, sparkling, reverent. "Takes a lot of courage to do that. Say the words out loud, let them be true. Takes a fuck of a lot more to serve them up to the world."

I swallowed glass, willing myself not to cry. I wanted to reply. I couldn't.

"I don't regret it," he continued. "In case you were wonderin'. Don't regret it for a second, hurting him. I regret it hurting *you*." His hand tightened around mine. "I regret it because it put a spotlight on you, a target on you that you don't deserve." His eyes simmered with rage, with guilt. "The good part of me says I should regret it purely for that, for putting any hurt on my woman. But that selfish, greedy, rage-filled part of me is infinitely glad I got to wet my knuckles with his blood. Not very evolved of me, Chef, but what can I say? I'm an animal deep down, protectin' what's mine."

Mine.

He still considered me his. After everything. There was none of the blame I expected, felt I deserved, blame that certain sections of the country were sure I deserved. No, none of that came from Kane.

"I'm scared," I admitted in a small whisper. "I'm terrified for you." That was putting it lightly. I wouldn't tell him about my nightmares, about sitting in the bottom of my shower, staring blankly at the tiled walls.

"Good," he said simply. "Means there's a chance of you being there waiting for me when I walk out of here."

"I'll be waiting for you," I vowed without a second thought.

"Promise?"

I heard it then. The fractures in his tone, the way it wavered. The strong, cocky formidable man in front of me faded out for a moment, and the vulnerable, abandoned and unloved boy appeared in his place.

This time it was me who tightened the hold on our intertwined hands.

"Promise," I whispered.

* * *

Sentencing was the next day.

The way this case had been fast tracked was very rare, Victoria told me. A good thing, considering bail had been refused.

He was given a year.

A *year*.

My blood drained from my body, and the whole world tilted when the ruling came down.

I noted the fury on Victoria's face, her opening her mouth—presumably to argue with the judge—the judge's sniveling, beady eyes narrowing on her, ruddy cheeks turning redder with obvious fury.

For the life of me, I didn't know what they were saying.

My eyes were on Kane. They hadn't left me since the ruling was announced.

He crooked his finger to me playfully, amongst the ruckus, as if we weren't in a courtroom where one year of his life was just stolen from him but at a crowded party where we'd been separated for a few seconds.

Though my mind was reeling, my body knew what to do—obey Kane.

I was already at the front of the courtroom, I just had to stand and walk a few steps. My limbs were jelly as I walked woodenly to him.

When I was within grabbing distance, Kane grasped the back of my neck and drew me to him. Our mouths met, tongues clashing, the world around us long forgotten. It was just me and him.

For one blissful, magical moment.

Until our private world was interrupted, roughly and violently... the banging of a gavel.

"We gotta take you now," a bailiff standing behind Kane said, almost apologetically.

Kane didn't move, his lips brushing mine.

"You've got to let her go," he urged.

"No, I don't. Not ever," Kane murmured to me. "You promise you'll be there?"

"I promise," I whispered.

"Then I'll see you. Love you, Chef." He gave my neck a squeeze then stepped back.

My body already ached from his absence. And it was the hardest thing I ever did, watching them take him away.

A terrified and knowing voice told me I'd never see him again.

$$Fourteen$$

IT WAS ONLY a handful of days later that my world imploded. Again.

Kane had been transferred to the prison where he'd be serving his time. The judge had said, given his 'light' sentence, violent, prior offenses and 'nature of the crime,' he deserved to be in a maximum-security prison. With violent offenders. Murderers.

Victoria had fought that tooth and nail. She'd ended up being held in contempt when she wouldn't let the judge shut her up. She'd then promised me she'd use all of her resources to ensure that Kane did not remain there.

I'd nodded, believing she intended to use any and all connections and talent she had, but I'd accepted that the system had spoken. Even though it was horrible, I reminded myself that many men and women were given much, much harsher sentences for lesser crimes on account of their socioeconomic status, skin color or religion. Kane was, as hard as it was to swallow, getting off easy in some respects.

He was being moved to a maximum-security prison two hours

outside of the city. She assured me that it would take a while for transport to get him situated, then I would be able to visit.

"Not that he'll be there long enough for you to make more than one visit," she promised.

Two hours away and locked in a cell. That's where Kane would be. For a year. I couldn't hold any food down at the thought of it.

The media was crazier than ever after the sentencing. Though the reception to me and my story was mixed, the outrage over the obvious bias of the sentencing was almost universal. People were outraged that one of their favorite celebrities was getting put away while a loud few were praising the judge for punishing violent criminals regardless of their status. Then there were those, who rightly so, were trying to get stories of loved ones heard who were locked away for longer than Kane for nonviolent crimes. It hadn't just become a pop culture news story; it also became the springboard for all sorts of conversations about the justice system and how it operated.

And on top of that, when I tried to get a hold of Victoria after obtaining life-altering information, I'd been informed she was temporarily incommunicado, and even her personal number went right to voicemail.

The rational thing would've been to wait. I trusted her. She wasn't going to leave me hanging. If I waited, she'd return my call and all would be well. As well as things could be. But I wasn't feeling very rational. Hadn't been for a while. And all logic fled my body when I found out what I had that morning. So I did a stupid thing.

I went to Brax's office. He was the only other person who had a connection with Kane since I hadn't seen nor heard from Knox. The man who'd spent his childhood protecting Kane was nowhere to be seen when he was needed most.

Not that Knox could've done anything. He wasn't a lawyer. Actually, I got the sense he worked completely above the law, which could be the reason for his absence yet not a compelling one for me.

My only choice was to go to Brax, as much as I hated it.

I'd waited in his lobby for over an hour because, "I didn't have an appointment." I knew Brax wasn't busy enough to warrant behavior like that, knew it was a power play, but what options did I have? My nails were bitten raw by the time he finally emerged from his office.

"Avery," he greeted me, straightening his tie. "Sorry for the wait. If I had known you were coming, I would've cleared my schedule."

A lie. We both knew it. But I ignored it, letting him usher me into his office.

"I need to see Kane," I told Brax, not bothering with pleasantries.

His stare was icy, that coldness I'd sensed from him, that menace that he'd masked poorly in front of Kane was now on the surface. I resisted the urge to back down. This man would not intimidate me. This was way too important.

"That's not possible."

"What do you mean that's not possible?" I demanded. "The prison has visiting hours. I called them, but they said I need to be on some kind of list?"

Brax rounded the desk then settled himself down in the seat, reaching forward to look at some papers. "Yes, considering Kane's celebrity status, we've had to make some arrangements, for his safety." He didn't look up at me. Didn't offer me a seat. Not that I wanted to sit down.

My hands were clenched at my sides. "I'd hope you'd make arrangements for his safety," I bit out. Kane was a big figure in my mind. Powerful. Not just physically. But there was something safe about him, a sense that he could never be hurt. Except that wasn't true. He was in prison.

A shiver raced down my spine.

"But I'm assuming safety precautions are primarily focused on protecting him from other prisoners, not his…" I motioned to myself.

Girlfriend sounded so immature. Kane routinely called me 'his woman,' though I felt silly, referring to myself in that manner.

I squared my shoulders. "I need to see him," I stated instead of getting caught up on labels.

Brax still didn't look up at me. "As I said, Kane's visitor list is short, and unfortunately, you're not on it."

That didn't make sense. Wasn't I given power of attorney? How had things changed so much so quickly? There was no point in asking the whys of it. I had one goal: to see Kane.

"Well, put me on it," I insisted firmly.

Finally, he looked up. His expression was still cold, but there was faux pity in his eyes now. "I can't do that. Kane has specifically entrusted me to keep you off the list."

My breathing stuttered. "What are you talking about? Victoria said in our first meeting that I was in charge of Kane's legal decisions, which I assume includes his visitor list."

"Victoria is not in charge anymore." He sighed dramatically, splaying his hands out on the papers in front of him. I hated the gesture and hated him. "I don't want to be the one to tell you this, I really don't. Of all of Kane's women, I liked you the most. The rest were obviously good-looking, but you're not like them. You've got more … substance." He slowly surveyed me, his eyes trailing up and down my body. "I was hoping that Kane would change his ways. But he's an old dog up to the same tricks. And I hate that this is part of my job description, but the motherfucker pays me well, and…" he shrugged in a 'what can you do?' gesture.

There was a high-pitched ringing in my ears. "Are you trying to insinuate that Kane was with other women as well as me?" Suddenly, my head was throbbing.

Another sigh. "I'm not going to say anything more." He looked down at his papers again. "I see you're already distressed enough, and I thought you were smart enough to know the score. You know Kane's reputation. But I guess he pulled the whole 'my woman' thing again and gave you the wrong idea."

He leaned back in his chair.

"It's not the first time, and it won't be the last, unfortunately. I do wish you the best."

He was dismissing me. Like he was better than me. The sniveling prick.

"As much as I'm sure your word is good, forgive me if I wouldn't prefer to hear the words from Kane's mouth." I straightened my spine. "Even if what you say is true—"

"It is," he interrupted.

I gritted my teeth against the rage brewing in my stomach. "I'm sure it is," I said tightly, not believing a word he said. "But I have other matters to discuss with him."

Brax arched a disbelieving brow at me. He was trying to make me feel small. Small, desperate and unimportant. I'd had many inferior men try that shit with me.

"You can discuss the matters with me, then I'll pass them on."

In his fucking dreams.

"These matters are private," I replied, wanting to shriek yet keeping my tone calm yet unyielding. "And as I said, I'd prefer to speak directly with Kane."

Brax rose, walking around the desk with a cocky gait before leaning against the side of it to regard me. "Let me guess," he folded his arms in front of him. "He told you he loved you. That this was 'it' for him." I struggled not to wince when he used air quotes.

Kane had said both of those things, but they were things couples in love often said. Brax was screwing with me. I knew it.

Maybe because he didn't like me—weak men didn't usually like women they couldn't bully—or just because he could.

"Again I'd—"

"I know." He clicked his fingers, again interrupting me. "He said that he wanted to sell his penthouse, get rid of all the playboy shit, artifacts of an old life and buy a little cabin in the woods of Vermont with you. Except he never took you to his apartment because it was being 'renovated,' so you actually don't even know where he lives."

"Do you think of the future?" Kane asked, his finger lazily trailing over my areola.

My entire body shivered, and need built in the base of my spine, even though we had just finished having magnificent sex.

I struggled to focus on the question. "I think of the future insofar as how the weather in certain growing regions of the country will affect crops and, therefore, quality of fresh, local produce and, therefore, my menu."

Kane's hand settled on my chest, over my heartbeat which was jackhammering, despite the calm tenor to my voice.

His chuckle was low, deep and sultry. "A woman after my own heart. My view of the future is pretty much wondering how much powder they're gonna get in New Zealand during the winter and if I'll piss off my sponsors if I blow off summer games here."

"Not exactly the same." I glanced up at him.

He tucked hair behind my ears. "Same spirit. We think of the future only in regard to how it affects our day to day. But you don't think about ... white picket fences, kids, dogs?"

I let out a half-hysterical laugh.

Kane wasn't smiling.

"I look like the June Cleaver type to you?" I asked him.

"You look like you." He dragged his knuckles down my cheek. "And you're a woman who ensures that she gets whatever she desires in life."

"That most definitely isn't a picket fence or dogs."

"Kids?" he murmured softly.

My heart skipped. This conversation was getting serious. Fast.

"No," I told him honestly. "I don't think I'd be a good mother. I

shut off too many emotions too young. I'm too selfish. Too regimented with my routine. I wouldn't do well with the havoc children bring."

It's something I'd thought of sparingly over the years. Since it was getting to be the time for me to freeze my eggs if I wanted them in the future.

I didn't voice my fear that I'd fuck up a child, fail at motherhood. The fears that had stopped me from considering if I really wanted it.

"You do pretty fucking well with the chaos I bring." Kane's gaze and tone told me he was serious. "And you are far from selfish, as my cock would attest to."

I smiled. "Kind of different, don't you think?"

His eyes swam with something I couldn't decipher.

"Do you? Want kids?" I found myself asking a question I didn't want the answer to. Afraid his answer might show how different our futures would be, further putting a time limit on this relationship.

He didn't respond straightaway, I could see him thinking. He wasn't going to pacify me; he was going to give me an honest reply.

"Maybe," he said as my heart dropped. "Maybe if I wasn't so fucked-up. If I didn't have mommy issues that I recognize are not completely dealt with. Maybe if I didn't enjoy picking up and leaving on a whim. Maybe if I'd had a better father." He chuckled without humor. "So no. No kids."

"But I like the idea of Vermont." He stared at me.

I stared back, perplexed. "Vermont?"

He nodded. "A cabin, one I built with my bare hands." He winked. "Or one I pretended to build with my bare hands while paying a very talented carpenter. Land where I could build a custom dirt bike track. A vegetable garden for you, in addition to a huge fucking kitchen, of course."

"For me?"

He nodded. "You think I'm pretending to build a house for little old me, Chef?" He stroked my jaw. "It's all for you. You'll open a restaurant. People will come from all over the country. The world. We'll fuck out in the woods."

I let his words wash over me. I couldn't decipher whether it was just a pie in the sky fantasy or if he was really serious. He looked serious. He was planning a future for us. In a cabin. In Vermont. In any other circumstance, a man planning a future for me would set my hackles rising.

But with Kane, it didn't.

A cabin, a vegetable garden, woods. Yeah, that sounded ... nice.

A restaurant that was mine, really mine, where I didn't have to cater to anyone for publicity, for articles in magazines.

Kane nuzzled my neck. "I'm not sold on Vermont. Or the cabin. Anywhere is fine, with you."

"I like a cabin in Vermont," I said in a small voice.

It was the closest thing to commitment I'd ever done in my life.

It terrified me.

Because it felt right.

"Vermont it is," he pressed a kiss to my lips.

A brick landed in my stomach. That was not an easy guess. Brax wasn't saying that to fuck with me—well, the arrogant tilt to his lips told me he was—but what he was saying was true. Because Kane had told him about the promises he'd made of a future that quickly turned out to be bullshit.

Brax didn't even try to hide his shit-eating grin as he saw the blood drain from my face. "If it makes you feel any better, you're the second woman this week who had to hear that her plans for Vermont were going to have to be put off. Indefinitely."

I tasted ash, certain I was going to throw up. Not only were his promises of the future empty, they weren't even original. There was another woman—one I inexplicably hated even though none of this was her fault—who had thought Kane was hers. If I'd had my wits about me, I might've questioned where this woman was, why she hadn't spoken to the media after Kane's and my relationship was splashed everywhere. I did not have my wits about me, though. And a guarded part of me had been waiting for this, expecting the other shoe to drop.

Brax crossed the space between us, only able to get close to me because I was frozen in place.

His hands went to my shoulders in what appeared to be a reassuring squeeze, but the pressure was too much, to the point of pain. Well, it might've hurt if not for the agonizing split in my chest that left me feeling completely numb.

I wanted to run then. Run from the pain, the excruciating pain, from Brax's smarmy expression, from the blackness clouding my vision.

But I held fast.

I held on to him.

Kane.

To the moments.

All of the moments with him that I had as evidence that I wasn't just some other woman. That we were something real. And I held on to something else.

"Whether or not that's the case," I said, my voice surprisingly strong despite the tornado of emotions swimming through me. "He also has a right to know something else."

Brax's oily gaze remained on me for a few moments before realization dawned in his eyes. They went down to my stomach, full of nothing but a cluster of cells at that point. Yet my hands went there protectively, as if to shield the being inside of me from Brax's stare.

His eyes darted back up to me. Full of faux pity. "What a pickle," he tutted. "This makes things ... more complicated." He slapped his hands together, and I jumped at the sound.

Harsh.

He grinned at my jump, satisfied at the evidence that I was on edge.

I glared at him.

"So you see it's important that I talk to him," I stated matter-of-factly. Calmly.

He nodded. "I see. Unfortunately, even this..." I had to force myself not to smack him when he waved his hand at my stomach. "Is not enough to override his explicit wishes, I'm afraid. But I will tell him." He paused, pinching his chin. "You have sufficient documentation, I assume. I apologize that I can't take you at your word, but this isn't the first time this has happened."

I tasted bile. Not just from throwing up in the restrooms thirty minutes ago.

Willing myself to keep my expression even, my posture taut, I reached into my purse.

It took everything inside me to hand the small black and white photo over to Brax. My hands had clutched it even harder once his manicured fingers had fastened around it.

Silly.

It wasn't even of anything. Barely a speck.

But it had a heartbeat.

That speck.

Our child.

A beating heart. Already.

That little piece of paper was suddenly the most precious thing I owned. Tangible proof of something that felt utterly surreal, terrifying and sacred all at the same time.

I hadn't even been sure I wanted it until that moment.

Brax pulled harder to get the ultrasound photo into his meaty paws.

He didn't handle it with care, causing it to crinkle.

I suppressed a growl.

Brax's eyes lowered to the picture without emotion. "I'll ensure he gets this, and I'll be in touch."

He tossed the photo on the desk like it was nothing more than a receipt.

His blatant disregard for my situation was like poison darts, hitting their mark. I wanted to do more. Demand more. But I was totally powerless at that moment.

I wasn't Kane's wife. I had no claim to him. Had no other way of getting in contact with him.

Knox was my only other connection with him, the only person I truly trusted to get this information to him.

But he was 'in the wind,' Kane had said when I'd told him I couldn't reach him.

And I had the impression 'in the wind' meant he wasn't going to be found unless he wanted to be.

But he must've known about Kane. Though I knew the two had a complicated relationship, Knox wouldn't willingly abandon Kane like this.

He'd turn up. Even if I couldn't trust Brax, I could wait for that. That's all I could do.

I was completely powerless.

The realization made me wobbly on my feet, but fuck if this asshole was going to see me as weak. So I kept my chin high and my gaze on his when I told him, "I'll be expecting to hear from you. Soon."

The grin remained. That knowing grin. That taunting grin. "Of course," he replied placidly. "You have a good day. Take care of yourself. Be careful. I know that this city can be dangerous at the best of times, especially with someone in your ... condition."

A threat. I didn't know why or really how, but it felt like a threat.

I didn't balk.

"I can take care of myself."

"I'm sure you can," he said sarcastically.

I turned my back, my step not faltering until I got home.

* * *

Brax was true to his word, something I hadn't expected.

I did hear from him promptly.

The next day.

I'd expected him to fuck with me. Make me wait, even if he did get in touch with Kane as soon as he could.

He was a small man who wanted power. And this was the most he'd ever had. I'd seen him watch Kane, seen him covet what Kane had. I'd trusted Kane's judgment, thought that there was a reason Brax was around, although I never trusted him.

I had to hold on to that trust in Kane, although it was hanging by a thread.

I didn't let any of my unease show on my face as I went back to Brax's offices. Didn't let him see evidence of the sleepless night I'd had, the worry and fear churning in my stomach.

His words had bounced around my brain all night. Had made me question everything. As if I hadn't already been questioning everything.

I wouldn't say I had many plans for my life outside of running my own kitchen, owning my own restaurant one day. Well, that was the plan. The main and only plan.

There hadn't been dreams of a man, a wedding, and most definitely not of a white picket fence. No plan to create a new family. I had a complicated enough relationship with my family as it was. No way was I going to try to make one of my own. I wasn't capable of that.

Then again, I hadn't thought I was capable of falling in love.

Yet I'd fallen hard and brutally for Kane.

I'd avoided feelings because I knew the power of them. Knew that losing love could ruin you. No way would I give away that power.

Then came Kane.

He made me feel safe. He made me feel like I wasn't going to lose him. That he wasn't going to ruin me.

Then there was the arrest. The trial, which was bad enough. The blame I carried around with me was almost devastating. It had caused me to be constantly sick to my stomach, throwing up everything I ate. Or at least I had thought it was the guilt.

In a million years, I wouldn't have thought that it might be a baby.

Our baby.

We were careful.

Not that careful, obviously.

Kane hadn't wanted a barrier between us. And nor had I. I wanted that intimacy. I was on birth control, and I trusted science even though I knew that nothing was 100 percent effective. Plus, I was over thirty—a woman's chances of conceiving at my age were less than 20 percent per month.

I'd considered the risk to be nonexistent.

I hadn't thought about how powerful Kane was, how equally powerful his sperm must've been. Not just to circumvent birth control but then to survive the stress of the past few months.

I had gone through the motions of my life as best as I could. Except I didn't do anything very well. Cooking was a shitshow. Pregnancy jacked up your tastebuds, it seemed. And then there was the almost round-the-clock vomiting. Luckily, my staff was the best in the world and able to run the kitchen without me. None had blinked an eye at my 'stomach virus' making it so I couldn't run point on dishes.

My team wasn't easily ruffled.

Still, I had no idea what I was going to do about the kitchen. If my sickness continued—which my reading told me it would, until the second trimester, at least—I couldn't work. I couldn't cook the quality food I was known for.

The mere prospect sent me into a cold sweat.

But I'd deal with that when it came. First, I needed to talk to Kane.

Brax had been lying. He'd caught me when I was vulnerable, had sniffed that out. But no way could he ruin everything Kane and I had in one conversation.

I'd been sure of that when he let me into his offices again, the same fake smile, same slimy demeanor.

"How are you feeling?" he asked, gesturing for me to sit.

I ignored that, staying standing. "I'm feeling like I don't need small talk. I need you to tell me I'm on the approved list to visit Kane." I had my ice queen persona firmly in place.

Brax's face softened into what was surely faux pity, but his beady eyes looked calculated.

"I'm afraid I can't tell you that."

"What the fuck do you mean?" I demanded. "You said you would speak to him."

He nodded. "I did. I spoke, told him about you, showed him this." He took the crumpled and ripped ultrasound photo out from inside of his jacket.

He'd ruined it on purpose, I was certain. Brax was the kind of person who wanted to ruin pure and wonderful things just because he could.

I let the rage burn my throat, but I kept my expression cool.

"And he gave me this, to give to you." He took out another piece of paper, this one smooth. Pristine.

Instead of handing it to me, he pushed it across his desk in my direction.

I gritted my teeth at his assholery. I took slow, measured steps to snatch up the piece of paper with steady hands, unfolding it and reading it.

Get rid of it.

. . .

I stared at those four words, a viscous sludge rippling through my gut.

My hands began to shake, gripping the paper hard enough to almost tear it in half.

Get rid of it.

Written in Kane's handwriting. I knew the messy, bold scrawl backward and forward. Had notes from him carefully preserved in a drawer beside my bed at home.

His handwriting. His words.

Get rid of it.

As if it were nothing. As if I were nothing.

My hand went to my stomach, and the paper fluttered to the floor. It didn't make a sound. I expected it to boom at the impact due to how heavy it had felt mere moments ago.

"I can arrange an appointment at a discreet clinic. I've been authorized to give funds to pay for the procedure." Brax's words seemed to be coming from a vacuum.

My head snapped up to meet his sniveling face. I was now released from any and all obligation to be polite to him.

"Go to hell," I said evenly. "You and your small, small mind and your gigantic ego can go to hell."

Then I turned and left, knowing I had nowhere to go, nothing left, but that I also had to protect the one thing in this world that was mine.

KANE

I clenched and unclenched my fists, willing my body to relax. I knew that she would assess every part of me in that sharp gaze of hers. She wouldn't miss a thing. Avery made it her job to become an expert at whatever she was interested in. And lucky son of a bitch that I was, she was interested in me.

Therefore, she'd seen me wired, she'd noted my lack of sleep and the energy of a caged animal I'd worked my ass off to shake. Thankfully, I hadn't been in any fistfights to establish dominance or some such shit. I'd been ready and willing to fight for a spot needed, but apparently, Knox had made arrangements since no one fucked with me. And I knew that was not because they were all motocross fans. Another way my brother protected me.

I was glad about it for many reasons, most because it would mean Avery wouldn't have something else to worry about.

I might not have made it my business to become an expert in everything I did, but I had made it my business to become an expert in her. Part of the reason I couldn't sleep— in addition to the paper-thin mattress, the stifling heat and the narrowness of the cell—was because I was haunted by images of her.

Running out into the alley, her eyes wide, pupils dilated like an animal that had become prey. The red mark on her cheek. The complete absence of the strong and sure woman I'd come to know. To love.

Her face after I was done beating Gerald to a pulp. Not horror. Not disgust in me. Not fear either. I couldn't quite decipher the expression. There was an emptiness in it that scared me.

Then the way she looked when she came to visit me. Pale. Gaunt. Bags under her eyes she'd tried to cover. Panic coming out of her very pores. Worry. And worst of all, guilt. She blamed herself. The fucking world blamed her. A conclusion that made me furious enough to punch through a goddamn wall.

The world was mad at a brilliant, interesting, talented woman for the crime of being abused. For the crime of knocking an asshole off his pedestal.

When it was *me* who did the knocking.

And I'd do it all over again.

But fuck, did I miss the taste of her. The smell of her. The warmth of her. I was well aware that she had the reputation of being an 'ice queen,' but no woman had burned hotter under my touch than Avery Hart.

Thinking of that, of her, her hair splayed out on the pillow, me inside her, eyes electric, wide, wild. The woman unrestrained ...that calmed me.

Three hundred and fifty-five more days.

I looked up when I heard the clang of the doors open, my smile ready.

But Brax walked through the door, the door closing and bolting behind him. I'd already seen him once before. How he'd managed to get in before Avery I didn't know, and it pissed me off. But he had things for me to sign, papers for me to go over, apparently.

"Where's Chef?" I demanded, standing. "Is she okay?" My mind whirled with things that could've happened, my fucking knees trembling at just the thought.

Brax smoothed his suit, taking his time to walk over and sit down across from me. And fuck if I hated that unhurried gait, that inflated sense of importance. I'd always known who Brax was—arrogant, power hungry, calculated—but it had amused me more than anything.

No one was perfect, and I knew better than anyone that we were a product of our trauma, never knowing what someone had gone through. I tended to give people the benefit of the doubt. Brax had been with me since the start. And as much as he could be a smarmy, sanctimonious prick, he'd never fucked me over.

"She's not coming," Brax said.

I was still standing. "I fuckin' deduced that. Why not?"

"You wanna sit?"

I sucked in a deep breath. "I want you to tell me where Chef is."

Brax sighed. It was long and dramatic and fuck, it ignited the embers already simmering in my gut.

"No one knows." He drummed his fingers on the table.

My heart rate went haywire. "What do you mean? Has someone—"

"No, it's not as dramatic as all that," Brax chuckled.

I wanted to plow my fist through his face for that chuckle.

"Although I would argue dropping everything, quitting her restaurant and leaving town is still pretty dramatic," he continued, unaware of how close I was to ruining his veneers.

Everything in me silenced.

"What?" I gasped.

He looked at me with pity in his gaze. "Man, I didn't want to be the one to tell you this. Fuck." He ran his hand through his hair. "I wanted her to be different for you, bro, I really did. I didn't think she was one of those clout chasers, in it for whatever they can get out of you. But she got her interview, got paid six figures for it, and now she's gone."

"Fuck off." I slumped into the chair. "She's not gone. Chef wouldn't leave. She promised."

"She came to see me a few days ago, before she left," he sighed again. "And her mind was made up."

"Bullshit," I spat, looking up at Brax. "She's not fucking gone. She'll be here."

Brax shrugged his shoulders. "I wish I had your optimism. And maybe she will be."

There was no maybe about it.

Chef had not gone. I knew that shit surer than I knew anything. She had promised me.

Fifteen

FOUR MONTHS LATER

AVERY

JUPITER, Maine was as good a place as any to hide. In fact, it could be described as one of the *best* places to run to.

It was idyllic, picturesque, settled on the rugged coastline, with idyllic, sea-weathered cottages. With well-maintained, colorful businesses on the cobbled main street. No chain restaurants or big-box stores to be seen. Everything was mom-and-pop, from the grocery store to the bakery that offered the best croissants I'd had inside and outside of France. Along with everything else in the pretty display cabinet.

The pastry chef was one of the most talented I'd encountered in my life. Which was saying something. When I'd first bit into her food, I'd told myself that I'd have to recruit her for the restaurant.

A thought that I'd had on instinct, a thought belonging to the person I used to be … before. The chef of a Michelin star restaurant. Someone with power, respect, a purpose.

Except I wasn't her.

I no longer had a restaurant.

Hadn't had any of the markers of my identity for the past decade.

Didn't have Kane.

It was the last thing that bothered me the most.

Not being in the kitchen, not feeling the hum of it, the heat… Yeah, it left a hole inside of me. But not like the gaping chasm I felt without Kane.

And at the same time, I felt an emptiness. I was growing. Growing with a child we'd forged. One that would forever serve as the reminder of what I'd had. What I'd thought was something special, everything.

And what I'd lost.

Except you had to actually have something in order to lose it. And Kane had informed me, through Brax, through those scrawled, heartbreaking letters, that I had never had it in the first place. Hadn't ever truly had him.

That had sent me into a dark hole for months. Even while being in the picturesque city of Jupiter. It helped that the cold and dreary days of winter matched my mood, and I was able to wallow. Though the oncoming of spring and the life and cheer it brought made me surly. I was supposed to be full of good thoughts, hope, being pregnant, but I couldn't find either.

The knock at the front door served to punctuate my bad mood. It was about to storm outside, the boom of thunder sounding in the distance, lightning flashing. No one was supposed to be out in storms, certainly not knocking on my door. I'd had a sign put up to leave packages at the door, avoiding social interaction.

I was distracted when I opened the front door, as I often was those days. It turned out that getting unexpectedly pregnant, uprooting your entire life to a place where you didn't know anyone, quitting your job—the thing that had comprised pretty much my whole personality—and trying to do it alone was distracting.

Go figure.

I had been lost in my spreadsheet of bedside bassinets. Beside each, I had listed the pros and cons, organized by price point—I was trying to weigh the best one based on various features of safety and comfortability.

I'd been at it for weeks. You'd think I would've been able to pull the trigger. I mean, it was a place for the baby to sleep. It was only very recently babies even had fancy bassinets to sleep in.

Babies had been surviving for thousands of years without $1,500 bassinets that rocked them and played white noise.

Yet there I was, agonizing over the sheer amount on the market.

I'd narrowed it down to five.

I'd been scanning the sheet, chewing on the end of my pen while laboring over a simple decision.

Me. Who could create a twelve-course tasting menu for New York's elite with the utmost confidence in myself and my choices. Me. Who had been in charge of a whole restaurant. Who could handle small fires, staff arguing with each other, sexism, long hours, constant pressure, physical exertion and second-degree burns.

But that was food. I knew food. I knew I was good at food. There were acclaimed reviews and Michelin stars to back that knowledge up.

There was absolutely no evidence I was good at picking out bassinets. Or being a mother.

Yet here I was.

Eight months pregnant, in a pretty cottage in Maine on the precipice of being one with no real choice otherwise.

"What. The. Fuck."

That was what I was greeted with upon opening the door.

And a six-foot figure dressed entirely in black, blocking out the storm-resistant sun, taking all my breath away.

Granted, it was easy to take my breath away those days since I had a six-pound—according to the most recent ultrasound—child squishing my internal organs and using my ribs as a kickstand.

But none of that was the reason for my gasp, for the stutter of my heartbeat, the weakening of my knees, the swarm of bees in my stomach.

Kane.

It was Kane standing in my doorway, staring at me, uttering three words drenched in fury as he pushed up his black Wayfarers to stare at me.

To stare at my stomach.

My hands went there automatically. I hadn't understood why pregnant women did that—constantly touched or rubbed their stomachs. I'd found it asinine. But when the previous flat area rounded, when I felt the flutter of small limbs that had now transitioned to soccer kicks from what felt like a large animal, I got it. There was a little human in there, one who already demanded a lot of my attention and had taken to pressing on my bladder when it got in their way.

A little human that I'd made.

With Kane.

Who was here.

Obviously out of prison.

And obviously pissed.

"What the *fuck*?" he repeated louder this time.

I flinched at the acrimony in his voice.

He'd never, never spoken to me like that before. His tone with me was always soft, teasing, playful, sensual. Never had he spoken so harshly.

I felt it. Everywhere.

Or I imagined I would, after the shock wore off.

"You got out early," I commented, my voice sounding vaguely detached. Kane had been gone for five months. Five months, three days and about twelve hours if you wanted to get technical.

Therefore, he should've still had about five months, twenty-six days and twelve hours left of his sentence.

It was a fairly benign if not logical observation, but it was obviously not the right thing to say.

"Oh, I'm sorry I got out early. Is that the reason why you weren't there waiting for me?" he asked. No, growled. "If I'd been inside for a year, without a word from you, without knowing if you were alive or fuckin' dead, let alone *pregnant*, you'd be there waiting for me, right? Like you promised?"

He was yelling now. Roaring, to be honest.

The force of his anger was a tsunami, washing over me. Yet somehow, I remained standing. I could feel my hands shaking, though. I wasn't afraid. Not quite. I was unable to fathom that Kane was here. That Kane was able to yell at me like that.

The sun, as if to match his mood, suddenly disappeared, storm clouds darkening the afternoon and booming thunder making me jump.

"I can't fucking believe this!" he yelled, rivaling the thunder for volume.

Rain started falling softly behind him.

"You don't get to yell at me," I replied quietly. I wanted to yell back. But I didn't have the energy.

"You disappeared after I was put in *prison*, not a fucking word!" he screamed, both hands on his hips as he paced up and down my front porch. The rain began coming down harder. "And I thought that was bad enough, considering what I thought we had, but for the first time in my life, I actually could not conceive of the worst-case scenario. Because never in my wildest fuckin' dreams would I have imagined the woman I loved would've not only abandoned me but neglected to tell me about *our goddamn baby*!"

He'd stopped pacing, leaning toward me to roar. In my face.

He was out of control. I could feel his frantic energy, taste the electricity of his fury crackling around me.

Kane was livid. Perhaps even dangerous. His fists were balled at his sides, veins of his forearms spiderwebbing down his arms. His nostrils were flared, eyes wide, pupils dilated, and his whole form was shaking with fury.

But I wasn't scared. He wouldn't hurt me. Not physically, at least.

He looked me up and down with absolute disgust. "Unless it's not mine."

If he'd hit me, it would've hurt less.

"It's yours," I said in a small voice.

"And that makes it so much fuckin' worse," he hissed, huffing out a long exhale through his nostrils.

I chewed on the inside of my mouth until I tasted blood.

"You're entitled to your feelings," I told him, keeping my voice even.

"Entitled to my fucking *feelings*?" His eyes bulged. "Yeah, I'm entitled to them. But that's not the response I want from you. That response isn't you. What I want is an explanation for this shit even though there isn't a sufficient explanation for trying to hide *my child* from me, for robbing me of watching you grow..." My heart panged, just a tad at the way his voice cracked abruptly.

His furious veneer wavered, gifting me with a glimpse of the man beneath the anger. The man who was sleepy in the morning, who was soulful in the moonlight, who had a soft side that hadn't hardened no matter how many times he'd thrown himself off cliffs, raced motorcycles or jumped out of planes.

Right then, he was ... hurt.

My insides were shredding, and hot shame poured over me.

"Were you going to hide the baby from me after it was born?" he asked, quieter now. "Were you going to keep my kid from me?"

My heartbeat thrashed in my throat, and I had the vague feeling I might vomit up my insides.

"You didn't want it," I replied, putting my hands over my stomach protectively.

A gesture that Kane instantly caught and made him stiffen, likely because he thought I was protecting the baby from *him*.

"I didn't want it?" he repeated quietly. "I didn't fucking know it existed!" He was back to roaring again, gesturing violently toward my stomach.

I recoiled, though I hated myself for it.

"Don't you dare fucking back away from me like I'm going to hurt you," he snarled, getting in my face. "You know I'm not going to hurt you. I'd never harm a hair on your fuckin' head."

I bit my lip harder, the metallic taste of blood grounding me.

"That doesn't make sense," I muttered, mostly to myself. "I tried to tell you. I mean, I did tell you, but you didn't want to see me."

"Who in the *fuck* told you that?" Kane asked, fingers at his temples.

I wrung my hands. Everything I'd built my life around these past few months was slowly falling apart. Not that the proverbial building itself was structurally sound in the first place.

"Brax," I said in little more than a whisper, the thunder drowning out his name.

"What? I can't hear you?" his voice was harsh, still much too loud, much too cold.

"Brax," I said louder, my throat thick. "He, um, I told him, and he told me that you wanted me to ... get rid of it."

Kane's mouth fell open, the tips of his ears going fire-red. I'd thought he was angry before. No, I hadn't seen anything yet. My stomach curdled with true fear. Kane was pissed off at me before, he'd been furious. But I was never in danger. I'd never seen a truly violent or deadly side to him, not even that day in the kitchen.

Until right that second.

"Well, Brax is going to fucking die," he seethed, almost to himself.

I shivered at his tone, what he said. He was not speaking in metaphors.

"Back to this." He motioned to my bump. All hardness rapidly left his gaze, a ... tenderness in place that almost brought me to my knees.

I was already having a hard time being upright, but that tenderness? That was ten thousand times harder to handle than his wrath.

"You know what we had, Avery," he shook his head. There was no tenderness in his voice. It was cold. Goose bumps erupted on my arms.

What we *had*.

Past tense.

Needless to say, I'd already mourned what we had. Or thought I had. My version of mourning was cursing his name throughout the day and hating myself for longing for him during the night.

But seeing him in that moment, understanding that there had been some kind of miscommunication and that he hadn't said what Brax told me made me mourn him all over again.

Because he had been mine. When I'd seen the two lines. When I'd been scared but also excited—deep, deep down. About having something with Kane. Something permanent. In that second, I'd imagined a snapshot of a life I could have.

With Kane.

Then reality came in and kicked our asses.

That life was gone, no matter what came after this. Because of me.

"You know what we had," he repeated, his eyes filled with emotion as he looked over my shoulder. "Yet you let Brax convince you it was nothing in *one fuckin' conversation*."

There was accusation there. Some of which I might've deserved.

I definitely shouldn't have made such a big, permanent decision based on secondhand information from an unreliable source.

And maybe part of the reason why I'd believed Brax so readily was because I didn't believe that Kane and I would last. And because I knew that I wouldn't survive him rejecting me to my face.

"He knew about Vermont," I told him, putting my hands on my hips. Maybe I had some blame in all of this, but I wasn't just about to submit. Pregnant or not, I had a backbone, and I was suddenly ready for a fight. Suddenly, I was ready for war.

Something skated over the outrage on Kane's face, rippled past it. Confusion? Shock? Who knew? I didn't have it in me to inspect Kane's expressions. Not when they were so full of contempt.

"You told him about Vermont, and he said it was a story you told all your … women," I continued, failing to keep the jealous bite from my voice.

It was better than the pathetic heartbreak that had been seeping from my every cell.

"And the note telling me to get rid of it was in your handwriting."

Kane stood there, staring, waiting. I didn't say anything else.

"That's it?" he eventually asked quietly. "That's all it took for you to give up on me, on us? To run away and take my child from me?" There was a slight snarl to his lip. He felt betrayed. "You didn't try to see me? Didn't talk to Victoria? I informed her directly that all decisions were yours to make."

I released my chewed-up lip to reply. "Victoria was out of reach when I found out."

"How long, Avery?" he screeched. "How long was she out of reach for? Did you wait one day, two? Did she call you back?"

I opened my mouth then closed it, unable to answer the rapidly asked questions, shot at me like bullets from a gun.

"I know she called you back because she fuckin' told me, after Brax delivered the news that you were gone," he seethed. "That you'd left me. I got in touch with Victoria, told her to find you because I might've been blind to what a complete piece of shit Brax is, but I knew not to trust the motherfucker with something so precious."

Something so precious. Me. Us.

He wasn't looking at me like I was precious.

"Did she call you back, Avery?" he asked, indignation carving off every word so they were pointed.

"I don't know," I admitted. The rain pounded louder now, the smell of the storm assaulting my senses, mingling with Kane's ire that was more powerful than the storm itself.

"You don't know?" he repeated, sounding so cold. Cruel. "How is it you couldn't know if your one connection with me, *the father of your fuckin' baby*, called you back?"

"I changed my number," I answered, my voice shrinking more with every moment.

"You changed your number." Again, repeating my answer in that tone.

I was looking down at the pots on either side of my front door. Distressed gray with dying blooms sitting in them because Kiera had arranged them, planted them, then demanded I keep them alive. As if doing anything beyond keeping myself and a baby thriving was doable.

"Look at me." The command was harsh, razor sharp.

If words could make you bleed, I would've been dripping on the floor.

Despite the pain, despite fearing I wouldn't be able to handle his gaze, I obeyed his command. And the disdain on his face shredded me further.

"Why would you break every thread you had connecting you to me on the word of one asshole?" he asked carefully.

A bead of sweat trickled down the side of my face. "Because someone leaked it, my number. I was getting calls, texts, death threats." It wasn't a lie. And it was awfully convenient that my number leaked right after my visit to Brax, before Victoria was able to get back to me.

I was suddenly realizing what was so glaringly obvious, it was worse than a 'twist' in a poorly-written detective novel.

Kane twitched at the 'death threats' part.

"It was all Brax." Shame spilled over me at my stupidity. "He orchestrated it all. To get me away. For whatever reason."

Not for whatever reason. I'd come between him and Kane. I'd seen him for what he was. So he'd wanted to punish me. Ruin me.

"Yeah," Kane said in a dead voice. "And you made it fuckin' easy for him. You didn't fight for us."

What was left unsaid was that I didn't fight for *him*. I could've wept in response to the pain he was veiling with anger and contempt.

"You gonna let me in, or you gonna continue to make me stand out here like a fuckin' unwanted houseguest?" he asked. No, demanded.

We had been hashing out something immensely painful and personal on my front porch. Luckily, I didn't have neighbors, my cottage located at the edge of town, down a long drive with the dense woods bordering my property, giving me the illusion that I was the only person left in the world.

Which is what I had wanted, to hide there. To rot there, maybe. Wallow in my pain and self-pity and absolute fear of what was to come.

I didn't say anything, just moved my body in answer. He took that as permission and shouldered his way past. I stepped back in time, wondering if he would've pushed me if I hadn't. Surely, he wouldn't. Kane wouldn't get physical with a woman, let alone a pregnant woman. Certainly not with me. Or so I'd thought. The old Avery wanted to call him out on that, tell him that despite his anger, he didn't get to treat me poorly. I wanted to tell him to leave just so I could breathe.

Yet trying to argue with Kane at that juncture would've been unwise. Considering the state he was in, there was no winning with him, even on my best day. That was far from my best day. And it was pouring rain, he'd come on his bike. He would get soaked.

Realizing my own mistake in quickly believing those lies and then being hit with how pissed Kane was at me, seeing him after all that time was ... a lot. No, it wasn't Kane's outrage, it was his pain that was hiding so poorly underneath his anger. I'd hurt him. Deeply.

I stood at the door for a little longer than might've been normal after he stormed through, holding on to the doorknob to stay upright and blinking at the motorcycle in the driveway.

I only caught myself when the sound of the back sliding door and the dog's rabid barking jostled me into the present.

I rushed to shut the door then ran down the hall to the back door before my dog could try to maul Kane. That was the last thing I needed. Not that Kane couldn't handle himself with an over-grown, untrained seventy-pound dog. The fight would likely be even. Or tilted in Kane's favor. He just had that aura about him that said he could handle any threat. Most especially now, furious and obviously just out of prison.

But still, the dog had teeth. Sharp ones. That could tear into Kane's skin, give him more scars. My stomach lurched yet again at the thought, because I'd come to the realization that he had plenty of new scars because of me, ones that weren't visible to the naked eye but ones that were bone deep, soul deep.

Instead of finding a dog and man brawl in my kitchen, I found the dog on her back, presenting her stomach for Kane to scratch.

"She's not barking," I stated the obvious. "Or jumping on you. Or attacking you."

"She's not." He didn't look up at me, still speaking in that cold, growly tenor.

It made sense. He wasn't exactly going to stop being angry at me from the time he walked from the front door to the kitchen.

"She barks at everyone," I said, watching man and dog together, the sight making both my heart and pussy clench … for different reasons. The pussy was obvious; I hadn't had sex in about … seven months. Kane looked better than ever in a simple black tee, ripped black jeans and boots. His bicep muscles stretched the fabric of his tee, looking like they'd grown a bunch in the time we'd been apart. His hair was longer too, and he had a dark scruff of stubble covering his jaw. With the tattoos, muscles and in all black, all he needed was a leather vest, and he'd look like an outlaw biker.

Despite Kane looking better than any man on earth had any right to look, it wasn't just that. It was him. Here. It was his smell. It was his huge presence in my compact, little cottage. It was his large, strong hands scratching the dog I'd adopted.

He was here. In the home I had been trying to create for the past five months. The home that hadn't been anything more than a house until he stormed through the door.

My eyes welled up, and I struggled to contain my tears.

Pregnancy hormones. That's what it was.

I cleared my throat loudly. "She's a rescue," I explained, focusing on the dog. "And she is … strong-minded. She doesn't stop barking or running around like an idiot unless I'm feeding her or I've tired her out with a long walk on the beach," I babbled. "And part of that tiring her out is me wrestling with her when another person or dog walks by."

I placed my hands on top of my belly, unsure of what to do with myself, how to stand, how to act in front of Kane. The man who I'd been more intimate with than anyone in my entire life had become a stranger to me.

When Kane looked up at me, his expression was blank. I had to stop myself from cringing at the sheer lack of warmth in it. This was the man who'd made me feel on fire and alive every time he laid eyes on me. The man who had made me feel like the only woman on planet Earth when he looked at me.

His gaze gravitated down to my stomach for a split second before he focused on the dog again. He gave her belly a rough pat before pressing onto his thighs and straightening up to a standing position.

Blanche jumped up as he did so, her tail wagging madly. I prepared for barking, jumping, plain old wild behavior.

"Go, sit," Kane commanded, pointing to the rarely used, fancy dog bed across the open plan area in the living room.

I'd tried that command about a million times, at varying decibels. Yelling didn't work. Nor did speaking softly and calmly. Nothing worked. Nothing that the sweet but befuddled dog trainer did worked either.

He informed me that he'd worked with hundreds of dogs and had yet to have one best him. She was his Everest.

Blanche didn't skip a beat. She trotted over to her bed dutifully then settled there without so much as a frustrated bark, curling up and chewing on the toy bunny that she'd been uninterested in before then.

I stared in amazement. "Aaron is going to be pissed," I said without thinking.

The energy in the room seemed to change. I looked at Kane whose eyes were narrowed and hands fisted at his sides. His attention glued me to the floor.

"Who the *fuck* is Aaron?" he asked quietly.

I kept my hands on my belly and stood my ground, despite my rapid rise in heart rate. "Aaron is a dog trainer." I nodded to the bed. "Her dog trainer. I've been working with her for a couple of months. Aaron is happily married and just sent his daughter Caroline off to college," I added, though I shouldn't have had to.

Kane was quite obviously mad at me. Things between us were severed, yet he also thought he could be possessive and wrathful at the mere mention of another man's name?

Kane didn't reply. Just stared at me for ten full seconds. I counted in my head as I tried to remember to breathe.

Then he nodded, looking around, taking stock of the house.

I wasn't skilled at decorating. At making places feel warm and welcoming. I was surprised my womb was welcoming enough for a baby to take root, but here we were. I was trying. With Kiera's help.

It was pretty much all Kiera. She came to visit when she had time—which wasn't often, but she'd occasionally jump on a plane to come for just a day—and in that time, she'd walk around the house with measuring tape, sucking her teeth and tapping on her phone.

The kitchen and living area were a result of her tapping.

Two, large deep-seated sofas were facing each other, the fabric a deep-green velvet. They were cluttered with contrasting-patterned, plush pillows, comfortable throws lying over the top of them. I'd tested out the comfort of the sofas many times, when I was too tired to make it to bed or if I had a day when my first trimester morning sickness decided to reappear.

The coffee table was round, in an effort to prepare for the baby proofing I'd inevitably have to do. There were varying sizes of beeswax candles—nontoxic because Kiera had also gone crazy to make sure everything in the house didn't contain chemicals that could harm the baby. Worn paperbacks were piled beside the cabinets. Not Kiera's doing, but me, desperate for distraction.

Baby books. All of them. Written by scientists, by doulas, midwives, spiritual experts—every side of the coin. I needed all the help I could get.

The fireplace was roaring because even though spring had sprung, I felt the cold more these days, despite my extra padding in the midsection area.

Paintings decorated the walls, all depicting womanly figures. Another thing that Kiera had insisted on, bringing 'divine feminine energy' into the house. I didn't quite understand what that meant, but I let her do it.

Apparently, it meant warm tones, a lot of candles, books, flowers, fertility statues and crystals. Which I instantly balked at. If my sister were here, she would've approved.

But my sister wasn't here.

She didn't even know I was here. Or that I was pregnant.

Nor did my mother.

Outside of Kiera, my doctor and Brax, *no one* knew.

And now Kane knew. He was glaring at me with unwavering intensity.

"You renting?" he asked, his tone cold.

No more yelling.

Somehow, that was worse.

"Excuse me?" I asked, confused by the question.

"The house." He waved one of his hands to gesture to the space around us. "You renting?"

"Um, no," I wrung my hands. "I, um, kind of impulse bought."

He stared at me. No change in his expression. "You impulse bought a *house.*"

His tone reminded me of Kiera's reaction when I'd told her about the house.

"It's my Thurdy gift," I informed her. "Did I use it right?"

There was a beat of silence at the other end of the phone. "Okay, I love *that you're using my term, but the concept has gotten a little lost on you. Because a Thurdy gift is something like a purse that costs as much as a used car, or maybe some hat that is only appropriate for the Royal Wedding even if you don't have any British friends. It is not a small, quaint and very Nancy Meyers vibes house in a seaside town!"*

She was yelling now.

Kane was still staring at me as I digested his words.

I chewed on my lip. His scrutiny was unyielding. I could barely breathe under it. "Well, I didn't want to be in the restaurant after … everything," I explained. "I tried at first, but I couldn't. Because of what happened, and because the smell and any and all food made me hurl then pass out." I was trying to make a joke at the end.

It didn't work.

Kane's gaze was even stormier. "You passed out in the kitchen?"

I swallowed past the boulder in my esophagus. "Not really. I mean, I caught myself."

A beat of silence passed as he just stared at me, me looking out the window when his scrutiny made my skin begin to itch. "You caught yourself," he eventually murmured, almost to himself.

My cheeks were flaming for some reason. I couldn't stand the silence, so I started talking again. I'd always been comfortable in silences, even awkward ones. My ability to withstand them was a power move, so I'd never balked. Until then. "It became clear the restaurant wasn't going to work, New York wasn't going to work. Without my kitchen, the city was …." Suffocating. A prison. A reminder of every memory I'd made with him.

"Unsuitable," I said finally, touching my stomach lightly. "And the apartment wasn't baby friendly." I didn't add that after Kane's sentencing, it became impossible and unsafe to be at my apartment. Due to the mobs, my number being leaked, my heartbreak. I'd pretty much gathered my meager amount of belongings, did frantic googling about small towns then just left. "So…" I didn't know what else to say, afraid to incite him even further.

"You bought a house. In Maine," Kane stated flatly.

I shrugged in response. "I did. I, um, like it here."

It wasn't a lie. Not really. If I had the ability to *like* any place, it would've been here. If I weren't numb and broken, I would've appreciated it. As it was, for the past five months, I had been numb and broken and couldn't really like anything. Therefore, Jupiter, Maine, was tolerable. The best I could do.

Kane clicked his tongue and looked out the window at the crashing waves. More silence followed. More coldness radiating from him.

I steeled myself to remain in the silence. No more babbling to fill it. It seemed to only make things worse.

"Can I get you a drink?" I eventually offered lamely, unable to stand the silence for a moment longer. "Coffee?"

Kane's head whipped from the windows. "You have a room for the baby?" he asked instead of answering my question.

I nodded, uncomfortable with the way he spoke of the baby. There was no warmth in his tone even though he seemed to have softened some. Same with his gaze when it floated to my stomach.

Even though it turned icy the second it returned to my eyes.

"Show me," was all he ordered.

I didn't have it in me to argue with him, to assert any kind of dominance in my own home. I didn't know what to do but turn my back and hope he followed me.

The thump of his footsteps told me he did.

I didn't pass out ascending the stairs, so I was obviously breathing. But for the life of me, I couldn't seem to feel the oxygen in my lungs. They were tight, burning, my stomach swimming with nausea. Worse than first trimester morning sickness. And that was saying something.

Kane didn't speak. But he was behind me. Right behind me. I could smell him, feel the heat radiating off his body as it almost brushed against mine.

I was aching for his touch. For the feel of his hands on my skin, his lips. His arms around me. But he hadn't touched me. Not since he arrived. He hadn't seemed like he *wanted* to touch me. Kane, the man who'd made it his business to have our skin touching before he even knew my name. That thought was a knife to my heart.

I thought I'd made my peace with Kane never wanting to touch me again. Never wanting anything to do with me. But that was when he was absent; it was so much harder in his presence.

"Here it is." I leaned in to turn on the light before stepping aside so he could walk through the door.

He brushed past me. The doorway was narrow, and I wasn't exactly small these days. Plus, he was even bigger than he had been before, all of him pure muscle. But somehow, he made it so even our clothes didn't touch. He didn't look at me either.

It speared my insides, but I stayed upright. Somehow.

Kane walked to the middle of the room, still silent, looking around.

Yet again, I couldn't stand the silence.

"I, uh, um, had high hopes about my ability to construct the crib," I explained, standing awkwardly in the doorway. "But as you can see..." I pointed to the cardboard that I'd given up on. Why I didn't buy the fancy stuff that came put together that people hauled in for you, I didn't know.

Kiera had tried to insist on decorating this room too, but this was the only room I'd pushed back on. I'd even let her do the kitchen. I'd had to. I could barely step foot in there except to take care of my basic nutrition needs. The ILVE Nostalgie stove, the Shun Hikari knives and the large island all taunted me. Showed me what I'd had. What I'd lost. Who I was. Who I wasn't.

But the nursery... it seemed like I had to do that. It was my job to take care of the nursery. I was the mother after all.

Mother.

Still, even with the baby now squishing all of my internal organs up toward my ribs, kicking me all night long and changing my body irrecoverably, I didn't think the label fit.

Father.

That's what Kane was. What I'd thought he'd refused to be. But he was standing in our baby's unfinished nursery, a stern expression on his face. Yet even with that expression, the label fit him, bespoke.

Kane remained silent, just focusing on the wood and the boxes for longer than was comfortable.

"Who carried these upstairs?" he finally asked.

I tilted my head at his question, confused. "What?"

He turned to look at me then. Yet again, I had to stifle a gasp at the lack of expression on his face. "Who carried these upstairs?" He gestured to the crib parts and the boxes.

"I did," I said, stating the obvious. "Well, the delivery guys did the dresser, thankfully. Just pushing that across the room was a workout."

I'd thought the air in the room was tense before, but it suddenly seemed to throb with ferocity.

Kane's eyes bore into me. They were no longer blank but bulging with rage.

"My *pregnant woman* carried this shit up *stairs* alone." He shook his head, muttering seemingly to himself.

My heart rate increased tenfold. "I mean, y-yeah," I stuttered. "But it's not like it's that heavy. I've spent my life carrying sacks of potatoes around restaurants and boxes of oysters through Manhattan."

His gaze was piercing. "You weren't carrying *my child* then."

The tiny hairs on the back of my neck rose. There it was. Even more menace. But also something else. Something I kind of liked despite the situation.

Possession.

My woman. *My* child.

But there was still distance between us. A coldness that rivaled the arctic in temperature.

My hand went back to my stomach. "She's fine, I just had a checkup," I reassured him.

Or at least I was attempting to reassure him.

He went stock-still. "Sh-she?" he clasped the back of his neck.

"It's a girl?" His eyes were on my stomach again. Yet his gaze was softer, reverent. Full of despair.

I sucked in a breath of air that felt like broken glass. "Yeah, I'm, um, not into surprises, or intense gender reveals. I like having a plan."

Not that knowing the gender helped my plan any. All it did was veer me away from onesies with trucks and dinosaurs on them. Not that I was overly bothered with dressing an infant in anything frilly and pink. I'd gone with muted tones that had good quality fabric and reputable reviews. No frilly dresses or clothing without zippers. I suspected I was in for a challenge merely putting on a diaper.

"A girl," he said again in little more than a whisper.

The despair in his voice made my heart ache.

His shoulders slumped as he rubbed a hand over his jaw. I'd never seen Kane like this. Never seen him so cold, unfeeling. And I'd never seen him look so ... defeated.

It was killing me. Because I was the cause of it. I wanted to go to him, wanted to comfort him, but there was a barrier between us. Invisible, but miles high and just as wide. Impenetrable.

More silence hung around us.

I didn't have anything left in me to try to fill it. I just stood there, leaning against the doorway, staring at the spot above Kane's head because I couldn't bear to look at him.

"I'm staying," he declared, breaking the tense hush.

I sagged in relief at him breaking the uncomfortable silence.

I nodded even though I was kind of surprised. Though I shouldn't have been. It was getting late, the storm was raging outside, and he was on a motorcycle. There were some hotels around, though that was likely too public for him. Where did I expect him to go after finding me here, pregnant?

Run. Maybe I expected him to run. Leave. Even if everything I knew about him told me Kane would never do that to me. Except I'd constructed a new version of Kane in my mind, the one Brax had born that day at his office, one that I'd let him poison my other version of Kane with.

"The sofa, it pulls out," I said, trying to find my bearings. This house was too small for a guest room. The upstairs had a large master with a bathroom, the nursery, another bathroom and a small linen closet. Downstairs was the living area, kitchen, bathroom and sun room. I'd liked that it wasn't big. I wasn't expecting visitors beyond Kiera, who made sure to get a top-of-the-line pullout even though she also scouted the best hotel in town. "I'll get some sheets."

"I'm not stayin' on the fuckin' sofa."

I paused at his tone, staring back at him. "You're not?"

"Avery, I got out of prison eleven hours ago. I haven't slept on a mattress thicker than a thin pillow for months. I haven't slept with my woman for months. I'm pissed as fuck with you right now, but there's no way I'm spendin' another goddamn night in a bed without you."

My knees were quaking, my mouth went dry, and my heart beat rapidly. Not from fear or despair. No, now it held hope. He called me his woman again. He might've still been looking at me with that horrible emptiness, but he was calling me his woman. He wanted to sleep in bed with me. I would no longer toss around a cold bed without the presence of the man I'd yearned for.

Even though that was what I'd hoped for, dreamed of, I hastened to erect a barrier of my own. One to protect myself. "Don't I get any kind of say in this?" There should've been some kind of bite to my voice. I'd intended to add bite. But the words came out small and hesitant instead.

I didn't know that woman. The quiet, timid woman whose heart was hammering like a hummingbird.

"No," Kane said simply. "No, you fuckin' don't." He looked at the crib pieces on the floor. "There good takeout places around?" he asked, kneeling down on the floor picking up the discarded, brand-new toolbox I'd bought in preparation for putting together all of this furniture.

My palms became sweaty.

It had been one thing to have to walk past this mess of a nursery that served as evidence of my failure to thrive on my own and create a space for my child. *Failed.* I hadn't done that in a long fucking time.

Or maybe that's all I'd done since Brax tried to tear us apart. Failed Kane. Failed myself.

Now Kane was here. And he could see it. That I couldn't even put a crib together for our kid.

"Avery."

Sadness pummeled me at hearing my name. I looked up to find Kane studying me. His brows were furrowed slightly. His expression still wasn't warm, but it wasn't iceman-cold either. But he was calling me by my name, not something he'd done since he first started using 'Chef' as an endearment. The loss of it felt physical.

"What?" I asked weakly.

"Takeout," he repeated. I couldn't be sure, but I swore that his voice was softer. "Any good takeout places around here?"

"Takeout?" I squinted at him, trying to get my mind together. "Um, yeah, there are a few places."

When I'd moved here, I was fresh out of the first trimester, and my appetite had slowly been coming back. Then it came back with a vengeance. But although I'd been starving for amazing food, I was also really tired. Like really tired. A physical exhaustion I'd never experienced even in my sleep-deprived career. Cooking a simple meal sometimes felt like a herculean effort.

I'd gone on a mission to find good food in this small town.

And I'd been pleasantly surprised at the variety and quality of the restaurants available. It made sense; this place was a tourist desti-nation, and the ocean was right there. The fresh seafood was abun-dant. There was a mix of casual, seaside eateries and more upscale restaurants. I'd sampled each and every one, more than once, and found myself drawn to the Shaw Shack run by a father and son fisherman team that focused on simple flavors done right.

In my opinion, they were missing the in-between type of restaurant. For when people wanted something a little more upscale than lobster rolls on paper plates but didn't want to be intimidated by a wine list and a tasting menu.

That was neither here nor there.

Here was Kane. In my house. In my nursery. Asking about takeout. He was here, but he wasn't. Not the Kane I remembered anyway. Although I supposed I wasn't the Avery he remembered.

"Pick your favorite," Kane instructed. "Whatever you think is good I'll like. Order a lot."

My brain scrambled to catch up as he glimpsed at the instruction booklet for the crib for a handful of seconds before tossing it aside and getting to work.

"I can cook for you," I offered, watching the muscles in his forearms move fluidly.

My desire woke up, and my mouth went dry while watching the muscles move, his veins bulging. Those arms had held on to me while I writhed in pleasure. Those hands had explored every inch of me.

When he paused, glancing up once again, my heart stuttered. It was there. Just a sliver, a mere speck of what used to exist before but impossible to miss. The heat. The spark. The warmth.

My body bloomed underneath even the scantiest sign of it.

"I want you to cook for me," he murmured, his voice rough, hungry. "And you will. But not now. I want you to go get your phone, a book, whatever you need. Then you're gonna plant your ass there." He nodded to the glider in the corner, the one piece of furniture that had come assembled. "While I put the crib together."

My vision blurred.

I tried to calm my breathing.

"Chef."I blinked through unfamiliar tears. The endearment. One that I'd heard thousands of times over the years from many people, but it never sounded better than it did coming out of Kane's mouth.

"Phone. Book. Food." His voice was gentler that time. Much gentler.

I held on to the words, tasks. I was good at tasks. I nodded then made my way to the door.

"Chef."

I paused, turning.

Kane's gaze was no longer cold. No longer empty. It was so full I could barely stand under the weight of it. Slowly, very slowly and very purposefully, his eyes went up and down my body. I felt every place it landed. His eyes lingered for a long time over the swell of my stomach. When our eyes met again, I was shaking, and I could've sworn Kane's eyes were shimmering.

There were things on his face, many things. Things that planted more hope inside of me. That made me think we might not be over. That he might still want me.

I held my breath as he opened his mouth, expecting him to say something earth-shattering, to give affection like he had so readily before.

"No ground beef. In the takeout. I've been put off that stuff for life."

I swallowed my disappointment. But I nodded.

"Got it."

Then I turned and left the room.

It was only once I was downstairs, clutching my phone while ordering takeout that I sank to the floor and gave myself exactly five minutes for self-pity.

Sixteen

WE ATE WITHOUT SPEAKING.

Kane sat cross-legged on the floor, taking bites in between putting the crib together. I sat in the glider, book untouched. The food would've been too, if Kane hadn't looked up within five minutes of the food arriving.

He didn't look exactly in my eyes, just at the plate in my lap, the fork.

"Eat," he ordered, the single word puncturing the silence.

I could've added to it, torn away at the thick wedge between us with words of my own. Could've argued against such an order, informing him that I would eat when and if I wished.

Yet I didn't.

I picked up the fork and put the food in my mouth. I couldn't say what it tasted like. Heartache. Regret. Pain.

Kane watched me for a few more mouthfuls, and when he was satisfied that I was heeding his command, he resumed his project.

We didn't speak again until the crib was put together, the food was consumed, and nothing was fixed between us.

I got up from the chair, with my plate, intending on grabbing

Kane's in order to take them downstairs, to clean and get some much-needed respite from his presence. Even though a large part of me didn't want him out of my sight, another part, a weaker, more vulnerable part, couldn't stand sitting in that room feeling his disdain coating me like oil.

"Don't you fuckin' dare," he commanded in a clipped tone as I stood.

I froze at the break in the deafening silence, so brutal, so harsh.

"What?" I asked. I was so angry at myself for the meekness of my voice.

Where was the Avery who spoke with confidence, with power?

She had been left in the kitchen at Inferno, in cinders.

"No way are you taking these dishes," he continued, not looking up from the crib. He was fiddling with a detail that I couldn't see.

"It's late, go and get ready for bed," he said, still not looking up. "I'll finish this, take care of the dishes then meet you in bed."

My heart faltered then beat what seemed like a million times faster than before.

He'll meet me. In bed. In my bedroom.

Even though he'd shown nothing but disdain for me. Even though I could feel in my bones that he hated me.

I was frozen in place.

"You need anything?" he asked. "From downstairs? Water. Tea. More to eat. Vitamins?"

"Vitamins?" I parroted.

"Prenatal vitamins. You need to be taking them."

My hackles went up. "I am taking them."

He'd said a lot of painful, hurtful things tonight. Most of it I deserved. But the insinuation that I somehow wasn't taking care of my baby... that I couldn't take.

His chin tilted as he regarded me.

"Okay," he said after a beat. "Water? Saltines or whatever the fuck to have by your bed in case you get nauseous?"

The tenderness of the offers were in complete juxtaposition of his overall demeanor, yet I felt softened by them, nonetheless.

"I don't get nauseous anymore," I told him. "First trimester, yes. I could only stomach mashed potatoes, on a good day. Second trimester I was able to add in some other things. I occasionally have an off day here and there, but now it's just radiating heartburn, restless leg syndrome, insomnia and migraines," I joked.

Kane didn't smile, though I didn't entirely expect him to.

"That shit isn't normal." A muscle flexed in his jaw. "Suffering like that."

I laughed, surprising myself. "I'm no expert, but I think that yes, suffering is a normal part of pregnancy and a preparation for motherhood."

Kane studied me for a long moment, too long. Looking at me without rage for the first time since he arrived.

"Water, tea," he eventually stated. "Go get ready for bed."

I pursed my lips, part of me wanting to argue just to get back on steady ground, just to even out the power balance.

But I kept my mouth shut. I imprinted Kane standing in the middle of my nursery in my memory, just in case he disappeared, then I turned and went to get ready for bed.

KANE

There were many places I imagined I'd be the night I got out of prison.

None of them, fucking none would've been in a nursery in a small house in coastal Maine.

Avery's nursery.

Thunder boomed throughout the night.

I focused on my breathing, willing my heart to beat evenly.

I glanced at the open door. There was no lock. I wasn't trapped. The air was cool. No officers, no yelling inmates, no stench of body odor and metal. I didn't have to be on guard, ready, waiting to see if Knox's protection detail had expired.

Most importantly, Avery was in the next room. I could hear her getting ready for bed. I wasn't wondering where she was, if she'd moved on to another man, if she was safe. She was there. With me. Pregnant with my baby.

My fucking baby.

Lightning illuminated the room. The crib I'd put together. The chair that Avery had sat in, watching me. There were rolls of wallpaper in the corner. Clothes with tags still on them sitting on top of the dresser. Impossibly tiny clothes.

I'd insinuated that the baby might not have been mine.

She'd recoiled as if I'd hit her. I felt pain, agony shredding at my insides seeing her flinch like that. Seeing her shrink before me. She didn't battle me. She didn't keep her trademark calm. There was none of that. None of my Chef. She wouldn't meet my eyes, she spoke timidly, froze like a scared rabbit.

I wanted to hold her. Fuck, I wanted to gather her in my arms and forget it all.

Maybe that was the right thing to do.

I couldn't, though.

I was too fucking angry.

But I loved her too much to leave. Ever.

I would never leave her. Never leave my baby.

But I didn't know how to forgive her either.

AVERY

I was in bed. I'd rushed my normally militant nighttime routine. Since I'd moved here, I'd been given something I hadn't had in years: free time. Endless amounts of it. Enough to make me insane. Nowhere to go in the morning. Nothing to prepare. No menus to design. No food to buy.

Only sorrow to digest, only a baby to grow.

Hence the dog. Hence me becoming addicted to reality TV and detective novels.

And the routines. Morning routine. Nighttime routine.

My en suite was overflowing with all sorts of body and face products courtesy of Kiera, who was sent endless amounts of things in PR. In my prior life, I sometimes indulged in a skincare routine, but most of the time I did nothing more than wash off whatever makeup I'd remembered to apply, brush my teeth and maybe slather on moisturizer.

Now I exfoliated. Used serums. Oils.

All pregnancy safe, thanks to Kiera's research. I hadn't even realized there were things you couldn't use while pregnant.

After researching, I realized that pregnancy was more about what you 'could' have. And even those things were highly debated.

Though I should've put double the amount of time in to make myself look good, smell good, considering I was getting into bed with Kane, I was in fight-or-flight mode. All I managed to do was wash my face, brush my teeth and tie up my hair.

I didn't want to get caught midway through my routine by Kane. I felt self-conscious, uncomfortable. I didn't know how to move around him. Didn't know how to occupy the same space. And soon, he'd be in my bedroom.

Nightwear proved to be a problem. A big problem.

I didn't take many things with me when I left New York. Yes, I left in a panic, but even if I hadn't, I didn't form attachments to material things. I took as many clothes as I needed for the immediate future, keeping in mind my body was going to change, and I'd have to purchase more anyway. I brought basic toiletries and my chef's knives.

And Kane's shirts.

He didn't have a drawer in my apartment, but he'd had things there. He liked me wearing his shirts when I wasn't naked, so he left worn ones. And I kept every single one of them. I hadn't washed them. Slept in them every night until they only vaguely smelled of him. I thought that's all I had left of him, tees with fading scents and painful memories.

Now he was here, and I didn't want to be caught in one of his shirts. Didn't want to show my longing for him when I couldn't be sure he felt the same for me.

But I didn't have anything else, unless I wanted to wear sweats —which I now owned copious amounts of. The other option was underwear. I'd been naked around Kane many times, but the thought of sharing a bed with him in my underwear, especially while exposing this new body … I couldn't stomach that.

His shirt it was.

I'd dive into bed, yank the covers up and hope that he only wanted to share a bed because of practicality's sake, and he hadn't slept on a decent mattress in months.

The thought stabbed me.

In the midst of this, it was somehow easy to forget that Kane had been locked away. Sleeping in a cage. Controlled. In an environment that I couldn't imagine.

Though I'd just told Kane my nausea had subsided, my stomach lurched, and I barely made it to the toilet before I emptied my stomach.

I brushed my teeth a second time then climbed into bed just as I heard Kane ascending the stairs.

The covers were shoved up under my armpits. Aside from lightning sporadically brightening the room, the only lights were the ones filtering in from the hall and the one I'd left on in the bathroom so he didn't bang into anything. Usually, I read, with the television on because I couldn't stand the stifling silence in the house. But I couldn't have both my bedside lamp and the TV on—too much light.

I was just frozen in my spot in bed, far too wired to sleep, too eager to know what this dynamic looked like beyond him being mad at me. Or maybe that's all this ever would be.

His footfalls were heavy on my hardwood floor as he rounded the bed to place a mug and a glass of water on the cluttered bedside table.

I did not do clutter before. Before, I had a scant amount of possessions, and everything had its place. Since moving to Jupiter, I was constantly buying books, baby things, trying to fill up the house, trying to fill up my mind.

I blinked as Kane leaned forward and somehow found the switch on the lamp on the first go, light flooding through the space.

He was there, right there beside me, face close to mine. His expression was still hard, guarded, but it wasn't entirely hostile. He held my gaze for ten seconds—I counted—before his eyes went downward to where I was still clutching the covers.

His head tilted, eyes softening.

His fingers clasped mine, gently taking the covers from my death grip. I released because he wasn't yelling at me, wasn't staring at me like he hated me, and he was touching me.

The gentle brush of our fingers was the first time he'd touched me since that kiss in the courtroom. My entire body responded. My entire body awakened. Like it had been wilting, hibernating all this time, and it needed him to bloom.

The cool air in the room kissed my skin as he took the covers completely off, exposing me in his tee, my large belly making it so it barely covered my panties, let alone any part of my upper thighs.

I was rigid underneath his gaze, my bones seeming to fill with lead.

He still held his shoulders tight, his entire form tense, but something in him relaxed. Defrosted. The turn of his mouth no longer formed a grimace, the crease between his brows smoothed as he ran his eyes along his shirt, gluing on to my belly a moment before trailing down my legs.

My heart slammed against my rib cage as his hand moved to the hem of my shirt—his shirt—pausing to glance up at me as if he were asking for permission.

I barely moved my head in a nodding gesture, pulse thrashing in my ears.

Kane's fingers grasped the hem then pulled it up, exposing the tight skin of my stomach.

I was religious about lathering it in oil and moisturizer morning and night. I hadn't thought I was vain enough to worry about whether or not I got stretch marks, but it was a humbling and terrifying experience to watch my body change without my control, so I was holding on to the small amount of control I could clutch with bleeding fingertips.

Though technically, stretch marks were largely dependent on genetics, not products. Whether it was my genes or the oils, the skin was taut, smooth, my belly button a definite outie now.

Kane let out a hiss of breath as his palms covered the swell of my stomach. He was staring at it in shock, in wonder. He kept the fabric of the tee underneath my breasts, not exposing them.

This touch wasn't sexual, not exactly. Though there was an undertone there. But that might've just been me and my crazy hormones.

Kane tore his eyes from my stomach, peering back up to me. They were watering.

I had to sink my teeth into my lip so I didn't start sobbing at that expression.

He didn't say anything, not one word, he just slowly, purposefully moved his face down then laid a gentle kiss on the skin of my stomach.

Then he placed his cheek there, barely putting any weight against me.

"This is your dad," he whispered to my stomach in a tone I

didn't recognize. Soft. Full of tenderness. Love. "I know I haven't been around, but I promise, I'm not going anywhere again. Ever."

It was an oath.

Not just to the baby in my womb but to me. It didn't feel like forgiveness, though. Not a threat either, but maybe a challenge. I couldn't be sure. I was overwhelmed by the emotions of the evening. From the emotions of the past nine months. Since I'd met Kane, if I wanted to get technical. Then there was the third trimester exhaustion that was nothing like being in a kitchen for twelve hours.

It was worse.

Luckily, Kane didn't have anything more to say. He just stayed there with his cheek on my stomach.

Not knowing what came over me—beyond the overwhelming need to make sure he was real—I risked lifting my hand and running it through his hair. The stakes were high, as were the chances of rejection. The way he was touching me right now was not about me, not about my body; it was about the baby inside of me. Our baby inside of me.

Instead of stiffening at my touch, Kane relaxed entirely. I continued running my hands through the strands, letting my heart rate even, letting myself lapse into a tense version of peace.

I couldn't be sure how long we stayed like that, but I would've been content to do it forever. Kane eventually lifted his head, looking toward me. Still, there was a shuttering in his eyes.

"I'm gonna go take a shower, then I'll be back." He was rubbing my stomach absently. "Don't go to sleep."

The order was spoken in a rasp.

Though there were many things different, unrecognizable about Kane, that tone was not. It sent me hurtling back in time, to my apartment, my bedroom, my sofa, my kitchen counter, dive bar bathrooms.

My libido, a thing that I thought was long dead, awoke with a vengeance.

"Heard, Chef?" he asked.

I sucked in an unsteady breath at the title.

"Heard," I replied, voice quivering.

He lingered there for a moment, looking at his hand on my belly, then pushed off the bed, walking to the bathroom.

I lay there, trying to calm my galloping heart as I heard the shower run, as he moved about in the room right next to me. He was preparing to come into bed with me.

I tried to catalog the evening so far, tried to process his anger, his hurt, his detachment. Betrayal. That was the biggest one. Not from Brax. Sure, that might've hit him, but Kane was smart enough to keep Brax at arm's length.

Me, though... me, he'd let in. He'd given me all of him, and I'd let someone else take it away and reduce it to nothing.

Then he'd sat in a prison cell for months.

It took significant effort for me not to get up and run to the bathroom down the hall to throw up again. Somehow, I managed.

By the time the bathroom door opened and Kane turned off the light, I had sipped at my tea enough to calm myself down and was not in danger of throwing up again.

Kane didn't speak when he walked out, but from a glimpse I stole, I saw he was in nothing but his underwear. He'd been muscular before but leaner. In the months he'd been gone—in *prison*, I corrected—he had packed on weight in pure muscle. He looked more menacing now. More dangerous. My tattoo was still on his left pec. He hadn't covered it up. My brand. My name. Seeing it burned my throat.

When the bed depressed, I leaned over in order to turn off my lamp. No way could I continue to look at him, feel the ache from all the changes.

A hand at my hip stopped me, a palm moving over my stomach.

"No," he ordered. "I want to see you."

He resumed rubbing my stomach, slowly, unhurriedly, impossibly gentle.

I felt the kick at the same time he did, from someone who had been suspiciously quiet this evening. Or maybe I'd been too overwhelmed to notice the movements.

Kane froze as a little foot kicked against his palm. Hard.

And again.

Despite the situation and my overall emotional state, I smiled. It had taken me a while to get used to the movements inside of me. I hadn't liked them at first. It felt strange and foreign and a far too real reminder that my body was not my own and that I would be a mother soon. A single mother.

But as the baby grew, as I watched her kick in ultrasounds, I felt reassured by my constant company, for a responsibility that forced me to keep going.

Kane still hadn't spoken, I realized. It had been at least a minute of kicking.

"We've got a night owl on our hands," I said, suddenly desperate to fill the silence. "Which isn't surprising, considering our nocturnal habits."

It sounded immensely lame, but I had no idea what else to say. I'd never in a million years thought I'd be lying in bed with Kane again, let alone with his hand on my pregnant belly as our child kicked.

Still, Kane didn't speak.

I held my breath.

"I had a lot in my life," he whispered. "Or I thought I had a lot. But after feeling this, I now know I had *nothing*." He tenderly rubbed his hand against my stomach.

I bit my lip so I didn't cry. I couldn't respond. I just let us lay there quietly until the baby decided it was time to rest. After, Kane kept his hand there for at least another five minutes. I didn't dare move.

"Chef," he rasped, a chill zipping through me at his rough stubble on my ear. Making me shiver despite the scalding warmth of his body.

"Your doctor clear you?" he asked, palm flat on my stomach in a possessive gesture.

"Clear me?" I asked, breathing heavily. He hadn't touched me anywhere intimate yet … but with Kane, everything was intimate.

"For this."

His hand dipped down, slipping into my panties where I was soaking for him.

I gasped, but he didn't go inside. He lingered, hesitant.

I tried to find sense. Reason. He was asking if I was cleared. For this. For him.

For sex.

My body erupted with need, excitement.

"Yes," I whispered. "I'm clear for … this." My doctor had indeed said that I was having a healthy pregnancy without complications. Despite being classed as a 'geriatric' pregnancy, I didn't have any restrictions including sex.

Why she specifically mentioned sex when I was so obviously single was anyone's guess, but the information was welcome now.

"It won't hurt the baby?" His voice was rough, concern and desire mingling. He rubbed my clit lightly, and my entire body jerked, impossibly sensitive.

"No," I breathed, already panting heavily. "It definitely won't hurt the baby."

My need was all-encompassing. My body was alive again, taut and aching for release. For Kane.

His mouth went to my neck. "Gonna have to get creative with positions," he murmured, still rubbing.

I gyrated my hips, reflexively moving for him, already seconds away from orgasm. Kane had always gotten me there easily, but this was unheard of even for him. Then again, I hadn't orgasmed in months. That part of me had felt dead.

Clearly, it was not dead. No, I was alive in a way I hadn't thought would ever be possible again.

"Kane," I whimpered. That was all I was able to get out before I broke apart, under nothing but his deft fingers, lips at my neck, body behind mine, warm, safe, hard.

My orgasms with him had been intense, always earth-shattering. But whether it was from the long absence, the intense emotions between us or the sensitivity of my body from pregnancy, I'd never weathered my body's reaction to this extent. Nerve endings I didn't know I had exploded in pleasure.

I was still shuddering with aftershocks moments later. Kane's mouth was still at my neck as I tried to catch my breath.

"Now you're warmed up," he murmured, his hands returning to my panties.

Though I was still delirious from the orgasm, I was ready to move to help him take them off. I was desperate for it.

That orgasm had done nothing but taken the edge off. I needed more. Needed him.

Kane was obviously as desperate as I was, because instead of rolling my panties down my legs, he ripped them apart.

Though we'd been plenty desperate for each other in the past, he'd never done that.

"This okay, Chef?" He angled me so I was lying on my side, leg cocked up to accommodate him, his hard length perched against my opening.

His body was pressed into my back.

"Yes," I hissed, bucking back to try to get him inside.

Though I could feel his need, taste it, he stayed there.

His lips traced my ear. "If it gets to be too much, if it hurts, you tell me right away."

He was worried. About me. About hurting me.

"I will. Now, please, Kane." I backed up against him again.

"Like that, Chef," he let out a low growl. "Hearing you beg for my cock. I've got half a mind to make you do it a little longer, but I need you. Need to fuckin' drown in you."

And before I could respond, he thrust inside.

I let out a muffled cry of pleasure and relief as he filled me. The angle was perfect, my body so sensitive I could feel every inch of him.

Once he was fully inside, he didn't move.

"This okay?" he asked, voice strained.

"Yes," I groaned. "Move. Please."

At my plea, he began moving. Gently at first.

It was nice, impossibly so, but I didn't want gentle.

"Harder," I demanded.

"Chef—"

"Harder," I commanded. "You won't hurt me, I promise. I won't break."

I didn't say you couldn't break what was already broken. I didn't say he'd be putting pieces of me back together. That was far too introspective at that moment.

I'd anticipated him arguing the point further, but his control broke, thrusting faster, harder.

I could've burst into tears at the relief I got from it, my body coming apart at the seams. His hands cupped my breasts, letting out a low hiss once he discovered how much bigger they were.

I made a sound between a moan and muffled scream as he tweaked my nipple through his shirt.

He kept pounding into me, and that, in conjunction with his fingers at my nipple, was enough to send me over the edge again.

He let out a roar as I took his release from him.

I didn't remember much after that, not him pulling out of me. Because the release had taken it all from me. Everything. It had uncoiled things in me that had been wound tight for months. It was the cure to the sickness invading my body. My eyes were drooping, and I lapsed into unconsciousness while he was still inside me, but not before realizing that though he'd had sex with me, he hadn't kissed me.

That felt important, somehow.

Before I could process it, I was gone, lost to a dreamless slumber.

Seventeen

WHEN I WOKE in the morning, it was to my sheets, my bed, the room that had been mine for the past five months.

For a second, I was sure I'd dreamed it, all of it. Even though some of it was a nightmare. The past five months had been a nightmare. And then Kane turning up in the rain, during a storm, dripping wet with anger and blame emanating from him... That had been both a dream and a nightmare.

But the sheets smelled of him. My body ached in a delicious way from what he'd done to me last night. I heard signs of life downstairs, the opening and closing of the back door, dog nails on the hardwood floor.

I slumped down onto my bed.

Kane *was* here.

Though our bodies had joined last night, a closeness that I'd never had with anyone else, there was still distance between us. Kane had left the bed before I woke. I slept like the dead these days and hadn't even stirred. In our life before, he never left the bedroom without waking me. Yet another glaring and painful reminder of how things were different.

Steeling myself, I held on to the headboard in order to get out of bed. Now that I was larger, my center of balance was way off.

He'd claimed me back last night. Without question, he'd made me his all over again. Even without kissing me. That was purposeful, I thought, not giving me that.

Yet in the harsh light of day, things were different. I was his, but somehow, I wasn't.

I felt self-conscious. Awkward. I sorely regretted throwing on the tee he'd been wearing yesterday. I hadn't been able to help myself. It was soft and it smelled like him. It strained over my stomach, showing all of my leg and the boyshorts underwear I'd pulled on.

I'd forgone a robe because I was suddenly not icy-cold anymore, and I'd been anxious to run down to the kitchen. I was desperate to ensure that this wasn't a dream.

It hadn't been.

Kane was here. In my kitchen. The picture of masculine perfection.

He was dressed in running clothes and covered in sweat. He'd obviously brought in a bag of clothes at some point. My eyes traveled over the ridges in his abs, visible as his tee clung to his torso. I licked my lips at the memory of the feel of him, his sculpted abs, his weight, his warmth, the fullness of my body with him inside me.

But he wasn't here. Not entirely.

My step stuttered as his eyes fell on me. They did a slow sweep of my body, again lingering for a long time on my stomach.

Suddenly putting on his tee felt like a mistake. It was too presumptuous.

Yes, I was carrying his child, and yes, we'd had sex last night. But that didn't mean we were *together*.

He'd been in prison for five months. He said he came straight here. He hadn't been with a woman in almost half a year. It must've just been a physical thing; he'd needed a release. Nothing was fixed between us. It wasn't that simple.

"I, um, should probably get dressed." I started retreating from the kitchen.

"Don't you fuckin' dare," he growled.

I froze at his tone.

But inside of my body I didn't.

My insides responded. Viscerally.

The air between us was charged, Kane pinning me in place with his possessive stare.

I was barely breathing.

"You hungry?" he asked.

I licked my lips. "Starving."

Kane's body jolted. And although there was a lot of unfamiliarity between us right then, I knew that response. I knew he was feeling the same desire I was. It was the fire in his eyes, the way his shoulders tightened, his jaw clenched.

But in a split second, all of that was gone.

"There's nothing in the fridge." He nodded to the sub-zero appliance.

I rubbed my forehead, trying to focus. "Yeah, I um, haven't gone grocery shopping. I eat out a lot. There's a bakery that makes croissants that will change your life. They hide three behind the counter for me; they're popular, and they're kind of my thing for breakfast these days."

Fiona—one of the owners of the bakery—had begun doing that when I started to show, and it became clear the croissants were important to me the one morning I arrived and they were sold out, and I almost burst into tears. Those croissants were my one little slice of joy in my lonely, scary new life.

Pathetic but true.

The women at the bakery—Nora, Fiona and Tina—had all

been welcoming, had even offered multiple times to have me over for dinner as I was new in town and was obviously alone.

I'd politely refused every time, although part of me wanted to be part of the friendship—the family—they seemed to have. But a few things stopped me, those things being the two hulking, handsome husbands of the women who adored them. Adored them with a ferocity that was too hard to look at.

Reminding me too much of what I'd lost.

I'd put myself away, on my proverbial island, in this house, walking on the beach for hours with my dog, reading books, watching mindless television, trying to plan for a life I hadn't expected. One as a single mother.

Kane was staring at me. He had been staring at me for a long time, while I'd been lost in thought. Brackets framing his mouth and the crease between his eyes told me he was worried.

I wondered how much of the last five months I'd shown on my face.

"Let's go get you your croissant, then," he said, although I was sure that wasn't what he'd planned to say.

I nodded, not moving, still staring at him. Blanche ran up to me, puffing and tongue wagging, nuzzling her face into my hand. Kane had obviously taken her on the run with him.

"First, you walking her alone is no longer happening," Kane motioned to Blanche. "You want to walk, we'll do it together. You're not getting pulled by her in your condition."

I opened my mouth to argue, but he wasn't done.

"As much as I enjoy the sight, you're gonna have to change into something different to go to the bakery," Kane waved to my clothing. "I'll need a shower too, but you can go first if you need one."

He was offering practical solutions to get ready for the day. Except that wasn't Kane. He wasn't about practicality. If we were together and needed a shower, we did it together. He carried me there, my legs wrapped around his hips, his mouth on mine.

Sure, such a thing wouldn't be practical given my overall size. But the shower off my bedroom was plenty large enough for both of us. Though small, the entire cottage had been renovated by someone with sense. The kitchen was big, and the bathrooms were all big enough for walk-in showers, full tubs and double sinks. Not that I thought I'd need the double sinks.

And maybe I wouldn't, since it was possible that Kane would never want to do something as benign and intimate as brush his teeth next to me again.

"I'll go first," I said, trying to digest everything.

I turned quickly so he wouldn't see my eyes well up.

"Chef."

I stopped, taking a breath to clear my expression before I turned.

Kane was standing in the same position, his eyes locked on mine.

He lifted two of his fingers to his lips then tapped against them.

The silent command made me gasp, made hope warm in my stomach.

I traveled the distance between us. He didn't move, didn't meet me halfway. Maybe that meant something. Maybe that meant nothing.

I went up on my tiptoes to reach his lips, laying mine on his. Still he hadn't moved to take over the kiss. It was all me. Until our lips touched, our tongues crashed together, and the kiss was no longer the peck on the lips I'd expected.

By the time it was done, Kane's hand was on my ass, inside of the panties, his other hand behind my neck.

Our bodies couldn't be flush because of my protruding stomach pressing into his flat torso.

Kane looked down at my stomach, his eyes hungry and possessive. He let go of my ass, stepped back then knelt down to lay his lips gently on the swell.

"Good morning, Baby Girl Rhodes," he murmured in an incredibly tender, incredibly sweet voice, speaking without any of the reservation he was using with me.

Which was good. I didn't want Kane taking his resentment toward me out on our child.

As if responding to her father's voice, a foot kicked against Kane's hand.

His eyes widened in wonder, then he smiled. Smiled with his whole being. Without any of the shadows that had been shrouding his face. "I can't wait to meet you either," he whispered, laying his hands on me a moment longer before looking up at me.

His smile was gone.

My heart panged painfully.

"You wanna be quick about getting ready?" he asked. "Our baby's hungry."

Another heart pang.

Our baby. Protective. Claiming.

Because I couldn't speak, I just nodded then turned to go get ready.

My tears mixed with the spray of the shower. And I couldn't decide whether they were from happiness or heartbreak.

KANE

I could barely breathe. Barely fucking think. My mind had been in a fog since the second Avery had opened that door. I'd been prepared to be mad at her. Ready to rage at her for running from me. For fucking abandoning me.

Just like my mother had.

Yeah, it was shitty of me, projecting all of my issues onto her when I knew she wasn't my mother. But I'd also told her about my mother, about the wounds she'd opened up inside me. Ones I'd hid from everyone but her. And I'd been livid about the fresh cuts she'd created herself despite knowing what she knew.

But then I saw her.

Her face flushed, different, softer yet harder at the same time. More vulnerable. So much more vulnerable.

And her stomach.

My child.

My fucking daughter.

Growing inside her.

Had been growing inside her while I'd been in a cell these past months. And I hadn't known. I'd fucking missed it. Months of it. I'd missed watching her grow. I'd missed taking care of my woman. The doctors' appointments. I'd missed carrying fucking furniture up the stairs. Getting pulled on a beach by a seventy-pound dog.

The thought of Avery doing all that.

Pregnant.

I flexed my fingers so I didn't put my fist through a wall.

I left Avery sleeping. She'd looked exhausted, so I didn't want to wake her. She needed the sleep. I'd battled over waking her up to fuck her last night, knowing that she was tired, that she hadn't been sleeping well—you could see it on her face. But my worse nature, my baser needs had overridden whatever shred of good was left in me. So I'd fucked her again, until she'd moaned for me, came for me then drifted off to sleep with my cock still inside her.

Yeah, she was fucking exhausted.

She hadn't even twitched when I'd gotten out of bed and gotten dressed this morning.

"You found her," was my brother's greeting.

Avery was getting ready, though it took everything I had to let her walk out of that kitchen wearing my shirt without claiming her

She'd walked in, barefoot, still hazy with sleep—I'd never seen her sleepy, and damn, she was fucking *gorgeous* sleepy—wearing my tee, the fabric straining over her stomach. Her perfect, round stomach. Holding our baby.

Yeah, after she walked over to me, so uncertain, nervous, kissing me. After tasting her, I'd wanted to take her on the kitchen fucking counter. Claim her all over again. But there was no food in the house, and she'd barely eaten last night. I needed to feed her. Feed both of them.

The feel of that pressure against my hand, harder than I'd expected, much harder... In all honesty, it had freaked me the fuck out, feeling it at first. I'd worried for Avery, that it must've hurt her. But she hadn't seemed bothered. The opposite, actually. All of the tenseness leaving her face when she kicked last night, a lazy contentment washing over her. Love. It softened all of her hard edges. And I hadn't thought my woman could be any more stunning.

"Found her," I agreed.

Knox had been the one to track her down. He'd done it in less than five minutes. I was sure it was through less than legal means, but I didn't give a shit. My brother lived his life how he lived his life. If he was ever caught doing whatever shit it was he did, he would get a fuck of a lot longer than five months in prison.

He wouldn't get caught.

And he'd die rather than be incarcerated. I knew that. He'd been in contact the second I got out. I knew the reasons behind him not being there for the trial—his specialty was not manipulating the justice system. But he had managed to manipulate the prison hierarchy to make sure no one so much as looked at me the wrong way inside.

"Good," was all he said.

My brother was a man of few words and not a romantic by any means, but I knew he liked Chef.

"She's pregnant," I told him.

I heard his swift intake of breath. From a man who was not

easily shocked. He hadn't dug that deep, then, hadn't hacked into medical records. Hadn't thought he'd needed to, maybe.

"It's mine," I continued.

"Of course, it is."

Again, a small inkling of what Knox thought of my woman. He knew she wasn't about to jump into bed with someone else while I was locked up.

I remembered accusing her of it belonging to someone else. As much as I was mad at her, she didn't deserve that kind of bullshit.

I cracked my neck. "Brax told her I didn't want it. Her. Asshole told her I said to get rid of it."

Knox didn't reply right away, but I could hear him breathing.

"You want it to look like an accident?" he asked. His tone was casual, deceptively calm. But I knew him, could feel the undertone of rage.

Not just rage. Killing fury. We dealt with our childhoods in very different ways, but both avenues fed that desire to dance with death. Mine was just on motorcycles, snowboards and whatever else I could find.

Knox's way of dealing was through literal death. Although I'd never flat out asked him, I knew my brother had killed before. Regardless, I didn't consider him a murderer. The people whose lives he ended must've been the worst of them. Must've deserved it.

My brother had had it worse than me. He protected me from a lot of abuse that scarred not only his body but his very soul.

He'd kill Brax. He'd do it for me, and it would never tie back to either of us. He wouldn't lose sleep over it either.

Though I ached for the man responsible for the pain behind my woman's eyes to stop breathing, I needed to face him first. Feel his bones crush under my fists.

"I'll deal with it," I told Knox, hearing the shower turn off upstairs. "Just get him here."

Avery was naked upstairs. My dick stood at attention at that thought. Her sexy body, full with my child.

My fucking child.

I still hadn't quite processed it, even though I'd slept with my hand on her stomach all night, had felt our baby move underneath my palm even as Avery slept. I hadn't slept. Not a fucking wink. No way was I going to miss a second of feeling that. Hearing Avery breathe peacefully next to me. Smell her.

No fucking way.

And I was worried if I gave in to sleep, that I'd wake up on a thin, lumpy mattress in a damp cell.

It was the memories of that cell that had me wrenching myself away from Avery's warm body in order to run down the beach. Even in her bedroom, cozy and warm, even wrapped up in the scent of her, I felt as if I were suffocating, trapped. The run along the beach had helped—the salty air, the crisp breeze, the open sky and the burning of my lungs, my limbs getting rid of the excess energy.

The lanky dog running beside me had loved it too, stupid fucking tongue wagging all over the place.

The place, Jupiter, was nice. I had to admit that. I'd always liked small towns, loved the ocean. It had a quiet, peaceful feel to it, this place. Not overrun with tourists, not bought out by commercial conglomerates. And the house, the cottage, down a long rambling drive, surrounded by woods but opened up to the ocean off the back porch... So not what I expected of Avery but somehow perfect. Small, unique, warm. I could see her, at the stove, cooking our daughter breakfast.

"It's a girl," I told my brother. "I'm going to have a daughter."

My mouth went dry at the thought. I was going to have a little girl. And I couldn't be fucking happier.

Although I was going to be in trouble if she was half as beautiful as her mother. Which I knew she would be.

"I'll get you a shotgun for Christmas," Knox replied.

I barked out a laugh.

It was genuine. I hadn't laughed in ... how long? The night before I was hauled away in cuffs, probably.

"Seriously, happy for you, brother," Knox added.

I clutched the phone.

"We haven't had much real shit to celebrate in this life," he continued. "Certainly not family. Glad you've got it."

What went unsaid was that he'd never have that. That he wasn't capable of having that. Because of what happened to him. What he'd protected me from.

"You've got to come and meet her," I urged.

"Sure thing. I'll be there, shotgun in tow."

I managed a grin. This one hurt.

"Glad you're out," he said.

"Me too."

Then we hung up, because I knew my brother; that's all he could say. Knew that he was beating himself up plenty about my months in the pen.

I took a long breath after putting my phone down on the counter, staring out at the ocean. It was calmer today, the sky a pale blue, no clouds, no hint of the storm that had raged throughout the night.

This was the place Avery had chosen. Her escape? Her hiding place? Her sanctuary?

Whatever it was, I decided that Jupiter, Maine, would suit us just fine.

Eighteen

AVERY

I GOT READY QUICKLY, anxious to get out of the house. Despite the situation, I was actually starving. As a holdover from the first trimester, if I didn't eat within an hour or so of waking up, I was sick. The clock was ticking.

And there were the suffocating walls of the house with me and Kane in it. The anger from last night was still there, a living, fire-breathing thing that had not been resolved nor addressed yet.

Because I wanted to give Kane privacy, I went downstairs to let him get ready after throwing on a cotton dress. I had never been a dress person, but I'd become one out of ease. Dressing a bump in a warm spring, approaching summer, I needed simple and breathability.

My hair was much longer now. Before, I'd had a standing appointment in New York, getting a trim every six weeks. Obviously, I couldn't make that appointment anymore. And I didn't have the energy to sit in a salon chair with a stranger while making idle conversation. Especially since a pregnant woman was a magnet for people wanting to converse with a stranger. It felt like I was a carnival game. In line at the supermarket, the doctor's office, the gas station. Everyone wanted to know how far along I was, what the gender was, did I have a name. The questions were endless and infuriating.

At least the people of Jupiter, Maine, didn't seem to recognize me from the photos posted all over the media during Kane's trial. Granted, I looked different being very pregnant, my face rounder than it was with the extra weight, my hair longer. I wasn't unrecognizable, though. So people were either very polite, didn't know who I was or didn't care.

I didn't mind any of the above as long as I was left alone. And it seemed the media had yet to find me, which was a plus.

"You ready?"

I jumped from where I'd been standing at the window, watching the waves, contemplating.

Kane was in the arch separating the kitchen and living area.

His hair was still wet, curling around his neck. I marveled at the tattooed arms, stretching the sleeves of his black tee. They were larger, much larger than they had been before. They were crossed over a chest that was wider, broader. Even though the day was warm, he wore jeans, ripped at the knees, and Converse.

He seemed to be doing the same inspection of my outfit. Simple white cotton dress that should've gone below my knees but because of my stomach, it brushed mid-thigh, showing off legs that were now tanned from my endless strolling along the beach with Blanche.

Same with my face. I had freckles I'd never had before ... which made sense since I had spent most of my days inside a kitchen without windows, blasted with artificial light. Because of all the extra blood flowing through my veins, it seemed my now rounder cheeks were always flushed with color. And that made my green eyes look brighter.

"You look different," Kane said.

"Obviously," I replied, gesturing to my stomach.

He shook his head. "Not that. Even though I couldn't have known it until last night, you were born to walk around, heavy with my baby."

My breath hitched at the casual yet possessive statement. One I shouldn't have liked. I didn't believe women were 'born' to be anything but whatever they wanted to be. They certainly weren't born to be mothers. Unless they made that choice themselves.

But yet...

"It's ... something else," Kane rubbed his jaw, looking at me with an inquisitive gaze. He opened his mouth. Closed it. Shook his head. "Let's go," he stated instead of saying whatever it was he was going to say.

Nodding, I pursed my lips to not let my disappointment show.

"After you," he said when I stood there unmoving.

We'd gone from him uttering something profound, intimate, loving to bumbling about like strangers on a first date, unsure of how to act around each other.

I hated it.

Because we were worse than strangers, we were people who once knew each other intimately and now we were ... something else.

I held my breath, keeping a wide berth as I brushed past him in the archway to get to the hall that connected to the front door. Regardless, I was somehow engulfed in the smell of him mixed with my soap.

I swallowed down the burn of my arousal, since Kane seemed to be doing the same to his. Yes, he'd been hungry for me last night, and there'd been the kiss in the kitchen, but all of that was now packed away, locked down.

Outside, I inhaled the morning air, the dampness from the storm still hanging around, leaving humidity heavy in the air.

Before all of this, I wasn't someone who appreciated simple

things like spring mornings after storms. I wasn't someone who slowed down in order to notice things like that. Now I did reflexively, not by choice.

I'd felt like I was going insane my first few weeks here. Stuck in survival mode, I'd forced myself to meditate for ten minutes a day, even though I didn't believe it would do a thing for me. Being pregnant meant I couldn't self-medicate, so it was a last-ditch effort to slow my mind.

It hadn't worked at all at first. But slowly, it helped quiet everything.

Yet with Kane back, things were loud.

I stopped on the porch, staring at his sleek, black motorcycle next to the SUV I bought after researching what was best for fuel economy, accommodating things like a car seat and a stroller along with Maine winters.

"Keys."

Kane's voice pervaded the quiet morning.

When I looked at him, he had his palm out open toward me.

"Excuse me?"

"Keys," he repeated, tilting his head to my purse.

"We're not taking the bike?" I asked.

Before, we never went anywhere unless it was on the back of Kane's bike. Well, after his accident was a short exception, but he was back on before the doctors could approve.

Seeing it parked in my driveway sent a yearning through me. To be pressed against him, to feel the world speeding by.

"Are you fuckin' *kidding* me?"

The harshness of the words snapped me back to Kane, who had pushed his glasses to the top of his head to regard me, even more pointedly, before lowering his ridiculously wide eyes to my stomach.

"You're eight months pregnant. You think I'm puttin' you on the back of my bike, even courting the chance of somethin' happening to you or the baby?"

I looked down at my stomach, having forgotten momentarily that I was pregnant. I'd gone back to life with Kane before the arrest, before the baby, when there were no worries, no barriers between us.

"Aren't you supposedly the best rider in the world?" I joked, not intending on arguing the point, just desperate to sever the tension between us.

It didn't work.

"I *am* the best in the world," he growled. "But that doesn't mean I'm stupid enough to put my baby at risk. Keys."

The jovial man I knew was gone. An angry, bitter person standing in his place, palm outstretched.

I wordlessly gave them to him, striding to the car so he wouldn't see my watery eyes. Not once in my past life had anything brought me close to tears. Yet I was on the edge of a full-blown meltdown with Kane's presence mingling with the pregnancy hormones.

Part of me wanted to spar with him, to give him the coldness I was so well-known for. But bigger parts of me were exhausted, hurt, confused and desperate for Kane. And the guilt... It weighed too heavily on me to fight back.

Though I thought I moved quickly, Kane made it to the passenger door first, opening it for me.

I kept my eyes down.

"Chef."

Though I wanted to deny him any eye contact, feeling helpless, I looked up.

He was standing behind the door, hands resting on the top of it, gaze intent on me, glasses now down so I couldn't read the expression in his eyes.

His body was tense, jaw hard.

I watched his head rear back as he read whatever emotion I was failing to hide on my face. The stern frown on his lips, visible below his glasses, softened.

"Chef." His voice was inconceivably tender.

I ground down on my molars. All I wanted was this version of him, yet now that I'd been presented with it, I couldn't handle it.

"We've got to go," I snapped. "If I don't eat within an hour, it makes me sick."

Not a lie, but the coward's way out.

Kane nodded slowly and looked like he was going to say something, but I climbed in the car. The second he got in the driver's side, I leaned forward to turn the radio all the way up.

I was doing all I could to avoid conversation, to avoid him. Yet some small part of me wanted him to turn the radio off, to face me and talk.

But he didn't.

Not for the whole drive.

KANE

I hurt her.

It was plain to see. The naked pain on her face.

Fuck, it almost took me to my knees.

That wasn't Avery. She wore her strength like armor, an unbreakable expression on her face meant to tell the world that she couldn't be hurt.

Even with me in the beginning, she wore that mask. Except when I was inside her, when she was alone with me. It was a gift she gave me, that vulnerability, that openness.

It was a crime, the worst I'd committed, to betray that openness.

That's what was different about her. Not the sun-kissed skin I wanted to explore every inch of. Not the freckles on her face I found so fucking pretty it hurt. Not the stomach, round with my baby that pierced my fucking heart every time my eyes landed there. No, there was no more barrier. All of her defenses had been ... shredded.

She was defeated. Lost.

I hadn't seen it last night because I was wrapped up in my own fury. Fury that I thought she deserved. I knew now that not an ounce of blame laid on her doorstep, yet I'd brought it here.

And I couldn't take it back. Couldn't undo the hurt. Though I spent the short drive to 'town' racking my brain on how to.

Avery spoke only to give me curt directions to her bakery, turning the music up to almost ear-splitting volume once done.

She needed space. I decided to give it to her, though it went against all my instincts. I wanted to pull the car over, pull her onto my lap and kiss her until she looked like my Avery again. Until she melted for me.

I wanted to be inside her again, tell her how much I loved her. But that wouldn't work, and not just because she was logistically too large right now to fit between me and the steering wheel.

"I get sick if I don't eat within an hour of waking."

Something related to the pregnancy, obviously. Another small example of how she'd changed, how I needed to take care of her. Another marker of just how much I'd missed.

I didn't know what she craved, what made her sick, what hurt her. She'd mentioned heartburn and some other things, but I didn't learn that myself.

My hands clenched against the steering wheel thinking about how much I'd been robbed of.

While I was plotting Brax's death, I absently looked at the town we were driving through. I didn't see much beyond the darkness and lights as the storm was rolling in yesterday. Plus, I didn't have the capacity to appreciate the scenery as I was riding toward the woman I thought had abandoned me. I'd come for a confrontation, yeah. But also, because I had nowhere else to go. After being stripped bare to show all the things I couldn't escape while locked up, all I wanted was to go home. Even when I was furious with her, Avery was my home.

In the bright light of day, Jupiter, Maine, was fucking charming. There was no other word for it. Right on the ocean, houses dotted sparsely on the coastline, all small, quaint, well maintained. Main Street was lined with small, unique stores, not a Starbucks to be seen. Everything gleamed with fresh coats of paint, colorful flower boxes.

It was all so fucking wholesome.

Not at all where I thought I'd end up.

But my woman had bought a house here. My *pregnant* woman.

So this was where we'd be.

AVERY

I had managed to pull myself together by the time we parked the car. Kane had somehow got a spot right out front, unheard of even at that relatively early hour. It was almost summertime, which I'd learned was the peak time for tourists to visit. But even when I arrived in the late winter, locals still swarmed to the bakery, all wanting fresh pastries and coffee.

Therefore, parking out front was typically all but impossible.

Unless you were Kane 'The Devil' Rhodes, it seemed.

I almost jumped out of the car the second he put it in park, not wanting him to do the whole opening the door for me thing. Didn't want to give him a chance to touch me, to look at me in that tender way. I almost sprinted to the entrance. Unfortunately, I could only manage a brisk walk in my condition, and even that was no match for Kane's unhurried, long strides.

To my frustration, he made it to the entrance to the bakery first, opening the door for me. I didn't look up at him.

I was sending all the messages that I wanted space, yet Kane did not give it to me. His hand rested on my lower back and stayed there as we walked into the bakery and lined up. My stomach was in knots. And it was also growling for pastries as the scent of bread, sugar and cinnamon perfumed the air.

Every morning it smelled slightly different, since every morning Nora, the owner of the bakery, would bake something dependent on her mood or what she was craving at the time. Nora was warm, shy, pretty and friendly. She owned the bakery with her best friend Fiona, both of whom had tried to engage me in more than small talk, tried to befriend me and neither of them had seemed to give up, despite my not-so-subtle rebukes.

It was probably sensible to befriend people in what very well could be my new hometown, especially since both of them were mothers and likely knew more than I did—which was exactly zero —but I didn't have the strength. I couldn't answer questions about my life before here. Couldn't answer questions about my plans for after I had the baby.

Which was one of the many reasons I hadn't even told my mother or sister about the pregnancy. For the very first time in my life, I'd stuck my head far into the sand of denial, and just now, it was being wrenched out.

I was mulling over all of this as we waited in line, doing my best to ignore Kane and his hand on me. He was looking around, seemingly casual, at ease, just as he had been in the past. But I caught the slight downturn of his lips, the tightness of his shoulders. He was on guard, tense. Whether it was because he was waiting for someone to recognize him, because it was the first time he'd been out of prison and in a public place for months or even if it was because of me, I couldn't know.

"You the baby daddy?" was Fiona's first question when Kane and I made it to the counter.

Fiona's gaze was sharp, probing, wary and vaguely threatening. I'd never seen such an expression on the pretty Australian's face. She was always warm, genuine, greeting me with a friendly smile. She looked at her husband with a much sweeter smile, one that made me want to look away from all the intimacy in it. Then she gazed at her daughter, who was always in her husband's arms with utter adoration.

But I'd never seen the woman look even vaguely hostile.

Until now.

Now looking at Kane.

Clearly, she was not impressed with the muscles, the handsomeness. She wasn't even intimidated by the new aura of coldness and danger that blanketed him. Nope.

She didn't seem to look like she recognized him. And she hadn't let on that she'd read any articles on who I was either. I'd been so sure that the entire world was closing in on me that I forgot there were plenty of people just living their lives, too busy to get caught up in tabloid scandals.

Thank God. I needed anonymity.

Kane, on the other hand, seemed to be ... surprised at the blatant hostility without any room allowing for his fame. His face went blank, eyes a little wide before he recovered.

Kane's arm was tight around my waist.

"Yeah, I'm the baby daddy." Kane recovered quickly, meeting Fiona's stare with an easy smile.

She tilted her head, not anywhere near charmed by the megawatt smile. "And you've been *where* the past five months?"

My body stiffened, and I opened my mouth to cut in, if only to avoid the drama of the situation, and my stomach was actually rumbling.

"Babe," a low voice interrupted Fiona's interrogation.

I hadn't noticed Kip rounding the counter until he was grabbing his wife and laying a kiss on her.

I'd never seen Kip without a backward baseball cap on, sandy-blond hair escaping from it. He was in paint-stained clothing most of the time or a tee sporting the logo of the construction company he owned. He was ridiculously handsome, tanned and had crinkles at the edges of his eyes that reminded me of Kane.

Though the logical part of me felt happy to see two obviously good people in the kind of love I didn't think existed, it had been extremely hard to look at it. I'd averted my eyes and ignored the burn in my throat that had nothing to do with pregnancy heartburn.

Right then, with Kane at my side, it felt infinitely more uncomfortable. He was there. But he wasn't. We were in front of two people who seemed utterly in love without complication or pain, and it made our issues all the more heartbreaking.

Kane was watching the two people essentially making out in front of us.

It was important to note that Kip had their baby, June, strapped to him in a baby carrier, and she appeared to be sleeping.

He let his wife go, but not before gently tucking her blonde hair behind her ear in an exceedingly touching gesture that somehow felt more intimate and precious than the make-out session from moments ago.

Kip turned to acknowledge me with an easy smile. "Avery," he winked. "Looking absolutely beautiful. Glowing, in fact. You better take me up on building your crib and installing the car seat; I'm practically an expert now."

I wanted to smile, I really did, but it felt traitorous with the man at my side.

The man who Kip had just noticed, his smile freezing and his blue eyes going wide.

"Holy fuck, you're Kane Rhodes," Kip exclaimed, hands on the bottom of the baby in the carrier. He spoke loudly, almost yelled, yet the baby didn't so much as bat an eyelash.

"Dude, I'm a huge fan. *Huge*." He leaned over, presumably to shake Kane's hand, but Fiona grabbed on to her husband's wrist.

"Uh-uh," she tsked. "We are *not* huge fans. Not of men who

abandon their pregnant women for months at a time." Her tone was hostile yet coated with a protectiveness that made me feel warm.

It was all so strange. We weren't friends, I'd made sure of that. But there she was, nostrils flaring and seemingly ready to go to battle for me.

Kip's demeanor instantly changed, looking stricken. I didn't know the man well enough to decipher the subtleties of his expression, but he looked almost hurt.

He looked down at his sleeping daughter.

Turning to her husband, Fiona's expression changed too, softening. "Babe," she whispered soothingly. "Not the same."

The two shared a look that again felt intimate, special.

"You don't know that," Kip retorted. "Things are always much more complicated than they seem. And I think you'll find out that Kane has a pretty good excuse as to where he's been these past few months." He gave Kane an empathetic smile. "Glad to see you're out, bro. And *now* I know why you look so fuckin' familiar, Avery," he added, eyes on me. "I probably would've figured it out sooner, but little June here doesn't like to sleep unless she's right here." He peeked down at June again. "And my brain is eating itself these days." He winked at Fiona. "But it's worth it. So fucking worth it. Trust me, you won't die from lack of sleep. Not immediately anyway. You may see the effects when you're seventy or some shit, but we're living day to day here, baby."

He leaned over and kissed his wife on the neck. "And may I say, you look so fucking hot today. You'd think you got at least a full five hours." He looked at me and Kane. "Five hours is considered sleeping through the night in our house. Anyway, look how hot my wife is. Wouldn't she look even hotter pregnant like you, Avery?" His eyes rushed to Kane. "Not that I'm calling your woman hot, well, objectively, she is. But I can only have sexual feelings for one woman on this planet." He craned his head toward Fiona who was smiling and shaking her head.

"First of all, no more children. One and done," she playfully scolded Kip. "Second, stop talking so much about sleep. Avery doesn't need that bullshit. Better to be blissfully unaware of the horrors that await you." She smiled at me. "Kidding. Kind of." Fiona's sharp gaze returned to Kane. "And I am not distracted by all this to decide I like you just because my husband seems to go all douchebag bro over you. Actually, that'll be a strike against you, not that you need any more. So even though my husband seems to know, I'm going to ask you... Where have you been?"

Fiona was quite obviously a dog with a bone. Again, despite my complicated feelings toward Kane right then, I opened my mouth to speak up for him, to save him.

"I've been in prison," Kane answered before I could. There was no edge to his tone. No irritation at having to explain himself to a woman he didn't know. "I went there because I beat a man half to death. A man who laid hands on Avery, and that was after he tried to assault her. A man who did much worse in the past before I was there to protect her, but that's her story to tell." He grasped my hip tighter. "My piece of shit manager spouted poison in her ear that he will never finish paying for, not even when worms eat his corpse, so I didn't know about the baby until last night."

His hand drifted to my stomach, rubbing my bump protectively. My heart did cartwheels.

"And trust me, I've been wondering for the past thirteen or so hours whether I would go back and not punish the bastard who laid hands on my woman and stole these months from me or if I'd do it again to make absolutely sure he paid."

Kane spoke the words quietly but with confidence, with emotion that seemed to seep from every vowel. Violence, guilt, anger, and determination all mixed together.

Fiona stared at him, struck silent for a handful of seconds before she recovered. "Okay, I like you," she decided, as if she heard heartfelt declarations every day. She reached under the counter, getting my croissants. "Now, I'll get your coffee ready and whatever other sweet treats your badass heart desires. We'll have you over for dinner one night but be forewarned: we eat at five on account of the tiny terrorist." She pointed to the baby carrier. "I have a feeling you're gonna get on just fine with the badass dad crew." She jerked her head at her husband who for some reason was grinning wildly. "Rowan will like you."

"We'll bring you the coffee," she said, pushing the croissants across the counter. "You two obviously have a *lot* to talk about, and now I have to gossip with my husband about you." She winked, and I took the croissants and walked away, more out of shock than anything.

Kane was close behind me as I sat at the one table that was free, Kane pulling out the lush, bright-pink chair for me.

We sat in silence for a bit as I stared at my croissants.

"Pink bakery," Kane observed, looking around at the space that was indeed decorated in shades of pink.

Everything was simple, white-framed art on the pale-pink walls, elegant, charming and definitely girly.

"Not something I thought would be your style," he continued, eyes darting to me. There was a familiar, playful glint in them that made my mouth dry like it had in the beginning.

I pushed one of my croissants over to him.

"Taste this, and you'll understand why it's everyone's style."

He looked from me to the croissant. "I'm not eating that. It's yours, you need it."

I quirked a brow, looking down at the two remaining croissants in front of me. "I'll be just fine with two, and those will change your life."

Kane's playful glint was gone. "I like my life exactly how it is, don't need to change shit, and I'm not takin' food from my woman and baby."

My smile died on my lips. I didn't know how to cope with the new Kane who yo-yo'd back and forth so quickly.

So I didn't say anything, I just ate my croissants.

Fiona was right, we had a lot to talk about. But we didn't speak the entire time we were at the table.

THE ENERGY on the car ride home was heavy. Oppressive. Just like the air this morning after the storm.

I kept going over the speech he'd given Fiona, the way he'd offered so much information so freely. The more I thought about it, the more I felt like he wasn't saying all of that for Fiona's benefit or Kip's. It was for mine.

Kane drove unhurriedly back to my place without asking for directions. First, though, he took a lap of the town, glancing at the streets, shops and the ocean as we drove past. He was taking stock of his surroundings, I guessed.

"What are we doing here?" I asked when he stopped at the grocery store.

"Chef, you're growing our baby, your cupboards are bare," he informed me as he parked. "We're getting food."

I nodded, unable to argue. I'd walked through the aisles with him like a zombie. He didn't ask me what I wanted; he just piled the cart high with ingredients that I would've picked in another life. It seared my insides, the simple, domestic act. We'd done this in New

York while joking, touching. More than once, he pulled me into an abandoned aisle to make out with me. There was none of that.

We just shopped, he paid and didn't let me carry a single bag. I didn't bother arguing about that either.

I didn't ask him what he thought of Jupiter, Maine. Part of me didn't want to know. It was peaceful, idyllic, without the chaos and danger of the city. He wouldn't like it. It wouldn't offer him the things the city did.

I could no longer offer him the things I did when I was a hotshot chef in the city.

We arrived back at my place, though it was still strange thinking of it as that. My cottage wasn't colorful and cheery like the rest of the coastal houses. Its exterior was shades of black and gray, giving it an almost moody appearance—which I'd been drawn to. That, along with the charm of it, the renovated kitchen and bathrooms, its proximity to the sea and privacy. And it had passed all building inspections with flying colors, was well maintained and wouldn't need another roof for about ten years, barring any natural disasters.

Not that I imagined being here for ten years. Though theoretically, that was the goal, right? Somewhere quiet and safe to raise the child of the world's most famous daredevil.

My palms itched with thoughts of the future, at the thought of preschool, of playgroups, PTAs... motherly things that I'd never thought I'd be part of.

I stewed on that as my sandals crunched over the gravel of my driveway, transitioning to the stone pavers that led up to my front door.

Kane followed me, arms laden with bags, not saying anything as I unlocked the door and walked into the living room. Blanche barked in greeting, running up to me. I petted her dutifully, grateful for something to do because I had no plans when I walked in.

While Kane unloaded the groceries, I spent as much time as I could petting Blanche. Unfortunately, she was a traitor and trotted over to Kane for ear scratches once he was done.

I turned around to look at him, watching as he lavished Blanche with attention. I was standing awkwardly in the middle of the room, unable to think of what to do with myself. Running sounded good. Yes, running out of the room was the best choice. Or apologizing. Had I done that? Apologized for abandoning him. Yes, that was what I needed to do. Although this thing between us was complicated, I knew in my heart that I'd failed him by believing Brax so easily.

I opened my mouth to say sorry, but Kane spoke first.

"This place," he twirled his finger around the room. "You got a mortgage?"

I nodded, taken aback by the question.

He clicked his tongue, eyes stormy. "Okay, we'll call who we need to call. I'll take care of the mortgage. I'll get another car in the morning too. Yours paid off?"

I nodded again, trying to process exactly what he was saying. I had a more-than-healthy savings since I was paid well for my job and hadn't had overhead beyond my rent-controlled apartment.

I bought the car in cash because that's what I'd deemed most sensible. The house was another story. The cottage might've been small and quaint, but it was still an oceanside property on two acres of land. Jupiter was becoming a desirable area. Therefore, the price tag on the seaside cottage was more than modest.

Even for me, it was too much. I might've been a well-known chef cooking food for billionaires, but I was far from one myself. I hadn't capitalized on my position by selling my name for cookware or recipe books.

Maybe I should've. Because now I was unemployed, with a mortgage and a baby to take care of … forever. Yes, my savings would keep us afloat for a time, but not forever.

Babies were expensive. As I'd discovered while trying to buy all the things I 'needed' before her arrival.

Except there was Kane, speaking about things like 'taking care of the mortgage,' insinuating he'd be 'taking care' of us.

When twenty-four hours ago, I'd thought he was in prison and didn't want me.

"Good," he said to himself. "Your insurance cover the baby visits? Hospital? And please tell me it'll be at a fuckin' hospital."

"What's wrong with a home birth?" My back went straight, suddenly defensive at him coming in here and 'taking care' of everything. "Plenty of women do it. Millions, actually, for thousands of years."

Kane's eyes thinned to slits. "Yeah, I'm sure it's great for plenty of women. And if it's somethin' you want, then I'll hire a doctor, buy out all the hospital equipment they use in labor and delivery and make it happen here."

He wasn't joking.

Not even a little.

Although I was tempted to continue baiting him with the home birth thing and stress that my labor experience was just that … *mine*, I didn't have the energy.

"I have a hospital organized," I said sharply. "It's close, has a top-tier neonatal unit, my OBGYN will be there, and I've already toured the facility, finding it more than adequate."

Kane looked vaguely less tense at the mention of the hospital, though his posture was still rigid, brows still furrowed, arms folded across his chest.

"Your OB, I'll need to meet them." Pacing, I could practically see the wheels turning in his head. "You need to make an appointment, get the ultrasound thingy. I want to see her." His eyes grazed my stomach, filling with a warmth he hadn't looked at me with since his arrival.

It was touching and devastating at the same time.

I fought against the urge to chew on my lip as I battled with emotions that slammed through me with the force of a hurricane. I struggled to grasp on to something familiar, safe.

"You're making a lot of demands." I rested my hands on the swell of my stomach.

Kane kept his gaze there. "Yeah, baby, I am," he carded a hand through his hair. "And expect a fuck of a lot more. I've missed out on a lot, and I intend on making up for as much as I can. I intend on taking care of you." His eyes went from my stomach upward. "Both of you."

Wasn't that everything I'd wanted? Everything I'd dreamed of when I first saw those two pink lines?

Maybe.

But a lot had changed since then.

And yes, maybe Kane wasn't the man I'd thought he was, but he had left me. Even if the logical part of me knew it wasn't by choice, I still felt that abandonment, that need to guard my heart.

"But you'll have a parole officer," I said, being cruel. "I'm assuming you're not supposed to be out of state."

His lips pressed into a harsh line as he exhaled loudly. "No parole officer, Avery. Victoria has been working overtime getting dirt on both the judge and the D.A. who prosecuted me. She found plenty of shit to get me out, and she's working on a whole lot more, but all I care about is I'm out."

A shadow crossed his face, and yet again, I was overcome by the reality of what Kane had endured the past months.

Caged. He'd been caged like an animal. Possibly treated worse than an animal.

Bile crept up my throat.

Struggling to maintain my composure, I held his stare. "You're going to stay. Here." I wasn't sure if I was making a statement or asking him a question. "Don't you have events, interviews or whatever you need to do?"

Kane closed his eyes for a moment, pinching the bridge of his nose. "You think there's anywhere else I'm gonna be but here? With you? Then you really must not know me, Avery."

There he was again with my name. It felt like a weapon, hurled at me in place of the soft term of endearment.

"I know you." I took a seat at the breakfast nook, my swollen feet needing a break. "Or I thought I did. But I didn't know any of this was going to happen. Especially not this." I pointed to my stomach. "I'd never planned on falling in love, certainly never intended on having a family. There's too much to lose. But then you..." I drew in a deep breath. "We were a whirlwind. Too good to be true. And when it happened, when Brax told me what he told me, I thought there it was, the other shoe dropping."

"And you gave up. And ran," Kane said flatly.

I rubbed my eyes, struggling between guilt, shame and defensiveness. Did I deserve all of his contempt? Maybe.

"I guess I thought you didn't want me—us," I corrected, touching my stomach.

Kane's eyes softened at the corners slightly, but his posture remained rigid, his jaw hard. "I have wanted you from the moment I saw you. You've been mine since I laid eyes on you, and you will be mine long after I become dust." His intense gaze zeroed in on my belly. The fluttering I felt there was not just in my mind but from the limbs of a child who somehow felt her father's gaze.

"Both of you," he whispered roughly.

My vision wavered at his words, and I fought against the tears that threatened to fall. Kane was staring at me in a way that made me ache for him, that gave the impression he was going to cross the void between us.

A vibration broke the moment.

Kane startled, pulling his phone out of his pocket then glancing at it.

He sighed, tapping buttons.

"I've got to go," he grumbled.

He looked at Blanche, who was sitting by his ankles, waiting patiently for his attention.

"You look after your momma," he ordered her, as if the dog could understand such commands.

Then he walked to me, moving quickly so I didn't have time to brace myself. He grabbed the back of my neck and plastered our mouths together.

The kiss was hard, passionate and claiming.

And over too soon.

He didn't linger near my mouth. No, he bent downward, hands on my bump. "You stay safe and warm in there, baby girl. Your daddy will be back soon." Warmth spread through my limbs at how incredibly sweet he sounded, whispering to her.

He glanced up at me. "I won't be long. I'm coming back. I'll *always* come back, in case that wasn't clear." He kissed me again, closemouthed and firm.

Then he walked out.

KANE

Leaving Avery for even a moment caused panic to swim deep inside of my gut. I'd been separated from her for months. Which in it of itself had been fucking torture. And that's when I'd thought she was waiting for me.

But knowing that she'd been growing our baby, that I'd missed that, that I would never get that time back, that made me desperate to have her with me at all times. I was afraid to fucking sleep because I didn't want to miss a moment with her. I thought of the pressure of little limbs against my palms. I didn't want to miss a moment with *them*.

But some things needed to be done.

Knox had moved quickly. He was efficient as fuck in business, but when it was personal, he was almost superhuman.

"This isn't going to take long," I told the man in front of me. "You've already taken enough from me."

I leered at Brax. He had a black eye and a bloody lip. We were on a deserted road in the woods outside of Jupiter.

Brax was standing. Barely.

"I told you not to lay a hand on him," I said to my brother.

Knox shrugged. "He slipped and fell. Clumsy motherfucker."

I almost smiled. I wasn't quite capable of smiling yet, especially with this fuck in front of me.

"Kane." All bravado was gone from Brax's voice. He was sniveling and weak now.

"My brother offered to kill you for me," I said conversationally, walking around him.

Brax had already been pale, but his eyes widened, and his skin sallowed even further. His beady eyes darted side to side as he contemplated running. There was nowhere to run to; we were far off any main roads, any houses. Knox chose this location, and Knox had done his research, controlling every single variable.

Brax wasn't a dumb fuck; therefore, he knew running was futile. And though I'd never shared anything about Knox with him, he was also smart enough to recognize a predator when he saw one.

"I didn't take him up on it because I didn't want your life to be on anyone's conscience."

I didn't look at my brother. I knew he would've been shooting me an expression that I'd be able to read without words. My brother didn't believe he had a conscience. A soul. He thought he'd sold both a long time ago.

I thought differently. But I'd given up on convincing him of that.

"In addition to that, you're not worth the effort it would take to dig your grave," I added.

"Have to agree to disagree with you on that one, brother," Knox stated in a flat tone. His expression was blank, soulless. Even though I knew my brother was much more than the sum of his parts, much more than what the underworld and our past had turned him into, that look sent shivers down my spine.

I didn't let that show, though, focusing my gaze on Brax, my fists clenched as the devil on my shoulder urged me to change my decision, let Knox take care of him once and for all.

But I was going to have a daughter. I didn't want to end a life. Not even Brax's. I didn't want that. I wanted to show my brother there were other ways to deal with things than violence and death.

"You stole from me," I told Brax quietly. "Somethin' more precious than anything I could ever own. You stole time from me, you stole moments I'll never fuckin' get back. I'm going to take *everything* from you."

I clenched and unclenched my fists. The dragon inside of me was clawing to get out, but I muzzled it.

"Everything," I repeated. "I've made calls to ensure you won't work for anyone in our industry ever again. You've been blocked from all clubs, all parties, all those fuckin' lists you were desperate to get on."

I looked at my brother. "And I've had some help to ensure that all of your bank accounts are no longer bursting with money you've hoarded or embezzled. There's enough there, to survive on." I looked him up and down, sneering at his $1,000 loafers. "If you know how to survive without caviar and fuckin' champagne."

I shook my head. "I know how superficial you are, how fuckin' shallow. I know all you care about is status and money. And with all that being gone, that'll be worse than death. I sentence you to a life where you mean nothing to no one, and you've got no way of hiding what a piece of shit you are." I paused, my eyes scanning his face. "On second thought…"

My fist plowed through his nose, savoring the satisfying crunch of it breaking. I reveled in the pain my knuckles felt from the contact with bone.

Brax fell onto the dirt, out cold.

"Thought you were taking the high road, no violence and all that," Knox commented.

I shrugged. "What can I say? The low road feels good sometimes."

Knox's head bobbed up and down in a slow nod. "Yeah, it does."

My brother's voice sounded haunted, underneath that steel, emotionless tone he'd perfected. They were tattooed in there, those ghosts, those demons. Because of the road he'd taken. And fuck if I felt helpless to see it, my brother getting further and further away from me.

We walked toward our respective vehicles, leaving Brax unconscious in the dirt. Knox was going to drop him somewhere far away from Jupiter, inform him of what might happen to his balls if he thought about selling my location to the press.

"How's Avery?" Knox asked.

I massaged my hand. The ache was dull, satisfying. I thought about the woman waiting at that cottage for me, with a dog, a fucking dog she'd said she'd never get, a dog that the most authoritative woman I'd ever met couldn't control.

I thought of the ocean, that kitchen, the warmth of that house that already felt like a home.

"She's good," I replied. "She's fuckin' gorgeous pregnant."

"Don't doubt it," Knox replied as we reached my bike. "You got a due date?"

I flexed my knuckles. "Don't have all those details, yet. Things have been a bit ... messy."

"I can imagine," he said, his normally impassive tone showing a hint of amusement. "You find that out, send me the details. The number you've got for me is clean now. If it isn't, you'll hear from me."

He paused, looking at my face—really looking. Despite him being my brother, I felt a prickling at my spine under his gaze. I could recognize a predator too.

"How you handling it, being out?" he asked, tone as soft as was possible for a man like Knox.

I gritted my teeth. He was worrying about me. Yet again. He'd seen the state of me after I got out of prison the first time around. It wasn't pretty.

"I'm handling it," I told him.

It wasn't a lie. Yeah, I wasn't sleeping. Yeah, when a room got even a little balmy, my blood pressure skyrocketed. Yeah, I was stripped raw from feeling like that helpless fucking kid again. But it was all still fresh. I'd get over it. I had to get over it. I had people to take care of.

"It's a lot," he pushed. "Shit that goes with being in. And out. And with you being a dad—"

"I'm handling it," I cut him off, not ready to open that can of worms.

Knox nodded, respecting the boundary.

"Thank you." I didn't miss his flinch when I clapped him on the shoulder. Knox wasn't good with human contact if it wasn't violent. "For making sure I didn't get shanked or anything in there."

I watched as Knox gritted his teeth, causing a muscle in his cheek to tick. "Well, someone had to. You're too fucking pretty for your own good."

I shook my head and laughed. "Seriously, brother. Know you probably had to call in some markers."

"Worth it," Knox replied. "That's the reason I collect markers after all."

I knew that he was shutting down the conversation. It was

getting too close to specifics related to his life in the underworld. One he was diligent about protecting me from.

Not for the first time, I grieved for the life my brother might've had, the relationship we might've had.

"You sure you're good, taking care of that asshole?" I motioned back to where Brax was lying in the mud.

"Oh, yes. Consider it my baby shower present," Knox's eyes gleamed. "Now get back to your woman."

I was already aching to. It had been less than an hour, and anxiety was building in the back of my spine. What if something happened? What if she'd fallen? Gone into labor early?

I picked up my helmet, ready to get back.

"Gladly will, once I get the promise you'll come meet your niece when she's born."

Knox stilled. Me requesting a promise was as good as an oath to him. Knox didn't make promises he couldn't keep. And though he'd been there for me in many ways throughout the years, vanilla, family shit like meeting babies was outside of his wheelhouse.

I saw him consider my request, waited, half expecting a refusal. I wouldn't be mad. Knox did his best, gave me what he was capable of. I took it because he was my brother, and I loved him.

"I'll be there," he said finally. "You call me, I'll be there."

I smiled at him.

"I'll call you the second she enters the world," I said, climbing on my bike.

"You may not need to," he quirked a brow. "She might cause an earthquake or hurricane or some shit. I've got a feeling she's going to be powerful."

I turned on my bike. "Oh, I know she's gonna be powerful."

AVERY

I didn't know what to do in Kane's absence.

Which, of course, was insane since I'd been without him for months and about thirty-five years before that. And yet...

When he left, I'd stood in the middle of the living room, Blanche sitting contentedly at my feet as I stared into space, listening to the rumble of Kane's motorcycle and then the silence once it drove off.

To be fair, I hadn't exactly been a productive human since I arrived in Jupiter. Yes, I'd done the research to get a reliable car, I'd negotiated the best closing deal on the house, got a sensible mortgage, homeowner's insurance, all of those things.

Yet once I'd gotten all the relevant things with the house sorted, once Kiera had furnished it and left, I was alone.

Not entirely. I was never really alone with the baby growing in my stomach. But I had free time. Oodles of it.

Which I spent adopting a dog, aimlessly walking the beach, reading baby books, researching baby products and watching reality TV.

And wallowing. Yes, plenty of that.

None of those things seemed to be prudent any longer.

I couldn't really wallow or long for someone who was no longer gone. Yet Kane *was* gone. Part of him, at least. The part that smiled easily, called me Chef with warmth and fire, who always had a cheeky glint in his eyes.

Yes, I was still longing for him. And there was the chance he'd never come back.

On that thought, I forced myself to take action.

I went to the kitchen and opened the fridge, looking at the bursting interior—Kane had gone a little crazy.

And then I did something for the first time in months. I cooked.

* * *

I didn't hear the roar of the motorcycle. Nor the opening of the door or the thump of his boots against the hardwood.

Blanche did, though, jumping up from where she was pressed against my leg where I was standing at the stove, barking to say hello to Kane.

"Quiet," he commanded in an authoritative tone.

Blanche obeyed.

I saw him ruffling her coat out of the corner of my eye. "Can't have you barking at anything and everything when we've got a baby in the house," he muttered to Blanche.

My stirring faltered at the mention of 'baby in the house,' but I kept going.

Yes, I was aware that I was pregnant, buying baby things and had even seen her on various ultrasounds, but it was becoming extremely daunting—terrifying—knowing that there would be a baby in this house, reliant on me to keep her alive in less than a month.

"You're cooking."

"Risotto," I replied as I glanced up. "With a basil pesto. The few plants I haven't killed." I nodded to the lush basil. "And focaccia. Charred chicken for protein. Nothing fancy."

Kane regarded me. "It smells fuckin' fancy. Truthfully, it smells like the best thing I've smelled in my life."

I pursed my lips. He wasn't being cold. He was almost being ... friendly.

"Don't speak too soon." I returned my focus to the risotto, pouring some cream into it, knowing it was done before I even tasted it. I sprinkled fresh grated parmesan on top before taking it off the heat and seasoning it one last time.

"My taste buds have changed since being pregnant." I worked on autopilot, spooning the risotto on the two prepared plates, drizzling on the pesto then placing the chicken and more parmesan on top. "So this could very well be horrible. You are under no obligation to eat it."

"My woman cooked risotto for me when all I've had is instant noodles and ground beef that may have come from a cow at some point," Kane said, right beside me.

I didn't jump but almost did. I'd been so consumed by plating I hadn't noticed him move across the kitchen.

He was close. Not touching me, but our bodies were a hairsbreadth apart, his scent mixing with the basil, the cream, the sharp cheese.

And there it was again.

My woman.

"Need me to do anything?"

I glanced up at him, giving him a pointed look. "You know better than to ask that. Sit. I'll bring it over." I waved to the small breakfast nook that looked out over the ocean. There was also a larger dining table, but I liked looking at the ocean.

"No," Kane said.

Hands on my hips, I gave him a patented Avery Hart, head chef glare. "What did you just say?"

He didn't so much as blanch. "You heard me, Chef. Finish what you need to finish, then you go sit down, and I'll bring everything over."

"Kane," I sighed in exasperation. "I'm pregnant, not terminal. I can carry plates."

"I know." He dipped a finger in the pesto, his pink tongue darting out to lick it off. "But you just cooked a whole ass meal, on your feet for at least an hour when you haven't done that in months. Your center of gravity is off. You could make it over there with plates, but I don't want you to." He jounced his eyebrows "And this smells like it promises to be the best meal I've had in months, and I don't feel like eating it off the floor because my pregnant woman got clumsy."

"I'm not clumsy." I narrowed my eyes, though my insides danced at his warm, teasing tone.

The corner of his mouth turned up. "I'm not chancing it. Finish plating, Chef."

I glared at him then went back to work wiping and garnishing the plate. "Getting ordered around in my own kitchen," I muttered, forcing back the smile wanting to curl my lips at him calling me Chef again.

"I won't make a habit of it."

"You better not." I looked at the plates. Not exactly Michelin star, but I already knew it was good. Great, really.

"Okay, go sit your ass down."

I tilted my head up to gawk at him. "I thought you weren't making a habit of ordering me around."

"I lied." I caught the twinkle in Kane's eyes before he leaned down to kiss me on my nose, cradling my stomach lightly. "You're too cute when you're pissed. Now go, I'm hungry."

I swallowed my smile and heeded his order, feeling lightheaded. It had nothing to do with being on my feet.

* * *

"Well, that was the best thing I've eaten in my fuckin' life," Kane declared, leaning back from his clean plate.

Mine was clean too.

It was pretty good.

It felt nice to cook again. To feel hungry again. To enjoy food, my one passion.

"I bet the baby fuckin' loved that," Kane continued, looking downward. "Is she doing somersaults in glee right now?"

My previously relaxed energy disappeared.

Dread invaded my bones.

"I haven't felt her move," I whispered, horrified.

Kane reached over, his hand settling on my stomach. "What do you mean?" he asked, rubbing again.

My blood pressure boomed in my ears. "I mean, I haven't felt her move in … since you left, since you said goodbye. Hours ago."

Hours.

"I was distracted," I whispered, guilt thickening my words. "With you, the mortgage stuff, the 'taking care of us stuff,' the apology you're owed. Then the cooking, and I got … swept away. How could I not notice she hadn't moved?"

The room began to spin.

"Chef." Kane's hands rose to either side of my neck, his eyes on mine.

"Breathe," he commanded.

I struggled to obey.

"Again," he murmured, rubbing behind my ears with his thumbs.

I mimicked the way he drew in a long breath before pushing it out, the spinning of the room slowing then finally coming to a stop.

"Okay," he said calmly. "She moved this morning, that's good. You said she's a nocturnal baby. How often does she normally move during the day?"

I focused on him, forced myself to think analytically though tears burned the back of my eyes. "A lot. I mean, she is nocturnal, but she usually gives me a few jabs throughout the day to remind me she holds dominion over my bladder."

I rubbed at my stomach, carefully prodding as I had done in the past to get a responding kick.

I held my breath.

Nothing.

Heat began slithering up my neck as I began panicking again.

"What can we do to get her to move?" Kane asked me pragmatically.

"Um, something cold. Ice cold. Sugary."

Kane didn't wait for more details, rushing to the fridge, getting a can of soda, dispensing ice into a glass then filling it.

My hand was shaking when he handed it to me, clattering against my front tooth when I brought it up to my mouth.

I gulped down the entire glass without tasting it. In the past, when I'd been concerned about lack of movement, it had taken minutes for something sugary and cold to wake her up.

We waited, Kane trying to talk to me and me muttering things back, trying to distract us while we waited, hoped.

Nothing.

The world swayed again. I looked at him, vision blurry. "Kane," I whispered, my voice drenched in fear.

His own expression remained even, calm, unworried. He took the glass from my hand, not having realized I was still clutching it.

"Okay, Chef. I'm thinking we call your doctor on the way to this hospital you've been telling me about," he said placidly. "Then I'll get the tour I want, and maybe I'll get to see our girl without waiting for an appointment."

Not waiting for my response, he helped me off the stool. His movements were unhurried as he snatched my purse from the counter.

"Is there anything else you need?" he asked, still holding on to me.

I shook my head, unable to think straight. My hand was still on my belly, rubbing, waiting for those telltale kicks. Nothing but quiet, stillness.

I could've vomited all over the floor. But that would've delayed the trip. Hospital. We needed to get to the hospital. The quicker the better.

My trademark cool had well and truly gone. I barely remembered Kane walking us through the house and getting me in the car.

He rifled through my purse then handed me the phone. "Can you find me the number for your OBGYN?" he asked me softly.

I squinted at the screen, my fingers shaking as I scrolled. "I can't talk to her," I shook my head, realizing just how close I was to a breakdown.

This was it. The other shoe dropping. Not Kane abandoning me and my baby but being reunited with him, tasting a future with them, then it being stolen.

Bad things happened every day. People died. I'd experienced that with my father. A brain aneurysm. Quick, unexpected. Unavoidable.

Fathers died.

Babies died.

I was going to experience that. I was sure of it.

My vision tunneled.

"That's fine, Chef," Kane took the phone from my hands before he leaned in to kiss my cheek and buckle my seat belt. "I'll talk to her, you just give our girl a stern talking to about getting sleepy in the womb. Tell her to save it for after she's born."

I smiled weakly as he closed the door then jogged around the car. He started it, phone pressed to his ear as he reversed.

I stared blankly at the woods passing us by, clutching my stomach. I heard snatches of conversation as Kane spoke to someone at my doctor's office.

"This is Avery Hart's fiancé." At the time, that title didn't so much as register. "I'm the father, yes. Avery hasn't felt movements all day. Not since about ten thirty this morning." A pause. "Yeah, we've done that. I'm taking her to the hospital now, to check." A pause. "Okay, great. Thank you."

He put the phone down.

"What did she say?" I looked at him, searching for signs of alarm.

There were none. His jaw was slack, one hand on the steering wheel, and now that the phone was down, the other settled on top of my bump.

Still no movement.

My lungs pinched.

"She said the baby is probably fine, but it's a good precaution to just go check." He spoke in a relaxed voice, eyes fixed on the road. "If there are any worries, she'll be there, but again, she doesn't expect there to be. This kind of thing happens all the time."

I massaged my temples. That didn't pacify me. Doctors were supposed to reassure worried patients. But she couldn't know the baby was fine. Not like I knew it wasn't.

I didn't speak the rest of the drive, I couldn't. All I could focus on was the horrible stillness inside of me.

* * *

There was already a nurse waiting for me as we walked up to the Labor and Delivery department of the hospital. She was smiling, warm, unhurried in her movements. I was doing all I could not to vomit all over her.

Kane helped me put on the gown they supplied because I struggled with my clothes, my hands shaking. He too didn't rush through anything, his forehead was free of creases, no signs of worry in his eyes. He helped me onto the bed, the nurse returning as soon as I got there.

"Now, let's wake up that baby," she said with optimism in her voice.

Kane stood beside the bed, holding my hand as she strapped large bands around my stomach and attached them to a machine.

I was staring into space, wondering how I was going to cope

with loss in front of Kane and this cheerful nurse. What would happen next? Would I have to give birth to a baby who would never take a breath?

I could barely remember how to breathe as the nurse asked questions, Kane answering them all for me.

She fiddled with dials, and as soon as she had everything calibrated, a definite and loud thump sounded.

My hand flew up to cover my mouth.

Kane stiffened.

The nurse laughed. "That always wakes them up."

I gasped as another loud thump sounded against the background of a steady patter.

Kane's head darted to the nurse. "That's her heartbeat?" he asked in a husky voice.

She nodded. "It sure is. And those loud thumps? That's her dancing in there."

He rubbed his jaw, eyes wide in amazement.

"She's okay?" I asked the nurse, feeling another kick. My mind was spinning. I'd already started grieving her, and yet there she was, kicking. I wanted to burst into tears.

"We'll monitor you for another half hour or so," the nurse told me as she typed on her tablet. "But her heart rate looks great, and her having an immediate response to the machines is reassuring."

That wasn't enough for me, I wanted to say. I needed to see her. I needed to see her moving on the ultrasound. But I stayed quiet, somehow unable to advocate for myself when it used to be one of my biggest strengths.

"We'll need an ultrasound," Kane spoke from beside me, his voice no longer as carefree as it had been.

The nurse glanced up. "If there's cause for concern, certainly, we'd do one. But this is a low-risk pregnancy, and everything looks great, so there's no need."

"There is a need. For me. For her." Kane nodded to me. His voice made it clear that this was not up for debate.

The nurse looked between us, obviously contemplating. Then she nodded. "I understand. It's not policy, but I'll pull some strings, talk to your doctor." She looked at my chart. "I know her; she'll be fine with authorizing it."

"Thank you," I whispered.

I was talking to Kane more than her, but she nodded then left.

Kane kissed my head. There was a steady beat in the background, punctuated by a thump here and there when she decided to kick.

"She's dramatic, it seems," I said dryly, somewhat embarrassed at how quickly I was ready to spiral and also somewhat shell-shocked at how close it had all come to falling apart. It felt so fragile. This life.

Kane's eyes were glued to the monitor. "Wonder who she gets that from," he muttered.

I rolled my eyes. "I'm not the one who jumps over things for a living."

He rubbed my stomach. "She's gonna give me a run for my money. I can already tell, Chef."

Our banter seemed comfortable, almost familiar.

I looked at him, took in his profile, his gaze still centered on the fluctuating numbers reporting her heartbeat.

I opened my mouth to say something, but the nurse came back in.

"We'll get you to the ultrasound room now," she said.

And the moment was gone.

It was time to see our daughter.

* * *

"She's perfect," the ultrasound tech said.

I didn't know if it was because they were just kind, if they knew who Kane was or had sensed my hysteria.

It didn't matter. We were staring at our daughter. I wasn't at this visit alone, wasn't staring at a black and white image feeling utterly numb.

Kane's hand was in mine, and his mouth was open in slack-jawed wonder. Tears stained his cheeks, and he didn't even try to hide them.

As she tended to do when the ultrasound wand was near her, the baby kicked and jumped.

"Holy *fuck*!" Kane yelled, obviously not feeling pressured to speak in soft whispers because of the atmosphere like I had.

He squeezed my hand. "Do you see that, Chef?" He was still speaking way too loudly. "She's going to be an athlete."

I shook my head, smiling apologetically at my doctor, but she was grinning too.

"She's an active one, that's for sure," she agreed as she squinted at the screen, making a series of clicks. "She's measuring about a week ahead, weight looks to be six pounds eight ounces already."

"Six pounds!" Kane shouted again. "Jesus, how is she going to fit, getting out of there?" He looked in my general crotch area.

My cheeks flamed even though I'd been wondering the same thing.

"Nature is a wonderful thing, Mr. Rhodes," my doctor said with a good-natured smile. "I'm glad you got to see your daughter."

Kane's shit-eating grin disappeared, his expression suddenly serious. Reverent. He brought my fingers to his lips.

"Me too, Doc," he murmured. "Best moment of my life right here."

I fought tears of my own.

"Just wait until you hold her in your arms," my doctor said.

"I'll never be putting her down," he vowed.

* * *

"Thank you for being so calm," I said to Kane as we drove home.

He was holding the steering wheel with the ultrasound photo clutched against his hand, as if he were afraid to let it go.

"Calm?" he repeated, looking from the road to me. "I wasn't calm, Chef. I was two seconds away from a goddamn heart attack. I've never been more afraid in my goddamn life."

I gaped at him. "But you were so composed."

"Yeah," he scoffed. "Because you needed me to be composed. You needed a lighthouse in the storm."

My mouth dropped open. A lighthouse in the storm. That's exactly what Kane was for me. Even though I knew he was still mad at me. Even though nothing was resolved. He'd seen me unraveling, and he hadn't hesitated to hold me together.

I didn't know what to do, what to say, so I just burst into tears.

And I couldn't stop.

Kane looked at me, horrified and shocked. He'd never seen me cry. I'd never cried. Not like this. I was bawling. Full body sobs, shaking, hiccupping, coughing, all of it.

"Jesus Christ, Chef," Kane muttered as he pulled off to the shoulder.

"I d-didn't realize h-how much I wanted her until today," I swatted at the tears racing down my cheeks. "I have been so caught up in being h-heartbroken, in pining f-for you, in pretending I wasn't pining for you, making s-spreadsheets, I d-distanced myself ff-rom her." I rubbed my stomach and she kicked in response, making me cry harder.

"Chef, breathe," Kane commanded, putting the car in park before unbuckling his seat belt and all but leaping out of the car.

My breath came in short pants, and I let out a snort that, thankfully, Kane didn't hear. My door wrenched open and Kane reached over, unbuckled my seat belt then moved me to a sitting position so he could rest his hands on my thighs.

"Chef," he repeated, more quietly this time.

"I didn't think I wanted to be a mom," I whispered. "But it w-wasn't an option to get rid of it because we made her. Even after I thought y-you didn't want her."

Kane's tender gaze made me want to hide my face in shame.

"I never wanted this." I pointed to my stomach. "I didn't think I was maternal. And then she didn't move. Then I thought she'd died inside me, and it felt like my life was over. Now it's real. She's our baby. You're here. And we could lose her."

My vision spun at all the things that could happen between now and her birth. Between now and the day I died. Illnesses, accidents, murderers, space junk hurtling from the sky.

"Chef, we're not going to lose her." Kane gripped my neck.

I swiped my eyes with my forearm, meeting his gaze. "You can't know that."

"I fuckin' can," he snarled. "I will go to hell and back. I will make deals with shamans, witches, demons, angels. I will raze this world to ensure that we do not lose her. That, I will vow. Nothing will happen to either of my girls. Never."

He was saying the words, but it felt like he was etching them into stone. Into blood.

Logically, I knew that Kane couldn't practice what he promised. I was a woman of science. I didn't believe in the supernatural.

But I believed in Kane.

"But you h-hate me," I hiccupped.

The hand at my neck tightened. "Avery Hart," he growled. "Open your fucking eyes."

I hadn't realized I'd squeezed them shut. Opening them, Kane's gaze was boring into me.

"I do not hate you," Kane rasped. He leaned forward to lay his lips on mine. "I was mad at you. I'm emotionally fucked-up with a shitty past. I felt abandoned. I lashed out. Because I love you. Because *you* are my lighthouse in a fuckin' storm, and without you, I was nothin' but rubble against rocks." He rested his forehead on mine. "I do not hate you." He ran his thumbs beneath my eyes. "You are mine. We have shit to work out, but it's nothing compared to this." He rested his hand on my stomach.

Baby Girl did somersaults underneath his palm.

He let out a laugh that sounded like it was mixed with a sob.

"This, the three of us, is my world," he whispered.

I couldn't stop crying. It was like a dam had broken, and I couldn't plug it up.

"I'm sorry," I sniffled. "I'm sorry I abandoned you. That I was so easy for Brax to fool. That I insulted what we had by giving up so easily. That's my own past. I know it. And you were locked up. Alone..." I let out a wretched sob at the thought of it.

"Okay, Chef, we're gonna pause the apologies." Kane sprinkled my moist cheeks with kisses. "You don't need to be getting worked up over this. We're gonna get you home. We're gonna shower, put you in my tee, then we're gonna go to bed. You can cry if you want, that's fine. But we're gonna save the heartfelt conversations for later. We've got plenty of time for that."

I tried to force my breathing to even. It felt like there was a beast inside of me, a hormonal, heartbroken beast. One I'd been repressing for years, and she had a lot of tears.

"You good to head out, Chef?" Kane asked me.

I sucked in a breath, trying to grasp on to the ice queen Avery Hart. I couldn't find her.

"I'll be fine," I lied.

Kane stared at me for a few seconds, his eyes flitting around my face. Eventually, he leaned forward to kiss me delicately. Then he kissed my belly. Then he rearranged me so I was facing forward in the car and buckled my belt.

Though I wasn't sobbing uncontrollably, I couldn't stop crying during the short ride home.

Without a word, Kane got out of the car, plucked me up from my seat then carried me inside.

"Kane," I hissed through my tears. "That's so dramatic. I can walk. I'm too heavy."

"You can walk," he agreed, unlocking the door. "And you're not too heavy. I want to carry you, so I'm going to."

And he did. All the way up the stairs. Then he peeled off my clothes and got us both into the shower. Still, I didn't stop crying. Not when we got out and he dried me off, peppering my body with kisses. Not when he used the oil all over my body, gingerly massaging out the kinks. Not even when we curled up in bed together, where I was warm and safe.

I didn't realize I had that much sorrow in my body.

It was off-putting.

Not to Kane, though.

He just held on.

Twenty

I SLEPT HARD THAT NIGHT, riding an adrenaline crash, I guessed. Yesterday had utterly exhausted me.

Kane had held me all night long. I had foggy recollections of jolting awake, his hands rubbing my stomach, my back, his voice in my ear. "You're safe, Chef. Baby girl is moving."

A large kick confirmed that, the relief of her movement coupled with Kane's warmth easing me back to sleep.

Kane had gotten up at some point because I woke in bed alone. My head was pounding, mouth dry, and I felt as if I'd been hit by a train.

I glanced to the bedside table where a large glass of water was sitting. I wrenched myself up to down it. Then I waited for my stomach to settle. I'd been so thirsty; I'd forgotten about the way my stomach lurched if I drank water on an empty stomach. A holdover from the first trimester still going strong.

I blinked at the time on my phone.

It was after eleven.

I'd slept almost twelve hours.

Never in my life had I slept in till almost noon, not even in my teenage years.

"Good morning to you too," I murmured to the soccer player in my stomach, obviously making up for the sleepy day yesterday.

I quickly made my way to the bathroom, since that kick jabbed right in my full bladder. Once that was done, I splashed water on my face, squinting at my reflection. I expected to look like a fright after hours upon hours of crying, but aside from the redness around my eyes, I looked fine. Good actually. My face had color and my eyes were bright, a more vibrant green than they'd been in months. My messy hair looked shiny.

It wasn't superficial, though; it was like a weight had been lifted off me. I didn't understand when Kiera had told me a good cry was almost better than a facial for the skin and a $700 an hour therapist for the soul.

I got it now.

But it might not have been the cry. It was more than likely the man I could hear downstairs.

I froze as I heard the voice of someone else.

Voices.

I frowned, quickly brushing my teeth and throwing sweats on.

I probably should've put on something else, but it was my house, and I still felt half asleep. And panicked. What if it were Victoria? Here to say there had been a mistake, and they were locking Kane up again? My fear was a physical thing, clawing at my chest.

The journey down the stairs took longer and longer these days, and I winced at the pain in my hips as I descended.

Voices.

I definitely heard voices.

It wouldn't be Kiera. She was in Bora Bora on some influencer trip. She was scheduled to come on my due date.

There was no one else who could've been in my house at eleven in the morning without an invitation.

When I walked into the kitchen, I blinked to make sure I was seeing straight. The woman in the kitchen was in her early 60s, her long hair fully gray and braided loosely. She wore jeans and a white T-shirt, a thick belt accentuating her hourglass figure. Her skin was lined from laughter, tanned from years tending to her garden. She looked ten years younger than she actually was.

A soft jangling sounded in the air when she moved her hands, coming from the many bracelets she always wore. A walking wind chime.

"Mom?" I rubbed sleep from my eyes. "What are you doing here?"

It was still a possibility that I was dreaming. That made more sense than my mother's presence.

"What am I *doing* here?" she asked, her tone bordering on shrill. Or maybe any tone would seem shrill when I was shaking off sleep, battling the pain in my hips and trying to dislodge a baby's leg from my ribs.

She put down the coffee that Kane had apparently made for her since he was standing in front of the coffee machine with a mug of his own.

I shot a scowl in his direction, making plans for his demise for not only letting my mother in but for making her a coffee and letting me walk down to her in the kitchen unaware.

Instead of responding to my scowl with a look of his own, he put his mug on the counter, strode over to me, grabbed me by the face and kissed me gently, his other hand rubbing my stomach. "Good morning, baby," he murmured against my lips. His eyes darted down to my stomach. "Good morning, baby," he repeated, still rubbing.

All thoughts of Kane's demise flew away, and my body went all soft and melty.

My chest warmed at Kane's ruggedly-handsome face, his easy smile and the soft way he spoke.

Yesterday had changed something. He'd changed. He'd come back to me. Mostly. I saw the remaining shadows in his gaze, he held himself just a little tenser than before, but he resembled himself more. He was changed, I reminded myself. Forever changed. We both were.

"Good morning," I whispered as he tucked hair behind my ear.

"Should we run down to see if hell has frozen over?" my mother's voice filtered through my haze.

I looked to her, trying to step away from Kane, but he merely tucked me into his body. I didn't fight it because it felt nice, warm.

My mother was looking between us, blinking rapidly against what looked like tears.

"Because my daughter, the career-oriented woman, force of nature, informed me at age seven that she would never fall in love or have children." She waved her hand violently, causing her bracelets to clash together. "You've never broken your word, not even at seven. Until now." She focused on Kane. "I already know I'm going to love you, Son, but you're going to have to get your hands off my daughter so I can do the thing she hates... Hug her."

Kane chuckled easily and kissed me before obeying my mother.

I stayed locked in place, mostly out of shock, but also because something foundational inside me broke, seeing my mother. She visited New York sparingly, and I went to New Hampshire for holidays. Or pretended I was going. Often, a 'work emergency' came up. When it didn't, I was there for the holiday, spent the night and was gone in the morning.

My mother was always affectionate during those short visits; that was her way. I endured it because I didn't want to be outright hostile. She was my mother, I loved her. I buried that under thick layers of indifference, denial and trauma.

But for whatever reason, the pregnancy hormones, the breakdown yesterday, Kane's presence, without the armor of the career I'd had for over a decade... I was no longer hiding from my mother. I didn't stiffen when she rushed over and pulled me into her arms.

I relaxed into her embrace, inhaling the perfume she'd been wearing since before I could remember. Roses and sunshine.

She hugged me tight, and just as I was about to cry again—as if I had any tears left in my body—she let me go to inspect me. Her hands cradled my stomach.

She was crying.

My mother was not shy about tears.

"You're beautiful," she declared. "Hello, my first granddaughter," she addressed my stomach.

My sister had two insane boys. They were my only experience with children, so I'd been relieved to learn I was having a girl for that reason alone.

My mother cupped my face. "You're glowing, my darling." Her eyes twinkled.

I let my mother hold me like that, and I held her stare, not averting my eyes away from any kind of connection.

Again, I felt a shift. And I didn't shy away from her.

She smiled, pinching my cheek.

"I'm making you both breakfast," she announced, letting me go.

Then she turned and went to the kitchen, leaving me standing there feeling thirteen all over again.

I stared from her to Kane, greeting Blanche as she ran in panting and eager for a head scratch.

"That dog is *precious*," my mother cooed. "Good for the baby's gut microbiome too, having a pet in the house."

I didn't bother to ask how she knew that, instead asking, "How did you know I was here?"

Mom pointed her wooden spoon at Kane. "I called yesterday. He answered, you were asleep. And he volunteered the information that he was the father of my grandchild and that you'd moved from

New York to a charming small town in Maine. Obviously, I jumped in the car the second I heard that. And here I am."

My head snapped up to Kane. "You told my mother about this, us, and didn't think to tell *me*?"

"Yep," he replied as if what he'd done was no big deal. "You consider yourself an island, Chef. But you've left it. The island. Both Manhattan and that place you isolated yourself on." He ran circles over my stomach with his hand. "You need your family now. Whether you realize it or not."

"I like him," my mother interrupted before I could yell at Kane some more. Or cry.

"Of course, you do, mother," I sighed. "He's immensely likable."

She grinned. "You say that like it's a bad thing."

"It is when I'm trying to be angry with him."

Kane squeezed me, lips still curled in that familiar smile.

"Well, you keep trying, and then sit your butt down there." Mom still had the wooden spoon, using it to point to the breakfast bar. "Kane informed me you have a ritual of getting pastries from the local bakery every morning, and I'm not one to get in the way of a ritual or of supporting a local business, but I'm going to add a little to the breakfast."

She turned to plate eggs along with toast, sausages and a bowl of fruit on the side. "Choline, protein, antioxidants," she chimed as she carried the plate to the kitchen island while Kane walked us both there.

"I can walk," I snapped at him, still mad about the entire situation.

"I know." He lifted me onto the barstool then kissed my neck. "This is just way more fun."

I struggled to keep my frown in place. Especially since my stomach growled at the large plate in front of me, croissants added by my mother after she set them down.

"Coffee!" she half shouted, turning to the machine and banging at it loudly.

I winced, thinking about the expensive machine.

"One cup." She pointed at me again, this time with the portafilter.

"I can make it," I offered, trying to get up to save my machine more than anything.

"Nope!" my mother sang. "You are going to let me take care of you even if I have to get your handsome man to tie you down in order to do so." She waggled her brows. "Unless he's already done that."

I squeezed my eyes shut. "And it only took five minutes for you to make a sexual innuendo."

My mother had not always been so sexually open. It was only in my adult years that comments like this came out. When I was younger, entering into womanhood, the topic was always taboo, awkward. My mother tried to talk about it with me, but she seemed as embarrassed as I was. And factoring in the distance between us after my father's death, the subject of sexuality and my relationship to it was stunted at best.

I'm not sure when the pendulum swung. Maybe when she started to get into more of her 'spiritual' side. Maybe it was meeting my stepfather, who was miles different from my biological father. Maybe it was Maisie coming of age, a full six years behind me and her treating sexuality as she did everything else, as if it were no big deal. She spoke about it with whomever she felt like.

Whatever the catalyst, my mother was overcorrecting with me. Too much.

I focused on my eggs.

"I won't have to tie her down," Kane answered for me. "Chef will let us take care of her. But I will take the suggestion about restraints; they're always fun."

I scowled up at Kane who was already flashing a mischievous

grin in my direction, the asshole. No doubt he'd caught how uncomfortable I was and wanted to push the envelope further.

Kane, quite obviously, had no hang-ups in the sexual department.

I kept my attention on my eggs as Mom moved around the kitchen, getting cleaned up and Kane settled beside me on the barstool, a plate of eggs in front of him too.

"I know it won't measure up to whatever fancy thing you can whip up," Mom said, for the first time sounding a little unsure of herself. "But it'll fill your belly."

All my complicated feelings toward my mother melted away, and I looked up at her. "This is great, Mom, seriously. I don't cook like this. Simple. Hearty. Just what she and I need."

The softness in which I spoke to my mother was unfamiliar. I'd made it my business to create a barrier between us, to speak to her in the cool way I did to those in my kitchen.

My barriers were down now, and I didn't have the energy to put them back up.

My mother's returning beaming smile made me feel warm inside in a way I hadn't let myself feel since my father had died.

Maisie is here too," she informed me. "She's just getting settled at the inn."

"*Maisie* is here?" I practically yelled.

"Naturally, she's here." Mom continued wiping the counter. "She's your sister, and you're about to have your first baby."

She spoke as though that explained everything.

"People have babies all the time," I returned. "I'm not special, nor do I require either of you to drop everything in order to ... what?"

"*Help*," my mother said softly. "In order to help. It would be a great gift, if you, Avery Hart, would let us do that."

I had been all worked up, ready to argue the point with my mother further. I had good examples in my head as to why they shouldn't stay. Maisie's two children, my mother's nice but not very self-sufficient husband, her volunteer work, the price of tea in China —anything to get them back home and in the compartment I'd neatly stored them in.

But my mother's simple, heartfelt request stopped me short.

I felt Kane's gaze beside me. I didn't look at him.

"Fine." I returned my attention to my eggs. "But we're not doing showers, parties, moon ceremonies, any of that. It's a birth. A child. Very exciting, but I don't want any fanfare."

"God forbid fanfare," my mother replied, a lightness in her tone.

I scowled up at her.

She held her hands up in surrender. "Eat your eggs. I'm done."

She turned to resume cleaning the counter, and after a beat, I resumed eating my eggs.

Kane's hand made its way to my thigh, then he squeezed. Tightly. I didn't look in his direction, but I reached my other hand down and covered it with my own as I finished my breakfast.

* * *

My mother was a whirlwind, as she tended to be. She was not one to remain idle. Even on my rare visits home for the holidays, she was always cooking, baking, cleaning, organizing things for donation, decorating.

It was good for me since there were few moments for her to sit across from me and talk, for her to get to know me. Not that she didn't try; I just didn't give her many openings.

Something about this visit told me it would be different. There were too many opportunities for openings now. I wasn't on a time crunch, there were no Christmas cookies to bake, nothing to decorate, no restaurant emergencies to conjure.

But there was a whole lot of baby stuff that needed organizing.

And you were supposed to wash the clothes before you put them on the child, I'd discovered. So she spent the morning doing that, after she cleaned up my meal.

Something that I hadn't realized I'd missed, my mother's cooking. It was the one connection I had with her that wasn't marred by the trauma of my childhood. She made everything from scratch—bread, biscuits, any baked goods. Our house always smelled of rosemary or cinnamon or apple pie.

I didn't understand the importance of that scent memory until now. Until it filled my house.

I glanced to Kane, to where he was on the phone.

Our home, I supposed.

He handed me papers I needed to sign about the mortgage while Mom was in the laundry room. "To authorize me paying it off," he explained.

I glared up from the pages. Yes, he'd mentioned this, and I knew it wasn't a passing comment; he'd really intended on paying off my house. I had planned on setting him straight on that, but we'd been busy.

"You don't need to pay off the house." I shoved the papers back. "I've got it."

"I *do* need to pay it off," he argued, pushing the papers back to me.

I frowned at him. "Just because I'm carrying your baby doesn't mean you get to take over my life."

"Taking care of you isn't taking over your life, Chef." He didn't come anywhere near matching my hostile tone. "And I know it's not feminist, I know you're independent and successful enough to cover the mortgage. But you've got the baby shit," he gestured around the living room, to the piles of things my mother and I were organizing. "You've picked the perfect place to bring her up. You got the vehicle. Please let me feel like I'm contributing. That I'm a part of this."

I gauged his words, deciding that they were utterly sincere. I knew Kane wasn't going to make me a 'kept woman,' yet it was hard to let go of my independence. "Contributing isn't paying off an entire house," I pointed out.

The corner of his mouth turned up. "It is if you're rich. Crass to say, I know. But I've been spending money on stupid shit for years, since I got handed piles of it. Let me put it toward our home, our future."

More gentle pleading. And my heart, previously made of iron—or ice, if you asked around in New York—was nothing but marshmallow.

"Fine," I reached for a pen. "But I'm paying insurance and property taxes."

Kane merely grinned and nodded in a way that didn't make me feel like I had won.

Before we could argue further, Mom danced into the room.

"Right, you," she pointed at Kane. "I have this." She waved what looked like a crumpled receipt with scrawled writing on it.

"A list. I need to get everything prepared." She looked to me. "You've done absolutely amazing at getting almost everything we need for the baby, my darling. Not that babies need much, really. A place to sleep, a diaper, a onesie or two and their mom and dad. And Grandma and Aunt too." She winked. "I would send this to Maisie, but she's probably already overloaded with things and won't have room for simple, practical items like nontoxic laundry detergent." She looked pointedly at Kane. "It should only have five ingredients. No fragrance unless it comes from essential oils. And I've got some food items on here so I can get started on the postpartum meals and some food to freeze for when I'm gone."

Kane didn't balk, just kissed my head then took the list from my mom.

"Got it." He folded the list inside his wallet. "Anything else?"

"I'll be requesting a ride on that motorcycle when you get

back," she said with a mischievous grin. "I hear you're the best in the world."

"Mom…" I began, shaking my head.

"I'd be honored," Kane said with a mischievous grin of his own.

I didn't bother to argue; it was clear they'd made up their minds. I just sank back on the couch and flipped through my latest pregnancy book.

"You need anything, Chef?" Kane asked.

"Peace and quiet?" I joked, though I'd had 'peace and quiet' for months, and I'd never want to go back to it.

Mom sat on the sofa with the laundry basket. "Oh, honey, that's gone for about eighteen years or so." She started folding onesies. They were amazingly tiny.

"She kissed peace and quiet goodbye the second she got on the back of my bike, Judith," Kane told my mother. "Love you, Chef," he kissed me on the head. "Love you, Mabel," he added, patting my stomach.

My head snapped up. "Did you just call her Mabel?"

Kane nodded. "Saw your shortlist on the laptop. I like Mabel." Then he left, not bothering to wait for my response.

"He just named our baby," I told my mother, shocked by that and the casual 'I love you.' Had he said that since he arrived?

"Mabel's a lovely name," my mother replied.

I sighed. It was. I'd wanted something unique, classic and not outrageous.

Mabel it was.

The bike thundered off and it hit me that it was just my mother and I in the house. I was reading and she was folding laundry, but I could feel it in the air. Things that needed to be said. And my mother was not one to procrastinate.

"I'm so glad I'm here, Avery," she said faintly, gingerly.

I put down my book to give her my full attention, even though my stomach knotted at the prospect of an emotional conversation.

"It broke my heart, pumpkin," she whispered. "First, seeing you in those magazines, seeing the pain in your eyes, feeling it. Then reading your words in that article, your story. What happened to you..." She sucked in a ragged breath, her composure slipping a little before she grasped a hold of it, squeezing my hand. "I'm so sorry that happened to you. And I'm also sorry that I didn't give you space to feel that you could come to me. That you didn't feel safe with me."

Though I thought I'd conditioned myself to erect barriers between me and my mother, her words struck me right in the chest.

"Mom, it's not that I don't feel safe with you. I just didn't want it to exist. I wanted to bury it down deep and forget about it."

Mom nodded somberly. "That I understand, my darling girl. And yet I wish that I could've been there for you. Not just for that, but for your entire wonderful life. I grieve that I wasn't. But I'm so very proud of who you've become. And now I'll be here to watch you become a mother. That's a gift that I'll treasure."

"I'm sorry," I told her, shame washing over me at how completely I'd shut everyone out without proper reasoning. "I'm sorry I didn't call sooner."

Losing my father had ruined me. I thought if I didn't let myself love my mother and sister the way I wanted to, it would hurt less if I ever lost them. A shitty, cowardly reason.

"Don't you ever apologize for your boundaries, honey," she replied. "You didn't know how else to cope. I wish I had been better at scaling the walls you built, but I was waiting, trusting that you'd come back to me. And you have. That's all that matters."

I bit my tongue. I didn't deserve such easy forgiveness, but I'd take it.

"Right." My mother wiped her eyes. "Let's get these upstairs and put away. You can direct me."

Just like that, the emotional moment was gone, and damn, was I glad.

* * *

Kane came back with everything on my mother's list. Tiny clothes were put away.

We were back in the living room, my mother humming contently as she dusted things. Kane was sitting with me, rubbing my feet.

The windows were open—my mother had opened them all. Every single one. She didn't like air conditioning; she called it 'artificial air' and had turned it off in favor of the gentle sea breeze that took the edge of the hot summer afternoon.

I had to admit, the way the curtains blew in the breeze and the smell of the ocean mixed with the flowers in the garden did put 'artificial air' to shame.

Since all the windows were open, I heard the crunch of gravel as a car pulled up, then I heard Taylor Swift. I knew it was Taylor Swift not because I was the kind of fan who could identify the song from a few beats. No, because my sister played it so loudly that I could hear every single word from the car stereo inside the house.

That was Maisie. Driving with all the windows down, her music so loud you couldn't hear her belting it out along with the chorus. She'd sing one in three words correctly. I'd told her countless times that she should learn the songs, but she'd only smiled and said she liked her versions better.

"Finally," my mother said from where she was dusting books.

"I bet she's been shopping. That Main Street has some great stores I've had my eye on, but I told her to wait for me and you so we could all go together." Mom glanced to Kane. "Maisie isn't great at waiting."

She said it fondly, with a smile and warmth that made my stomach prickle. There it was. That familiarity that mom and Maisie had.

Not that mom ever played favorites—Maisie was just more accessible to her.

When the music cut off, I stood, holding my breath.

The front door slammed shut, then the clang of a heeled boot on my floor along with the jangle of bracelets announced her arrival.

Maisie *looked* like a Maisie. She was the day to my night. Her blonde hair was always in wild curls or a messy braid or a ponytail half falling out.

She always had on big earrings, sundresses with cowboy boots, skirts, anything feminine and flowy, really. My sister wouldn't be described as a 'hippy' exactly, but she was definitely alternative, and she had only gotten more so as we'd grown, most especially after we lost our father.

Part of my 'rebellion' was being more serious, regimented and reserved while my mother and sister blossomed into their carefree existences.

A jealous, ugly part of me hadn't wanted Kane to meet Maisie. Not only was she younger and objectively more beautiful, it wasn't her appearance that threatened me. I knew Kane wasn't as superficial as all that; he'd been with plenty of women who were clearly prettier than me—Victoria's Secret models, for God's sakes. No, it wasn't Maisie's appearance, it was her spirit. Even though she was a mother of two, even though she'd spent a good majority of her motherhood as a single mother, she had a unique lightness to her. She was a wanderer, a magnificent free spirit.

If someone had to match up two people, it would likely be Kane and Maisie instead of Kane and me.

Yes, these thoughts were utterly illogical, but I couldn't help but have them. I'd crafted an identity of being one of the most impressive and successful people in my field. I'd been recognized globally, making me confident in many ways. Yet my baby sister always made me feel insecure.

"Oh my god, you're glowing!" she cried when she appeared in

the door, a huge smile on her face. She was on me in three long-legged strides. Though she knew I wasn't a hugger, she did what she always did when she saw me, pulling me into her arms.

And like always, she smelled of vanilla and violets.

She gave me a squeeze, a kiss on the cheek, then looked down. "You're carrying very low; it won't be long now." Her hands went to my belly, stroking gently. "Hello, little niece. I'm so excited to meet you."

"I'm getting an induction," I blurted instead of any kind of greeting, not asking about my own niece and nephew. It was rude, and I didn't know why I did it, but I had to get it out in the open before her or my mother had any grand ideas about home births or tinctures or whatever it was they thought was better.

Maisie's brow dimpled but she stayed silent. Nonetheless, I knew what she was thinking.

"I don't need to let nature or my body do its thing," I told her.

"I didn't say anything." Her hands were still on my belly. She wasn't shy about physical affection.

My eyes ricocheted back-and-forth between hers. "Yes, but you're thinking all sorts of things. And I'm telling you right now, I trust my doctor and modern medicine, and I like knowing I have a plan. I don't want you making me feel guilty because I shouldn't be messing with my body's process or whatever."

Maisie's expression softened. "Oh, honey, there is so much guilt baked into motherhood that I wouldn't dream of adding to that pie." She rubbed my bump once more before turning to Kane.

"You're Kane," she said, hands on her hips.

"And you're Maisie," he replied, an easy grin tilting his mouth.

She gave him a quick once-over, not even trying to hide it. Then she looked back at me. "He's hot."

"He's within earshot," I informed her.

"He's also likely seen a mirror," she countered. "So he knows he's hot. And it means good things for your child, because you're hot too. Not that her worth is tied to her looks."

I rolled my eyes good naturedly at my sister.

Her face turned serious as she looked back to Kane. "Thank you," she said sincerely. "For calling my mom, for bringing us here and braving her wrath." She jerked her head to me "We would've been heartbroken if we missed this."

The air in the room became heavy. There was no blame or guilt weaved into my sister's tone. She didn't have a malicious bone in her body and wasn't trying to make me feel bad.

Yet I felt bad nonetheless.

Feeling the warmth in the room, smelling the scents of Maisie's perfume, Mom's cooking, the ocean air, I struggled to find all the reasons why I'd pushed them out of my life.

Except the reasons never had anything to do with either of them. It was me. I'd changed. Because of Kane. Because of this baby.

I had a family now.

Whether I liked it or not.

And I did, like it. Which was the scariest thing of all.

Twenty-One

EVEN THOUGH KANE was sure Mabel was going to surprise us all by coming before her due date, there was no havoc or drama, no water breaking in the middle of a restaurant, no baby born in the car on the way to the hospital.

No, on the night of my induction, there was a dinner at home, one I made even though Mom and Maisie fought me on it.

"It's the last thing I'll be able to take my time cooking," I argued to them.

And Kane, usually—infuriatingly—on their side with most things pertaining to my 'care,' sided with me.

"You got this, Chef," he said, kissing my neck.

He was doing that more lately. Easy affection, affectionate tones. He wasn't punishing me anymore. Although he hadn't truly punished me since that first night. Maybe I was punishing myself.

Whatever it was, we were still tiptoeing around each other in a way. Relearning each other. I wasn't Avery Hart, chef, anymore. And for the time, it seemed Kane was no longer Kane 'The Devil' Rhodes either.

Through some miracle of fate, no one here had taken photos of him, posted anything. The media hadn't found him yet, and I knew they were looking because there were articles online.

I shouldn't have read them. I hadn't in the past, knowing they were toxic. Yet now, for whatever reason, in the rare moments I wasn't with Kane or my mother or Maisie, I was scrolling through the articles.

Kane Rhodes out of prison, conviction overturned... But where is he now?

Mixed reception on Rhodes's release from prison. Did he deserve to get out?

DuBois, currently under investigation for sexual violence charges, has 'no comment' on Rhodes's release.

Has Avery Hart, the Ice Queen, managed to put Kane's fire out? Where has he gone?

The respite wasn't permanent. Some determined reporter would find him. Someone would leak his location. Or he'd go back for an event, a game, the freaking Olympics for all I knew. Kane was a thrill seeker to his core, so he couldn't stay in Jupiter indefinitely.

That reality hung in my head too. My career, as I knew it, was over. There weren't any twelve-hour days at a restaurant. No more commanding a kitchen ... or my life, for that matter.

And I didn't know how I felt about that. I knew I already loved Mabel more than anything, that I wouldn't change my situation for the world, but the unknown future ahead of me made my throat uncomfortably tight.

"My only request is that I be sous chef," Kane murmured, bringing me out of my thoughts and into the present.

The present being a kitchen in Maine, with my mother and sister sipping wine at the breakfast bar, the ocean air blowing in, Kane Rhodes next to me, a baby kicking in my belly and a midnight admission to have the aforementioned baby.

"Sous chef?" I craned my neck to examine him.

He nodded. "You tell me what to do—chop, fry, whatever. I got you. You work your magic." His eyes glittered as something unspoken passed between us. He knew I needed this. We were both standing there, on the precipice of a completely new life. After tonight, nothing would be the same. So the simpleness of being in a kitchen, cooking with Kane, meant everything.

"I need onions diced."

"Yes, Chef." His eyes held mine for a long moment.

Then we cooked.

Our last meal as Kane and Avery.

The next one we had, we'd be Mom and Dad.

An insane idea.

Yet somehow perfect.

I hadn't wanted the epidural.

Not because I was some kind of martyr. I trusted modern medicine and firmly believed that women shouldn't have to suffer through labor when they'd already suffered through a pregnancy and would be suffering through the recovery and whatever other demands society had for them.

I believed every woman had the right to experience childbirth in their own way, with as little pain as possible.

But I'd also read up about the more prudent, realistic parts of labor. And I wanted it to be as quick and as efficient as it could be. Statistically, labor could last longer if an epidural was administered.

Also, I might've been arrogant about my threshold for pain.

I'd endured my fair share of it. My training ensured that my power of will was ironclad and that I never gave up. I set the expectation for myself that I wasn't going to get an epidural, and I'd intended to stick with it.

Which was an absolutely stupid fucking idea.

I had heard about people who said inductions were dramatically more painful than natural labor. I'd taken this into account, but I'd also thought that pain was pain. I knew logically it couldn't kill me, and I had my breathing exercises; I would focus on those, and I'd be fine.

And I was indisputably wrong.

I was in the tub. Initially, I hadn't planned on using the birthing tub. But it was one of the ways to help reduce the pain without drugs. Something I found to be pure bullshit after floating around in there, still three centimeters dilated after hours. After what felt like years.

Three centimeters meant that I had more hours ahead of me. Of that pain. Pain that felt like my body was splitting in two. My contractions had been coming every minute for ... God knew how long.

Kane was at my side, as he had been the entire time. Massaging my back, holding my hand, brushing hair from my face. He'd been steadfast, calm, tender. All of the things you'd want in a birth partner. Yet I barely paid any attention to him due to the pain. Even Kane 'The Devil' Rhodes couldn't manage to anchor me in that sea of agony.

"I need the epidural," I ground out to him from the tub.

There was a nurse kneeling beside me, her hands in the water, holding the two monitors on my stomach to ensure the baby was still okay. She was. Her heartbeat was steady. Apparently, she was as calm as could be while her mother was fighting for her life.

Kane's eyes were clear on mine, though I saw the edge of worry there.

We'd talked about this.

"If I say I need the epidural, you need to tell me no," I'd said while rubbing oil onto my stomach.

"Me, tell you no? Absolutely fucking not." Kane didn't even take a moment to consider his response, the words rushing past his lips as he swatted my hands away so he could rub in the oil for me. It was one of his favorite tasks. "If you're in pain that you can't handle and there's a medicine available that will make that pain go away, I am in full support of a professional administering it."

"I can handle it." I pursed my lips. "Women have been handling it for millions of years. But knowing that it's available in the back of my mind, I may falter."

"Chef, you won't falter." He paused so he could look up at me. "And again, asking for medicine is not faltering or failure, just so you know."

I let out a deep sigh. "Yes, whatever. But this is my request. That you remind me of my birth plan and that I can do it without the epidural."

Kane's brow furrowed. "I'll remind you."

"Someone get my woman a fucking epidural," he said to the nurses without missing a beat.

"Okay, honey. You stand up, and we'll get the anesthetist on the phone." I hated the nurse for sitting there and not being in unbearable pain. I hated everyone. Even Kane. Especially Kane. He did that to me.

Even the simple act of standing seemed unfathomable. *Breathing* was an effort.

Yet I found the ability, with Kane's help.

As soon as I stood, the pressure at my pelvis turned, morphing into something different than pain. Something much bigger.

"Something's wrong," I gasped.

Kane's expression remained calm, but I saw his pupils dilate.

"I feel like I need to push."

That was an understatement. It felt like my insides were about to all come tumbling out. The pressure... The pressure was unlike anything I'd ever felt.

Once I'd uttered those words, the nurses jumped into action.

Suddenly, I was out of the tub and on the bed, the nurse between my legs.

"Okay, she's here," she announced calmly.

"*Here*?" I shrieked. "But I was only three centimeters dilated. I need the epidural."

She glanced up at me with kind eyes. "You're all the way ready now, and we're past the point of an epidural."

My eyes bugged out. "Past the point? That's not real, that only happens in stupid romantic comedies."

She smiled. "Well, it's happening here and now. I'm just going to call your doctor."

She put the phone to her ear as more nurses filtered in, the energy in the room changing from calm support to purposeful preparation.

For labor.

Of a baby.

That I had to push it out.

Without drugs.

"I can't do this," I panted.

"Yes, you can, honey." The nurse looked at me with knowing eyes, with a belief in me that made no sense since she didn't know me. "You can totally do this."

"No I can't." I had thoughts of closing my legs, insisting on them cutting her out instead. They could do that, right? I could make them do that. I could threaten to sue them or something.

Why I was thinking about threatening to sue these lovely, supportive, hardworking women was a testament to how much agony I was in. I would do it in a heartbeat if it would make it stop.

A dry palm pushed the damp hair from my head before familiar lips pressed into the skin there. "You can do this, Chef," Kane murmured against my forehead. "You can do this."

His voice was firm, confident, full of certainty.

"You are powerful," he whispered in my ear.

I didn't feel powerful. Not even a little. I felt exhausted. The most exhausted I'd ever been in my life. My body felt as if it were so fragile it was made of cracked glass, ready to shatter at any moment. My hips burned, the bones grinding against each other, the pressure in my pelvis indescribable. My ass seemed like it was going to explode.

The nurses were moving around the room then, practiced, with a calm kind of urgency. One of them was on the phone with my doctor who was, apparently, stuck in traffic. More nurses came in.

They were getting ready for me to *give birth*.

Except I wasn't. I couldn't. I wasn't strong enough.

"Chef, look at me," Kane's voice filtered through my foggy mind, and I veered my gaze to him. He was right beside me, hands clasped in mine. Firm. Hard. Tethering me to the earth. "You are a warrior. You can do this."

He said it with such surety. Like it was an indisputable fact. Like he believed in me.

Everything inside me coiled as I felt my body ready for another contraction. It was like the ocean sucking the waves back in preparation for a tsunami. My breath came out of my lips in short bursts. "I am powerful," I repeated like a mantra.

The contraction crashed over me.

The nurse was between my legs again. "Now we've got to push."

She didn't have to tell me twice; I would do anything to relieve the pressure. The pain, I'd thought I'd prepared for that—I really fucking hadn't—but the pressure was completely unexpected. I felt like I was going to burst, like my pelvis was about to shatter.

"This is not natural!" I screamed. "Everyone in the birth classes said it was natural. Magical. This does not feel like nature. This is torture!" My sentences came out broken, fractured.

The nurses laughed. I wanted to punch them. "Nature has a way of torturing women, but you've got this."

A handful more contractions ripped through me, and each time, I pushed. "Practice," the nurse called it, but I wasn't practicing, I was trying with all my might to get that baby out.

To no avail.

Luckily, though, the pause between contractions was longer than it had been since active labor started. I got a brief respite, sinking back onto the bed, feeling half normal. Kane would kiss my head, blow cool air in my face with a handheld fan.

Things moved impossibly fast yet excruciatingly slow at the same time. I was in my body, more than I ever had been, people in the room filtering in and out of focus with each contraction.

And then my doctor was there, rushing in, switching places with a nurse, changing out pieces of the bed, squeezing my leg, telling me I was doing great.

At some point, they got me a mirror for me to see what was going on down there, to help with the pushing. I hadn't thought I'd want to see, but I needed it. I needed to. Kane did not.

"Stay by my head," I demanded, my breath coming in shallow pants as I rode the blissful wave between contractions.

"No way in hell." Kane leaned back toward me to kiss my head.

"I'm serious, Kane," I said through gritted teeth. "You do not need to see all that."

I was looking at the mirror out of pure necessity; even I did not want to see all of that. But I needed it in order to get this demon out of me.

Even in my throes of exhaustion, agony and general fucking madness, I understood I would never unsee myself fully dilated.

Kane, who was in no agony at all and nowhere near as exhausted —therefore having all of his mental faculties intact—would definitely not be able to unsee it. Though I didn't have much time to argue with him, I knew my reprieve was short lived and could already feel the swell of another contraction approaching.

"I'm serious," I gritted out.

Kane's brow flattened as he fastened his hand tightly on my leg, holding it up and in place for me to push, as though he could feel the crest of my contraction too.

"I'm serious too, Chef," he replied. "I'll give you anything you ask for. But not this. I am seeing our daughter come into this world. I'm watching your body perform this fucking miracle, and that is that."

I wanted to argue. I very much did. Especially about the whole 'miracle' part.

But I didn't have the energy.

I looked from Kane to the small patch of hair that was my daughter's head.

"Okay, this push, you're going to get her out," my doctor told me. "You're going to push with all your might."

"As opposed to the leisurely pushing I've been doing?" I asked sarcastically.

She only smiled.

A contraction built, and I felt my reserves of energy dwindle down to nothing. There was nothing left in me.

Except I had to.

So at the peak of my contraction, I went somewhere in my head. Outside of the room but still in it. And then I pushed.

With all my might.

And out came our daughter's head. All of it.

My doctor cradled it, and I looked at her, half out of my body.

"That's the hardest part, now let's get the rest of her out." She told me this so calmly, nonchalantly, as if she wasn't holding half of my baby, who was hanging out of my vagina.

I pushed once more then felt immense relief.

Out she came.

Screaming.

Beautiful.

Then she was on my stomach, getting cleaned off, using her lungs.

I blinked down at her. This baby, this living, breathing, crying thing that was mine. Ours.

My hands found her skin.

It was warm, still wet with vernix, but it was perfect.

I looked up at Kane.

He was crying. Tears ran down his face as he gazed at our daughter in wonder. Then he looked at me with worship.

"I pushed her out," I whispered. "Our baby."

His whole face softened some more. "Yeah, Chef, you did. You did fuckin' great." He leaned in to kiss my head.

"You want to cut the cord, Dad?" a nurse asked.

"Nah, that's grandma's job," Kane said, staring at our baby.

We'd already discussed that. Mom and Maisie were in the waiting room, and we'd instructed a nurse to go get Mom once the baby was born to surprise her with this. I knew she'd been fully expecting to be shut out of everything, as she had been all the other important moments of my adult life.

Mom rushed into the room, eyes shining and already wet with tears as she took in the scene.

For once, my mother was speechless as a nurse held out the scissors.

"Go on," I smiled at her. It had been a revelation to me, how hard my mother had tried to connect with me. How hard I'd tried to push her out.

So it was important to me that I gave her this. Gave us this.

Her tears landed on the scissors as she cut the cord.

Then the doctors did their work.

"We're just going to get her cleaned off and weigh her," a nurse said as she plucked Mabel from my chest.

I nodded, even though it went against every instinct in my body to have my daughter taken from me, even if it was just a few feet across the room.

Kane followed the nurses, a hairbreadth away from them, not letting our daughter out of his sight.

My mother came to kiss my head.

"Thank you," she whispered, tears in her eyes. "You did so wonderful, my baby."

I let a single tear slip, watching Kane's back.

"Yeah," I agreed. "We did."

* * *

The chaos of labor gave room to quiet. My doctor left after stitching me up and telling me she'd be back in the morning.

Stitches. Down there. It made sense since I'd felt the horrible ripping sensation as Mabel came out. Worth it, completely worth it.

A nurse got me up and helped me to the bathroom. I walked hunched over, totally in shock at how much pain I was in. I couldn't straighten.

She helped me onto the toilet, and I didn't have the energy to feel shame. She also showed me the process of putting a large pad in my disposable underwear, one that had a cooling feature, then she laid witch hazel pads on top of that to soothe.

When she helped me pull up the underwear, the relief was welcome.

Then I hobbled back to bed, one eye on Kane sitting in the rocking chair, his large finger tracing the nose of our tiny baby. They were in their own little world, his shirt off, pressing her skin to his.

Once I was settled, he immediately gave her up, settling her at my breast.

He helped me position her properly, like the lactation consultant who had been in earlier showed us. It felt unfamiliar. Strange. But also natural. I was awkward, afraid of holding her wrong, of breaking her.

Kane seemed more sure, more confident. Much more natural.

He gave her a kiss on the head then me one on the lips before he returned to his chair. Neither of us spoke, we just watched our baby drink then, eventually, fall asleep at my breast.

Carefully, oh so carefully, mindful of the tiny bundle and how any small movement made my pelvis light up with the fire of a thousand sons of bitches, I cradled her in the nook of my arm.

I left my breast exposed, too tired to cover it. One thing I lost that day was my modesty.

"You need to sleep." Kane's voice was soft and throaty and full of awe.

I glanced at him through half-lidded eyes, clutching the swaddled bundle in my arms. I looked down to her chubby cheeks, her closed eyes and the gentle flaring of her nostrils as she inhaled and exhaled.

"I don't want to let her go." My voice was hoarse from screaming during labor. I really thought I wouldn't be the kind of woman who screamed. But then again, I had no fucking clue how tough giving birth unmedicated was. I would've roared like a dragon if I thought it would've given me relief.

Kane didn't try to argue with me on that, but he again told me,, "Sleep."

"I can't sleep." I tilted my head down to her. "I don't want to drop her."

"You won't," Kane replied firmly, sitting straighter in his chair.

"How can you know that?" I was sure I wouldn't drop my baby, even in sleep, that there had to be some kind natural instinct to protect. But I also had been awake for over twenty-four hours and was more exhausted than I'd ever been in my life.

Kane pulled his chair even closer to the bed, though I hadn't thought that was possible.

"Because I won't let you," he assured me. "If you drop her, I'll catch her."

His eyes weren't bloodshot and there were no bags underneath them, even though he'd been awake for as long as I'd been. He was tired too. Granted, not as tired as I was on account of me being the one who went through childbirth.

But even still, he should've been fading. Kane wasn't. Kane didn't fade on me. His eyes were bright, determined, strong. His posture rigid.

He wouldn't let me drop our baby. He would catch her.

Catch both of us.

"I love you," I whispered. He reached out to caress my hand.

He might've said something, might've even said it back, but I didn't stay awake long enough to hear it. I'd been hanging on by a thread, running on pure adrenaline, gripping on to consciousness by my fingernails. Kane's words, his promise had been what I'd needed to let go, to trust that he was there, watching over us.

Twenty-Two

KANE

AVERY WAS FINALLY SLEEPING.

I'd managed to get Mabel from her arms and into the hospital bassinet without waking either of them.

I'd wanted to hold Mabel in my own arms, settle there with that weight—seven pounds eleven ounces—in my arms and simply watch her chest rise and fall.

But I needed to sleep too. I was aware that this was only the beginning of a long road of broken nights and early mornings. And I was prepared for it. Fuck, was I.

Even me, with an inflated idea of myself understood that biologically, I needed at least a few hours to carry me through.

I had a big responsibility now. A fucking precious one.

Husband and father.

Not technically the former yet, but that was just a matter of paperwork.

Avery had done all the heavy lifting so far; it was time for me to step up, now that I could.

I'd never felt as powerless in my life as I did watching my woman weather the pain of the contractions. I'd never wished so hard that I could take it away, take it on myself. But I'd never been in awe of another human like I was watching my woman bring our daughter into the world. I might've been powerless, but I'd never seen a woman more powerful.

My hand rested on Mabel's chest in the bassinet.

The foldout sofa in the corner of the hospital room called to me.

But...

I couldn't find it in me to drag myself away from her. From them. My eyes drifted to where Avery was sleeping. Sometime during my transition, she'd moved so her body was facing us, her hand reaching toward the bassinet, as if even in her sleep she'd sensed me move Mabel.

It felt as though a clamp tightened around my heart as it grew bigger than the ribcage that contained it.

Though I might've been exhausted and just a little bit enchanted by my daughter and my woman, that didn't mean I wasn't on guard. So my hackles rose when I heard the thump of boots out in the hallway. Too heavy to be the nurse's sensible sneakers.

I tensed, all too aware that we were around more people than we had been since I arrived in Jupiter. Though everyone had been fucking great, I knew that people were often looking to make a buck, for a way to make a name for themselves.

The price on my head was higher now as people speculated on where I went after I was released, after my conviction was overturned. All it took was one stressed-out hospital worker, overworked and underpaid, to see dollar signs in that.

And all it took was one motivated and sneaky journalist to find their way into a labor and delivery suite, to find my baby.

Defensives on high alert, I turned, ready to end whoever might have any thoughts of putting my baby in danger.

My brother entered the room.

He had a raised brow, communicating that he saw my stance, felt my aggression.

I relaxed instantaneously.

"It's past visiting hours," I greeted my brother, trying to slow my blood pressure. I'd gotten a taste of uncontrollable rage when DuBois put his hands on Avery, but now with Mabel, it felt like another well inside of me had just been opened. I feared it and welcomed it at the same time. I would take down fucking regimes if they threatened my daughter. Face armies with nothing but my bare hands to protect her.

"Those are just suggestions," Knox replied.

I shook my head, smiling and swallowing that cool rage.

He clapped me on the shoulder, a rare sign of affection from him. "Congratulations ... Dad."

I smirked at him in response, feeling fucking overwhelmed that that's what I was. Someone's dad.

Her dad.

Knox was holding something in his hand.

My smirk turned into a grin.

"Wouldn't have pegged you as a soft toy kind of guy, but it suits you."

My brother, in his black suit, wearing all his shadows and demons, was holding a pink bunny.

He ignored me and stepped forward so he could look in the bassinet.

When Mabel let out a squeak, I was quick to lay my hand back on her swaddled chest. She calmed instantly.

Knox didn't say anything. He just stared.

I was happy to stand in silence and stare at the most precious being that ever lived. Could've done it forever.

Knox leaned forward, and I tensed. Even though it was my brother, the one who would die to protect me and in turn, Mabel, he was still a predator. An ancient instinct in my body recognized that.

I knew that Knox saw me tense because that's who he was, but he didn't react.

He just placed that bunny in the corner of her bassinet, pausing his hand by her head, hovering as if to touch her before pulling it away, a fist at his side.

It hurt me, fucking killed, actually, that the simple act of touching his newborn niece wasn't possible for my brother. I couldn't read his mind, but I could guess that he considered himself too tarnished, too dirty, to sully Mabel.

"She's beautiful," Knox whispered.

I nodded. "More than beautiful."

We stood for a while longer. "She's gonna need an uncle," I encouraged quietly. "I know that she already has one who will protect her from all the monsters of this world. But I'm gonna ask that you give her one who will sit with her, have tea parties, whatever the fuck. If that's out of reach, one who will be there for Christmas." I glanced at my brother. "Time to find a way out of the shadows, brother. I want this for you." I motioned to Avery and Mabel. "More than that, you *deserve* this."

Knox didn't say anything for a long while. "One day, long fucking time ago, I might've deserved this. But not now. Not after what I've done. Who I am. You've gotta make your peace with that, brother. I'll protect her from the monsters of this world, but I can't sit and have tea with her because I am one of those monsters."

It hit me in the chest, the surety in which he spoke. And it hit me even harder that part of me might've agreed with him.

I opened my mouth to argue once I shut up the shitty part of me I was deeply ashamed of.

But Knox had already turned, heading out of the room.

I didn't try to stop him, just sighed, looking at my daughter then the pink bunny in her crib.

My brother thought he was beyond saving, but that pink bunny proved he wasn't.

He just couldn't be saved by me.

Or himself.

If there was anything I'd learned this past year, it was that the right woman could save a man, one who'd thought he was undeserving.

Two women, I corrected, staring at my daughter while hoping, praying, my brother would find that.

I continued watching Mabel for another hour.

AVERY

Our first night in the hospital was exhausting.

I snatched a few hours of sleep at the beginning of the night, but that was mostly it.

Mabel was restless. She constantly wanted to be held by me or her dad.

I was in too much pain to do things as simple as reaching over the bed to lift her from the hospital bassinet. It was infuriating, humbling and deeply distressing that I couldn't go to my daughter.

Kane did all the heavy lifting, even changed his first diaper. He did it like he'd done it a thousand times before, kissing Mabel lightly on the head, murmuring some lullaby.

I didn't have to lift a finger. Never mind that I physically couldn't do much more than shuffle off the bed, taking me about ten minutes to reach the ground. And when I did reach the ground, blood rushed out of me, puddling on the floor.

The first time it happened, Kane was so alarmed, he called for a nurse. I hadn't known exactly what to expect postpartum, but the pain, the magnitude of it, was surprising. Same with the blood, the nurses who came into the room every couple of hours to push on my tender uterus and flush even more blood out.

I was not wearing an expensive robe, propped up, nursing my baby while looking fresh and well rested, like popular culture portrayed.

My hair was matted, and I wore my bloody hospital gown until a nurse kindly suggested I change into the pajamas I'd brought with me.

My meticulously packed hospital bag was barely touched, other than the aforementioned pajamas. I had brought a plethora of toiletries including shampoo, conditioner, body wash and skincare products. The thought of standing for the period of time it took to shower made my stomach roil, so I avoided that. I barely managed to splash water on my face and brush my teeth.

My mother and Maisie arrived the next morning, looking far fresher than the two of us.

Well, I should say *me*.

Yes, Kane's clothes were slightly rumpled, his hair messier than his usual tousled style, and his eyes were slightly bloodshot. But he still looked handsome, roughish. Just ... softer now.

Then there was seeing him with Mabel in his arms. Yes, the sexual part of my body felt like it was shut down inevitably, but it might've made my womb clench if it weren't already aching from shrinking down to its pre-pregnancy size.

"This is the best thing I've eaten in my entire life," I moaned through a full mouth.

Maisie was holding Mabel, who calmed in my sister's arms right away after fussing over a diaper change.

She sang to her quietly.

I was eating the ham sandwich my mother had brought, wrapped in wax paper. Devouring it like a wolf might've been a more accurate description. I didn't know how starving I was until that moment.

I was still getting the hang of breastfeeding ... and to just being a mother while in large amounts of pain. The fact that they didn't give anything stronger than Motrin should've been criminal.

Kane continued to change tiny diapers with large hands, like an expert.

He fawned over me. Kissing me whenever he had a chance, jumping to help me to the bathroom, if he didn't have the baby in his arms. Gingerly transferring her to my mother or Maisie if he did.

And when the lactation consultant returned, he was right there, front and center, observing the latch and asking questions about positioning, nipple care and what I could and couldn't eat.

The answers to which he wrote down.

In a little blue notebook.

"It's my dad book," he explained proudly, waving it in the air. "It'll be the dad bible. I'm going to put every piece of advice we get in here."

There he was, Kane 'The Devil' Rhodes, waving a blue notebook around proudly, jotting down information about nipple care and the football hold.

"Google exists," I reminded him.

"Fuck Google," he muttered.

I smiled at him then at Mabel, who I was still struggling to believe was mine, that she'd come out of me. Sure, I had all the evidence, stitches and all, to reinforce that she was mine, but it was still surreal.

Soon, my mother and Maisie left to prepare the house for our arrival—whatever that meant.

Though we were covered to stay another night at the hospital, the nurses informed us that both Mabel and I were cleared to go home whenever we wanted.

I thought of the uncomfortable hospital mattress, the cramped bathroom and the constant noise. I compared it to my expensive bedding, soft mattress, large shower and house that I'd never thought of as a home until that moment.

I made the choice to get discharged. Kane had second-guessed it, worrying about me, which seemed to be his new full-time job. But I was insistent. I'd made up my mind. Home, with my comforts, would help make me feel grounded. Right then, everything was different, even my body. It was the still round but significantly smaller bump at my stomach that shocked me the most.

I hadn't been attached to being pregnant. I hadn't liked the restrictions that came with it, that people treated me like there was something wrong with me. I'd thought I'd love the freedom of having my body back, but I felt a pang of grief, of emptiness. Never was Mabel safer than when she was tucked up inside me. Now she was in this loud, dangerous world. I was more than mindful that Kane was recognizable, that there were many people who might see him roaming the halls, holding his daughter and think to snap a photo. The mere thought filled me with panic.

Yes, home and safe in our little cottage in our little town was much more preferable.

I was secure in that decision as I gingerly got dressed into the easiest and most comfortable clothes I had. Even that took three times as long as it normally would've.

Kane put Mabel in the butterfly-print onesie Maisie had declared her 'going home outfit.' I hadn't known such things existed. I would've left her in the hospital onesie and called it a day.

Still in our hospital room, Kane buckled her into the car seat—with the supervision of a nurse to ensure it was done correctly—doing it the same way he did everything thus far, with confidence and ease.

Mabel screamed bloody murder throughout the process, which had me horrified and panicked that he'd accidentally buckled a piece of her skin or bent one of her tiny limbs the wrong way.

The nurse informed me car seat screaming was par for the

course, and once she was up and Kane was swinging the seat gently, Mabel quieted.

Kane smirked. "She doesn't like to be strapped down and has to be constantly on the move. Who does that sound like?"

I smiled if only to mimic his ease, though I certainly didn't feel it. Not only did Mabel's crying do something primal and painful to my insides, but I did not feel at all calm. She was too small and her head lolled from side to side with a neck unable to support it. She was far too breakable. And I myself felt fragile, in pieces. Like a bunch of broken China inside a box. If you shook me, I'd rattle.

Then there was the issue that I could only take shuffled steps and had only just managed to walk with a straight spine.

We made the slow walk out of the hospital, the nurse following us to our car to ensure we installed the baby carrier into the base properly.

Then she just … left.

That was it. The last check, the last bit of help we'd get from the professionals. I stared after her as she disappeared through the doors of the hospital.

I had a sudden urge to run back—or shuffle painfully—then pound on the doors, begging to be let back in where the nurses were just a buzzer away. Because they knew things. Like Mabel choking on spit up was just fine. Or that blood gushing from me and puddling on the floor was normal.

I needed their confident, calming and most importantly, educated reassurance.

"Got you, Chef," Kane murmured, somehow having calmed the now sleeping baby and ready to help me into the backseat with her.

He didn't question my choice of seat in the car. I deduced that the front seat was too far away from her; I needed to be within touching distance and there to ensure that she continued breathing.

Positional asphyxiation. I'd read about that. It could happen in soft beds, car seats, if the infant was sleeping in one for too long.

Suddenly, the laundry list of dangers seemed suffocating and overwhelming.

Kane's gentle yet firm grip on me, helping me into the backseat, was the only thing that calmed my suddenly frantic mind.

He kissed me gently on the head, reaching in to buckle me and gaze at Mabel for a handful of seconds before closing the door quietly.

I reached over to her amazingly tiny hands, and she snuffled in her sleep, holding my finger tightly in her fist.

My chest clenched at the power of such a small gesture.

"Ready, Chef?" Kane asked, eyes latching onto mine in the rearview mirror.

I felt rather than heard the meaning in those words. He wasn't just asking if I was ready to leave the parking lot; it felt like he was asking if I was ready to leave our prior lives behind to start a new one.

No was the answer.

Absolutely not.

Her tiny fist flexed around my finger.

"Yeah," I whispered. "I'm ready."

* * *

Second Night Syndrome.

I only knew the name of it because Maisie had warned me, delicately, as she had everything, when we arrived back home.

She and my mother were there waiting when we came home, food ready, arms open to take the baby while Kane and I devoured the first proper hot meal we'd had in what felt like forever.

It was simple—pasta with red sauce and a load of veggies. My mom and Maisie had both been talking constantly about the 'warming' foods I'd be consuming for the next forty days and the foods needed to help repair my womb, balance my hormones and increase my milk production.

Usually, I rolled my eyes at their more eccentric views, but I'd been reading up on different culture's approaches to postpartum, and there was significant historical evidence to back up a lot of what they were saying.

So I did something that was rather painful for me—I let them take charge of all the food, refreshments and overall care.

I'd been eating pasta and sipping a mug of bone broth while Maisie told us about Second Night Syndrome.

Kane had been eating with one hand, scribbling in his notebook with the other.

Essentially, it was the baby realizing that they were out of the mother's womb and in the big, loud, cold and intimidating world. The first night they were, apparently, exhausted from the journey through the birth canal—not Mabel, though—and same with the following day.

Mabel had been slumbering peacefully in Maisie's arms as she explained it, my sister standing and rocking like an expert, sure of each one of her movements, of the way she held her.

I hadn't seen my sister in this light before. Hadn't allowed myself too. In my mind, she was the young mother, the free spirit who I struggled to connect to.

I'd brushed off whatever 'alternative' knowledge she'd muttered about, barely listening. I hadn't taken her seriously.

That was my mistake and cross to bear. Same with my mother.

Two women I'd shut out of my life who came running without resentment or blame when I needed them.

I'd ruminated over that the entire second night because I was awake for every moment of it.

Mabel seemed to be glued to my boob. Every time she fell asleep there and I'd thought it was safe to put her in the bedside bassinet—I hadn't ever decided on one; Kane had taken all of my meticulously constructed spreadsheets and made decisions on all the remaining baby items in about fifteen minutes—her eyes popped open, and she wailed until I put her back on my boob.

My body was still riding on adrenaline. I knew logically that I was exhausted, but I didn't feel it.

At first, Kane stayed up with me, rubbing my back, getting up to change Mabel when it was clear she needed it, thumbing through his notebook plus the baby books on his side of the table in search of things he could do to help.

"Go to sleep," I whispered to him as I watched the fatigue roll over him in waves, his bloodshot eyes drooping.

Those drooping eyes widened. "Absolutely fucking not," he whispered, looking at me and placing his large hand on Mabel's tiny head. The head that had come out of my vagina. Still insane to think about. But not that insane considering the aforementioned vagina was throbbing with pain to communicate that yes, a head the size of a small basketball had come out of there.

"You need sleep," I told him.

"So do you," he countered. "You sleep, I'll stay up to watch over you."

A sweet offer. A genuine one. Despite his lethargy, he would stay up to watch us so I could get rest.

"I can't," I told him truthfully, nodding down to my breast. "This isn't exactly the most comfortable thing in the world, and I'm wired. My body is producing hormones in order for me to deal with this. Yours isn't. You need sleep."

His brows furrowed. "You need help."

I shook my head. "You can't help me; your nipples are useless. Therefore, sleep. There is no point in both of us being exhausted. This parenting thing is a marathon, not a sprint. You need your energy." I held my finger up to pause him, holding my breast as Mabel moved slightly.

We were both silent, watching her in the low glow of the night-light I'd bought that doubled as a sound machine.

I'd learned that white noise replicated the sound of the womb. For me, it just grated against my senses.

Mabel settled back down after ten seconds. I counted.

"No arguing," I whispered to Kane. "Sleep."

He considered me, us. "Goes against all my better instincts to sleep while my woman is up with my baby."

"Well, for once, go toward your bad instincts, and sleep."

He shot me another troubled stare before he leaned in to kiss the side of my mouth. "Yes, Chef."

My body warmed at the endearment, taking me back to who I was, who we were, for a moment.

He kissed Mabel's head, curled up beside us, and was asleep within seconds.

It was a credit to how much he'd obviously been fighting against it.

I watched the two of them, my man and my baby sleeping peacefully, going over the past forty-eight hours in my head. The labor felt visceral yet blurry all at the same time. I stared at my phone, watching the time go by while forcing my eyes to stay open. Dawn. If I made it to dawn, then I had made it through the night. Then it would be morning. My mom would be up and Maisie would be there; there would be mothers to help.

Because me... I wasn't a mother. I didn't know what I was doing. This poor baby was trying desperately to drink from me, yet there was nothing there. I couldn't do anything but hold her to my breast and watch the sun start to kiss the horizon.

* * *

Kane awoke with a start just after six. He jolted up, his hair askew, eyes wide. "What do you need?"

His hands rushed to Mabel's head, which had begun moving around, her soft grumbles of disquiet calmed as her half-asleep father took her into his arms.

"Good morning, my pretty princess," he murmured against her head, inhaling deeply. His eyes met mine, cataloging me.

"You didn't sleep," he deduced. "And I did. What an asshole. Fuck, I'm sorry, Chef."

"You're sorry for sleeping?" I asked, a hint of teasing in my tone. It felt forced, that lightness, battling against the weight that settled against my chest at some point in the night.

"I'm sorry for sleeping while my woman stayed up with the baby, yeah." He brushed his hand through his hair, holding Mabel one-handed.

"I'll get up, you don't move a fucking muscle," he demanded. "You sleep. Now."

Without waiting for me to respond, he got up from bed with Mabel in his arms, walking in the direction of our bedroom.

"Kane," I called.

He turned, baby against his chest. Our baby against his chest. "Yes, Chef?"

"You're basically naked," I pointed out. My skin prickled at the visual.

He was only in his underwear, Mabel nuzzled against his bare torso.

"So?" he shrugged. "She doesn't care, and we know skin to skin is great for bonding these next few days. Plus, I like the feeling of her close." He pressed his lips to her head. "And I know you don't hate the view." He winked.

"All of those things are true." I was struggling to have what felt to be a normal conversation when my emotions were pinballing around my brain.

"And as long as you don't mind my mother and Maisie enjoying that view too—which they will, I'm sure. They have no shame—

then you go right ahead." I shifted in bed, wincing at the small movement and the pain it sent radiating to my crotch area.

Though they were staying at the inn in town, both of them had slept on the pull-out couch last night, in case we needed anything. My mother planned on staying there for the rest of the week. I'd thought it was overly indulgent, but considering the way I was feeling, it wouldn't be overly indulgent if she stayed there for the next year.

Kane stiffened as he clocked my wince. "What do you need? Painkiller?"

I scoffed as if the measly Motrin would do anything besides dull the edges of the knife carving away at my insides. "No, I need to use the bathroom." He did not need to know that I also needed to reassemble the pad and hemorrhoid patch concoction that the nurses had showed me.

Kane darted across the room, gingerly setting Mabel down in the bassinet beside our bed.

Her little face instantly screwed up as she made sounds of protest.

"Daddy is going to be right back," Kane told Mabel. "I'm just helping Mommy."

I reeled at the labels.

"That's us," I muttered. "We're *Daddy* and *Mommy*."

Kane grinned, his face light despite his exhaustion. "That's us, Chef. Daddy and Mommy."

He pulled back the covers, leaning down to put his arms behind my shoulders in order to help me from the bed.

"You don't need to do that," I argued, my voice strained with pain. "I'm capable of getting out of bed on my own."

Mabel's protests continued in the background, my teeth grinding at the sound of her displeasure.

"I watched you give birth without drugs." Kane carefully helped maneuver me so my feet touched the floor. "I'm well aware that you can handle the simple act of getting out of bed. But my masculinity cannot handle that my useless nipples can't do anything other than this." He pulled me up to standing, again carefully.

When Mabel's cries intensified, I felt it in my stomach. In my womb, cramping in sync with the wails. In my skin. My jaw clenched and every fiber of my being rebelled at the sound, something inside me screaming to go to my baby.

Despite the blood rushing to my already soaked pad, I made a beeline for Mabel instead of the bathroom.

Kane scooped her up before I could, one hand still on me.

How he could handle our newborn baby so confidently one-handed was anyone's guess. I still had trouble moving her from one breast to the other—with both of my hands.

Mabel continued to whine, but she seemed to calm somewhat in Kane's capable grasp. He then began to walk us to the bathroom.

"You need me to help in there?" He, to my mortification, nodded to the toilet.

I pursed my lips. "I think I can take it from here."

He paused for a moment then nodded.

I closed the door firmly behind me, resting my back against it and closing my eyes for a second.

I wanted, very badly, to sink onto the cool bathroom floor and sleep. A subtle cry from beyond the door sounded, then a soothing, low, masculine whisper.

There was no room for luxuries like sleeping on the bathroom floor. I was a mother now.

Taking a deep breath, I walked to the toilet.

* * *

By the time I emerged, neither Kane nor Mabel were anywhere to be seen. A rush of pure, unhinged panic hurtled through me.

I rushed down the stairs—as much as one could rush with their vagina stitched together—and found Kane in the kitchen with my mother, Maisie and Mabel.

Maisie was holding Mabel, Kane with two cups of coffee.

He was somehow dressed.

The thought of getting dressed and dealing with Mabel seemed impossible to me. I guessed he was Kane 'The Devil' Rhodes, so he could do such things.

Meanwhile, I could barely make it down the stairs.

Then again, he's not the one who just gave birth, I reminded myself.

"Chef, I was going to bring this up," Kane chastised, frowning with concern. "The doctor said you're not supposed to use stairs."

I tore my eyes from Mabel, seemingly content with my experienced sister, my heart yearning to hold her even as I enjoyed the break. I blinked at the sun streaming through the windows, remembering my lack of sleep then Kane's words.

I took the coffee thankfully. "Our bedroom is on the second floor; I have to use the downstairs," I sipped the liquid, hoping to hell it would work its magic.

Was it safe to have caffeine while breastfeeding? I searched my brain for the information, but all there seemed to be inside of it was that toy monkey playing the drums over and over again.

"You don't need to come down the stairs," Kane argued, breaking my mind-monkey's rhythm. "We've got you."

"And what am I supposed to do?" I asked. "Lounge around in bed all day?"

"I wouldn't call it lounging; I think they call it *recovering from having a baby*," Kane said dryly. "Remember the triple five rule? Five days in bed, five days on the bed and five days near the bed."

Even though the concept of bed seemed incredibly enticing right then, I knew from the previous night that bed did not equate sleep. And feeling stuck in a horizontal position when I wasn't sleeping, even if I was recovering, made my toes itch.

"Well, that's just ridiculous," I snapped. "I'm not spending ten days in bed."

I hadn't spent longer than one day in bed in my whole adult life, and that was when I had walking pneumonia, which interestingly, it is quite hard to walk around with.

Kane looked like he was going to argue, but my mother stepped in.

"Darling, Kane said you had a hard night and you didn't sleep," she deftly changed the subject. "Are you okay?"

The simple question asked in a genuine, loving and concerned tone, mixed with my mother's caring gaze and all the other ingredients in the postpartum soup made me, to my horror, burst into tears.

My mother scurried over to envelop me in her arms. I held onto her and let my tears come. I felt exceedingly small and weak and helpless.

"Oh, darling." My mother stroked my head, emotion bursting from her voice. "It's the baby blues. You're going to get just a touch if you're lucky, although even a touch feels like you've been run over by a freight train." She kissed my temple, brushed away my tears.

"It doesn't help that you haven't slept a wink," she added.

"I couldn't," I half sobbed, struggling to get myself under control. "She needed me. It seemed like the only thing I could do was put her on my boob, and I don't even think she got anything."

Maisie came over, cradling Mabel as she reached out to rub my arm. "It's just her stimulating your milk production. It'll ease up when it comes in. Well, until cluster feeding, but we won't talk about that right now."

My eyes bugged out. "Yes, let's talk about that right now," I demanded. I looked at Kane, eyeing me over his coffee cup with concern. "Where's your notebook? We're getting all the information.

"Sweetie, take a breath," Mom cooed. "You don't need all the information right now."

"I do," I argued. "I need all of the information. Because I can't do this. I can't be an amazing mother like you two." I waved my hands at them. "I can't do any of it."

To my horror, more tears streamed down my face.

"Babe, when you first walked into a professional kitchen, did you know how to make a consommé?" Maisie asked, transferring Mable to her capable father's arms.

I frowned at her, interested that she even knew what a consommé was. "No, not really."

"Exactly," she said, gently walking me to the breakfast nook. "You don't know anything about being a mother because it is your *very first day*." She sat me down. "This is not something you're expected to be an expert in. Not that there is such a thing as being an expert mother. This is something you mold into. And you will. For now, let me and Mom make you food, enjoy the sunrise, watch the ocean and hold her. That's all she needs. The rest will come."

My sister spoke calmly, sagely, as if she were the one who was six years older. She'd always brought the younger sister energy with her energetic soul. But then, I saw her for what she was: mother of two, a caretaker.

I'd always thought of 'mother' as an ordinary title. It was one of the most common in the world after all. Almost anyone could be it, do it. Or so I'd thought. I was beginning to realize it was the most specialized title one could have, something so beyond ordinary it was a joke.

I struggled to restrain a sob as Kane sat beside me and gingerly handed me Mabel. When she snuffled at my chest, Kane's deft fingers moved my shirt to help her latch on. He rested his hand on her head, the other on the back of my neck.

He didn't say anything. Nor did my mom or Maisie. The two of them made us breakfast while I sat with Kane and Mabel, the sun streaming through the windows, watching the ocean.

I'd never felt more fragile in my life. Never felt more present. Or more scared. I tried my best to mold into it.

"Marathon, not a sprint," Kane leaned in to whisper my words from last night.

I nodded then sank into him.

* * *

Kiera arrived later that day.

Thankfully, I had pulled myself together somewhat, having been all but carried back to bed with Mabel. The two of us spent the day napping and feeding, my mother and sister coming in with a steady stream of food and drinks.

"You need to keep your fluids up while breastfeeding," Maisie said as she fluffed the covers and opened the windows to let the sea breeze in.

"I'll go prepare your sitz bath," she added.

I clutched onto her wrist, careful of Mabel.

"Maise," I whispered.

She looked down at me.

"Thank you," I told her. "I know I haven't been the best big sister, or really a sister at all. And you being here, it means a lot."

Maisie's eyes twinkled as she smiled, covering my hand with hers. "There's nowhere I would be, Rey." It felt good to hear her use the name she called me when she was little. The age gap between us meant I'd merely tolerated her once the novelty of a new baby wore off, and she'd followed me around like a puppy, desperate for my attention.

One more squeeze then she was gone to prepare the sitz bath, later taking Mabel while Kane helped lower me into it.

The horrors didn't cease. Though Kane didn't seem bothered in the slightest. He put on an acoustic Unquiet Mind playlist, promised he'd be back in ten minutes then left me, giving me time to decompress.

And as promised, he was back to help me out and get me dressed, but then came hurricane Kiera.

She was laden with bags as she breezed in, declaring Mabel the 'cutest fucking baby to grace the planet' as she gave me a long hug. She hadn't met my mother or Maisie yet, but unsurprisingly, the three of them got along like they'd known each other for years.

What was surprising was that my best friend was so very similar to my mother and sister. Well, not surprising, maybe just that I hadn't noticed it sooner. Though I'd been shutting them out my entire adult life, I'd also been unconsciously searching for their energy.

Another deep, introspective thought ... one I normally would shut out, but I was a raw nerve those days. And in between my soul clenching doubts about my ability to be a mother, my tiredness and inescapable anxiety, I seemed to have time for existential crises.

Kiera stayed for a week, at a hotel on the ocean. She tried to help, but unlike my mother and Maisie, she was not a mother; that stuff didn't come natural to her. But she was there, a reminder of my old life. Who I used to be. Her presence was enough.

She left with promises to come back, but I knew part of her was relieved to leave. She felt out of place in my new life, new dynamic. I felt it, the shift in our relationship, like tectonic plates moving.

The goodbye was bittersweet. I knew Kiera would never be gone from my life, but her position was different now. I grieved that.

There was still another week left before my mother and Maisie left, and I felt the time moving like a noose around my neck, tightening with each passing day. Kane was amazing, helping in every way he could. He would jerk awake, back ramrod-straight, spluttering, "What do you need?" before he was even awake.

Mabel was a beautifully complicated baby. She required every second of our waking hours. She did not like to be sitting, or on her back. Whenever someone was holding her, they had to do laps around the house. Or walk along the beach. With, of course, Blanche in tow. Because wherever Mabel was, Blanche was. At the feet of whomever was holding her. And on the rare occasions Mabel was put down in the bassinet, Blanche laid directly underneath it.

Not that Mabel laid in a bassinet to nap often. Usually, it was in her besotted father's arms. He rarely put her down and routinely wore her in the baby carrier that had arrived as a gift from Kip and Fiona.

She fed often, and my breasts were only just recovering from breastfeeding. From the painful engorgement, where I grew three cup sizes. The cracked, bleeding nipples. The powerful let down. All of my clothes were stained with breast milk. Our sheets too.

Mabel fed hourly, on rare magical occasions, it was every two hours during the night. I routinely forced myself to stay awake, only to wake an hour later, Mabel resting happily on my chest.

I would punish myself for this, having heard and read about the dangers of bedsharing.

"You will feel guilt about it all," Maisie informed me when I told her. "You will find people or articles to reinforce that guilt. 'You're putting your baby in danger if you co-sleep, you're depriving them of comfort if you don't, you're giving them abandonment issues if you sleep train, you're not giving them self-soothing skills if you don't.' It will drive you fucking crazy." She rubbed my arm. "The decisions you make on your own are your best decisions. Like I said before, you've got a lifetime of decisions ahead of you that you'll question and second guess. But you're doing great."

It was one of many pep talks that Maisie offered, since like she predicted, I did question everything. I was paralyzed by indecision. I couldn't put Mabel in the car seat. Not only did she scream bloody murder when anyone did, I was tortured with thoughts that I was buckling her too tight. So Kane did it. Like he did all the practical things pertaining to her. I barely knew how to change a diaper that first week, still feeling like I was fumbling, all thumbs.

Me, who could effortlessly debone a branzino.

Mom and Mabel did all the cooking, because even though I yearned for the kitchen, my brain couldn't conjure up a single dish, let alone the steps to make that dish. They did all the laundry, the cleaning. They took Mabel in the early mornings and evenings so Kane and I could sleep. I'd creep downstairs to where my mother was still sleeping on the pull-out, the sun would be rising, my mother would be propped up in bed, waiting with her arms open.

I'd hand off a sleeping Mabel who would nuzzle into my mother's chest, then I'd do a zombie walk back to sleep. Only to wake up in a panic.

One morning, I sat up screaming, "Where's the baby?"

Hearing my angst, Kane had scrambled up and looked under the bed for her before we both realized she was downstairs with Mom.

That was not the first or the last panic-stricken moment. I'd woken many times in alarm, thinking she was tangled in the duvet. I tried to nurse a pillow another night.

And this was *with* my mother and Mabel's help.

I feared, truly feared, their exit.

When I communicated my panic to my mother, she hadn't so much as blinked in shock at the way I was not only willingly sharing this but being open and vulnerable with her.

"Trust your motherly instincts; you know what's best for her," she said, lighting touching Mabel's head.

My eyes snapped up at my mother and her well-meaning words spoken in a delicate tone. "My instincts?" I repeated in a harsh whisper so I wouldn't wake her. Though when she was in my arms, a tornado running through the living room wouldn't wake her. Carefully placing her in her bassinet was the only surefire way to jolt her awake.

"I don't *have* instincts when it comes to babies." I continued. "I have instincts when it comes to the correct time to take a blue cheese souffle out of the oven. When a Wagyu steak is perfectly rare. How long to sear scallops for." I looked down at the little smattering of dark hair. "And I certainly don't know what's best for her. I just met her. These people are experts." I tapped the nearest book. "These people have degrees and knowledge about babies. I know food, that's it. I do not know how to do this." My words were emphasized by a sob.

"Here's the secret, sweetie." My mother leaned forward to brush the tears from my face. "No one knows how to do this. We're all just pretending, making decisions that we hope are right. Doing our best." She looked outside, to where Kane was on the phone. "And you have the best man."

I followed her gaze, unable to disagree with her.

But even with the best man, I felt like we'd fail.

Twenty-Three

"WHAT ARE YOU DOING?"

I startled at the rough voice, the question spoken in a whisper yet boomed through the quiet of the house.

Quiet. Such a simple concept. One so elusive those days.

I turned to find Kane in the kitchen, wearing only his boxers. Not for the first time—nor even the hundredth—I marveled at the washboard abs, the six pack that was the same if not more defined than when I first met him.

He was pure sculpted muscle.

I was ... not.

Not that I'd spent hours in the gym in my prior life, but I was constantly on my feet, moving, lifting. I'd never been traditionally slim, but I was fit.

My body had regained somewhat of its previous shape thanks to breastfeeding and stress, yet I did not look the same. I was ... less firm now.

Once again, I thought about my body and whether it made me less attractive to Kane.

"Chef."

I blinked up from where I'd gone into a dreamlike existential crisis while looking at Kane's abs.

"What are you doing?" he repeated his question.

"I'm making chocolate mousse," I said, even though it was kind of obvious. I'd just finished whipping the egg whites and was folding in the melted chocolate.

My mother hadn't woken during this process, which I was thankful for.

"Chocolate mousse," he echoed. "At three in the morning. When you've had exactly one hour of sleep, and Mabel is going to wake up in another forty-five minutes for more food."

It didn't surprise me that Kane had calculated exactly how much sleep I'd had. He made it his business to catalog everything about me. How much water I'd drank, how much food I'd consumed, whether or not I was doing the prescribed sitz baths.

His little blue book was not just about Mabel but about her postpartum mother. He'd transitioned seamlessly into a caretaker for both me and Mabel.

And though I loved watching that with Mabel, it set my teeth on edge for me.

"I need to sleep," I agreed, continuing to fold. "Because my body, my cells, my blood, my brain all need sleep in order to function. But my soul, my insides need this." I gestured to the bowl with the spoon. "Need something else, need a reminder of who I am other than a mother who constantly feels like she's failing. And I feel like a failure for saying even this, that I need something else. But I need to feel like I was before. Like I know what I'm doing somewhere. Here, in the kitchen, I know what I'm doing. I feel in control. I need that."

Kane folded his arms across his chest. His muscles and tattooed rippled, and my mouth moistened, remembering those arms around me. Remembering sex.

I still hadn't been cleared for that. I wondered if Kane would even see me that way when I was. He had his hands on me whenever he could. But it was that careful, caretaking touch. No fire.

"Okay," he conceded, going to sit at the breakfast bar.

"What are you doing?" I asked. "Go back to bed. You need sleep."

He nodded. "I do. I'll sleep when my woman sleeps."

"There is no room for chivalry in the newborn trenches." I shook my head at his asinine notion. . "It's every man for himself."

"Not this man." His tone told me not to bother arguing the point further. But I wasn't functioning on all cylinders.

"What if she wakes?" I sighed. *Or what if she somehow rolls over and suffocates in the mattress without either of us there? It* was a thought I didn't utter, but it pumped nausea through me. It didn't matter that she didn't know how to roll yet. Such morbid and terrifying thoughts were commonplace then. I tried to brush my concern aside but couldn't. I almost abandoned my mousse to run up the stairs to check on her breathing.

"I got her, Chef." Kane tapped the monitor I hadn't noticed him carrying, as if he could see the terror on my face. "I'll watch over her. You finish." He jutted his chin to my bowl.

I gulped painfully, struggling to even trust the man who loved Mabel just as much as I did with her wellbeing, but I managed.

I went back to the mousse, forcing myself to make slow, practiced movements although I felt the overwhelming need to hurry through the steps like I felt the need to rush through everything else. Meals. Brushing my teeth. Showers where I heard phantom baby cries.

Measured calmness, that's what was required. It used to be muscle memory. Now I had to grit my teeth, sweat dampening my brow as I compelled myself to be meticulous.

When the mousse was put in a glass dish and into the fridge to cool, Kane jumped up.

"Okay, Chef. We're going outside to sit for a spell," he said, holding onto my hip.

The simple touch grounded me. His scent, his naked torso. All of that awakened something deep inside me, that desire too tired to come all the way to the surface, though.

"I need to clean this up." I flicked my wrist to the minor mess I'd made. I'd gone into autopilot, keeping the kitchen clean and tidy, but there were still dishes to be done.

"You need to come outside with me," Kane commanded. "You need some fresh air."

I wanted to argue with him, but Kane had a tone that brooked no argument.

I let him lead me outside, inhaling the crisp air. Summer was still holding on, but the bite of fall could be felt at two in the morning.

My eyes scurried to the screen of the monitor Kane was holding.

"She's good," Kane promised me.

He then sat in the chair on the deck. I went to sit in the one beside it, but Kane pulled me onto his lap. Delicately, though. Not roughly like he had before. I was mostly healed, but my body was tender. Kane knew that, and handled me with care.

I stiffened at first, conscious of my new body, my extra pounds. Kane's arms settled around me, and like a balm, they settled me.

The sound of the ocean crashed gently against the silence of the night.

"I've worked in some of the toughest kitchens in the world," I said. "I know that doesn't sound like something to brag about—"

"It most certainly is something to brag about," Kane interrupted, rubbing my arms.

I rolled my eyes. He was not about to let me get one self-deprecating thought in, even when he was struggling with sleep deprivation.

"Those kitchens break people," I continued. "The environment, the stress, the treatment from the head chef, others trying to get ahead of you. There is a reason why my profession is fraught with drug addictions and mental breakdowns. It is not for the weak."

"You're not weak."

"I used to think so." I rubbed my eyes, trying to hold on to my train of thought. "I not only survived all of that, but I didn't become an addict, didn't suffer any kind of mental breakdown or throw knives at waiters like some of my contemporaries had.

"I used to think that because I didn't crack in those kitchens, nothing would break me. When you were locked away, when I thought that you didn't want me..." I looked up at the house, the tranquil light coming from it, then down to where Mabel was still sleeping on the monitor. "When I thought you didn't want her, I was close to losing it. I didn't, though. I lost my mind a little, not having my kitchen, my city, my order, but I managed. And then you came back, and I thought that there was nothing more that could break me, certainly not a little baby who sleeps most of its life." I smiled at the black and white image of our sleeping baby. "Or is supposed to sleep." I glanced back at Kane. "But that's what I feel. Broken. Not because I don't want her, us. I want both of you more than anything. But I truly am doubting whether I'm capable of it."

I expected Kane to immediately rush to assure me of how capable I was, to lift me up as he had throughout this entire experience, but he didn't. He didn't say anything at first, he just ran his hands up and down my arms, considering.

"Yeah, I get that," he nodded. "I feel it too. Not broken exactly. But fuckin' terrified. And, babe, I've been in scary situations. Not just jumpin' shit or riding motorcycles or crashing motorcycles. I've been in bad situations with bad fuckin' people. And some part of me always figured I'd handle it somehow." His fingers stroked my hair. "Now, with her, I'm scared shitless. I don't know how to handle her; all I know is I love her so fucking much it hurts my bones."

He too glanced down at the monitor, clenching it so I could see his knuckles whiten under the pressure. After a handful of seconds, he glanced up to me. He looked at me lovingly. Gone was the resentment and contempt he'd arrived there with. We hadn't even properly spoken about the events that occurred. It had felt so pressing before. Now it didn't seem to matter as much.

"And you," he murmured, tucking loose hair behind my ear. "I see you givin' all of yourself, your very insides, to being the best mother you can be, then driving yourself crazy thinking that's not enough. And I want to help. Want to tell you I'm constantly mystified by you, in awe of you. That sometimes, I just watch the two of you together and want to find a way to wrap you up and protect you both because I love you so fuckin' much."

He glanced down at the monitor again.

"But I can't." His eye twitched. "I can't wrap her up and protect her from the world, though I'll try my fuckin' best. And I can't fix you when you think you're broken, even though I see you overflowing with brilliance. So I'll wait."

He kissed my neck. "I'll be here, and I'll do whatever needs to be done to help you feel less broken. First off, you're gonna do something I know you're not used to. And granted, I'm no expert, but I'm thinkin' the key to all of this is not trying to do everything yourself. You don't gotta suck it up and figure out a way to white knuckle it. Your mom and sister are here for that reason. And yeah, there's a lot of messy history sittin' at the door, waiting to be unpacked, but it can wait. For now, let them help. Let me help. And for fuck's sake, give yourself some goddamn grace."

Tears burned my eyes, and I struggled to contain them.

I wiped angrily at my face. "I've cried more since she was born than I have my entire life," I hiccupped.

Kane wiped another tear. "Again, babe, you're close to it, but you're not Superwoman. You've gone through the biggest identity shift you probably ever will in your entire life. Plus, the hormone drop. So I'll repeat my earlier statement. Give yourself some goddamn grace. Humans cry. Even ice queens melt." He winked at me.

I let out a sound between a sob and a laugh.

I watched Mabel's body move ever so slightly in the monitor, recognizing it as the telltale sign she was about to wake.

My body seemed to hum with exhaustion, if such a thing were possible.

Kane looked down at the monitor. "Let's go get our girl."

Once I was settled in bed, he brought her upstairs, and the second I was done feeding her, he expertly transferred her to his chest.

"I got her. How about you get some sleep? You know it'll be two more hours until this boob hound is back at it," he joked with a smile.

"You need sleep too," I mumbled, my lids already drooping.

"Uh-huh. Unfortunately, I'm not Superman either, so I do need mortal things like sleep," he pressed a kiss to my cheek. "I'll put her in her crib soon, but we're gonna cuddle first." He laid his lips on Mabel's head as he gently patted her back.

And that's how I fell asleep, watching Kane cradle our daughter.

True to his prediction, she was awake two hours later.

We were on the sofa. We being me and Mabel and my mother.

Some TV show was playing in the background. I'd tried to follow it but had started and stopped the first episode about three different times, rewinding it because even though I was staring straight at it, I couldn't for the life of me remember what it was about.

Mabel was curled up on my chest, napping. In her short life, she had not napped anywhere that wasn't on me or my mom or my sister or her father. Maybe that was why she was so opposed to the bedside bassinet that I'd toiled over purchasing. Even if that was the case, even if I could stand to set her down instead of having her heavy warmth on my chest or her little hands clenched in mine, none of my family would be able to heed that request.

I was resigned to being nap-trapped, lying on the sofa, trying to concentrate on watching a show, trying to keep my eyes open since I knew that even if I attempted to fall asleep, I wouldn't be able to. My mind didn't let me.

Kane was on a call in the next room. Life had completely stopped for me. Life being anything resembling what I had before Mabel came into the picture. I'd made it clear to Heidi that I wasn't coming back to the restaurant. Ferris was now head chef, a bittersweet moment for sure. I trusted him with the kitchen, knew that he was capable and great food would still come out of there, but that change made it permanent. I wasn't going back to New York.

Beyond the job, New York wasn't me anymore. I knew that in my heart of hearts. Jupiter felt like home now. It felt like the right place to raise Mabel, even when a small part of me was struggling to accept our new reality.

A quiet, coastal town that was a three hours' drive away from my mother and sister.

For now and for the foreseeable future, this baby on my chest was my life. I'd made as much peace as I could with that, but my mind stewed over Kane.

He was speaking with a new manager now. Though he'd tried to downplay it, he'd been getting a lot of requests for interviews, sponsorships, invitations to events, requests to compete in races.

Kane had disappeared after getting released from prison, but the zeitgeist had not forgotten about him. No, he was more in demand now than ever with entire websites and social media accounts dedicated to 'finding' him.

I knew this because in the early hours of the morning, when Mabel had decided she absolutely was no longer sleeping in her bassinet and would only settle on my chest, I kept myself awake by scrolling those sites and accounts.

And maybe I'd driven myself a little crazy.

Although our lives were anything but peaceful right then, we had enjoyed privacy in Jupiter that was almost unbelievable. I didn't know if it was the magic of small-town people or sheer dumb luck, but not one reporter had come sniffing.

I was aware that we could not hide forever. And although he was amazing, Kane's life had not stopped in the same way mine had. His body, hormones and brain chemistry hadn't been permanently altered. He was still Kane 'The Devil' Rhodes, but now he was also Kane 'The Dad' Rhodes. And the former would be hungering for the things that kept him sane.

After mulling over all of that for some time, I looked around the room, thinking wistfully about a gleaming stainless-steel kitchen, fresh ingredients, music playing over the speakers and unlimited time to cook.

"I'm not wishing this away," I said to my mother while patting Mabel's booty. "But is there going to be a time, any time when I can do more than hold a baby, change a baby, feed a baby, put a baby to sleep and then figure out a way to get a moment to myself?"

It felt selfish and wrong asking these questions, shame flooding through me over it. But part of me felt suffocated in the demands of motherhood and desperately needed to know how my mother had survived it. To know that there was an end.

"In the beginning, all you want is a moment to yourself," Mom said, folding a onesie. "Then slowly, you get them. Snatches, here and there. Not enough to do much more than shower, eat, change clothes, brush your hair. Soon, sooner than you think, you'll have more moments to yourself, more moments to do things than just tend to basic needs. And then after that, much sooner than you think, you'll have endless moments to yourself, when your girl is out there in the world without you, and you'd give anything imaginable, you'd give away all those moments to yourself, for a second of this." She gestured to the baby on my chest. "Though it doesn't seem like it now, it'll happen."

I opened my mouth then closed it, trying to formulate something to say. My brain was slowly eating itself.

Mabel began whining as she woke, writhing atop me, her little face screwing together in distress.

At the first sound of her wail, Kane's footfalls sounded in the hall.

"I got you, baby," he murmured, taking her from me before I could blink, kissing my head. "I'll take her for a walk, get her some air."

I wanted to argue. Her cries seemed to communicate that I was continuing to fail. Yet I was determined to get through this. To be the perfect mother, despite my sister assuring me such creatures didn't exist.

Despite this, I got up with him, helping him get her settled in her bassinet in the stroller, my mother coming in to tuck a blanket over her since she was convinced that Mabel was always cold. I rolled my eyes but let her, knowing Kane would whip the blanket off if Mabel looked so much as balmy.

"Love you, Chef," Kane murmured.

My mother and I watched Kane walk out the door then down the drive with the stroller. I might've watched them until they were nothing but a speck in the distance if it wasn't for my mother talking.

"Honey, most men, in the newborn phase, need a good jar of harden the fuck up. Women are born with it. Men usually have to buy it."

I cocked my head in the direction of my mother, my jaw hanging open in shock. My mother did not curse. She said 'sugar' instead of shit and routinely chastised me for cursing—as an adult.

"He does not have to buy it." She pointed to Kane. She rubbed her chin while looking out the window, as if searching for the right thing to say.

I was not ready for the bomb that my mother dropped next.

"Your father, he left for about six months after you were born."

My head whirled from where I'd been watching the empty driveway in a daze. "*Left*?" I gasped. "What does that mean?"

"The first few weeks are tough," she said instead of answering the question. "As you well know. Tough is much too kind a word for it. They're hell. Your whole world is turned upside down. You don't sleep. You have a wound the size of a dinner plate inside you. Your hormones are haywire. And that's just *you*. You feel all this and have to take care of a baby. Men struggle with this transition. The changes in you, their life and the lack of attention that they get."

She clicked her tongue, walking back over to the sofa to fold onesies, as if she couldn't just stand there.

I followed her stiffly.

"Your father didn't expect it. Any of it" She kept folding, periodically glancing up at me. "He didn't know the reality of it, and he, well, he couldn't handle it. So one day, he packed a bag and left."

I gaped at her again, unable to fathom the words coming out of her mouth. My father abandoned me and my mother. That absolutely could not be true. My father was kind, caring and had adored us. He didn't so much as raise his voice to us, not once. He never wanted to hurt us.

As complicated as my relationship with my mother was, I knew she would never lie either.

"He came back, obviously," she continued. "When he realized what he'd done, what he was doing."

"And you took him back," I said numbly, trying to reconcile a man who left his wife and newborn baby with the man who coached my soccer team, who read to me nightly, who gave me my love of food.

"Of course, I did," she said. "I loved your father. Even if I hated him for a while for doing that. And of course, I loved you more than I could've hated him. The reality was, I needed him. His help, his support, his financial contribution to give you the life you deserved."

I tried to digest all of this. Tried to put myself in my mother's shoes. If Kane left me and Mabel because it was too hard for him... My blood sizzled at the mere thought. Panic clutched me at how deeply that wound would cut me.

Kane would never do that. But if he did, there was no way I could take him back. Though I was financially solvent, had a profession, a name for myself. My mother had been a stay at home mom since I was born. She hadn't had anything to fall back on.

"I didn't tell you this for many reasons," she said after a long sigh. "First, because you were too young, and maybe because I was trying to forget myself. And because your father was your hero, I would never take that from you, never take him from you."

I stared at my mother. I took in the softness to her eyes, the delicate lines on her face. The kindness that she had never let the world carve from her.

"You let me believe he was the hero when it was really you," I choked out. "*You* are the hero, Mom."

She smiled back at me, and the emotion between the two of us was almost impossible to handle. I couldn't go from being Avery Hart, ice queen, childless and loveless to Avery Hart mother, in love with Kane Rhodes, to also having somewhat of an emotionally healthy relationship with my previously-estranged mother.

Too much.

Way too much.

Luckily, my sister was the queen of timing, the thump of her music as she pulled up the driveway announcing her arrival.

"That's why there's such a big age gap between me and Maisie," I realized, hearing the closing of her car door.

Mom looked toward the door, nodding. "I wanted another child, but I couldn't do it alone. It took a long time for me to trust him again."

"Does she know?" I asked quickly, knowing Maisie would be in the room in moments.

My mother shook her head. "I didn't think she needed to, that she should. You're both strong in different ways. Maybe it's a mistake telling you this now, maybe it's a mistake keeping it from her. I'm just doing my best."

I saw it then, the look I saw in the mirror every day, what I'd never recognized in my Mom. Doubt. Fear over failing as a mother.

I reached over to squeeze her hand. "You're doing great."

The moment lingered between us, and I felt the connection between us grow, something that was just ours. It always felt like her and Maisie had things I couldn't have, but now we had this.

The front door slammed shut.

"I come bearing sugar!" Maisie cried. And thankfully, the moment was broken.

Twenty-Four

KANE and I didn't have much time to talk those days. Well, we talked plenty. We talked about Mabel's bowel movements, the amount of diapers we needed, bath time, wake windows, naps, when her last feed was, how long a particular bottle had been left out. I primarily breast fed, but Kane urged me to pump every now and again to get a break. Not that it was a break. My breasts would get engorged if I missed a feeding.

We didn't have conversations like we used to. Long, soulful discussions about our dreams and our demons. He didn't wax on about his feelings for me, though he still made a point to tell me he loved me at least once a day.

Our relationship was different, there was no way around it. Our chemistry still lingered, at least a whisper of it. But both of us were too tired for much else. When I had the energy, I mourned that, worried if we'd get it back since we hadn't been together long enough to create a foundation to come back to.

The worry was exacerbated by the news of my father. That pulled the rug out from under me. I had to reevaluate the man I'd loved so fiercely. And whatever Freudian bullshit was at play, it made me rethink things with Kane.

How my feelings and past with my father were tied to my present with Kane was anyone's guess. But my father was the man I/ trusted most in the world, and to learn that had been built on a lie shook me.

I told Kane about it, even though part of me wanted to keep it hidden, bury it back down and pretend my mother had never told me.

But already, the knowledge was corroding my insides, and the thought of keeping something like that from Kane, when he hadn't kept anything from me, felt wrong.

I told him in whispers, after the baby was put down, glancing back at her, trying to fathom my father walking out on a baby that small.

His baby.

Me.

In my life, I'd never questioned if my father had loved me. Adored me.

After I finished, Kane's eyes traveled to the bassinet too, as if he were thinking the same thoughts.

"Babe... *Fuck*," he said, scrubbing a hand down his face.

"Yeah, my thoughts exactly." I blew out a long breath, still unable to process the information. My mother had expressed regret for telling me after she'd watched me intently throughout the night.

"I didn't mean to load your shoulders with even heavier weight," she murmured after dinner. "I thought it would help you understand that even the most wonderful people—and your father was a decidedly wonderful person—struggle immensely with this stage in life. Instead, I stole your hero, made you question everything. Something you're learning now is that as a mother, you're constantly wondering what the right decision is. Right now, it's regarding swaddling, feeding, napping. And then when they're older, it's over what

truths to omit and which to tell. As you can see, I'm still getting it wrong."

Again, I felt blown away by the weight of motherhood, yet another thread weaved my mother and I closer.

Which I appreciated.

"You didn't get it wrong," I told her. "I'm glad I know now."

I wasn't lying. Not exactly.

"I'm sorry," Kane said as he rubbed my back. "This on top of your adjustment to life as a mother... It's a lot. What can I do? How can I help?"

"Even the most amazing man can't help me with this," I sighed. "And you are the most amazing man. But you are not able to fix this, get my body, or my bladder control, back."

I hadn't meant to say that last part. I wasn't an overly shameful person and didn't get embarrassed over bodily functions, but I also didn't want Kane knowing about my bladder control, or lack thereof. He'd already seen me fully dilated. That was enough.

Kane didn't look perturbed about the bladder control comment, though. Although he was nice enough and smart enough to school his features if it did freak him out. "Your body doesn't need to be fixed," he framed my face with his strong hands. "Your body grew our child, brought her into this world and is now keeping her alive. You absolutely should not worry about your bladder control or your hemorrhoids."

There was a low ringing in my ears. "I didn't say anything about hemorrhoids," I gasped, horrified.

Kane chuckled, obviously not as smart as I'd credited him for considering he was laughing at me at that moment. "Babe, I read everything and anything I could on not just pregnancy but the childbirth process. I wanted to know exactly what your body was going through so I'd know how to help. I know about hemorrhoids. They're completely normal, and again, evidence of our child being brought safely into this world."

"This conversation isn't happening." I hid my face in the crook of his neck. "I'm not talking to my super-hot, super-muscled boyfriend about hemorrhoids."

Kane pulled me up to look at him, his brow furrowed. "You can talk to me about anything."

"Anything except hemorrhoids," I corrected. "Though the prospect is a bit worrying right now. I would like you to eventually fuck me again and find me attractive."

Kane's brows flattened, his mouth turned down and his eyes went downright stormy.

He grasped my neck roughly, reminiscent of the way he used to grab me before I birthed a child and ruined my vagina.

Even ruined, my vagina responded to the touch.

"That is the last fuckin' time I'm gonna hear any kind of bull-shit to that end," he growled. "I have always found you to be the most breathtaking creature to walk the earth. And then you grew my child. You brought her into this world. I truly didn't think I could love you, worship you, more. Than I did. Than I do. Every day. As I watch you grow into this. Blossom into this."

He nodded at the bassinet.

His grip tightened. "And I know that you're processin' this shit with your father and it'll probably bleed into doubts about me, so let me tell you... I'm not leaving. I'm never leaving. I'll have it inked into my forehead if you need me to."

I smiled. "That won't be necessary."

"The offer stands." He kissed my head. "You believe that, though, don't you?"

I nodded my head, even though I didn't. Not entirely.

I was unraveling.

Slowly.

Or rapidly, depending on how you counted time.

Before then, before Mabel, I could make decisions without hesi-tation. Menus, staffing, ingredients. Now, the simple thought of how many layers she should wear to bed consumed me. I went back-and-forth, debating with myself. I questioned putting her in her car seat—was she angled correctly, was she buckled too tight? Not tight enough?

Every decision was agonizing, as though it determined whether the world would end or not.

I know everyone noticed me struggling. It was impossible to miss. And that was eating me up inside too. Looking weak. Even if logically I knew this was chemical, hormonal.

My mom and Maisie were leaving the next day. I could barely eat due to the dread I felt about that. My mother was in the kitchen, making the last of the freezer meals that were neatly labeled and dated.

Maisie was in the living room with Mabel, and Kane was getting groceries. I'd taken a shower, forcing myself to make it long, knowing my sister had it covered.

My hair was wet because I couldn't bring myself to take the time to dry it. I wore my new uniform of pants with an elastic waist and a linen, button-down shirt, easily opening to feed Mabel.

I made my way through the graveyard of baby products that promised to calm even the most distressed child. Swings mothers on the forums swore by, bouncers that countless women recommended, playmats that were meant to entertain and help with neck strength. Hundreds if not thousands of dollars' worth of products marketed to desperate parents who would pay anything to calm their baby.

Mabel didn't like any of them. She liked to be in her father's arms the most. Then whomever else was around. Currently, it was Maisie, standing, swaying back-and-forth, watching some show on the television.

I watched her for a moment, her skirt moving fluidly with her movements.

There was still a rift between my sister and me. A clean break between us, the slice practically surgically sliced since the day our father died. We dealt with it in entirely different ways. She and my mother had seemed so vulnerable, so delicate that I took it upon myself to be a fortress, to keep the family together by shoving my grief away somewhere where the pain became a distant part of me that I gritted my teeth to ignore as I watched my mother and sister weep at my father's funeral. I'd let tears escape my eyes in short bursts, quickly wiping them away in order to nod and smile at the many people who had come to pay their respects to my father.

He'd been a popular man. So popular that they ran out of room at the church where the service was being held and had to set up screens for the people lined up outside.

I hated them all. His friends, milling around our house afterward, drinking, eating, talking. But I'd also been glad to have them filling up the rooms so I didn't have to feel how empty they were. It gave me a distraction.

The people left, eventually, but my coldness stayed. It grew. I stayed away from Maise and Mom and left as soon as I could. Yet they were there for me when I needed them.

I cradled a coffee my mother had handed me before she went to do yet another load of laundry.

"How did you do it?" I asked Maisie over the mug. "I'm trying, but I ... can't. I'm falling apart."

It was the first time I'd verbalized that.

"You created a person inside of you," Maisie replied, not looking at me like I was weak, broken. "You cultivated fingers and toes, a liver and a brain, reproductive organs. All the grandchildren you'll have were in your womb. You made an entire person and all the organs to sustain her life. Your own organs rearranged themselves in order to accommodate that person. And when it was time for her to leave, your pelvis stretched, your body opened to its limit, and not only did she come out, but the life you produced was wrenched from inside you. You experienced the biggest hormone drop any human will have … ever. Your insides are forever different. You don't get out of motherhood unchanged or unscathed, sweetie."

She kissed Mabel's head.

I ground my teeth, her kind words scratching against my irritated skin. She freely gave tenderness, kindness to me. Kindness I felt I didn't deserve.

"You must hate me," I said.

"Hate you?" Maisie repeated, still rocking. "You're my sister. I've hated you plenty," she teased.

I rolled my eyes. "For not being there. When Hank and Wyatt were born."

Her grin left her face. "You were there. You sent gifts. Great gifts."

"Yeah, I spent as much money as I could to cover up the shame of my absence," I admitted, watching her with Mabel. "I didn't drop everything to come to you, cook for you, clean for you, be there for you. I sent gifts."

I screwed up my nose, horrified with myself.

"Great gifts," Maisie corrected. "That bougee baby carrier was worth its weight in gold. It was the only place Hank napped for the first five months of his life and saved me from being shunned in a dark nursery for contact naps. Absolutely no back pain from all of that carrying, despite him being a big boy. And when he did finally make it to his crib, you got the eco-friendly, nontoxic one plus the breathable mattress."

"Don't do that," I pleaded. "Don't try to make me feel better." It was making me feel worse, much worse, her efforts to quell my regret.

"I wasn't there," I said firmly.

"No, you weren't." She reached out to hold my hand, her other stabilizing Mabel on her chest. "And I don't hate you for it. Not even a bit. I know you wanted to be there. But I also know that you weren't ready to be there. And simply, you weren't a mother. You were only you. Avery Hart. Chef."

Mabel started to whimper, her cries decidedly hangry.

Reflexively, I began unbuttoning my shirt, my breasts already tingling from the sounds of her weeping.

Maisie shifted Mabel to me, not even blinking at my bare breasts. I never thought I'd be showing my nipples to my sister and mother so often, but there we were.

When Mabel was latched, Maisie moved around the room, tidying things.

We sat in silence, our conversation on hold until she finished cleaning and came to sit beside me. She watched Mabel feed for a handful of seconds, her face compassionate.

"Your life was calculated chaos," she said. "Regimented rush. You were constantly on a schedule, often doing multiple things at once, always thinking three tasks ahead, never taking a moment to breathe. And motherhood is like that. But there is no calculated chaos, no regime. It is a free-for-all shitshow." She grinned. As if this was funny. "You inhale your meals, you hurry through showers, bathroom breaks and basic hygiene routines. You rush sex. If you even have enough energy to have it. And some people, some mothers, can sink into that, can thrive off it. Most do not. Because your cortisol is constantly peaking, you're constantly in fight-or-flight mode. And sometimes, babies like Mabel come along." She looked down to my daughter with absolute unconditional love. I had that for my nephews, but I'd buried it, hadn't let myself feel it, let alone show it. "They give you no choice but to stop, be in the moment. They make you sit there, with their weight on your body, their hand in yours, and there is no more rushing. There is only surrender. You breathe. You read. You think. You watch their face, examine their perfect features. Honey, you think it's a curse, but Mabel is giving you the gift no one on earth, except maybe that man of yours, can give. Peace. You just have to embrace it."

"Embrace it," I parroted, looking down at Mabel's head.

"It's a process," Maisie said. "And we'll be back."

"Promise?" I looked up at her. "I know I haven't said it, I know I don't deserve to say this, but I need you."

She put her hand on my thigh. "We need you too, Avery Hart. And we're not going anywhere."

KANE

I was struggling.

Fuck, was I struggling.

Luckily, I was managing to hide it because the last thing I needed was Avery to see it. She needed to focus on two things: herself and our baby. I could see it, eating at her, the need to be perfect, to do it 'right' all while her brain and her hormones were waging a battle against her.

It hurt me, physically hurt me to see Avery struggling and not being able to do a fucking thing about it.

The one thing I could do was not pile on more or complain. She had it so much fucking worse than me. She slept less because she was up feeding constantly and didn't wake me. Another source of guilt... I managed to sleep through some of Mabel's wake ups because I was so fucking exhausted. Avery had told me many times that there was no point in me being awake too when I couldn't 'do' anything.

I disagreed. I could change the diapers, reswaddle, resettle Mabel. I could make Avery's life just a little bit easier.

And I could pull myself together.

I thought I'd been through it all, thought I was tough. I played the tough guy pretty fucking well, but being a father? Yeah, that made a man of me.

Leaving the house, even with Judith and Maisie there, felt like a betrayal because I didn't want to leave Mabel and Avery. Worse, I felt guilty as fuck because a small and fucking selfish part of me was thankful for the break, to be able to get on my bike and ride past the ocean and just fucking breathe.

Horrible. Selfish.

I wouldn't take them away, not for the fucking world. But I'd give myself less of a fucked-up childhood so I knew how to step up for them.

I had no father figures beyond variations of stepfathers who came in and out of my life, ranging from apathetic to sadistic. A mother who stayed in the picture long enough to fuck me up royally. Not to mention the other abuse.

I hadn't told my mother about her granddaughter yet. We weren't close like that. Especially after seeing Judith, the perfect grandmother. My mother wouldn't be that. She'd find a way to make it about herself, she'd find a way to make me take care of her. And I didn't need that. Avery didn't need that.

I'd considered myself evolved—I'd gone to therapy, accepted my trauma, whatever the fuck. But if parenting had taught me anything, it had showed me all the ways I still needed to parent myself.

And I had to. Fucking had to. Not just because I planned on being there for every moment of Mabel's life, and Avery's too. But I planned on Mabel adoring me, never questioning my love for her or her mother.

I had to pull myself together.

"It's Kane 'The Dad' Rhodes!" a voice exclaimed, making me jump.

I'd been sitting on my bike, helmet in my lap, staring into space. Who knew for how long. I was supposed to be out on a pastry run, not fucking wallowing in self-pity.

I glanced to where Kip was sauntering out of the bakery, coffee in hand. I'd seen him and his business partner Rowan a handful of times around town, mostly at the bakery since their wives owned it, and they made it their business to be near their wives, something I'd come to understand about them.

Part of me knew we'd get on well. Both seemed nice enough guys—Kip a little more outgoing than Rowan–but I saw they were good people. Though I was a little gun shy with letting anyone into my life since Brax. Yeah, my internal alarms had warned me to be careful with him, but I'd thought he was harmless.

And he'd almost ruined my fucking life.

My fists clenched, thinking about him, and I wondered, not for the first time, if I'd made a mistake in not taking my brother up on his offer.

"You look how I felt for the first year of June's life, brother." Kip grinned at me in a way that told me the expression was second nature to him. He slapped me on the shoulder as I got off the bike.

"Fatherhood," he sighed. "It's hard."

I hummed in agreement.

His hand, still on my shoulder, tightened, and his eyes narrowed on me. "No, bro, it's *hard*. I've been in combat. I've had people shooting at me, I've been this close to death." He held his thumb and finger millimeters apart. "But I'll tell you, fatherhood is harder than war."

I looked at him, not able to tell if he was joking or not.

He shook his head, the haunted look leaving his face. "But it's worth it. I promise. And it gets easier." He took a long sip of his coffee, seemingly in thought. "Kind of. I know you guys are still in the newborn trenches, and let me tell you, I know they're fucking trenches, but once you're out, we'll come over. Me and the wife and June. We'll show you there is life after this." He squeezed my shoulder again, quite obviously unafraid of physical affection with a man he barely knew.

"For now, copious amounts of coffee, sugar, and for fuck's sake, don't ever tell her you're tired. You're apt to get your face metaphorically clawed off, if you're lucky. No matter how tired you are, they are 1.000 *percent* more tired."

He winked then turned to leave.

I looked at the pink bakery I'd become a regular in, my bike parked on a Main Street that could only be described as quaint with what I was almost sure was spit-up on my shirt.

I was exhausted—obviously not more exhausted, never more exhausted than Avery—not from an all-nighter, not from training for the Olympics, not from crashing at the X-Games and narrowly avoiding death. Nope, drained from an eight-pound baby who liked to be held and fed and hated sleeping anywhere that wasn't on her mother or me.

The crisp sea breeze seemed to be the only thing keeping my eyes open.

I'd never felt more alive in my life.

And despite my struggle, my bone deep fear that I was going to fuck up, I wouldn't have it any other way.

Twenty-Five

AVERY

THE FIRST THREE months didn't pass in a blur like people said they did.

Mabel was diagnosed with colic, with her constant crying ramping up the day after my mom and Maisie left. I was aware 'colic' was a catchall term for a baby who appeared to be healthy but was in obvious discomfort.

I tried everything. Nothing worked.

Every day dragged into an eternity of dirty diapers, of burp cloths, of milk-stained clothing, engorged breasts, crying and sleep deprivation.

And every day was a variation of the same. With the one key difference: what calmed the baby one day didn't necessarily calm the baby the next day. More likely, it served to distress her more.

And although I thrived on routine, that was not any kind of routine crafted on Earth. Often, I would've sworn that in the middle of the night, amongst the cries and the grunts and the feedings, that that routine was crafted in the depths of hell.

Kane no longer had the magic touch. Because when you have a colicky baby, there was no magic except in the blissful fifteen minutes —if you're lucky—we got a day when our baby was content, ready to look at us and occasionally even gift us with her precious smiles.

Aside from that, magic was somewhere else, at Hogwarts or wherever.

No, for all Kane's considerable talents, calming the baby was not one of them. His magic was to stay calm when she wasn't. To speak to her with adoration, kiss her head, rock her, walk around the house for hours. Not once did I see him get frustrated with her, lose his temper, look at all like he was going to go out for a pack of diapers and never return.

That was a feat in itself. Because in my darkest of moments, I'd thought about getting in my car and driving off. Not forever. Just for ten minutes.

Ten minutes of peace. Ten minutes when I wasn't trying to stop the baby from crying or tense, knowing it was inevitable that the baby would start crying again.

I would look at her—her tiny nose, the cute fingers, the rosebud lips—and find it impossible to believe that something so perfect existed. That someone so precious was mine, ours.

And then I'd struggle to stand over the weight of it all, over the failure I felt because I couldn't fix her. Not with a change in my diet, not with all the natural remedies, not with medications I hesitated to use because she was just so tiny. Not with the special exercises, ways to hold her, massages. Not with the swaying swing nor the vibrating contraption for the bassinet.

"How do people do this?" I cried, juggling the baby because when I spoke, I paused slightly, and therefore, her sleeping form registered the change in movement and decided to rouse to inform me of how I'd fucked up.

I held my breath as she fought against the swaddle for a moment then settled. I kept holding my breath to see if she was really asleep. It seemed, for the moment, she was.

I braved looking back to Kane, breathing again. "Like, seriously. People walk around with children every day, and I've never given it much thought. I hate to admit it, but I never considered that being a parent made you overly strong or special in any way. Now I think every one of them needs a fucking medal for dealing with these creatures." I gestured to the baby with only my eyes, every other part of my body dedicated to the specific combination of movements required to keep her asleep.

Kane smiled, and I loved him for that easy smile. I also wanted to punch him in the face for that smile.

"Don't you know, baby?" he murmured, reaching to take Mabel from me. I chewed on my lip as she moved, whined and then curled into her Dad's chest. "I've already got medals." He started to sway like the expert he was.

"I would say go nap, but I understand now that you're physically incapable," he said. "So how about you go sit outside, breathe the sea air and have a glass of wine. Or tequila."

I would've rolled my eyes at him if I hadn't been so tired. "It's ten in the morning."

He blinked, a slow blink, him looking at the clock in confusion the only signifier that he might've been as frazzled as I was. "I could've sworn it was five in the evening at least," he muttered. "Oh well. Time means nothing, so have the tequila. Or a cup of tea, if you want to be more traditional. I don't judge. Just give yourself a break."

I gnashed my teeth at his suggestion.

Now that my mother and sister were gone, there was always something to clean up, something to do. Endless amounts of laundry; Kane was always folding something.

I itched to do something productive, to cook something. But

my limbs were leaden, and my brain could not think of a single thing to make.

"Chef," Kane urged, and though I stilled liked it, sometimes the title felt like a taunt rather than an endearment. "Go outside. Breathe. I'll let you know when she needs you."

A look passed between us. One full of knowing, yearning, exhaustion and longing. I longed for Kane's arms around me and for my body to be able to appreciate the touch.

I imprinted the image of him standing there, cradling an exceptionally tiny baby against his chest, etched with exhaustion but also unflinchingly handsome.

Blanche, as always, was pressed against her father's legs, as close to the baby as she could get.

For another moment, I lingered. All I'd wanted was a moment to myself, yet now I hesitated to take it.

But eventually, I did, walking outside and staring at the wide-open ocean. I hadn't considered myself to be a beach person before I moved there. In fact, with rising sea levels and hurricanes, I thought it would be prudent to be inland when and if I ever settled down somewhere. Not that I ever considered settling down.

But there, in that town, with the rush of the ocean soothing the edges of my frayed nerves just a tad, I couldn't deny I understood the appeal.

* * *

We had our first fight.

It was inevitable.

We were both criminally sleep deprived, both in raw emotional states, both still dealing with traumas that we hadn't properly dealt with.

I felt Kane's prison sentence seeping from inside of him. When he looked panicked every time he was in a room with a closed door.

If the house got too warm. Sometimes just a faraway look in his eyes when he was holding Mabel.

I didn't know how to talk to him about it. I felt guilt over that. Felt responsible. And I wanted to fix him, just like I wanted to fix Mabel.

But that was impossible. People couldn't be fixed. Especially not babies. She was an intelligent baby with big feelings and only one way to communicate. I knew that logically. Yet every time she cried, I couldn't help but feel like it was an emergency, like I'd missed something.

My nerves were frayed, and though he seemed to be hiding it better than me, I knew Kane's were too. Without my mother and Maisie, the house descended into a disorganized mess of diapers, wipes, burp cloths and coffee cups.

We were constantly behind.

"Maybe we should hire some help," Kane suggested one afternoon.

I stared at him, from where I was folding a onesie. I didn't know why it needed folding instead of shoving it into the drawer. It's not like Mabel cared if it was wrinkly, and we barely went anywhere for other people to see. "No."

He paused from where he was piling our plates from lunch, preparing to take them to the kitchen.

My mother's freezer meals were a godsend.

"Accepting help isn't failing, Chef," he said mildly.

My head snapped up. "I'm aware of that, Kane," I spat. "But this is it. This is my job now." I gestured to the onesies. "Plenty of women do it. Thousands. Without help, without a hands-on partner. I just have to … figure out how in the hell they did it."

It seemed like some big secret everyone was hiding, how one survived the 1,001 household tasks that needed done plus the 1,001 baby care tasks while also eating, sleeping and personally grooming oneself. An unachievable equation.

"You don't have to figure it all out," Kane reminded me. "We have the luxury of differing schedules and financial security to design our own lives. We don't have to be stuck in Groundhog Day forever."

I paused, chewing on my lip as I weighed his words. "Is this because this is too vanilla for you?" I couldn't stifle the snark suddenly coloring my tone, buried for who knew how long.

"What do you mean by that?" Confusion tugged down his lips.

"You know exactly what I mean by that, Kane." I slammed a folded burp cloth down much harder than necessary. "We haven't had sex. Not once, even though I was cleared by the doctor. You are stuck in a house most of the time. With a lovely yet constantly crying baby and a woman who does not resemble the one you crossed the room at a party for. This isn't us fucking in a dive bar in New York," I hissed, inexplicably furious at him although he didn't deserve it.

I let out a hollow laugh. I'd gone off the deep end. This was a breakdown, one that had been slowly building and fueled largely by the knowledge of my father. Yet I couldn't stop it. "We won't be living like that anymore. Or I won't be. This is our life now. Not an adventure for you. This isn't going to be death-defying, full of excitement. Our lives now revolve around responsibility, bedtimes, naps, bathtimes... This is going to get boring for you. I am not the same person who can be led around on the back of a bike, a woman with freedom. I'm not her anymore. This isn't going to be enough for you."

I am not going to be enough for you, was what I left unsaid.

Kane's face had been impassive when I started speaking, but by the time I was done, he was scowling, eyes blazing with fury.

"You really think that little of me?" he asked quietly. "Think that I'm so fuckin' shallow that what I want for the rest of my life are empty adventures?"

I opened my mouth, realizing how cruel I'd sounded. He didn't let me speak.

"You don't get to say what you think isn't enough for me." I bristled at how cold he sounded, putting the dishes down on the coffee table. "You don't even get to insinuate that a life where I'm a dad, where I get to watch our daughter grow, learn, laugh, discover is too fuckin' *ordinary* for me. And you sure as shit don't get to tell me that watching my woman become a mother, care for our little girl, isn't fuckin' enough just because I don't get to fuck you in a bar anymore." He stepped forward. His face was menacing, his wired energy practically oozing from him. "And, Chef, I don't think my days of fuckin' you in bars are done. If they are, that's fine with me. Any way I get to be inside of you, feel you clench against my cock, is just fuckin' fine with me. And on top of that, any day I get to wake up with you, drink coffee with you and our daughter is the *best fuckin' day of my life.* You thinking that I need more than that, need more than you, is total fuckin' bullshit."

Again, I opened my mouth to say something, to say anything, but before I could, he walked away.

He didn't slam the door shut behind him, but I got the feeling he would've if he could've.

Nor did I hear the sound of his motorcycle leaving.

So after calming myself down enough to breathe evenly, I went to look out the window to see what he was doing.

His bike wasn't there.

He must've pushed it down the drive so the noise didn't wake Mabel.

Even in his fury with me, he protected our daughter. Like always.

Regret, painful and all-encompassing, hit me then, the organ beneath my sternum aching. I'd just belittled him as a partner, and more importantly, as a father. I'd insinuated that he didn't have the depth to love something pure and simply.

Yes, I'd voiced my greatest fears, but they were more about myself than Kane.

I wanted to race after him, wanted to crack open a bottle of tequila and drown my sorrows. I wanted to crawl into bed, cover my head and welcome oblivion.

With a squawk, Mabel not so gently reminded me I could do none of those things. I was a mother. So instead of immersing myself in the luxury of sorrow or any kind of breakdown, I tended to my daughter and hoped that Kane would come back.

* * *

Kane came back.

It was never a question, really. He gave no indication that he was going to leave us. He was not that kind of man.

Yet I was still off-kilter from the news of my father. He hadn't seemed like that kind of man either. Not in a million years. Yet he left.

Add to that severe sleep deprivation, and I didn't trust my own mind, let alone the mind of someone else.

Yet Kane came back. Less than two hours later.

My entire body relaxed, as did Mabel's, but that could've been out of sheer exhaustion from crying every moment Kane was gone.

He sauntered through the door, anger still hardening his face until he saw our daughter. He took her from my arms wordlessly.

"She eaten?" he asked, his voice void of emotion.

That flat tone hurt me, but I deserved it.

I nodded.

"She slept?"

"Not a wink."

"Okay, let's get you to bed, little one," he murmured, kissing Mabel's head. Before leaving, he looked at me. "I love you, Chef.

Still need time, but we'll talk later. Then we'll have angry makeup sex."

On that, he turned and ascended the stairs with our baby.

* * *

"Are we going to talk?" I asked in a whisper, mindful of Mabel sleeping in the bassinet beside us. She'd grown accustomed to the noises of us getting ready for bed, but it was a crapshoot as to whether a whisper would wake her or she'd sleep through me dropping an entire glass of water on the floor. No rhyme or reason.

We'd gone about our routine after Mabel woke up from her last nap—changing her, entertaining her, me cooking while Kane walked with her out on the beach. Us sitting together taking turns holding a crying Mabel, me ending up breastfeeding her at the table while eating my meal one handed, quickly, barely tasting the food.

Then dishes, then bathtime with the calming music, massage and Mabel screaming on and off throughout the routine.

Then her bedtime.

Routine. A variation of the same every day. With Mabel keeping it interesting as to whether she treated us with dazzling smiles or informed us how pissed off she was with the routine or life in general.

It was why I was worried, terrified, of the future.

"Nah," said Kane. "I'd rather fuck you."

My insides somersaulted as I looked at his face, seeing naked hunger on it. All of the desire he used to look at me with was there, and more.

Suddenly, my heart was stuttering, and fear cinched my lungs.

I glanced over to where Mabel was sleeping, arms thrown up above her head.

"With the baby in the room?" I whispered.

He let out a low chuckle, yet it was sexual too. "Yes, Chef.

Hopefully, she's out for the count, and considering that's how we made her, I don't think she'll mind."

Though I had thought about sex often since Mabel was born, I hadn't thought much about the reality of having sex in front of her. Granted, she was sleeping and had no idea what sex was, but still.

Before I could contemplate further, Kane's lips were on my neck, hands on my hips, slowly moving me across the bed, away from Mabel while covering my body with his. The simple weight of his body on top of mine, his erection pressing against me was all I needed to remember that my body was more than a machine that created breast milk.

"I haven't tried to fuck you, Chef because I've been waiting for you to come to me," he murmured against my neck.

His hands ran down the sides of my body, making me shiver.

"You've gone through a change that I can't begin to understand," his hands continued moving up and down. Soft, tentative.

"Your entire life has been consumed by the needs of another human for the past four months," he added, lips traveling up my jaw. "I didn't want to be another person you felt you needed to give more to."

He pulled back so I could see his face in the low light from the sound machine.

"I never thought you would equate that to me not desirin' you." His lips gently pressed on mine, his hands gliding underneath the hem of my tee to skim the bare skin of my hips then my stomach.

I tensed, knowing that that area was forever changed.

Surely, Kane noted my tensing, but maintained his slow skimming, up my stomach, over the parts that had stretched to accommodate Mabel, to the places where my insides had moved, where my abs had separated.

"I have never desired you more," he told me, kissing me deeper.

There was no immediate fire, no overwhelming, desperate,

animal need. That was there, kindling deeper down. This was a slower build, purposeful.

His palms grazed over my breasts, my nipples peaking at the light touch. I arched upward into his hands as I kissed him back, joyous to be awake in this way, even amidst my exhaustion.

Kane kneaded my breasts before bringing his hands back downward, to where I was wet for him.

"This, here, Chef is all I need," he rasped, toying with me over my panties. Just as my toes began to curl, Mabel punctuated this by passing gas loudly in her sleep.

Both Kane and I froze, looking toward the bassinet, waiting for the telltale flail of legs and arms to announce she was awake.

But nothing happened.

She snuffled then went back to sleep.

Kane and I looked back at each other and burst out laughing. Muted laughter, of course.

When our eyes met, something passed between us. It wasn't hot or electric, no inferno of carnal desire. But it was something deeper, simpler yet more profound. A recognition of what we were together, what we had together.

"I think maybe we should go to the bathroom," I suggested, panting slightly. "I'm not quite ready for us to do that with her right there."

Kane chuckled again, low and throaty, pushing his erection against my soaked panties.

I gasped.

He didn't verbally respond to my request.

At once, we were no longer on the bed; we were up, my legs wrapping around Kane's waist.

Our mouths met as he ambled quietly across the room, me rubbing myself up and down his length, his hand on my ass.

I detached from his lips only long enough to check on Mabel as we passed. Still sound asleep.

Kane grabbed my face, turning it back toward him so he could kiss me again.

We made it to the bathroom, Kane closing the door.

"It turns me on so much how quietly you closed that door," I breathed against him.

Kane laughed. "So it's not my muscles, tattoos or general air of danger, it's my ability to shut doors quietly."

I smiled against his lips. "At this point in our life, yes. That trumps them all."

He pinched my ass playfully.

Then he set me on the counter of the bathroom. I gasped at the cold marble on my skin.

"Arch up, Chef," he ordered.

I did as he asked so he could quickly slide off my panties before stepping between my legs, freeing himself.

His touches in our bed had been slow, unhurried, almost lazy.

Now he was moving much in the same way I ate my food—rushed, trying to get it done before Mabel started crying.

The urgency was strong within me too, knowing Mabel could awaken at any moment, and as desperate I was to connect with Kane, I knew I couldn't continue through that.

I clutched either side of his head. "Slow."

His ice-blue eyes found mine as I felt his breathing even somewhat, the frantic energy melting off him. He gave me a lopsided yet horny smile. "In case you were doubting how fuckin' desperate I am to get inside you, Chef, it's very fuckin' hard to heed your command." I watched the cords of his neck tighten.

"If it feels different—" I whispered.

"Stop right fuckin' there," he growled, pressing his cock against my entrance.

I gasped.

"It's not gonna feel any different," Kane continued. "Because it's you, Chef. It's my woman. Warm, wet, welcoming. My. Fuckin'. Home." As he spoke, he slowly pushed into me.

I mewled at the intrusion, taut in preparation for pain.

That area had basically been beaten up recently. So I'd been afraid of this. Kane was not small.

The simple act of taking steps or using the bathroom had been painful. Sex felt dicey.

But beyond a slight tug of discomfort, there was nothing but soul-wrenching pleasure.

Kane's forehead laid against mine once he was fully seated inside me.

"Are you okay?" He didn't move straight away. "Does this hurt?"

"No," I hissed. "Move."

He made eye contact with me. "Yes, Chef."

Then he did as I'd instructed.

Not as hard and furious as he had in the past. Instead, he gave me slow, deep, powerful thrusts.

I sank my nails into the skin of his back.

It felt like coming back. To a different part of myself. The sexual part. The desirable part. The part that was Kane's. That deserved pleasure. Coupling.

It was exquisite.

It wasn't the earth-shattering, erotic fireworks of before. It was something deeper than that. My orgasm didn't take me apart and put me back together. It was warm, washing over me, melting all the tension in my body.

It was coming home.

And Mabel was kind enough to wait until we were done to wake.

Twenty-Six

I'D TOLD Kane that I was fine with Mabel on my own. I'd lied. Obviously.

He had a life to get back to. There were pressing matters, meetings with lawyers, figuring out what his future looked like. There were contracts he'd already signed, sponsorships to discuss. And media to pander to.

I'd convinced him to do an interview in Portland with a magazine in order to quell the craziness and hopefully buy us more time. We knew our luck was going to run out. Soon. I could feel it. And maybe if he did an interview, it would help feed those hungry, desperate people scouring the earth for Kane.

Firstly, because if they found Kane, they found Mabel. And my fear, my anxiety was only just starting to dissipate. I no longer thought she'd died in the night if she slept too long—granted, it was only because I had a device on her foot that monitored her heart rate. I was slowly able to do things without bone-rattling terror. The mere thought of a world of people swarming to catch a glimpse of our daughter... I knew that was the driving force behind Kane leaving. He would move heaven and earth to protect her.

Secondly, I needed to prove to him that I was capable of caring for her without him. So he didn't have to look at me with such concern when he ran out to get milk.

And thirdly, I needed to prove to *myself* that I was capable of being with Mabel on my own because it was destroying my ego that when Kane was out getting milk, I was fighting for my life.

Kane had only left an hour ago yet had sent me countless text messages. As had my mother. And Maisie. And Kiera. Because, apparently, Kane had all of their numbers.

I planned on killing him for highlighting my vulnerability when he got home.

The hour had passed without event ... so far. I'd even managed the unthinkable: putting Mabel down for her nap in her bassinet. There were many things to do, yet I'd just wandered around the house, jaw tight, unable to think about what to do with myself.

I'd been staring at the monitor on and off. Partly to check on Mabel, also to check on Blanche. We'd tried, unsuccessfully, to get her from the room when Mabel was sleeping, in whispered commands, but even Kane couldn't make her budge.

He had done what the dog trainer couldn't, there was no more barking, no more pulling the leash. But where Mabel was concerned, all bets were off.

Kane had decided to just leave her. I, on the other hand, was petrified that Blanche would somehow snap and decide to try to eat Mabel, hence my laser-like focus on any small movement on the monitor.

No, Blanche had never shown so much as a smidgeon of aggression toward our daughter, but my intrusive thoughts knew no logic.

I tensed the moment Blanche's head lifted from where it had been resting against her feet.

Seconds later, a soft knock sounded against the door. Thank God the delivery person had finally read the sign we not so subtly put up to request no one ring the doorbell.

I went to the door, expecting to pick up one of the many middle of the night purchases I'd made while breastfeeding and researching things that would help Mabel sleep easier.

But it wasn't a package.

"Fiona," I gasped, staring at the woman on my doorstep.

Both she and Nora had sent gift baskets and texts and pastries and offers to come over to watch the baby—which I'd thought was extremely nice, but I wasn't comfortable with that. Because they were essentially strangers. Nice, interesting and warm strangers, but strangers nonetheless.

I was not prepared for them to see me like that. I wasn't prepared to see myself like that, but I had no other choice.

Both my mother and Maisie had urged me to take them up on the offers, to connect with them and make mom friends.

I'd smiled and pacified them but hadn't intended on doing it. Not now or in the immediate future. I was trying to survive; I didn't need to socialize too.

Yet there she was, at my doorstep. And unless I wanted to slam the door in her face, I had no choice but to socialize.

Fiona looked me up and down. I could only imagine what she saw. My hair was piled on my head, and I was pretty sure I'd brushed my teeth today. I'd fed Mabel before her nap and hadn't bothered with a breast pad, so I likely had stains on my white tank. From milk and the tomato pasta I'd just shoveled in my face.

Fiona, however, looked flawless. Her short blonde hair was effortlessly shiny and curly. Her slim figure was encased in a stain-free white tee and jeans. She had no bags underneath her eyes and looked vibrant and alive. "You need a village, girlfriend," Fiona declared, pushing her way through the front door, canvas bags hanging from the crooks of her arms.

"I know it's risky, bringing food to a chef, but I figured that you wouldn't be worrying too much about the Michelin Star quality of it since you don't have to make it or do the dishes," she informed me as I dumbly followed her through the living room into the kitchen.

I couldn't even remember if I'd closed the front door, and I was too tired to go back to check.

Fiona unpacked foil packages, each of them with white labels on them.

"I'll put some in the fridge and the rest in the freezer," she continued as if I'd spoken a word to her aside from breathing her name in surprise.

She paused with her hand on the fridge. "Is the baby sleeping?" she asked, looking around, expecting to find a baby hidden somewhere.

I nodded. "If she wasn't, you'd know," I said with a grim smile.

Fiona's eyes were kind, understanding, and the mere look made me want to dissolve into tears. "Do we need to be quiet?"

I shook my head. "Mabel will sleep through anything. The surefire way to wake her up is to put her down in her crib, and I managed that already."

I thought bitterly about all the movies and shows that depicted babies being put into cribs, gooing and gahing while their parents kissed them on the head, turned off the light and closed the door.

Utter bullshit.

Fiona nodded, opening the fridge then clanged things about as she rearranged its contents. "Good. Babies need to be able to sleep with life going on around them." She closed the fridge. "And as for the other thing? Despite what all the sleep training gurus and whisperers tell you, it's luck of the draw. They come preloaded with personality and willpower. Some can be trained, sure. Others are just little bastards." She went to a bag where she retrieved baked goods and coffee, which she handed to me.

I stared at Fiona for two seconds, then I burst into tears. Real tears. I was shocked and disgusted at myself, but I couldn't stop.

Before all of this, that would've been my worst nightmare. I was uncomfortable with emotions, tears especially, and always delegated the shoulder pats and kind words to my sous chef whenever someone broke down in my kitchens.

But I was a world away from commanding a world-class kitchen with a will of steel and emotions locked down tight. That thought, of course, only served to bring on more tears and a very ugly sounding sob.

"I'm s-sorry," I hiccupped. "I'm just ... I'm reading all these books." I thrust my hand out to the kitchen island where I'd been pouring over the countless books I'd purchased that promised twelve-hour sleeps, calm babies and set routines.

"I've followed them to a T," I continued. "I'm a chef—well, I used to be a chef—" I was overcome by another bone-racking sob. "Before I became a mother, I was a chef. And I know how to follow directions. Precisely. My brain slotted things into place effortlessly. Having sixteen elements of a dish ready at precisely the same time was child's play to me. Pardon the pun." I laughed with a maniacal edge. "Now trying to figure out when exactly I should feed her and put her down for a nap seems akin to rocket science. It's obviously me. Because millions..." I tapped the cover of the book, "*millions* of copies were sold to mothers who were obviously more competent than me and managed to do it all. Yet I'm not. I'm failing."

There it was. The two words that haunted me most.

I'm failing.

Fiona, thankfully, didn't do anything like bring me into her arms for a hug when I cried. That would've made me feel worse. She had just stood there, face free of judgment and listened to me. When it was clear that I was done, she spoke.

"I'm not an advocate for burning books," Fiona said. "In most circumstances, it's a crime." She picked up the book on the counter then walked to the living room.

She piled my dog-eared, tearstained parenting and baby books in her slender arms, marching toward the backyard.

I followed her because she was talking about burning things and had picked up a lighter from where it sat on the counter beside a candle Maisie had left to 'purify the air.'

Fiona walked past the patio set to the outdoor pizza oven that had been a big part of selling this place to me. I'd envisioned making pizzas with the sea breeze kissing my face, my baby happily watching me from a bouncer.

Not once had that thing been fired up.

Until now, with Fiona dumping a bunch of books in there then setting it alight without a second thought.

I watched with horror and satisfaction as the fire ate away at words that had taunted me with my failures.

Fiona didn't speak straight away, she just watched the books burn.

"Some babies are book babies." She waved to the fire. "They can respond to methods 'experts' concoct. Others are not. Our baby June is not a book baby. It sounds like Mabel isn't either. I'm saving you months of overthinking and insanity."

I watched the flames, not speaking.

'You've got to survive the gauntlet." She turned to face me as if she hadn't just lit a fire in my backyard.

I was still clutching the baby monitor, so I glanced at it to find Mabel still sleeping.

"The first year of your baby's life is the gauntlet," Fiona explained. "Which is the first year of your relationship. Your new relationship. Where it isn't just two people, hot sex and independence. There's sleep deprivation, screaming, crying, dirty diapers, postpartum depression, sleep regressions, teething, illnesses." She huffed out a breath, waving smoke away from her face.

I vaguely wondered if I needed a fire extinguisher. Not that I was overly worried. Small fires, I had experience with.

"I mean, I didn't think I was a mother who would be preoccupied with nap schedules," Fiona continued. "I watched my overly anxious and slightly insane—in the best way—friend have a baby. Nora obsesses over everything, but she did not obsess over naps or sleep. Her baby slept through the night from *eight weeks*. I took her life as a blueprint for mine. And I love her so dearly, but once our girl June was born and she came out screaming and ready to fuck shit up, I changed my tune."

She shook her head with a smile on her face.

"I wanted to punch my best friend and her perfectly sleeping baby," Fiona chuckled. "I wanted to punch the husband I was sure I adored for daring to sneeze after I finally got the baby down for a nap. Like who the *fuck* did he think he was, sneezing like some bachelor? Hold it in. I don't care if you crack a rib."

I barked out a half laugh at that. Although Kane did indeed close doors quietly, he'd also become quite a butterfingers suddenly. His phone, plates, knives and forks routinely clattered out of his hands and onto the hardwood floor.

He was always apologetic, ready to run to calm Mabel if he woke her, but it did make me want to strangle him, just a little.

"Anyway, marriage is supposed to be built to survive the first year. But it tests you. Granted, our marriage didn't begin with love, it began with immigration fraud, but that's a story for another day." She waved her hand dismissively as my interest piqued.

"I went through a lot for my baby June," Fiona gazed at the ocean. "I thought I would never be a mother. And I thought all of my loss and pain would inoculate me from the woes of being a first-time mother. I wouldn't resent the lack of sleep, the radical change in my identity, my body, my everything. Because my baby was precious. But let me tell you, that's all bullshit. She's precious, but it was hard. I love my husband more than anything, but there were times I considered calling a lawyer. But that was sleep deprivation and postpartum depression."

She stepped forward and squeezed my arm.

"I knew who you were the second you walked into the bakery.

Not the fame shit, I knew you were a stone-cold bitch—in the best way—who had had her heart broken. Like recognizes like and all that. I get that you want to do it alone. Prove it to yourself. But you're a resident of Jupiter, Maine, honey. We like you. Therefore, consider this the welcome committee barging our way into your life. We're gonna be friends. Our babies are gonna be friends, our husbands are already basically boyfriends."

Another laugh burst from me.

Fiona smiled. It was warm and lit up her whole face.

"I respect the fight of doing it alone," she continued. "But it's time to wave the white flag. We're here, and we're not letting you do it alone. Because, babe, I consider one of the greatest crimes another mother can commit against another is to not help another when she's able. So hold the fuck on, bitch, we're here to help."

I couldn't bring myself to argue.

I didn't want to.

So I held the fuck on.

Fiona unpacked the food, spoke a mile a minute, helped with Mabel when she woke and didn't leave until Kane arrived home.

And for the first time in a long time, I felt like I could handle things.

* * *

And so the rotation of the Jupiter women started.

Nora was next. Pregnant herself, she came with her husband Rowan and their daughter Ana. Rowan I'd seen at the café a few times. He was tall, muscular and absurdly handsome. He also seemed to only smile for his wife and daughter. He lit up for them. It had hurt to look at before.

Those days, not so much since I had a man who lit up for me too.

Rowan was a man of few words, but he was also a man unafraid of crying babies, handling Mabel with the ease and care of a skilled father.

"I'll take her outside." His voice was deep, serious, and just a little intimidating, even to me who was not easily intimidated. "Fresh air. It's good for them." He looked at me. "Also, you won't be able to listen out for her cries and convince yourself it's your job and only your job to go to her."

He winked knowingly at me. I got the impression that a wink from Rowan was rare and likely not to be repeated.

Then he looked at Kane. "I'm thinking we'll have a beer. You got any?"

"Oh, I've got beer." Kane told Rowan before his eyes grazed mine. "You good here, Chef? Need anything?"

I shook my head. "Go drink beer, do man things." I was trying not to marvel at how Mabel immediately nuzzled up against the strange man holding her, settling there effortlessly. I feared that if I looked too hard, I'd ruin it; she'd realize that five seconds ago, she was majorly pissed.

Kane kissed my forehead then my lips before going to the fridge and getting two beers.

Both Nora and I watched the men leave. Ana had already run off to the toy and baby product graveyard to find something to play with.

Nora looked me over. "You go have a shower or a long bath or scream into a pillow. I'll whip us up a cake."

I gaped at her. "It would be incredibly rude of me to leave a visitor here on her own. And I doubt I have the ingredients to 'whip up a cake.'" I struggled to catalog the contents of my fridge and pantry when that used to be second nature to me.

"It's most certainly not rude. Actually, I would consider it rude if you stand here and make small talk with me when I'm guessing it feels like your brain is melting from the inside out from lack of sleep." She smiled with empathy. "And you let me worry about the ingredients." Though everything about the woman was sweet, serene, there was adamance in her tone.

I glanced to the glass doors, out to where I could see figures on the beach. A pang hit my chest because Rowan's prediction was right; I couldn't hear whether Mabel was crying or not which sent my heart rate skyrocketing. Yes, she might've been perfectly content right then, or she could've been screaming her head off.

"They're fine," Nora said after following my gaze. "I know a lot of men are arguably useless at this stage, but I got a good one. A great one. And I'm taking an educated guess that you did too. Mabel could not be safer out there with two progressive, feminist, alpha, girl dads. So go." She shooed me with her hands.

I didn't do well with taking orders in my own kitchen, hadn't in years. Yet the kind, soft-spoken baker managed to obtain my submission with no argument.

So I did go upstairs. No screaming into a pillow or long bath-both felt too dramatic and indulgent respectively. But I did enjoy a long shower, not a rushed one where I heard phantom baby cries and came out with one leg shaved and unrinsed conditioner in my hair because I was convinced Kane needed help.

Even though he never needed my help.

I shaved both legs. Rinsed out the conditioner. And when I got out, I still didn't hear cries, so I added the indulgence of blow drying my hair and putting on three steps of skincare instead of slapping moisturizer on my face with a shaky hand.

By the time I came downstairs, in clean clothes and feeling a lot saner than I had in a while, a smell not dissimilar to Nora's bakery was wafting through my house.

Still no baby cries.

And walking into my living room, it was no longer an obstacle course of baby products. Everything had been put away into the wicker chest I'd intended to use as storage but hadn't had the time or energy to use yet. Especially when I was taking them out and putting them back three times daily, at least.

Ana was sitting cross legged with blocks and some books that I'd bought, thinking that they'd entertain a four month old, not realizing that they were for older children. Apparently, it even said so on the box. Nora, to my horror, was folding laundry.

"You don't have to do that." I rushed to take the basket from her.

"Sit," she protested in that soft, commanding voice. Again, I responded to it without meaning to.

I sat beside her, my fingers twitching to take the laundry from her.

"Tea," she said, waving a baby blanket to the now uncluttered and sparkling-clean coffee table. "I took a gamble when I made it, and I think it may be just the right temperature now. I don't know about you, but I didn't finish a hot drink for months after this one was born." Nora nodded her head to the sweet girl playing peacefully.

I longed and dreaded Mabel getting to the age where she could sit alone, playing without me constantly entertaining her and ensuring that there was nothing she could choke on in the vicinity.

"You don't have to do all of this," I said, taking the tea then motioning to the room.

"Yes I do," she replied. "It's the duty of a woman who has gone through and survived the first few years and now has wisdom and free time and all of her hormones back under control. Well, kind of," she snickered, rubbing her stomach. "But seriously. We women, we mothers owe it to each other to make sure we don't do this alone. That we have help. My sisters-in-law did it for me. It's a sacred, precious gift, and I consider it an honor to be able to pay it forward. You'll be able to one day too."

I sipped my tea and considered her words. I struggled to imagine a time when I'd be able to do something like this for someone else when I could barely shower and shave both legs while doing so.

"You will," Nora reassured me, seeming to read my mind. "For now, enjoy the tea, and don't feel like you have to force conversation with me. I'm quite happy here." She patted her belly, still small but pronounced.

Nora was tranquil, quiet, not quite shy but definitely introverted. Her daughter seemed to be the same in a lot of ways. Until Kane and Rowan emerged from outside with Mabel, and she screamed, "Daddy!" like he'd been gone for months instead of an hour. He passed off Mabel to Kane expertly in time to catch the daughter who was sprinting toward him.

He twirled her in the air where she screamed in delight before nuzzling into his neck and whispering something in his ear.

I looked over to Kane, who was pressing gentle kisses on our daughter's head, murmuring something to her.

"It's enough to make your ovaries explode," Nora stage whispered, gesturing to our men

I smiled and couldn't disagree with her.

After that, we ate the best carrot cake I ever had, and I watched Nora, Rowan and Ana with disbelief at what awaited us. A little person. A family. Although we already were a family, I realized.

Next on the rotation were Tina and Tiffany, the most unlikely yet perfect couple. Tiffany was hot-pink velour sweatsuits, bleached blonde hair out to *there*, acrylic nails and bright pink lipstick. Tina was heavy metal, tattoos, short, cropped hair, no nonsense, no bullshit.

Tiffany doted over Mabel, and Tina did the same but with less enthusiasm. She then declared she was going to cook us freezer meals—since I had discovered they were the 'thing' for new mothers —and demanded Kane and I go nap.

I opened my mouth to say I couldn't nap in general, let alone with two strangers—albeit nice ones—in my house, one of them holding my baby.

"Nap," Tina ordered. "No lip. We'll be up when the baby is hungry or I'm just tired of the screaming and cooing." She tilted her head to Tiffany.

I was going to argue, but the weight of my exhaustion made that seem impossible. Kane took my hand, just as exhausted but able to hide it a little better.

"Come on, Chef. They've got this," he said, though I saw his eyes linger on Mabel protectively for a beat.

I knew it was just as hard for him to leave Mabel.

Blanche was there, Mabel's constant protector. We knew she'd never let Mabel from her sight.

The logical part of me, Avery Hart, chef—the part that was quickly disappearing—let Kane take my hand and pull me upstairs. We needed all the rest we could get in order to be decent parents.

"I'm not going to be able to nap," I told Kane as he got us into the bedroom where I slipped off my clothes as he pulled off his tee.

"Give it a go, Chef." He pulled me into bed with him.

I relaxed into his arms, letting them settle around me. Moments later, I was out, only to be woken by Kane's lips at my ear two hours later.

Tiffany had brought in a whining Mabel to be fed. The freezer was stocked, the house smelled of Tiffany's perfume, and the place was spotless.

Then they left.

Then next was Calliope.

I'd seen her around the bakery a handful of times but hadn't interacted with her a whole bunch. Although for some reason, I gravitated to her somewhat more than the outspoken and extroverted Fiona or the feminine and shy Nora. She always wore a slash of red lipstick, sharp eyeliner accentuating her dark eyes, hair slicked back into a bun, showing off angular features. And she was always in black with high heels, looking like she was going to a high-powered business meeting instead of walking around a small coastal town in Maine.

When I heard she'd been in New York until recently, I understood why I was drawn to her. The no-nonsense attitude, the slight chill, the overall confidence. She reminded me of who I used to be.

I didn't know much about her other than that she was Rowan's sister—the resemblance was uncanny—and she had worked on Wall Street before moving to Jupiter.

She was the last person I wanted in the rotation because it shoved an uncomfortable truth in my face... That I'd never be like her, or even close to being like her, again.

But she arrived at our doorstep one Saturday evening.

"You're going out," she declared, stepping her red-soled shoe through the doorway. "Where's the baby?"

I pointed to the living room where Mabel was in her $300 baby swing she barely tolerated for longer than five minutes, watching fruit dance along the screen of the TV.

I was vaguely embarrassed about this put together woman coming into our house, seeing me with Kane's tee and boxer shorts on at five thirty in the afternoon, my kid in front of the TV.

I'd told myself I wouldn't expose Mabel to screens—there was all sorts of research to show that it wasn't beneficial to kids under the age of two. But I'd found something the studies didn't mention: it gave me five minutes of respite. I could enjoy a hot coffee, breathe, use the bathroom, sit on the sofa and stare into space.

Those fruits were the best thing ever invented.

"Good, great, she's distracted." Clearly, Calliope didn't have judgment over the TV being on. Kane was sitting on the sofa, watching out daughter with that tender look on his face.

Calliope pointed to both of us. "You're going out," she repeated. "Go get ready. I'll sit with her."

I sucked in a deep breath. "I can't expect that of you." What I didn't say is that I couldn't leave my daughter with a stranger. I'd barely left her with my mother.

"You're not expecting anything. I'm telling you you're going out," she said. "And I know you don't know me, I don't have kids, but they're pretty foolproof at keeping alive at this age. For short periods anyway." She shrugged with a mischievous glint to her eye. "I'm an aunt to about a thousand of the little fuckers and have babysat them all without major bodily injury. You can call Nora for references if you wish, or you can get ready, go out, have something to drink, or have sex in your car on the beach. Whatever tickles your fancy." She waved her hands. "The most important thing is you get out of this house and away from singular identities like mother and father and have a couple of hours as whoever you feel like being."

While I digested her words, Kane was grinning, quite obviously on board with the idea despite his overall protectiveness of Mabel. He almost jumped on strangers for staring at her too long, yet he was okay with the Jupiter tribe, it seemed.

"I'm breastfeeding," I said lamely. "She needs a bottle."

"Well, pump one," Calliope flicked her fingers to the breast pump on the coffee table. I couldn't remember how long it had been there.

She made it all seem so simple, so I struggled to find any other reason why we couldn't leave our baby with an almost stranger.

"Go," she ordered, settling on the couch close to Mabel.

And although her sister-in-law had been much quieter and gentler with her orders, it'd had the same effect. I heeded them.

Twenty-Seven

"WE SHOULD GO BACK INSIDE," I said the second that I got on the back of Kane's bike. He'd suggested we take it, and I'd jumped at the chance. Initially, I'd jumped at the chance. The thought of being pressed against Kane, the fall air biting at us as we tore down the road... It promised an exhilaration I had loved in the past.

But now I was dressed, in jeans—no elastic waist to be found—and in a simple, long-sleeved top, makeup on and hair haphazardly curled. I was wearing shoes. Low heeled boots. Real people, adult clothes.

I'd longed for such things. Just like I'd longed for time with Kane, a ride on the bike. But straddling the bike, my body was frozen as I stared into the windows of our house. The curtains were drawn, so I could see light filtering out, and I swore I could hear a baby calling out for her mother.

Never mind that she couldn't even form words yet.

"We are not going back inside," Kane stated, putting a helmet on my head.

I scowled at him. "We don't know her." I pointed to the house again.

"We know Rowan, we know everyone else she is family with, and I know she has great taste in automobiles." Kane motioned to the sleek car parked in our driveway. I couldn't say much about it other than it was red.

I put my hand on my hip. "Seriously, we're trusting our daughter with someone because they drive a nice car?"

Kane gripped my hips. "We're trusting our daughter with someone because we know she's good people. We're trusting our daughter with someone because in order to get through this, we need to start trusting people, letting them in, letting them help. I promise you, Chef, it's just as fuckin' painful for me to leave Mae, and I miss her like goddamn crazy already. But we need this."

I chewed on my bottom lip. He wasn't wrong. I knew he wasn't. Even though my mother and Maisie were only a three-hour drive away and promised to make the trip as often as possible, they had their own lives. We did need to find some semblance of a support system here in Jupiter if we intended on it being home. As much as I loved Mabel with all of my being, I also understood that being a better mother meant sometimes taking time for myself.

I stared at him, then the bike.

"We don't have a will," I realized, horror buzzing beneath my skin. I'd had a list of things to get organized once the baby was born —life insurance, a will, a college fund. None of that had been done. "Or life insurance."

"Unless you're planning on taking me to a secondary location and murdering me, I think we're okay," Kane replied.

"We're parents." I smacked his shoulder. "We get into a crash on this thing and leave Mabel an orphan, there needs to be a plan in place for her care. I'm going to go back in and write a will."

I climbed off the bike to do just that, but Kane caught my wrist, pulling me back to him.

"Chef, you're not going to write a will tonight, and we're not going to crash."

"You can't know that," I argued, panic well and truly seizing my lungs at that point.

He arched a brow. "I've got more than a few medals to communicate how I can know that."

"I'll remind you, I've seen you crash," I told him. It was a low blow, but I was frantic.

Kane didn't seem bothered, merely grinning. "An anomaly. One never to be repeated." He put his hands on either side of the helmet. "Get that you want to take care of our girl, and I also get that your brain is your worst enemy right now. So how about we give it a break with a ride, me fuckin' you either in the bathrooms of a dive bar or over this very bike on a beach somewhere. We get a drink, come back then write wills."

My mouth filled with saliva at the thought of sex, public sex with Kane. Since the first time, we'd caught moments to ourselves when we could—in the kitchen while Mabel napped, in the living room, pretty much in various rooms of our house while the baby slept. Each time we were quiet, rushed, mindful that she could wake at any moment.

Though the new, fragile part of me that was now a mother urged me to go inside, I held onto Kane's gaze and let him put me on the back of his bike.

* * *

Once we got going, Mabel was a constant worry at the back of my mind. Though that worry quieted under the purr of the bike, the exhilarating speed of us hurtling down coastal roads. My arms tightened around Kane, dipping my fingertips under his tee then down to the waistband of his jeans.

Then ... lower.

His cock was hard underneath my palm.

There was a thrill in resting my hand there. I wasn't going to move it; I didn't think that was responsible. But the potential of my doing so was enough.

We didn't ride very long. Kane pulled the bike off to a side road then into an empty beach parking lot. The sun set earlier that time of year, so the dusk made it so we were barely seen when he shut the lights of the bike off.

As soon as he did that, Kane hoisted me off the bike, helmet flying off.

He didn't speak as his hands dove into my hair, tugging the tie from my hair then pulling at the strands.

I kissed him back with the same ferocity. There it was... What we'd been muting, tempering in the house with a sleeping baby. Now there was nothing but open air, waves crashing against rocks and sand, the low hum of a car driving past, the hazy illumination of our shapes from headlights.

We were almost entirely obscured from the road. A passing driver couldn't see us, but if you pulled into the parking lot you could.

My heart pounded.

Kane's teeth were at my neck as his hands plunged into my jeans.

I gasped as he bypassed my panties and went right in.

He let out a low hiss as his fingers found me wet.

He didn't say a word as he unbuttoned my jeans, forced them down and turned me around, hand going to the small of my back and pushing me down.

My palms steadied themselves on the seat of the bike, nails scratching at the leather.

Kane steadied me with one hand on my hips as he freed himself then without pause, he slammed into me.

He'd been careful before this, mindful of my body, worried about me healing.

He wasn't worried about anything now.

We weren't Mom and Dad. We weren't anything but two animals under the moonlight.

He bunched my hair in his hand then wrenched it back.

My scalp radiated with glorious pain as the rest of my body succumbed to inconceivable pleasure.

He continued pounding relentlessly. My mind went hazy as my body shuddered and exploded over and over again.

How many times, I couldn't know. Eventually, Kane growled, roaring as he released into me.

We were both panting heavily when we were done. My limbs burned.

Carefully, Kane pulled out of me, slowly raising my jeans back up and buttoning them while I steadied myself on the seat of the bike.

He turned me around, kissing me gently on the lips. I could feel his smile.

"Hottest piece I've ever had, Chef. After giving birth to my baby..." His hands ran over me. "Fuck..."

I couldn't help but smile back, my body singing with electricity.

"How about we get a drink, greasy food, then repeat this on the way home?"

I couldn't think of anything better.

I held my breath as we walked in the door of the house. It wasn't completely dark, but all the overhead lights were off, and only the soft lamplight from the living room illuminated the house. The TV was on, and Calliope sat on the sofa. Not looking at it—instead, tapping on her phone, a glass of wine in her hand.

She glanced up at us. "This is my first one." She held the glass up. "I didn't sit here and get drunk with your baby, don't worry. Though it was tempting; you have good wine." She drained the glass then stood up, glancing between the two of us.

She wore a knowing smile. "You had fun." Not a question, and somehow, it communicated that she suspected we took her advice about public sex.

I didn't blush nor feel embarrassed, for whatever reason. Maybe it was because I was thoroughly satisfied or because I felt comfortable with Calliope.

"Fuck yeah, we did," Kane beamed back at her. "We're gotta send you a fruit basket or something as a thank you."

She shook her head, reaching down to snag the bottle of wine and shove the cork back in it. "This will do," she said, shaking it.

"Where's the baby?" I asked suddenly, as if I were just noticing Mabel wasn't there.

"Sleeping," Calliope replied. "She's been down since about seven-ish."

I stared at her. "Down?"

"In her bed."

"In her bed," I repeated, dumbfounded. "How did you do that?"

Mabel did not just 'go down' in her bed. There was rocking. Feeding. The arm drop test, a tense transfer. And then only 50 percent of the time it worked for an hour, at most, before the whole dance started again.

"She was tired. I fed her, burped her, put her in her swaddle suit thing and read her a story. Told her it was time to sleep, put her down then left the room."

"Did she scream?" I asked, unable to hide my shock from my tone.

Calliope arched a well-manicured brow. "Not a peep. Babies don't try that shit with me."

I gaped at her. If she were anyone else and I wasn't presented with the evidence of a quiet house and presumably sleeping baby, I would've called bullshit. Babies bowed to no master, except, it seemed, Calliope Derrick.

"Thank you," was all I was able to say.

"I'm not gonna say 'anytime' because I'm not *that* good of a person, but we'll make it a habit. And truly, anytime." She gave me a wink then sauntered out the door, bottle of wine in hand.

Both Kane and I stood there, listening to the muted hum of her Porsche leave the driveaway.

And as if she sensed her leaving, Mabel's low cry sounded.

Both Kane and I looked at each other then laughed.

"I got her, babe," he said, kissing my head. "Go get ready for bed."

"She may be hungry," I reminded him, feeling my breasts for their fullness.

Kane waved to the kitchen. "Pump is sterilized and ready to go. You pump a bottle, then go get ready for bed. I got our girl."

"You need sleep too," I sighed.

"I needed your pussy, the sound of you and the feel of you coming. I can survive off that for at least another twenty-four hours." He kissed me hard on the mouth.

"Pump," he ordered. "Skincare, teeth, sleep."

I did as he asked. And Mabel was up in another handful of hours. But I managed it, feeling refreshed, feeling less alone in Jupiter.

I had a family with Kane and Mabel.

And I had a village thanks to everyone else.

* * *

There were hard days, days when nothing more than coffee and Kane got me through. Even in the midst of those hard days, there was beauty. Mabel's newfound voice, shrieking with glee as her cries of distress lessened. I was slowly getting less tense during her periods of contentment, no longer bracing and ready for a meltdown. I was ... enjoying her. Enjoying motherhood.

Moreover, I was enjoying Kane as a father.

Though *enjoy* was an insufficient word for it.

He was endlessly patient with her, laying with her on a sheepskin rug most of the day, playing, reading, kissing her. He was besotted.

And he was an animal when it came to protecting her.

Especially since her existence and his location had officially become public record.

We'd known it was a matter of time, so Kane had begun making preparations for a media circus long ago. Our property—both our names now on the deed—had fencing all around it. Kane had bought the additional acreage on either side, both conveniently empty lots. The front of the driveway had a gate that required either a code or a clicker similar to one for a garage. That was the most recent addition, and all of the Jupiter crew were given the code since there was always someone popping in.

We couldn't fence the beach since it was technically public property. But someone would have to walk for miles in order to make it to our property from the beach access. There were security cameras everywhere, motion sensors.

And then there was the dirt bike track that Kane was building on one of our new properties. He had said countless times that he was happy to be retired from competing and though he seemed sincere, I was still overcome with doubt.

"You don't go from a life of excitement and constant movement to this," I argued, gesturing to him on the ground with Mabel.

"If you're really fuckin' lucky, you do," he countered.

I had been silenced then, overcome with emotion that I still didn't feel equipped to deal with.

He said he was building the track in order to 'fuck around,' and apparently, get Mabel ready for her debut on two wheels. Though my anxiety about her general wellbeing was crippling, the image of her on a dirt bike racing through the woods didn't spike fear inside of me. It made me smile, thinking of the mischievous and adventurous traits it was already apparent she'd inherited from her father. And I knew he'd be right there beside her.

The media was another story.

We weren't even aware the picture had been taken, a rarity for Kane. Whenever we were out in public—which was more often now that Mabel had adjusted to being in the world and had calmed somewhat—he was on guard, watching strangers with hyperawareness, aware of who had a phone even pointed in our direction, anyone who looked at Mabel too long.

And plenty of people looked at Mabel.

She was, objectively, the most beautiful baby to exist.

She had her father's dark hair, a full head of it since birth. Though it was inky black on the day she was born, it had lightened up over the past few months, strawberry blonde in the sunlight. There was enough of it now to tie into pigtails. Which Kane did. Every day, he sat with her and brushed her long hair, carefully and precisely tying two bows on either side of her head, redoing them until they were perfect.

She also got Kane's wide, ice-blue eyes framed by dark lashes. She got my porcelain skin tone and my nose, small and delicate. Her rosebud lips only got fuller, and she had the chubbiest cheeks I'd ever seen.

Yes, she was gorgeous. And when you saw a baby with pink bows in her pigtails, being carried by a ripped man covered in tattoos, wearing all black with his hair tied back in a low bun and a look of utter devotion on his face, you stared.

We got used to it. Became a little more relaxed.

And then the photo happened.

Kane, holding Mabel. Thankfully, her face wasn't visible, just the bows of her pigtails, but it was enough.

One day, our life in Jupiter was quiet, sleepy, comfortable. The next, reporters had descended. They formed a mob at the entrance to our house, the location had somehow been leaked.

They'd been at Nora's bakery, swarming Kane, Mabel and me when we tried to enter. My blood pressure took off, and I panicked with the suffocating feeling of people closing in.

Kane, who had been clutching Mabel to his chest, had stiffened with fury, wordlessly handing her off to me as someone flashed a camera in her face.

I saw the clench of his fist, the writing on the wall. His expression was much the same as it had been in the kitchen with Gerald. But it was somehow ... worse. More dangerous. Mabel was the most precious, innocent and pure thing in this world, and people were trying to tarnish her, capitalize on her. I felt consumed by rage, an insatiable need to unleash violence upon anyone near her.

Except there were too many people. And if Kane hit one, it would be immortalized in a photograph forever. His conviction had been overturned, but that didn't mean something else couldn't happen, that he couldn't be taken away from us again. But I also couldn't stop him from defending our daughter.

The door to the bakery opened, and Rowan rushed out, making a beeline for me and Mabel. Curling an arm around my shoulder, he hurried us inside. Not even vicious paparazzi dared block his path.

Kip came too, stepping in front of Kane. "Allow me, brother," he said with a grin before punching a photographer in the face.

Then there was the incident at our house a few days later.

We'd been shaken by the scene at the café, but I'd finally stopped jumping at shadows. It helped, knowing Rowan and Kip were hard at work scaring every photographer off Main Street.

Kane had given statements via his publicist, giving not so veiled threats that he'd ruin the careers of any publication who published photos of Mabel.

There was not much more we could do other than ride it out.

Interestingly, this was the first time that I was calmer than Kane since Mabel's birth. He was a thundercloud, stomping around the house, muttering about siccing Knox on every paparazzi in the vicinity.

I had left him to his mutterings, sitting outside with Mabel, feeding her.

Until a stranger with a camera came up the steps from the beach.

I didn't so much let out a gasp before a flash of black came past me along with a yell to get Mabel inside.

I did so, heart galloping. Just as I closed the door, I heard a loud boom.

With a slack jaw, I realized that Kane was holding a shotgun and had fired it. I wasn't sure if it hit the photographer or not. I surely hoped it didn't.

Mabel whimpered, so I kissed her head, trying to calm her while watching Kane race down the beach.

My breathing didn't regulate until I saw the photographer upright and running. For about two seconds before Kane tackled him.

Heart in my throat, I watched as Kane's arms flailed, and his mouth moved rapidly before the photographer scampered off.

Kane walked back into the house, shotgun in one hand, camera in the other.

Closing my jaw seemed impossible.

He dropped both then took Mabel into his arms. "How's my baby?" he murmured softly.

I just stared at him. "Where did you get a shotgun?"

"Baby gift," he replied. "From Knox."

I nodded, dragging a hand through my hair. That made sense.

"I don't think that photographer is going to be quiet about that," I told him.

Kane kissed Mabel's head. "I hope to fuck he isn't. I told him to inform his friends they wouldn't get a warnin' shot next time."

I closed my eyes, drawing in a deep breath. There was no point in even trying to dissuade Kane from such things. A stranger had taken a photo of me nursing his baby. He was lucky there had even been a warning shot.

Not long after that, there was a call from the gate. The sheriff, Finn, had arrived.

Kane greeted him with a smile and the offer of coffee.

Finn accepted it, friendly enough as he sat at the breakfast bar and smiled at Mabel. She smiled back, which was rare for her. She was an immensely happy baby with her father and me but was picky about which strangers she smiled at.

She was a mix of Kane and me, my ice and his fire.

After five minutes of small talk, Finn casually said, "Got a report of an attempted shooting from this property."

"Is that right?" Kane replied just as casually, holding Mabel upright on the counter.

Finn nodded.

"They happen to mention they were trespassing and takin' photos of my woman nursing my daughter?" He spoke in a calm tone, but it was impossible to hide his underlying fury.

Finn's face became stony, no longer the friendly neighborhood sheriff. "They did not," he murmured, putting down the coffee cup. "You got a permit for that?" He jutted his chin to the shotgun that Kane hadn't even bothered to hide.

I'd have to have a conversation with him about deadly weapons being left around when there was a baby in our house close to crawling.

"Yes," Kane lied easily.

If the gun came from Knox, there was absolutely no way he had a permit.

"Pftt." Finn took another sip of his coffee. "Well, then I'm going to have to inform that photographer," he snarled, "that he's lucky I'm not charging him and inform him that I'll have that same sensibility with any of his friends."

The message was clear. The town of Jupiter, law enforcement included, was on our side. Everyone had closed ranks around us. This didn't immediately stop the circus, but it helped assuage it.

Our life continued on.

Twenty-Eight

MY FINGERS WERE ITCHING.

They had been. For a while.

They itched for knives. For pans. Pots. Minor burns.

A culinary kitchen.

And not rushed meals I threw together, panic racing through my veins even though Kane promised he 'had' Mabel. I was unable to slow down in our house. I knew that everything I was experiencing were common traits of motherhood—the sense of constant urgency, that no task could be done properly, only rushed through. It would all pass, my sister and the books promised. But this new way of life felt cemented into my personality.

I tried to grit my teeth through it.

But I was grinding them to dust.

Kane and I were sitting in the living room, the television playing in the background. Kane liked TV now. He was partial to The Real Housewives. Go figure.

Mabel was sleeping happily on his chest.

I was tucked into his side, her gentle breath caressing my face. My favorite thing in the world.

Kane had bought digital photo frames and peppered them around the house, each one loaded with pictures of her we'd snapped. I was watching that, not The Housewives.

"I love her," I whispered, looking from her to the frame playing a slideshow of Mabel's short but wonderful life. "I love that I'm her mother," I continued, wringing my hands in anticipation of this confession. "But I don't love *being* a mother." I avoided Kane's eyes. "I mean, I don't love being *only* a mother. It doesn't fit me. I feel like I fail her because I can't be here all the time every day without losing my mind. I need something more. I need a kitchen. I need to create food, and I need to be something else in addition to being her mother. And I feel like there's something wrong with me for not being content with just taking care of her."

There it was. I said it all. All of those shameful thoughts that had been simmering during the short months I'd been her mother. The short months that felt like years and seconds all at once.

My gaze blurred as I watched the pictures switch, saw her adorable, chunky face grow more beautiful, more aware, more inquisitive with each passing slide. More shame piled onto me as I watched, overcome with love.

There must've been something wrong with me if I couldn't be utterly fulfilled by being there for that perfect human being.

Kane's fingers at my chin forced my gaze to him. I readied myself for judgment, disappointment, looks I no doubt deserved. But on his handsome face was only tenderness.

"Need you to stop talkin' shit about my wife," he rasped in a low tone.

I scrunched my nose in confusion.

"I'm not your wife." I voiced the first thing that came to mind since it was pretty important. "I know I'm sleep deprived, but even I would've remembered if we'd gotten married."

He smirked, the expression boyish and roguishly sexy simultane-

435

ously. Although I was exhausted, overwhelmed and emotional, I felt that smirk right in the pit of my stomach.

"Yeah, well, we've gotta rectify that. Soon." He stroked my bottom lip with his thumb. "Not a traditional guy, but I'm a possessive one. Want you to have my name. Want you as mine in every single way possible."

Yeah, I felt that one again. In a big way. Evidently, my vagina was not as exhausted as the rest of me.

I didn't know what to say to what was essentially a marriage proposal. Except he wasn't proposing anything.

Not that the idea of lifelong commitment was completely out of the blue since we had a child together, and the man professed his love for me daily—but it still made my heart flutter.

And I was not a heart fluttering kind of woman. Especially when it came to things like marriage. I was sure I was immune to society's obsession with marriage and women's determination to celebrate the 'big day.'

Turned out I was just like everyone else.

All it took was a sexy daredevil with our daughter's name tattooed on his chest—right beside his 'Yes, Chef' tattoo—and her sleeping in his arms to make me feel it.

"In my mind, you're mine forever, in every kind of way," he continued. "So I already consider you my wife. And I won't take anyone talkin' badly about her. Even you." His eyes narrowed. "Especially you. Not gonna hear you talkin' shit about the best mother I know." He looked down at the dark head of hair nestled in his arms. Everything about him became kinder, more patient, liquifying when he touched his eyes to our baby.

Another heart flutter. A really big one.

"Our daughter is going to have the best example of what she can do with her life. How she can define herself. Watchin' you care for her, navigating this time in our life, has only made me love you in ways I never thought possible. I watched you bring her into this world, no fuckin' drugs, all grit and willpower." He smiled. "My warrior, Chef. But, Chef, cooking is who you are too. I'd never dream of takin' that away from you, of makin' you feel like you're defined by one thing. Actually, this is kismet. Go look on the counter." He craned his head in that direction.

I frowned, kind of because I was trying to fight the onslaught of tears, but also because I didn't know where he was going with this.

Though I didn't want to leave the warmth of Kane's body or the scent of our sleeping baby, I was curious.

I got up, picking up the manilla envelope off the counter that I hadn't noticed till then. Granted, our house was organized chaos, and I barely noticed that I was walking around with my boob still hanging out an hour after feeding Mabel; a manilla envelope could easily get lost in the fray.

"What is it?" I asked.

"Open it and find out." He stood, expertly depositing sleeping Mabel into the bassinet we kept in the living room. Magically, she stayed asleep.

"I don't like surprises," I told him, my heart hammering in my chest.

"Well, I'm never gonna beat knockin' on this door and findin' my woman eight months pregnant, so you can live with that one," he teased.

There was no resentment in his tone. I knew Kane wished he had been there from the start, but he'd long since let go of any anger he had toward me about the whole pregnancy thing. Regardless, I still hadn't let go of the guilt.

My fingers tore open the envelope, then I retrieved the stack of papers, bleary eyes scanning over them. "What is this?"

"It's a purchase agreement," he said. "I know people tend to do leases, but I like it here, like the thought of raisin' our daughter here. And I believe that this is a forever kinda thing. Although if the location doesn't work, we'll either sell it or turn it into something else and find you something that does work."

I blinked rapidly. "Work for what?"

"Your restaurant," he replied as if it were obvious. As if I'd regularly spoken about opening a restaurant as opposed to the few offhand comments I made before Mabel, therefore, another lifetime ago.

"My restaurant?" I repeated.

"Yes, Chef." His eyes danced with joy.

I looked from the papers to Kane then back down again, focusing on the address. It took a second to compute, but if I wasn't mistaken, it was an old boathouse on the wharf that I'd always looked at dreamily.

"Needs some work," Kane shrugged, as if he were reading my mind. "Rowan and Kip start Monday, if you agree, that is. Also got an architect on standby so you can tell them what you want, and they can make it happen."

Palm over my mouth, I tried to process everything that Kane was saying.

"Did I fuck up?" His easy grin had dimmed. "The location not fancy enough? I just saw it when we were out walkin' with Mabel, and I felt like it was you. But—"

I held my hand up to silence him. It was shaking. "It's perfect," I whispered.

"I know you're not the kind of woman who likes to let go of control." He put his hands on my hips. "And me takin' charge and makin' a big decision like this for you could be considered as a toxic male move. But you're the boss here, Chef. I'll willingly submit to you, stay at home and take care of our daughter, while you go and bring home the bacon."

He winked.

I struggled to stand under the weight of everything he was saying, everything he was giving me.

"You'll give up your career?" I clarified.

"Already done."

I stared at him. He was serious. "But that's your life. You're Kane 'The Devil Rhodes.'"

He chuckled, brushing hair from my face. It was probably crusty or sticky with spit up.

"No. *You're* my life," he corrected. "*She's* my life." His eyes roamed to the bassinet, where there were no tiny legs flailing or hands scrambling for escape, no cries of 'pick me up.' I had a rogue thought to go check her breathing before Kane turned my attention back to him.

"My identity was never in the bullshit I did to keep the demons quiet," he said. "It was how I thought I made myself a man after everything I went through. I've come to realize that how I make myself a man, the best man I can be, is by being a husband and father."

The next day, we got a marriage license.

The day after that, we got married.

Then construction started on Tides, my restaurant.

* * *

It should've been the end.

Or more appropriately, it should've been the beginning of a whole new life. One that I finally felt I was getting the hang of. I was making my peace with the chaos that came with being a mother.

On one of Maisie's many visits—she brought the kids and her husband who was goofy and doted on both her and the children— I'd been cooking while she and the kids entertained Mabel.

Mabel, who was now entertained, who giggled—*giggled*! Who cried still, since it was the only form of communication she had, but cried to communicate her needs rather than to scream at us like we were doing something wrong or the world was too loud or she was in discomfort or for whatever reason babies with colic cried.

The press left us alone for the most part. There was the odd reporter on Main Street when we went for walks or to get pastries, but Rowan scared any and all away from the bakery when they tried to enter.

And no one in the town had given an interview, shared any information, so they eventually scattered off for the next story.

Not that there weren't stories. People had been transfixed by Kane when he was flying through the air on a motorcycle, winning Olympic medals, dating supermodels and generally being mischievous. But now that he'd 'settled down,' and had a baby girl, people seemed even more enchanted. By his love story, his happily ever after.

Yes, I was a little enchanted too. We were finally sleeping more. Not through the night, no, of course not. But we were getting three to four hours ... in a row—that counted as eight hours in my book —which meant I was slightly saner.

Mabel napped in her crib, sometimes for a full *hour*. She still enjoyed most days slumbering, cuddled up to her father.

The house was filled with her laughter, her smiles. I had slightly more time to do things for myself. Especially with the never ending visits from the Jupiter 'posse'. Nora, Fiona, Tina, Tiffany and Calliope.

Kane had his bromances with Kip and Rowan going strong, the three of them taking the kids out and about so we could sit in Nora's garden drinking or eating or just doing things that weren't wiping faces, cleaning diapers or feeding children.

Nora welcomed a second baby girl without fuss or disarray. She seemed content, well rested and not at all on the edge of a mental breakdown like I'd been those first weeks. It baffled me that she'd done it again by choice.

Fiona seemed to feel the same as me. We were both content with one child whereas Nora wanted many.

These new friendships meant that Mabel would never feel lonely, though. Not with all of the children she'd be surrounded by, not to mention her cousins, who adored her and had just left with a tearful goodbye and promises to return soon. My mother was scheduled to arrive the next day.

Kane had already contracted Kip and Rowan to start work on a 'guest house' for family on our property. He wanted them to feel welcome. He'd spoken about adding on to our petite cottage, but I'd refused. I liked it exactly how it was. Small, compact, perfect for two adults, one child and one dog.

He had told his mother about Mabel, and she'd visited. She'd been timid, hesitant and when she did speak, she spoke a lot about herself. She'd held Mabel, but she'd seemed uneasy, uncomfortable, Kane's jaw hard while watching them together.

It wasn't an altogether 'nice' visit. It hurt me that Kane didn't have what I had with my mother. But he'd made his peace with it.

As much as anyone could.

We hadn't seen Knox. I knew that bothered him more than his mother's indifference.

He'd thrown himself into the role of 'stay at home dad,' though I had urged him to do something other than that, like write a memoir. His new agent let it slip that he'd been offered many book deals. Kane was a literary lover and had an extraordinary story.

He was in Portland then, meeting with publishers, on my urging.

Tides was opening in two weeks. I had been toiling over the menu all throughout the day, writing and rewriting it. My decision making struggles were not just reserved for baby related things; it seemed they had seeped into an area of my life I had previously thought was untouchable. Unbreakable.

Doubt gnawed at me that this restaurant was a mistake.

"I didn't hear your bike," I called to Kane as the door opened then closed behind him. "She's not sleeping. You didn't have to push it up the drive again," I laughed.

Mabel laughed along with me from her highchair, squeezing a piece of banana in her little fist, elated at the resulting mush.

It was a process, my accepting the mess that Mabel had to make in order to discover food, to learn. To understand that most everything I made ended up on the floor and that the bigger mess she made, the more delighted she was. Until it came time to clean her up. Then she made it clear that she thought we were trying to torture her.

Yes, it was a process. But one I was starting to enjoy. Motherhood started to feel comfortable, like it fit, like it might've been made for me instead of something that I was trying to cut myself into shape for.

Some days were harder than others. But I had Kane. He was unflinching in his support of me, of us. There were times, moments, when he did things that communicated the ways in which his life hadn't changed and I had. Small things. It was hard not to turn them into larger things, to not catastrophize our entire relationship and its trajectory. To believe that he wanted me to be nothing more than a wife and mother.

Except he'd proven the exact opposite was true. Yes, he'd bought me the restaurant—which I still battled with my feelings about. But it wasn't because he wanted to own me or be my 'boss,' to hold it over me. It was given freely, a part of myself he was giving me back.

And he was happy to be a stay-at-home dad, to 'retire' from his title as 'The Devil.' Granted, he was still planning on taking sponsorships here and there to 'bulk up Mabel's college fund,' even though it was already bursting.

I knew he didn't want to entirely let go of the opportunities because part of him was still the poor boy struggling and going hungry.

He'd communicated that one night. "Except now I know you'll feed me, Chef," he murmured against my neck.

And I was working on that. Feeding him. Feeding us. Feeding myself. The restaurant was truly coming together. I had finalized a menu after testing it, retesting it then changing it completely. It had taken me four times as long as it used to, but that was okay.

I'd interviewed for staff, gotten licenses, approved the interior layout, had the time of my life designing my kitchen. It was a little extravagant considering it was going to be a mid-scale restaurant in a small town, but Kane had insisted on it, and I'd found it hard to argue.

I was dying to be in a kitchen that was mine, to reclaim a little bit of my old identity and mesh it with this new one.

I had spoken to a therapist who diagnosed me with postpartum anxiety—not an uncommon thing with high achieving women, apparently. The transition from the control we had to perfect our everyday lives to the utter chaos that was parenthood and the chasing of a perfectionism that didn't exist was a bit of a recipe for disaster.

It was nice to have a label, a diagnosis. There were many things I could do to combat it, though the 'make sure you're getting enough sleep' was a laughable concept.

I thought about her death often. About the myriad of ways she could be taken from us. Suffocating in her sleep, choking, some obscure sickness, a food allergy. The list of things took my breath away and panic crawled over my skin knowing how fragile she was. How helpless I was.

But I was learning to let go of things, to not try so hard to control everything since an eight month old was uncontrollable. I tried to trust that nothing would happen to her.

"Babe?" I asked Kane, still looking at Mabel's smile. At the time, she was craning her head to the hall to look for her father. She was obsessed with him and usually let out squeals of delight whenever he arrived home, even if he had been gone for less than an hour. He'd been gone since early morning, so surely, she'd be screeching.

Seeing the bond between them, seeing him grow as a father, made me feel simultaneous joy and pain while thinking about the own father I'd lost. I'd forgiven him, finally, my father. Not that I'd had any other choice. Dead men were forgiven easier.

My inner thoughts were not punctuated by Mabel's squeals. Instead, the smile died on her face as she stared at the hall with a tilt to her head and an uncertain expression.

My blood immediately chilled, and I froze in place. Call it what you will, motherly instincts, intuition, but I knew the person standing behind me was not Kane.

I held my breath, looking around for something, anything to use as a weapon. My phone was across the kitchen, as were all the sharp and pointy things. Out of the grasp of little fingers. The only thing in reaching distance was a rubber spoon that Mabel was waving in her grubby hands.

That was then I noticed Blanche's absence. I'd let her out to the bathroom minutes before. Under protest, she'd left her spot beneath the high chair where she had proximity to Mabel and snacks from whatever Mabel dropped. I searched for her outside and saw the slash of golden fur, lying lifeless on the deck. My mouth dried with terror.

"Isn't this cozy?" a voice sneered.

I turned, unable and unwilling to have my back to him. I'd recognized his voice immediately, of course.

Brax.

He looked a lot different than the last time I saw him. No bespoke suit, no fancy haircut or fake tan. No smarmy grin.

He was disheveled. Much thinner than he had been and pale, gaunt almost. His hair was mussed and longer, a thick layer of patchy stubble covering his jaw. His gray tee was rumpled, hanging off him.

And he was holding a gun.

I sucked in an unsteady breath and moved my body so Mabel was completely behind me.

Brax was there. In our kitchen.

I'd asked Kane what happened to Brax since he'd sworn to 'kill him' in a way that seemed very literal. Kane had replied by saying that he was 'taken care of.' That had seemed ominous, but a quick Google search couldn't find a missing person or obituary anywhere, so I was relieved that Kane wasn't at risk of incarceration for murder.

I hadn't given it much thought beyond that. We had other things going on.

"You ruined my life," Brax snarled, taking another step into the kitchen.

Every muscle in my body went taut. I kept my focus on him as Mabel started protesting my back being to her. My stomach lurched at the situation I was in. An obviously angry, desperate and armed man was in my kitchen with me and my baby. Defenseless.

Kane was supposed to be home soon. He'd messaged that he was making the drive home what, an hour ago? Two? I couldn't remember.

But even if he did come home, what could he do? His shotgun was locked away upstairs, in a safe as I had requested. But he was much more physically fit than Brax, and the sheer rage he'd feel protecting his family would save us. That I knew.

Except he wasn't there to save us.

"You need to leave. Now," I demanded, conjuring my best ice queen voice. "Right now. You're breaking and entering. Leave before it's something you can't come back from."

Brax laughed. It was an ugly sound with an edge of mania. "It's not breaking and entering, you dumb bitch. The door wasn't even locked. You think you're untouchable here."

I didn't ask how he got past the gate; it was an insignificant detail at that point. He'd gotten past it. He was there.

He took another step forward. I pressed myself into Mabel's highchair, and her banana covered hands clawed at my back.

"You're not," he continued. "You're not going to ruin my career either. I get *that*." He waved the gun in Mabel's direction, and acid burned my esophagus. "If I get the first scoop and picture of the famous child, I'll have my in."

I stared at him, understanding that I was looking at a completely unhinged man.

There was no point in reasoning with him, in pointing out that kidnapping our daughter and essentially selling her to the media—I think that's what he meant, at least—was going to get him his job back.

Kane had done something to ensure he lost everything, that much was clear. And instead of doing some serious inner work, he had laid the blame at Kane's feet. And at mine. And clearly, he'd let his mind become unhinged enough to come here. To my home. Where my daughter was.

"Step aside now," he said, waving the gun.

"You'll have to kill me." I was proud that my fear wasn't evident in my tone and that I was able to stand straight despite my legs feeling like mush. I knew I had to stay strong, so I stared at Brax, not letting go of his gaze. "Kill me. That's the only way that you're getting your filthy hands on my daughter."

Even saying it, thinking of him near her, made me want to vomit.

I wasn't afraid of death. Not in the slightest. But I was afraid of my death meaning Mabel was in danger. Alone. With Brax. That scared me to the core.

My mind was clear, yet my heartbeat crashed against my ribs. Protect my daughter, at any cost. That was the goal. Buy time. Kane would be home. If it was before I was shot or after it didn't quite matter. All that mattered was that he was there to save Mabel.

With the gun centered on me, his cold gaze transitioned from madness to hatred. "I'll do it,' he murmured. "I'll gladly do it. Won't it just add to the story? It'll hit him where it really hurts." He rubbed the top of his head with his free hand.. "But then he'll twist it. He'll be the hero, the grieving single father, again on top. Even more popular than he was." His face screwed up, and he pinched the bridge of his nose. "Nah, I'm not doin' that." He shook the gun again. "Get out of the way."

I planted myself, wishing I could grow roots in the tile, turn to stone so he couldn't get around me. Couldn't get to my daughter.

I was bracing myself. For pain. For the loud gunshot. To die protecting my daughter.

But only a small pop sounded then a large thump as Brax's body hit the floor.

I stared down at the growing red puddle on the tile. Blood. Coming from Brax's head.

Then I looked up to the form in my kitchen.

Knox.

He had on gloves. Holding a gun with a silencer. At least that's what I thought it was. It looked similar to ones in movies. But somehow larger, heavier.

I took in a shaky breath. Then another. Knox was there. With a gun. He'd just killed Brax moments before Brax was going to kill me and take my daughter. Those were the horrifying facts.

Then I turned to face Mabel, a large smile on my face. "Let's get you in front of fruit while I talk to Uncle Knox," I told her in an overly high-pitched voice.

She squinted at me then peered around at Knox. I tried to hide the dead body from her view, though she didn't seem to notice it. She was focused on her uncle, who stood frozen in the doorway, eyes locked on her.

There was no smile on his face, no softening or warmth to his expression that most people had with her. No, his face remained an impassive mask.

Mabel did not cry out in fear. No, she *beamed* at him.

Knox recoiled, presumably in shock.

"We'll say hello in just a minute," I promised her, lifting her from the high chair, swirling us around then quickly stepping into the living room where I deposited her in her 'DJ Booth'—what Kane called the stationary container she could stand in. I kissed her head then switched on the fruit video, forcing myself to remain calm as I walked back into the kitchen. Knox had thoughtfully found a kitchen towel and was using it to stop the blood from spreading.

He didn't speak, didn't ask me if I was okay.

We both just stared at Brax's body.

I'd never seen a dead body before. Though I still had the vague taste of bile in my mouth, I forced myself to keep it together. That was not the time for hysterics.

"We got two options," Knox finally said. "You call the cops. You're gonna have to say it was either you or Kane who did that." He motioned to the bullet hole. "I, for various reasons, cannot be on the radar for things like this."

I nodded, understanding, even if I was naïve to what it was Knox actually did for a living.

I thought about that. It was self-defense. Quite obviously. But that would result in attention. A whole lot of it. A national media storm, even if we weren't charged in any kind of way.

Our life would once again be plastered over every news site, every channel. *Mabel's* life.

Not only would she have the history of a famous father, but death, murder would forever be attached to her name.

My stomach lurched again.

"Or..." Knox continued. "I take care of it. No one ever finds him. Nothing ever traces back here."

I eyed him, taking in his demeanor. He didn't seem shaken at the slightest by killing someone. I was plenty shaken, and it was taking my years of training to keep calm. That and the little being in the other room did not need her mother losing her shit.

"I can't ask that of you," I said, my voice raspy and thin.

"You're not asking," he replied. "I'm offering. Consider it a wedding present. And an apology. I've been keeping an eye on him, making sure he didn't do anything like this. I got … distracted." His eyes went faraway for a split second before refocusing on me. "He shouldn't have ever made it inside this house. That's on me."

I shook my head. "That's on *him.*"

Knox's lips were a thin line. He didn't agree.

I sighed. I wasn't going to convince him.

"We don't need more attention," I said finally, decision made. I was willfully deciding to break the law Acquiescing to be an accomplice to murder. I'd go to jail if this was ever discovered. Mabel would be without me. I was trusting Knox with not only my life but with Mabel's. It should've scared me more, but I trusted him, implicitly.

He nodded once, head tilting to the sound of a motorcycle in the drive.

Mabel shrieked, knowing that sound.

The thump of Kane's boots sounded as he bounded through the door. "Chef—"

He halted as soon as he could see into the kitchen. Horrified, his eyes went to me, to the body, to Mabel in her play center then finally to Knox.

"I'm taking care of it," were Knox's words.

And he did.

Our wedding present from Kane's brother included body disposal and crime scene cleanup, apparently.

And that was our ending.

Kind of.

Epilogue

JUST BECAUSE THE villain was dead and the family was saved didn't mean we got a happily ever after.

After murder in our kitchen, life went on.

It had to.

My restaurant opened to glowing reviews. Each night, every table was filled, the reviewers, food bloggers and 'influencers' raving about it. Kiera had come for the grand opening then stayed for a little while longer. Both to bask in the joy that Mabel was and to recharge herself. I could see that my friend was burning out. Her social media life had catapulted, so she featured in a constant stream of posts, events, videos. Though she pretended that this was all she'd ever wanted, I knew my friend, and she was fraying at the seams.

Not that she admitted that to me. Which wasn't a surprise since I knew she was watching me for signs of unraveling. She didn't know about the big secret, no one except Kane and Knox did, but she saw me, saw the results of it.

Which was part of my not so happy ending.

I had a thriving business, was back in the kitchen, was married to a man I loved, and most of all, I had an amazing, healthy baby girl and a family I'd reconnected with.

And I'd only just started recovering from postpartum anxiety when a former enemy came into our home, armed, and threatening to steal my baby. Brax had been ready to kill me before my brother-in-law shot him and dragged his body away somewhere it, presumably, would never be found.

A counterbalance to our happy ending.

It turned out that almost dying in front of your infant daughter, having the prospect of her being in the hands of a madman and seeing that madman die was pretty traumatic.

I knew in theory that I was dealing with heavy stuff. But I expected to be able to compartmentalize the event, to tuck it away somewhere deep, where it wouldn't affect me.

I'd excelled at that, organizing things neatly in my mind to ensure that they never leaked into other parts of me.

Yet my mind was not organized.

Before the event, and most certainly after, my mind was muddled. Was any mother in possession of a stable mind, even on her best day?

Although Mabel had finally started to sleep in her crib in her nursery, I could no longer stand her to be even a room away from me. I'd watch the monitor obsessively until my eyes could no longer stay open. Then I'd wake up in a cold sweat, scrambling to her room in order to make sure she was still there, still breathing.

Kane was there during all of this, rubbing my back, murmuring that he'd watch over her so I could get some sleep.

I trusted him with my life, with Mabel's, but I still couldn't let go.

I'd begun to bring her into bed with us, aware of the controversy surrounding such things, but I couldn't sleep, could barely breathe without feeling her warm body next to mine, my hand on her chest, feeling it rise and fall.

Kane didn't protest; he was willing to do anything and everything to get me sleeping. To help. I knew he felt powerless, that he was battling his own demons about the event.

Blame.

He carried a lot of it.

For not being there.

For not killing Brax in the first place.

He needed Mabel next to him just as much as I did.

My doctor prescribed me pills to help with the anxiety. I didn't take the pills. Not solely because I didn't think I needed them, but because a warped part of me felt that was letting Brax win.

Mabel still slept in bed with us. I still struggled with working the kitchen at Tides every night. I had the control I craved. Got to work in a space where I was sure, certain. An expert.

Yet all I did was long to get home, wistful over missing her bedtime.

Kane had given me a gift with the restaurant, an incredibly thoughtful one based on who I'd been before. And at face value, it was all I'd ever wanted. My mother had been right: all I yearned for were a few moments to myself. But once I had a kitchen to myself, all I wanted was our living room and its cemetery of toys and diapers.

Then there was the reading I was doing. Upon Fiona's advice, I had gotten rid of all of the parenting books, but now I was pouring over books on trauma in childhood and how it impacted them as adults.

The first three years of a child's life was when they set the emotional foundation for their entire personality. Their emotional brain developed. Any trauma during those three years could follow them into adulthood.

Mabel hadn't technically *seen* anything; I'd been in her line of vision initially. But she'd heard the conversation, and although she likely hadn't understood the words, I was sure she might have tapped into the overall vibe.

Kane was less worried about her emotional health and more worried about mine. Which I guessed made sense.

"She's resilient," he tried to reassure me for the hundredth time. "She's got an entire life of love ahead of her, a father who will move heaven and earth to ensure that she doesn't endure any trauma for the rest of her life."

I pursed my lips. I wanted that too. But my sense of hope seemed to have died with Brax.

"Right now, that's gonna be easy since I'm never fuckin' leaving her side again," he continued, his voice thick with shadows that followed him since that day. "So let's get you right, Chef."

"I'm fine," I said immediately.

He raised a brow. "You watched a man die. You faced the prospect of death yourself..." His fist clenched, and his body shook with rage.

If Kane could find a way to turn back time and beat Brax to death, I knew he would've.

He took a visibly deep breath, forcing himself to calm.

"You were moments away from death," he whispered. "That's going to affect you. You tell me how to fix it. How to fix you."

"You can't," I sighed. "And I can't fix how it affected you. We just … get through it. Together."

Despair shone in his eyes. I could taste his sense of powerlessness. But he nodded, grabbing my neck and pulling me so our foreheads touched.

"Forever," he vowed.

* * *

Mabel was in her own bed.

A win for the night.

Especially since she'd been in there over an hour. I wasn't working at the restaurant. I'd managed to arrange things so I was only there every other night. Though I yearned to be home full-time, I knew that I needed the kitchen too. Just not every night. Which I could do now that I trusted my team enough to go a night without me. I was there for hours every afternoon, prepping, but I always made it home for bedtime.

I'd also done something stupid. I added to my plate. With Maisie in mind. During her last visit, I broached the idea.

"Freezer meals?" she questioned as she cut up cucumbers for our salad. Her hands were never idle.

"You'll help me design them, using simple ingredients. They'll be like a ... made to order menu for new mothers who don't have the time or energy to prepare healthy meals."

I'd been brewing this idea for a while and had spoken to Kane about it. Unsurprisingly, he'd instantly been supportive and had already made calls to the people I needed to be in contact with to make it happen. Though I had plenty of my own connections in the culinary space too. I'd also put out feelers and had several companies jumping at the chance to have my name on this.

But it wouldn't be just mine. It would be Maisie's too.

"Partners," I said. "Both of us."

Her eyes welled. "You're serious."

I nodded. My sister had her hobbies, friends, but she'd devoted her life, her early twenties, to being a mother. She'd worked part-time when she was a single mother but now she didn't need to. Though she seemed perfectly content, I sensed that she was looking for something new, another purpose as her boys grew older.

"If you don't want to, don't feel pressure." I suddenly felt self-conscious. I had only just started to get to know my sister again; this was presumptuous. Business and family didn't mix. It was a recipe for disaster.

"I want to," she clutched my hand. "I love the idea, Avery."

So the 'Made from the Hart' company was born. Kind of a corny name, but I liked it.

We were still in the development stage, figuring out production, scale, packaging, ingredients. But I had a good feeling about it. This was not cheap cookware I was simply putting my name on. This was something immensely personal. This was family. This was my way of helping other mothers who desperately needed it.

And my way of creating something with Maisie.

It added to my pressures, but I was learning to delegate. To switch off from my business and be present in our home.

I'd cooked for us. Nothing fancy, shrimp scampi with herbs from our garden.

Kane was inside doing the dishes, having banished me to the porch with a glass of wine and orders to relax. As if such a thing were possible.

Even with all the changes, the nightmares and anxiety lessening, I still hadn't learned how to relax. There was always something to be done. With the restaurant, the house. Then I had to eat, shower, sleep. Even with help, the to-do list was never-ending. Even with all the help.

It did take a village.

And I needed it.

But then there were the nights of Mabel splashing in the bath, reading stories with her father and us putting her to bed. There were nights of quiet meals and easy conversation, an old yet hot attraction simmering between us. We hadn't devolved to the 'roommate stage' like everyone scaremongered us into expecting.

There were days and nights when we spoke only about bowel movements, nap times and feedings. But we were still each other. Somehow.

The door opened, then Kane emerged, his cheeky grin lit up by the last rays of sunlight. For a moment we were in a crowded party, eyes meeting across the room, electricity buzzing between us.

My body responded just like it had that day. Viscerally, passionately.

"You look relaxed, Chef," he observed, coming to grasp my hips then seemingly effortlessly pulling me out of the chair, sitting in it himself then repositioning me on his lap. My body practically purred at the contact.

I leaned into him, inhaling the scent of him mixed with the sea breeze and a faint whiff of Mabel's spit-up. It comforted me. All of it.

"I am relaxed," I told him honestly.

He stroked my head. "Well that foils my plans. I had expected you to still be tense. So I planned on peeling off your panties, making you sit in front of the ocean, in front of me while I ate your pussy and the waves drowned out your screams.

I stared at him.

"You're serious."

"I'm always serious about your pussy," he replied, leaning in to nip my neck.

I glanced at the monitor which showed Mabel sleeping peacefully. I then gazed over to the empty beach.

It was unlikely that we'd get caught, seen, but it was possible.

An old flame of excitement sparked within me. One that was born in a dive bar in New York. One that hadn't died with motherhood, with my identity shifts. One that hadn't died with Kane.

"Is that an affirmative, Chef?" Kane asked, hunger in his tone.

I looked from the ocean to his eyes. "Oh, it's definitely a yes."

And that was how I ended our night, with Kane's face between my legs, bringing me to exquisite orgasm.

There was a lot ahead of us, a whole life together.

And for the very first time, I was in the moment.

And that moment was pretty darn good.

KANE

They were both sleeping. Curled up together in our bed, faces inches apart. I etched that image into my memory, wishing it could push out all the other terrible ones, the one that had me up at two in the morning when I should've been in bed with my wife and daughter.

Brax.

On the ground of our kitchen—Avery's kitchen. Her one solace, sanctuary, poisoning it with his presence, his death.

Mabel, mere feet away, squealing in glee at me while the dead body of her would be kidnapper cooled.

I squeezed my eyes shut then opened them, my blood pressure accelerating with the image burned into the backs of my eyelids. Yeah, there were plenty of other ingredients in my trauma soup— my past, my prison sentence—but they paled in comparison to my wife and daughter being in danger and me not being there.

It took great physical effort to leave the room. I ached to stay there, watch them for the rest of the night, but the roof was too close, the walls beginning to close in. I took my phone, having set up another monitor in our room so whenever I had to leave it, I could watch them sleeping. Blanche was pressed up against the bed, even more clingy to both of them after what happened.

I fucking swore, if dogs could feel guilt, she was coated with it. Brax had poisoned her. He'd known about her, had been watching us, and had lain in wait for Avery to let her out.

It was a fucking miracle she survived.

We exchanged a look as I left, her silently telling me she'd watch over them. Or that's what I liked to think.

I walked through the dark house, willing my mind to quiet.

I was free.

Our daughter was safe in her mother's arms. There were no threats.

Yet I walked into every room, checking.

Nothing.

The ocean air hit me as I went outside to the deck, breathing it in, wishing my breath to steady. The sky and the sea yawned in front of me, comforting me with their endlessness.

My entire body tensed at the dark form emerging from the shadows, my heart clenching and the dragon inside of me roaring, happy, ecstatic about the threat, the chance to prove myself, to let go of this fury.

"Easy," my brother said as he came into focus.

"You gotta stop doin' that shit," I gritted out, my fists staying clenched.

"What am I gonna do? Ring the doorbell at two in the morning?" he asked dryly.

I shook my head, sitting in our outdoor chairs.

He sat beside me.

"Baby and Avery sleeping?" he asked.

I nodded, rubbing at my jaw.

"She doing better?"

I nodded again. "She's doing fuckin' great."

I knew she didn't think so. Knew she punished herself for every one of her feelings she considered weaknesses. But she was a great fucking mother. An excellent chef, had bridged the gap between her and her mother and sister, had made friends, laid roots in Jupiter. I considered that to be something to be in awe of. Which I was. Every day.

"Good," Knox replied.

We didn't say anything for a long while, listening to the waves crash in the darkness.

"How do you do it?" he finally asked.

I looked at my brother's profile, seeing him in the dim light. He looked ... different. Almost tortured.

"Do what?"

He continued looking at the ocean. "Love someone."

My jaw dropped. He was tortured because he was in fucking love. My brother. The man who considered himself a monster. And he was wrecked over it.

Fuck, I was elated. Or I wanted to be. It wasn't going to be simple for him. It was going to be wrought with pain. That much I understood. I yearned to ask questions, a shitload of them, about this person who'd ensnared my brother, scaled his countless defenses.

But that was not the time.

"It's not somethin' you do, brother." I clapped him on the shoulder. "It's something you ... surrender to." I smiled at him. "Know you're not exactly practiced in surrender."

He laughed without humor. "No. I'm not. And I can't. I won't ruin her life."

I opened my mouth to tell him no way in fuck was that true, but he stood, running his hands through his hair in an uncharacteristic gesture.

"This was a mistake," he muttered. "All of it."

Again, I opened my mouth to try to bring him back, to help him. But he was already turning his back.

I watched him walk toward the beach. It wasn't my job to save him. I hoped to fuck whoever this woman was, that she could do it.

I glanced down at the monitor, to my sleeping girls. I prayed my brother would find the strength to surrender like I had, because there was nothing in the world like it.

Then I took a breath, stood. I went back inside, curled into bed with my baby and my woman and thanked my lucky fucking stars that I got this gift.

Finally, sleep came easily.

Acknowledgments

This book took me a year to write. I cannot believe it took me that long. Well, I can, since I was taking care of a tiny human in that time also.

I consider myself to be so infinitely blessed to have the career I do. Not just because I get to write about my daydreams and call it a 'job' but because I can take time off to heal after giving birth, to soak in the first year of my baby's life.

Writing this book was so hard in so many ways. So healing in others. It's deeply personal and I wrote our birth story almost word for word. I feel so lucky to have a tangible time capsule to look back on now that our little girl is growing at warp speed.

Being a mother is so very hard. And doing it while trying to work is that much harder. Not just because my brain did seem to start eating itself from lack of sleep. Because I felt vague panic every moment I was away from our girl, even though she was in her very capable father's care.

I wouldn't have been able to write this book if not for the people in my life helping me along the way.

Taylor. My husband. My baby daddy. My best friend. Thank you for shooing me out of the house to write. For doing bedtime while I wrote about a hero who did all the things you did and continue to do for our baby. Thank you for being patient with me as I navigate this identity shift. Thank you for calming me down when I spiral. Thank you for bringing home three king size Milky ways when I tell you I had a hard night. Thank you for continuously giving me inspiration to write.

Juni. Our little June Bug. You made me a mother. You make me a better person every day. Everything I do now is to make you proud. Make you happy. I consider it my greatest honor and achievement to be your mum.

Mum. Thank you for supporting my dreams, for talking me through motherhood, for being there to cut the cord, to hold your granddaughter while we got much needed sleep. Thank you for giving me such a wonderful model of motherhood to look up to.

Aunty Vicki. We didn't have a village here so you flew across the world to help give us one in the first weeks of Juni's life. That is so infinitely precious to me. I consider myself so lucky to have a family full of strong women who show up for me and Juni.

Dad. You never got to meet your granddaughter. I know that you would have adored her. I know you're watching from somewhere, so proud of her. Unfortunately, you are the reason I know how to write about loss. I feel lucky to have had you as my dad but I wish every day I had you for longer.

Annette. You have been there for me through so much. You help me with everything book related, everything life related. You're such a special person.

Jessica. You're such a talented author, such a great friend. Thanks for always being there to vent, to proof my blurbs, to help inspire me.

Kim. The best editor out there. Thank you for surviving the pregnancy hormones, for being so flexible with me and helping to make this book be the best it can be.

Cat Imb. Your light is so bright, your heart is so big and your talent is endless. Thank you for creating covers that make me want to write a book worthy of them. Thank you for being my friend. I adore you.

Ginny. Thank you so much for always being there. For loving my characters as much as I do. For telling me what I need to hear. You are the best.

My girls. Harriet, Polly & Emma. You're half a world away but distance means nothing. You've all gotten me through some of the hardest times of my life and I'm so so lucky to have you as friends, as sisters.

And last but not least, **you, the reader**. Without you, dear reader, I would not be here. I would not be creating stories as a job. Thank you for making my dreams come true.

About the Author

ANNE MALCOM has been an avid reader since before she can remember, her mother responsible for her love of reading. It started with magical journeys into the world of Hogwarts and Middle Earth, then as she grew up her reading tastes grew with her. Her love of reading doesn't discriminate, she reads across many genres. She can't get enough romance, especially when some possessive alpha males throw their weight around.

One day, in a reading slump, Cade and Gwen's story came to her and started taking up space in her head until she put their story into words. Now that she has started, it doesn't look like she's going to stop anytime soon, with many more characters demanding their story be told as well.

Raised in small town New Zealand, Anne had a truly special childhood, growing up in one of the most beautiful countries in the world. She has backpacked across Europe, ridden camels in the Sahara and eaten her way through Italy, loving every moment.

Now, she's living her own happy ever after in the USA with her brilliant husband, their precious daughter and their two dogs.

Want to get in touch with Anne? She loves to hear from her readers.
You can email her: annemalcomauthor@hotmail.com
Or join her reader group on Facebook.

UNQUIET MIND

Echoes of Silence

Skeletons of Us

Broken Shelves

Mistake's Melody

Censored Soul

GREENSTONE SECURITY

Still Waters

Shield

The Problem With Peace

Chaos Remains

Resonance of Stars

THE VEIN CHRONICLES

Fatal Harmony

Deathless

Faults in Fate

Eternity's Awakening

Buried Destiny

RETIRED SINNERS

Splinters of You

THE KLUTCH DUET

Lies That Sinners Tell

Truths That Saints Believe

STANDALONES

Birds of Paradise

Doyenne

Midnight Sommelier

Hush - co-written

What Grows Dies Here

A Thousand Cuts

New Hope, Old Grudges